Ilsa Evans lives in a partially renovated house in the Dandenongs, east of Melbourne. She shares her home with her three children, two dogs, several fish, a multitude of sea-monkeys and a psychotic cat.

She has completed a PhD at Monash University on the long-term effects of domestic violence and writes fiction on the weekends. *Broken* is her sixth novel.

www.ilsaevans.com

BROKEN

ILSA EVANS

Pan Macmillan Australia

First published 2007 in Macmillan by Pan Macmillan Australia Pty Limited
1 Market Street, Sydney

National Library of Australia
cataloguing-in-publication data:

Evans, Ilsa.
Broken.

ISBN 978 1 4050 3777 8 (pbk.).

I. Title.

A823.4

Typeset in 11/15 pt Birka by Post Pre-press Group
Printed in Australia by McPherson's Printing Group

Papers used by Pan Macmillan Australia Pty Ltd are natural, recyclable products made from
wood grown in sustainable forests. The manufacturing processes conform to the environmental
regulations of the country of origin.

To Michael, Jaime and Caitlin.
For making everything worthwhile.

Courage is fear that has said its prayers.
Dorothy Bernard

*S*he'd worn white to her wedding. Huge clouds of frosted white that billowed around her in the wind like fairytale snow. Against her waist she held a bouquet of milky roses that dripped with clusters of tiny white gypsophilia. And the limousine was white too, inside as well as out, so that when the door opened and she looked out at the guests milling around the church steps, she merged perfectly into the background but for her red-lipped smile. An elaborate concoction of alabaster and lace.

Just before she entered the church, the photographer darted forward and took a shot when a gust of wind wrapped the white satin around her body like a sheath, picking up the veil and spreading it across the cloudy sky behind.

In the photograph, now living in an embossed gold frame, she has one hand up trying to harness the fly-away veil, and the other holding her bouquet down by her side so that the blooms brush against the cobblestoned portal. And she is still smiling, a broad, open-mouthed smile that shows all her teeth and beams a message of delight so uninhibited that, even trapped in time, it remains infectious.

Because everything lay before them. Not only the rest of that day, with its intoxicating focus and whirlwind celebration, but an entwined future that could be clearly seen ahead. And they would be joined now not just by the strength of their emotions, but by priests and promises, and a piece of parchment that could be framed in matching gold.

ONE

Most of that first day Mattie spent cutting out motivational sayings from a desk calendar with an old pair of nail scissors. Inspiring couplets and illuminating quotes that she trimmed with fierce concentration and then stuck with sticky-tape onto the refrigerator door. *The future depends on what you do in the present. It is hard to fail, but it is worse never to have tried to succeed. Happiness resides not in possessions but in the soul.* She used her teeth to tear the tape because the nail scissors were too blunt, so that it stretched and curled with ragged edges that vaguely irritated her.

The desk calendar was the only item left behind from the unit's previous tenants. Everything else had been taken – curtains, toilet paper, even the light-bulbs. Jake had laughed hugely when he saw this and, on his next trip from home with a carload of her belongings, brought a spare sixty-watt light-globe that he deftly fitted into the lounge-room socket. Shedding light on the proceedings. But as soon as he left to collect the children from school and take them home, Mattie flicked the switch off. Then she tore a page from the desk calendar to write a shopping list but was distracted by the italicised blurbs that accompanied each date.

It was dusk by the time the calendar was stripped of relevance, and the pile of boxes in the lounge-room cast a jagged shadow that licked across the floor towards her feet. But it wasn't a threatening darkness, not the type that made her nerve-ends dance anxiously, but instead had an inevitability that was quite soothing. So Mattie poured herself another glass of wine and settled on the burgundy microsuede beanbag in the corner to watch the gloom graduate from shades of dove-grey to a pervasive gunmetal colour that she could almost breathe.

This was the first time that Mattie had ever spent a night away from her children. *They* had left home for occasional sleepovers with friends, and the odd night with a relative, but Mattie herself had always been there. She took a sip of wine and wondered what they were doing right now. Jake said that he was taking them out for dinner, to lessen the impact, so she supposed they were excited, and happy, and enjoying themselves. But she wished that they were here, with her instead.

And if they were, she would *have* to start unpacking. She would *have* to arrange furniture, and fill cupboards, and hang clothing, and switch on the light. And she would have to find a brave face and rally them around. They'd turn this whole debacle into a glorious adventure, and build a giant's castle out of the empty cardboard boxes. A castle that reached almost to the ceiling, with tunnels and caves and secret hidey-holes.

But they weren't here. They wouldn't be here until Sunday, two whole days and nights away. And it was the humming silence that was the strangest thing of all. Not the unfamiliar rooms, the boxes, the encroaching darkness – but the silence. Because Mattie wasn't very used to silence. Two noisy children and one noisy husband made for a household where continual sound was just part of the tapestry that made it a home. Even during the worst of times, there was always music in the background or the sounds of the television set broadcasting a parallel world. A parallel world that was probably just like hers anyway, one where nothing was quite as it seemed and noise drowned out the whispers of dissent.

There was a portable television set sitting on the floor by the boxes, but for now Mattie preferred the silence. She didn't want to watch other people going about their daily lives as if nothing momentous had happened; instead she just wanted to bury herself in the beanbag and fade into the darkness. Because it fed her misery in a way that noise and laughter wouldn't have, so that she could dwell within a despair that was almost self-indulgent.

Mattie would have stayed like that, silent and still, for the rest of the evening but along with the darkness came a crisp spring chill that her jeans and t-shirt did little to dispel. So, before it got too dark to see, she unpacked only one box, the one marked 'bedding', and delved through the contents until she found the thick, checked Onkaparinga blanket with the satin edging. Her share of the matched pair that had been a wedding present ten years ago from her father, back before Alzheimer's honeycombed his brain and they buried his shell in the local cemetery. Mattie kicked her runners off and then flipped the blanket out, wondering melodramatically if she would ever be able to match it or whether it was now doomed to end its days lamenting the loss of its identical twin, its soul mate. She grinned at herself, without humour.

After pouring another glass of wine, Mattie tried to wrap the blanket around her shoulders Indian-style, but as she dragged it across, something sharp scratched her arm and pierced the soft flesh inside her bicep. She dropped the blanket in surprise and, licking her finger, dabbed it against the beads of blood tattooing her skin. Now she could see that there was a note pinned to the satin edging, so she undid it clumsily and held it close to make out the words.

Mattie – I'll <u>always</u> be here.
Love you, Jake

Mattie stared at the note for a few moments while the drops of spit-smeared blood elongated across the cut and began to trickle down her arm. Then she stuck the pin into the nearest cardboard box and folded the note up, making sure the edges were aligned. She took it out into the kitchen where she put it on top of the fridge and then, grabbing a tissue, mopped up the thin trickle of blood from her arm. She folded the tissue over and held it against the cut, hard, until the bleeding slowed, before fixing a bandaid in place. It was a bright purple Harry Potter bandaid, with the youthful wizard astride his broomstick and waving a magical wand through the air.

Mattie went to the sink and washed her hands, working up a rich foamy lather with a bar of soap she'd placed there earlier in the day.

After she rinsed, Mattie went back into the lounge-room, wrapped herself in her blanket and started to cry. Fat, silent tears that tracked down her cheeks and dripped onto the blanket to soak into the thick weave. And even though part of her despised the tears and the self-pity, she simply couldn't summon the energy necessary to rise above them. It was too enormous a step. And too final. The unit, the move, the light-globes, the unpacking – *especially* the unpacking. Because, folded amongst the odds and ends of clothing and crockery and ornaments was all her other baggage. All the guilt, the recriminations and the nostalgia that come when you pack up a decade of marriage and try to close the lid.

And besides, if she didn't unpack the boxes and assemble the couch and make up her bed – if she didn't scribble across the blank slate of this unit with *herself* – then she could always change her mind. She could simply ring Jake and tell him she was on the way. Because she'd made a mistake. A big mistake. A *huge* mistake. And it was a call he would probably be expecting because, although this was the first time that she had gone so far as to rent a unit, this was certainly not the first time she had left. Twice before she'd gone to a hotel, returning the next day only to pack but being persuaded to stay instead. Her other, and most recent attempt had resulted in a prolonged stay at her mother's house, where her kind-hearted bewilderment, the children's wide-eyed watchfulness and Jake's misery brought Mattie back home within a week.

And she knew the reason he had – eventually – become so accommodating about this latest move was that he didn't really believe she'd see it through. So if she picked up the phone now, right *now*, and rang home, his voice would smile with relief, and a certain smugness. And she could be back there within minutes. With her family. Jake would light the open fire in the lounge-room while she curled up on the couch with the children and watched the flames. And she could reunite the Onkaparingas and instead wrap herself with hearth and home. A place where she knew every nook and cranny, and the pictures on the walls spoke of their shared past, and where all the furniture had a tale to tell that only they understood. And they'd celebrate her return with champagne while he teased her about her silliness and, after the kids went to bed, they'd make love on the carpet while the embers washed their bodies with a smouldering glow.

But she didn't make the phone-call. Although tonight would be marvellous, and tomorrow, and probably even the next day also, sooner or later she would be back in that bad place. And it wouldn't matter that she knew every nook and cranny, because none of them would be safe. For some of the tales living within her home had been written with her blood, and her sweat, and her tears – and she didn't want to hear them anymore. So she didn't make the call, but she didn't unpack the boxes either.

*T*hey hadn't lived together before marriage. Not because of any moral objections, but simply because it wasn't practical. Even staying with each other had been less than ideal. Mattie shared an already overcrowded flat whilst Jake rented with two other males who, although friendly enough, made Mattie feel awkward with their flashing eyes and hearty innuendo. So it wasn't until they married that all the little mundane differences, only discovered through cohabitation or time, began to surface. Like the fact that Mattie admired a garden with untamed, luxurious foliage, while Jake preferred it orderly, lined with pine-bark and edged with miniature fencing. Then there was the shower stall, where Mattie drove Jake mad with her inclination to scatter products across the floor. And she enjoyed board games like Scrabble and Pictionary, while he preferred strategy games like chess. And Mattie liked to dance, but Jake didn't. And she also loved to lie in on the weekend, whereas Jake would leap out of bed at 6.30 am but liked to nap on a Sunday afternoon, especially after sex.

But the hardest thing to come to grips with, for Mattie, was Jake's meticulous planning. He valued budgets and goals and key objectives, and she suspected that he saw her occasional impulsiveness as a character flaw, or a sign of immaturity. But, over time, they learned to give and take. On the weekends, Jake brought her breakfast in bed and they read the newspaper together. And they bought a wire shelf to hang from the showerhead, and shared the garden – this section for him, this one for her. Occasionally she'd even get him to dance with her around the lounge-room, and he called her his 'Waltzing Matilda'. And, for their first anniversary, Mattie bought Jake a compendium of 64 computer strategy games. All the traditional ones like chess and draughts, as well as the newer ones like Freecell and Tetris and Spider Solitaire. And she gave it to him with a silver embossed anniversary card that read: 'To Jake with love. Forever.'

TWO

The next morning Mattie woke with renewed determination. Her neck was stiff from sleeping so awkwardly and her eyes were grainy from the wine, but with the light that now streamed through the curtain-less windows came a sense of optimism that invigorated her with its buoyancy. Mattie relaxed and let it flood her, smiling as it met the residue of last night's despair and dispersed it condescendingly. She snuggled down underneath the blanket and watched the daylight dapple over the mottled brown carpet, illuminating scores of tiny dust particles spiralling through the air. If anything, the unit looked even more lacklustre during the day but this didn't affect Mattie as it had before. Instead she felt strengthened by possibilities and armed by a sense of survival. Besides, when all was said and done, it was only a one-year lease and she was confident that by then she'd have sorted out what she wanted, and where.

She stripped off her jeans and dropped them on the floor. Then, dressed in just her t-shirt and knickers with the blanket draped across her shoulders, she went into the kitchen to give her hands a wash and put the kettle on. The Harry Potter bandaid had come partly unstuck so she pulled it off and threw it in the bin. Then she bobbed down to read through the motivational sayings on the fridge again, nodding when she came to one she felt particularly apt. *Happiness resides not in possessions but in the soul.* When the kettle boiled she made herself a cup of coffee and then, spooning baked beans straight from the tin, she did a tour of her new home.

The floor plan was simple. The front door led straight into the lounge-room with the kitchen to the left and a tiny passage ahead that had a bedroom up the far end, a bedroom off the middle and then a toilet and bathroom off the other end. The lounge-room itself was fairly spacious, with just one triple bank of windows close by the mission-brown front door. Cream walls and white ceilings. Somehow comforting in its traditional unexceptionableness.

The kitchen was also big, with white formica cupboards around three of its walls and room for a table and chairs against the fourth. A window behind the sink showed an elevated view of the backyard, which could only be reached through the laundry at the far end of the kitchen. Mattie went through to the back door, unlocked it and walked out onto the small wooden veranda. There were six steps down the stairs to the yard, and then only eight steps across to reach the far fence. It was tiny. Mostly concrete, with just a small patch of grass in the centre. And she knew the children were going to be extremely disappointed, accustomed as they were to a spacious property with room for trees and trampolines, swings and sandpits, adventures and imagination.

She took a spoonful of baked beans and ate them pensively. They'd just have to be creative, and she would have to help them. Perhaps some pot-plants, or a tent – or even a puppy. Mattie's face brightened at this last idea, because it had definite possibilities – something to sweeten the deal, encourage them to call this place home. A golden retriever, a cocker spaniel, or a border collie. Any one of those breeds known for their loyalty. That could turn from a gentle pet into a snarling, jugular-ripping protector in the blink of an eye. She smiled at the thought.

Mattie closed the back door and turned the key before heading towards the little passageway behind the lounge-room. She had already worked out that it took three large steps from the lounge-room door-way to reach her bedroom at the end, three very small ones to reach the children's, and three medium ones to reach the bathroom to the left. She opted for the latter and then leant just inside the doorway, still eating her baked beans. The bathroom was compact, functional and predominantly white. White tiles over a white bath near a white vanity unit with the shower stall at the far end. One of the vanity's corners had been snapped off at some stage, leaving a jagged curve of chipboard on display, and a few of the tiles were cracked with the grouting interspersed by deep grooves. The missing grouting and the chipboard grated on her but overall it was liveable. And that was the main thing.

From the doorway, Mattie could see her reflection in the mirror. A small, slim figure clad only in a loose red t-shirt and a hint of floral knickers. Facial features a bit on the thin side but in proportion, with a cloud of short, dark, wavy hair, even messier than usual. A slightly too-wide mouth that turned down automatically but still smiled well, and good teeth, except for a side molar that was tinged with grey through nerve loss. A frown line that punctuated the once smooth space above the bridge of her nose. Dark brows and thick dusky lashes framing dark brown eyes that stared back at her trustingly. Show us the way and we will obey.

Leaving the bathroom door open, Mattie turned and flung open the bedroom doors as well, because the whole unit had the musty, damp cardboard smell that came from lack of occupation. Both bedrooms were almost identical – the same two-door wardrobe set into one wall, the same double bank of windows lidded by clanky white metal venetian blinds, the same mottled carpet as the lounge-room, and the same standard cream and white paintwork.

Lengths of polished pine lay on the floor of the children's room, waiting to be assembled into a set of bunks, and a pine tallboy sat by the window with a small pine desk next to it. Mattie had purchased the furniture through a local second-hand store, and Jake had spent all yesterday morning collecting and delivering it for her. The same store had supplied the double bed mattress and base that was in her room, and the old-fashioned white dressing table with its huge round mirror and chunky wooden drawers.

And that was all the furniture she could afford. All she'd taken from the house was the modular couch from the family room, a nest of walnut side tables, and the old pine kitchen table and chairs from the shed. A fair and reasonable split of the possessions they'd collected over the years would only take place if this 'trial' separation became permanent. That was one of the rules, same as with their savings. But Mattie had been willing to agree to almost anything to obtain Jake's assistance, because only in movies were women able to leave with just one suitcase that miraculously furnished an entire new life. In reality there were all the complications of a negotiated fair share, and the needs of the children, as well as the fundamental minutiae of baby photos, and certificates, and old school reports, or even the set of blankets that had been a wedding present from a now dead father. The truth was that it was hard to leave without some level of cooperation from the other partner. Life could become very difficult, very quickly, without that.

Mattie touched each of the walls in the children's room, for luck, and then took the three steps required to reach the lounge-room. One, two, three. She headed into the kitchen, threw the half-empty can of baked beans into a plastic bag she'd tied onto a drawer handle, and dropped the dirty spoon into the sink. She stared at it for a moment and then rinsed it off, along with her coffee cup, before drying them, putting them away and washing her hands. Then she took two headache tablets, swallowing them dry so that they rasped painfully down her throat, and stared out of the window at the tiled roof next door as she worked on reigniting her optimism. Once this was achieved, Mattie took several deep breaths and decided that the children's room was the priority. That way, even if Jake turned up early, it would send a message that she could accommodate them. That she was able.

Two hours later, and after several false starts, she had the bunks assembled and positioned in a corner of the bedroom. The tallboy fitted fairly neatly into the alcove by the wardrobe and, after discovering that the venetians were faulty, she had used drawing pins to position a set of spare royal blue sheets over the windows to act as curtains and keep out the light. The beds were made up with military tightness and a soft toy was placed neatly on each pillow. A fluffy loose-limbed dog with a red polka-dot bandanna on Max's and Harmony Bear, a smiling purple-blue Care Bear, on Courtney's.

But the soft toys were indicative of a problem that slowly emerged as Mattie unpacked the boxes. Neither was a new or even an old favourite, instead they were just two of a pile of cast-off and outgrown possessions that Max and Courtney had packed for their mother's new home.

There were no electronic games here, no treasured teddies, no Harry Potter books, no current fads, no collections. And the pattern continued within the boxes they'd packed with clothing. Outgrown tracksuits, stained t-shirts, hand-me-down jumpers. Despite being told to pack a box of clothing and a box of toys each, everything special and favoured had clearly remained behind. In fact, the boxes contained nothing more than if the children had been asked to clear out their rooms for a garage sale. There was not one item here that they would miss if they never saw it again – or if they never spent one night here, in their mother's new home.

Mattie picked up a book called *A Child's Garden of Verse* and ran her finger gently over the cartoon depiction of a blonde, tiara-topped princess on the cover. She tried to put herself in the children's shoes: being informed that your parents were separating, however amicably, and that you would now be spending four nights a week elsewhere. Neither child had displayed much emotion at the time, and neither had asked one question about the unit since they'd been told. Perhaps they, like their father, never thought she would go through with it.

Mattie tossed the book to one side and hefted herself to her feet with a sigh. She would just have to prove to them – all – that she was serious. That this was serious. She pushed the problem away and concentrated on placing the books neatly on the shelving, arranging them by size and ensuring the spines aligned. She livened up the arrangement with a few judiciously placed stuffed toys and a resin musical carousel that Courtney had been given by her grandmother the year before. Then she left the remainder of the toys in the boxes and put them inside the wardrobe as temporary toy-boxes.

When she had finished, Mattie stood in the centre of the room and looked around with pride. Certainly there was plenty more to be done – posters for the walls, doona covers for the beds, proper curtains for the windows, but the room looked comfortable and inviting and *used*. And she thought the children were going to like it. Especially with a puppy.

Before Mattie could move to the next room, the doorbell sounded shrilly, piercing the silence with an intensity that made her flinch.

Close on this, however, was the sudden realisation that only one person knew where she was living. A realisation that propelled her to the front door, flinging it open with a huge, welcoming smile. Which collapsed as she was confronted not by who she'd been expecting, but by her sister.

'Mattie!' Hannah's eyes widened, then flicked down to Mattie's bare legs and back to her face. 'Are you okay? What's going on?'

'How'd you know where I was?'

'I rang Jake. He said you'd *left*.' Hannah shook her head in disbelief. 'Mattie, why? What's going on?'

Mattie looked at her sister expressionlessly and then opened the door wider, moving aside as she did so. 'You'd better come in.'

Accepting this invitation hesitantly, Hannah stepped over the threshold and then paused to gaze around the lounge-room. She was a tall woman, more angular than her sister, but with the same dark colouring. Her hair, rather than being free to wave like Mattie's, was worn long and pulled back into one full-bodied plait that hung down the centre of her back almost to her waist. As always, she was dressed conservatively but well. A v-neck cream jumper with a swirling pattern of cableknitted browns, and chestnut-brown tailored slacks with a matching pair of heeled boots. She looked exactly like what she was – a happily married, relatively affluent woman made unconsciously smug by her circumstances.

Hannah took a few moments to scrutinise the room, her silence clearly conveying her opinion. She finished by staring pointedly at the abandoned cask of wine by the burgundy beanbag and then turned back to her sister, her disapproval tempered by bewilderment. 'I don't understand.'

Instead of answering, Mattie walked into the kitchen and lit the gas under the kettle. Then, still wordlessly, she started to assemble the coffee plunger for herself and a mug of tea for her sister. It wasn't that she disliked Hannah, or normally avoided her company, but she'd anticipated at least a few days to settle in before having to explain to family. And besides, they had never been girlfriend-like close, never whispered secrets or giggled together, or joined forces against their parents. Eight years older, Hannah had married before Mattie reached her teens, and then even the maternal interest she'd shown in her younger sister was displaced by the birth of her own daughter the following year. So now Hannah was forty to Mattie's thirty-two, with an adult child, whilst Mattie's two were still in primary school.

They always remembered each other's birthdays, and those of their respective families, and even met occasionally, with their mother, for lunch. And when Mattie first married, Hannah had made a concerted effort to establish regular get-togethers between the two couples but, as these things often do, they petered off over time.

'Does Mum know?' Mattie asked, placing the mug of tea in front of her sister, who was now seated at the kitchen table, still looking around with critical incomprehension.

'No. Not yet.'

'Well, could you hold off telling her?' Mattie sat down opposite Hannah and laced her fingers around her mug. 'Just for a week or so. Till I settle in.'

'But *why*?' Hannah almost whined the words and then, as if hearing herself, took a deep breath and continued in a more measured tone: 'I just don't understand. Why would you give up all *that* for all –' she waved one hand around the kitchen rather disparagingly – '*this*.'

'It's not as simple as that.'

'Then explain it to me.' Hannah looked at Mattie imploringly. 'I *want* to understand. Just like I wanted to last year when you went to stay at Mum's for that week. But I can't understand if you won't tell me, can I? I mean *something* must have made you do this. Is it Jake? Did he have an affair?'

'Of course not.' Mattie drew back, affronted.

'Then what *is* it? Does he treat you badly? Or abuse you? Or mistreat the kids?'

Mattie shook her head at each of the suggestions, frowning. '*Nothing* like that.'

'For god's sake then, Mattie! Look, this is what I see, and it's up to you to tell me if I'm wrong. I see a woman with a nice husband, nice house, nice kids. But somehow that's not enough.'

'It's not like that.' Mattie tried to find the right words but they hovered just out of reach and she fell quiet in frustration.

'Yes, it *is* like that. And you're going to lose everything because of what? A whim?'

'You talk like I'm throwing them all away. I'm *not*.' Mattie leant forward in her eagerness to make Hannah at least understand that. 'Jake and I will still be seeing each other. It's just a . . . well, a scaling back. To give us a chance to work some things out. And hopefully after a year, everything will be back on track.'

'That makes even *less* sense. Why even shift out if you're still together?'

'Because, see . . . don't you ever feel that you're too *close* to something to work it out? That you need to take a few steps backwards to get perspective?'

'Sure.' Hannah looked at her derisively. 'With new curtains maybe. Not with my marriage, for god's sake.'

'I suppose not.' Mattie sat back again and sighed. Because it was impossible to put into words what she barely understood herself. And impossible, anyway, to expose the belly of her pride. After a few moments of silence, she muttered: 'I just need space, that's all.'

'Then why can't you get space *inside* your marriage?' asked Hannah sharply.

'Because . . .' Mattie paused, staring down into the tan-coloured liquid within her mug as if an answer lay there. 'Maybe because Jake smothers me.'

'Smothers you?' Hannah threw up her hands in frustration. 'He *loves* you! God, I wish Stuart would pay me the attention you get from Jake! You don't know how *lucky* you are. Really, Mattie, you don't.'

'Probably not.'

Hannah sighed and shook her head as she gazed around the kitchen again. Then she glanced back at her sister. 'Look, I know Jake can be a bit domineering. I've seen that. But if that's the problem, Mattie, then I've got to tell you that from where I'm sitting it's largely your fault.'

'*My* fault?' Mattie stared at her sister, visibly wounded, but Hannah continued regardless.

'Yes. Look, I'm not saying that he isn't one of those assertive-type guys, but to a large extent he's *had* to take charge because, well, it's like you've stepped back from everything, *especially* over the past few years. I mean, even Mum's noticed.'

'Nice to know you both discuss me behind my back,' snapped Mattie.

'I'm not going to deny that.' Hannah reached forward and folded one of Mattie's resistant hands within her own. 'But we only do it because we're worried, you know. *Truly* worried. To be honest, I think you need help.'

Mattie flinched. Hannah wasn't the only person to have said that. In fact she'd heard it so often that it was beginning to echo through her life, undermining her choices and making her question any certainty. She drew her hand back and laid it on her lap.

'And what about the kids? Have you thought about them?'

'I've thought about little else,' replied Mattie slowly. 'They'll be staying from Sunday night till Thursdays with me, and then the rest of the time with their father. I'm going to get them a puppy.'

'What about money? What will you *live* on?'

'If you must know, I've got an appointment at Centrelink on Monday.'

'Centrelink!'

'Yes. Just until Courtney's finished preps, then I'll get a job.'

'Do you know how much you'll get from Centrelink?' Hannah looked aghast. 'It's a *pittance*. You'll never live on that!'

'Well, I'll have to, won't I?'

'Not if you just went back!'

'No!'

Hannah glared at her sister in frustration and then, as Mattie simply stared back stubbornly, she shook her head again and sighed. After a few minutes during which neither spoke, Hannah undid her plait and, after running her fingers through her thick hair, redid it deftly. It was a ploy she had used for years to give herself time to think. As soon as she finished, she flicked her plait back and stood up, taking her handbag from the table.

'I'm going to do as you asked and not tell Mum for a week. But –' she shook her head as Mattie went to speak – 'I'm not doing it to give you a chance to settle, I'm doing it in the hope that, after a week, there won't be anything *to* tell her. That you'll have come to your senses by then.'

'Not going to happen.'

'You never know.' Hannah looked at her and sighed again, this time ostentatiously. Then she walked across the room towards the doorway, pausing at the fridge to stare at the motivational sayings plastered across it. She raised her eyebrows and glanced at Mattie, who simply rose and led the way to the front door, opening it and standing to one side.

'Thanks for dropping in.'

'Look after yourself, Mattie.' Hannah suddenly leant forward to kiss her sister on the cheek but Mattie flinched instinctively and Hannah's lips just brushed her skin like the dry, feathery wing of a butterfly.

Mattie flushed, embarrassed by her reaction. 'Sorry.'

'That's fine.' Hannah gazed at her for a moment. 'Do me a favour, Mattie. If you won't talk to me, talk to *someone*. Please. Even if it's just a friend.'

Mattie nodded, knowing it wasn't going to happen. 'Okay.'

The late spring breeze came rushing up behind Hannah and rustled against her back, separating tendrils of hair from around her face and fluffing them out. For an instant she looked very much like her younger sister, an impression that was heightened by her evident uncertainty about what to do next. The moment passed without either sister recognising it, and Hannah started down the path towards her bronze late-model Volvo before turning back one last time.

'You act like I'm against you but I'm not. I'm only worried for *you*. That you'll end up losing everything.'

'I know.' Mattie nodded and then looked at her sister searchingly. 'But what you have to understand is that the other way, I was losing *me*. And that means that I would have ended up losing everything anyway.'

Hannah stared at her for a moment and then shook her head, puzzled. 'I'll just have to hope, for your sake, that you know what you're doing, because I really don't understand. At all.'

'No, I don't suppose you do.' Mattie watched as her sister unlocked the car and got in. Then she spoke under her breath. 'And you ought to be *glad* you don't. Because I wouldn't wish that on anyone.'

*T*hey held their first dinner party while house-sitting a work colleague's home and waiting to move into their own. Meticulous planning went into every detail – who to invite, what to serve, which music to play, how to decorate. In the end they invited eight people, a mixture of friends and family. And they dressed the table with wedding presents of crockery, cutlery and crystal. Mattie raided the garden for huge sprays of wattle and fernery for a centrepiece, and Jake folded the serviettes into little opera houses that squatted before each carefully laid place setting.

For starters they served some type of seafood dish, Mattie couldn't remember what exactly. But the main course had been delicious – a creamy chicken and asparagus dish that Jake found in a recipe book and cooked to perfection. They presented it with a green salad and crusty bread rolls. And for dessert there was chocolate and rum mousse topped with whipped cream and curly slivers of dark chocolate.

The evening was a huge success. Sublime, sociable, relaxing. After dinner they took their glasses out to the patio where they sat and talked about plans and promises. There was a magnificent lavender bush by the French doors, and the pungent, cloying smell of the fresh lavender seemed almost more intoxicating than the wine. And Mattie had basted in her pleasure, buoyed by the idea that this evening would be the first of many where friends were always welcome and good food and wine simply oiled the contentment that was her life.

After everybody left, Jake and Mattie went back outside and listened to music. And when Meatloaf came on with the song 'Two out of three ain't bad', they took it in turns to sing it to each other, only harmonising when it came to the chorus. By the end of the song they were both laughing so hard they could hardly get the words out.

THREE

Mattie started peeling and slicing potatoes at the kitchen sink just after five o'clock on Sunday afternoon, flipping the pallid segments into a large pot of boiling water on the stove. It had been a busy day, but the dividends were evident throughout the transformed unit. A huge grocery shop had filled the cupboards and provided odd necessities like scissors and light-globes and pot pourri to banish the last of the stale smell. Even though it severely dented her available funds, the investment had been well worth it, bestowing a sense of permanency hitherto largely absent. Now everything that needed to be unpacked was unpacked, with the boxes flattened and stacked in the laundry. And although the furniture was sparse, the walls bare and the windows covered with odd spare sheets, it felt as if she had now *stamped* the rooms. Marked her territory. A few cushions, some framed photos, an open book, the rich smell of food cooking – and a cluster of featureless rooms suddenly metamorphosed into a home.

Mattie opened the oven and stirred the casserole of braised beef in red wine, breathing in the rich aroma with satisfaction. As she slid it back into the oven and closed the door, a car could be heard decelerating outside before it turned off the main road and then coasted slowly down the driveway with a throbbing purr. Mattie immediately froze, waiting tensely until the car passed, the sound fading as it continued on down the driveway towards the two rear units.

Mattie relaxed again, rolling her eyes at her reaction. But she'd been

like that all afternoon, with her stomach tensing every time she heard
a car slow down. Twice, when the car hadn't moved on quickly, she'd
rushed to the lounge-room windows to draw the sheet-curtains back
just enough to see that it was only other unit-dwellers stopping at the
mailboxes to retrieve their weekend junk mail. And she couldn't understand why she felt so nervous. Why, when she was only expecting her
own family, was she feeling all the adrenalin-charged expectation of a
first date? She'd even dressed carefully, trying to balance nonchalant
casualness with something flattering, and finally settled on jeans she
hadn't worn in years that were now a bit tight around the buttocks,
and a clingy shell-pink long-sleeved shirt. Now all she needed was her
family.

Mattie washed her hands briskly and then went into the lounge-
room to sit on the couch armrest and peer behind the sheets. She played
a game in which she counted cars, with the tenth car bound to be them.
Then the twentieth. Thirtieth. Maybe the fiftieth. She became aware
that her forehead had beaded with perspiration so she ran into the
bathroom to reapply her make-up. Then back into the lounge-room,
one, two, three, convincing herself that Murphy's law had kicked in and
they'd arrived while she was gone. But they hadn't. In fact they didn't
arrive until nearly seven, when the potatoes had long boiled, and the
casserole had been turned down to a thickened simmer.

Courtney exited the car first, pausing on the pathway to gaze at
the unit blankly. Mattie repressed the urge to fling open the door and
envelop the child in her arms. Instead she stayed where she was, a
voyeuristic witness to her daughter's first impressions. Courtney was
six, a small dark-haired girl whose baby plumpness was still evident
in her sturdy legs and rounded belly. She was a child to whom open-
ness came naturally, who disliked subterfuge, and artifice, and secrets.
Unless she was the instigator.

Apart from his dark hair and eyes, her brother was very different.
Although not a devious child in the sense of being deceitful, he nevertheless displayed an instinctive wariness that sometimes made him
seem that way. But Mattie knew this was more because he just seemed
to *feel* things more profoundly than most other children. It was like

his soul had no protection and the only defence he could muster was avoidance.

Mattie watched, a lead weight pressing against her gut, as Max finally scrambled from the front passenger seat and joined his sister on the path. They'd obviously dressed themselves – Max in a pair of patterned board shorts and a black windcheater with orange lining, and Courtney in her favourite pink tutu topped by a red cardigan. Her long hair was caught up in a rather crooked ponytail that was barely secured by an extravagant pink and gold hair-tie. Both children looked back towards the car, unsure of what was expected of them next. By now their father had also emerged and was removing their schoolbags from the boot. Mattie stared at him, trying to reconcile her pleasure at seeing him with the fact that she was here in the first place. Nothing made sense.

Even in terms of looks, they were a matched set. Like Mattie, Jake had olive skin and dark brown hair, a virtual guarantee that both their children would inherit the same colouring. The only difference was that Mattie, Max and Courtney all had brown eyes, while Jake's were an unusual shade of bluish pewter-grey that shone when he was amused and dulled flatly when he was annoyed. He was a tall, almost thin man with large hands and feet and distinct grooves either side of his mouth that deepened when he smiled. At thirty-three his hair had the beginnings of a prematurely receding hairline, a family trait that Jake was rather self-conscious about, often spending an inordinate amount of time and money on differing hair products, a conceit that Mattie found rather endearing. Dressed more tastefully than his children, Jake was wearing jeans and a navy polo shirt with a light blue inset panel across the chest. As Mattie watched, he slammed the boot shut and grinned across at their indecision, saying something that she couldn't hear and gesturing towards the front door. Seconds later the doorbell rang, its shrillness making her jump even though she was expecting it. Mattie took in a deep breath, waiting until it filled the uncomfortable hollow beneath her ribcage before going to answer the door. But before she could, it swung open.

'Hey there.' Jake grinned and held up her spare key. 'Still got this from the other day so I thought I'd save you the bother. How's it going?'

'Good. It's good.' Mattie stood there awkwardly.

'Mummy!' Courtney squeezed herself past and flung herself on her mother. 'Mummy! I *missed* you.'

'Oh god, Court.' Mattie bobbed down, the tight jeans protesting, and wrapped her arms around her daughter amongst the pink tulle. 'I missed you too. *So* much.'

'C'mon, it's only been two days.' Jake shook his head with mock disgust as he dumped the schoolbags on the floor and then reached down into one of them and pulled out a bottle of champagne. 'Here you go. House-warming gift. Chilled and all.'

Still keeping one arm around Courtney, Mattie took the bottle and smiled at Jake with surprise. 'Thanks. That's really nice.'

'That's me. Really nice.'

She looked at the bottle, truly touched by his thoughtfulness, and then to hide her emotion, peered past Jake towards the doorway. 'Where's Max?'

'Right here.' Jake stepped inside and revealed Max, who had been standing behind him. 'It's just he's got a bit more self-control than you two. Haven't you, mate?'

'Yep.' Max met his mother's eyes briefly as he shuffled inside next to his father. He glanced around the room expressionlessly and then stared down at his feet.

'I know it's not much.' Mattie looked at him ruefully. 'But we can fix it up more. Hang some pictures, maybe even paint the walls if the landlord lets us.'

'I don't think it'll help.' Jake gave the lounge-room a cursory look. 'Still can't believe you couldn't do better than *this*.'

'Well I couldn't.' Mattie stood up, still keeping an arm around Courtney but with her eyes on Max. 'Do you want to see your room? I've been working on it all weekend.'

'Okay.'

'Me too!' Courtney finally disengaged herself and jumped back. 'Where is it?'

'Up here.' Mattie led the way up the small passage and into the kids' bedroom. She stood back as they entered and then watched their faces

apprehensively, well aware that it didn't measure up to the other bedrooms. At home.

'Can I have the top bunk?' Courtney clambered up the ladder and
bounced on the top excitedly. 'Can I?'

'We're sharing?' Max sounded stunned.

'I *told* you that,' replied Mattie defensively. 'There weren't any three
bedroom units around. Not that I could afford.'

'And she didn't want to wait for something better,' added Jake, who
had come to stand in the doorway. 'Too eager to be shot of me. Which
is my cue to leave.'

'No!' The word came out like a gunshot and Mattie immediately flushed. 'I mean, I thought that, maybe . . . you'd like to stay for
dinner?'

Jake looked down at her with obvious amusement. 'And I thought
the whole point was to get *away* from me.'

'Not quite . . .' Mattie petered off as she glanced at the children, who
were both listening expectantly.

Courtney flipped onto her stomach and slid off the top bunk, a
pair of Barbie knickers flashing before she landed on her feet and the
tutu settled into place. She ran over to her father and wrapped an arm
around his knees. 'Please stay, Daddy. *Please.*'

'How can I refuse *you?*' Jake grabbed his daughter under both arms
and swung her up, settling her around his waist. She squealed with
delight and smacked a kiss against his cheek.

'Okay then,' Mattie said, injecting heartiness into her voice, 'let's celebrate with the champagne!'

'Celebrate?' queried Jake, raising an eyebrow at her.

'Well . . . you know what I mean.'

'Rarely, my dear, rarely,' said Jake, in his best Rhett Butler voice.

Max, who had watched this exchange silently, flicked one more
glance around his new bedroom and then squeezed past his father and
walked back into the lounge-room. Jake put Courtney down and she
ran after her brother, to start a mild bickering over the ownership of the
top bunk. Mattie followed them with more measured steps and turned
into the kitchen, where she put the mashed potatoes in the microwave

and pulled the casserole from the oven. Jake came in and leant against the doorframe.

'Need a hand?'

'No, it's all done.' Mattie examined the beef, noting with disappointment that the edges had started to congeal thickly. She trickled some water from the kettle into the casserole dish and stirred it vigorously. The water formed beaded rivulets through the red wine sauce, refusing to merge, while the chunks of meat separated into stringy threads.

'Mmm, looks appetising.'

Mattie flashed her husband a suspicious look but he just grinned back, the furrows on either side of his mouth stretching into smiles themselves. The microwave pinged so she removed the bowl of mashed potato and placed it on the table, which she had set earlier with four places. She gave the casserole one more hopeful stir and then gave up, putting it on the table also.

'It is hard to fail, but worse never to have tried to succeed,' Jake read from the fridge, and then glanced across at Mattie. 'Is that what you call leaving me? Trying to succeed?'

'No. That is, I —'

Jake gave her a wry smile. 'Just teasing.'

'Oh.'

'By the way, I like your jeans. Advertising your wares already, are you?'

'Only to you,' replied Mattie quickly, with a grin.

'Let's keep it that way, wench. And now, how about I open the champagne?'

Jake proceeded to do just that, the frothy liquid bubbling over the top as he rushed it to the sink. They both laughed and Mattie passed him two flutes.

'Is dinner ready? I'm *starving*.' Courtney bounced into the room, her ponytail flipping from side to side as she tried to take everything in.

'I'm not surprised. Look at the time.' Mattie glanced quickly at Jake, hoping he didn't take this as criticism, but he was busy mopping the champagne spillage off the floor. She turned back to Courtney. 'But it's ready now. Sit down and I'll fill your plate.'

Jake stood with an exaggerated groan and threw the dishcloth into the sink. Then he took his champagne over to the table and pulled out a chair. 'Max! Dinner's ready!'

Mattie sat down and took the cover off the casserole dish, ladling some up for Courtney. As Jake spooned mashed potato next to the beef, Max came in and slid into the spare seat quietly. He looked at the meal, flashed an expressionless glance at his mother and then stared down at his plate.

'Max said I can have the top bunk.' Courtney started mixing the beef and potato into a brown and cream swirl. 'He said he didn't care.'

'Well, I do,' said Mattie, loading her own plate. 'And I'm afraid Max gets the top bunk anyway. He's two years older than you.'

'That's not fair!' Courtney dropped her fork with a clatter and stared at her mother, instantly infuriated. 'He *said* he didn't want it. And I do!'

'That's not the point –'

'The point is,' Jake interrupted smoothly, 'the manufacturers recommend the bunks for eight years and over. And you, my love, are only six. Not –' he lifted a hand as Courtney opened her mouth – 'that you would be likely to have an accident, being particularly flexible for your age. But rules are rules. Besides, given that your mother was the one who put it all together – just think of me. I wouldn't be able to sleep at home knowing that you were risking your life each night over here.'

'Daddy,' giggled Courtney, mollified by this argument. 'What's flexible mean?'

'It means agile and cute. And in need of sustenance. Which means food. So eat up.'

'Thanks.' Mattie smiled at Jake as she passed the ladle across. Then she leant back, taking a sip of champagne while she regarded her son with some concern.

'Did you have a good weekend, Max?'

'Yep.' Max nodded his head without looking up.

'How did Auskick go on Saturday?'

'Okay.'

'Max!' Jake's sudden exclamation made everyone jump, including Mattie. 'For god's sake, answer your mother properly! It's like trying to get blood out of a damn stone!'

'It's all right.' Mattie shook her head at Jake. 'It's just all new for him. He'll talk when he wants to. Won't you, honey?'

'Yep.' Max was flushing. 'I mean, sure. I will.'

'I had a good weekend,' piped Courtney, flicking an overly bright glance from one parent to the other. 'But I missed you, Mummy.'

'We've already established that,' said Jake dryly.

As everybody else settled in to their meal, Mattie realised she had no appetite. Even the thought of trying to swallow mashed potato or the overdone beef made her feel ill. So instead she sat back, sipping her champagne and watching the others. Courtney, whose capacity for large meals was amazing for one so small, ate steadily, pausing every so often to glance around the table and reassure herself that her family seemed content. Max, on the other hand, kept his head down as he pushed his food around his plate, the set of his face a clear indication to Mattie that tears were just below the surface but being held rigidly in check. She sighed and glanced quickly at his father who, if he noticed the boy's distress, was not letting on. He looked up, caught Mattie's eye and grinned. A huge grin that was like an embrace, trapping her breath within her chest and making it ache.

By the time dinner was finished and the dishes were washed, it was already past the children's bedtime. Mattie tucked them into the bunk beds, with a promise to Courtney that the moment she turned eight, she'd be able to swap places with her brother if they were still in bunks, which Mattie fervently hoped wouldn't be the case anyway. For once she didn't stay to read them a story, using the excuse that it was late and they both had school tomorrow. But the truth was, she was too conscious of Jake, drying the dishes in the kitchen, and the chance that, once finished, he would simply call out a goodbye and leave. And she didn't want him to. So she kissed both children on the forehead, cheeks and chin, brushing Max's hair back and whispering that everything would be all right. Then she closed their door before walking (one, two, three) back through the lounge-room to the kitchen and picking up her champagne from the table.

'Finished already?' Jake stacked the dried dishes on the bench. 'What, no story?'

'Not today. It's too late.'

'Happy?'

'Pardon?' Mattie knew what he meant but the suddenness of the question took her by surprise.

'Are you happy?' Jake opened the cutlery drawer and slid knives and forks inside with a metallic clatter. 'You know, here. Was it worth it?'

'Worth what?' Mattie stalled for time, trying to play it safe.

'Worth the effort. Worth the money. Worth fucking up our family.'

'I haven't –'

'Yes you have. At least have the guts to admit it. Have you even *noticed* your son's face since we got here? Does he look like a happy kid to you? And what about Courtney? She tries to act all frigging bubbly but really she's just worried sick that her family's falling apart. So I'm asking you if it was worth it.'

Her muscles suddenly turning to liquid, Mattie flopped down onto a chair and stared at Jake. How could she explain that it wasn't about worth, or about trading her happiness for the misery of others? Especially when the guilt she felt was razor-sharp. And, at the same time, her despair was framed by anger. Anger that she should feel so bad for trying to survive, anger that the children's welfare was such a potent weapon, anger that she could feel her eyes filming with tears and there was nothing she could do to stop them.

Jake turned his head away and shook it. 'This is hopeless. I'd better go.'

'No!' Mattie's voice came out in a strangled squeak.

'Look, Mat –' Jake slid into the seat opposite her and, wrapping his hand around one of hers, looked at her earnestly – 'I don't want to upset you, and I don't want to have another fight. I'm bloody *sick* of them. But I can't help the way I feel. And watching what you're doing to the kids is tearing me up. It really is.'

'I know.' Mattie stared at her hand, so small within Jake's long fingers. He had piano-player hands. Rugged with muscle and elongated bones. Capable of extremes.

'But I promised that I'd shut up about it, didn't I?' Jake traced a line across the back of her wrist with one of his fingers. 'Give you the time you needed. Yet here I am going off at you first thing.'

'Doesn't matter.'

'Yes, it does. I'll shut up, okay?'

'Okay.' Mattie watched his finger start to draw little circles around each of her knuckles. They tingled, imprisoned by a sensory loop.

'But you have to understand my frustration too.'

'I *do*.' Mattie dragged her eyes up to his face. 'I *know* how hard this is for you.'

'Do you?' Jake grinned at her lopsidedly and then sighed.

'Well, I try to.'

Jake lifted up her trapped hand and kissed it lightly. 'I suppose that'll have to do then, hey? So I'll leave you to your little hovel, and I'll head off home to my mansion.'

'Don't rub it in.' Mattie smiled, her relief at his light-heartedness bringing with it a new sheen of tears.

'Just say the word.' Jake kissed her hand again before releasing it and stood up, stretching. 'Okay, so I pick up the kids from school Thursday, is that how it works?'

'Have another drink before you go.' Mattie held the champagne bottle aloft. 'You can't bring someone a present and then make them drink it alone.'

'Can't I?'

'No, it's terribly bad manners.'

'Why do I get the feeling you want me to stay?'

'Maybe because I do.'

'Let me see . . .' Jake sat back down and watched as she refilled their glasses. 'You spend a fortune renting a poky little flat to get away from me, but then you don't want me to leave? You're going to drive me crazy, Mattie.'

'Sorry.'

'So when you say you want me to stay –' Jake picked up his glass and took a sip – 'do you mean just for another drink, or do you mean . . . longer?'

'I mean longer,' replied Mattie without hesitation. And it was nice to know something for certain when everything else was confusion. She didn't know where she was going or even what she wanted if she got there, but she did know that she wanted Jake to stay tonight. To finish off the champagne and then go to bed and hold her tight. Make love. Fill her with security, and leave no room for doubts. Injecting something familiar into a life that was suddenly anything but.

*T*hey had already put a deposit on their own home before the wedding, and two months afterwards were able to move into a brand new clinker brick in Mont Gully, a relatively new suburb in Melbourne's eastern suburbs nestled between Wantirna and Boronia. Mattie's preference had been for nearby Box Hill, where she had grown up, which boasted numerous beautiful old-world Californian bungalows with deep verandahs and stained-glass windows. But, as Jake pointed out, for the same price as one of those they were able, with the help of their bank, to buy a twenty-five square, four bedroom, two bathroom house on a new estate. A house that nobody had lived in before them, a house that they could decorate to their own taste, with a garden they could start from scratch.

They did the long workday commute to the city for the first year. Driving in together, parking in the basement car-park beneath Jake's accountancy firm, and Mattie catching a tram up to her secretarial job in the Defence Department near Spencer Street. Then Jake joined a firm in Ringwood and for a while Mattie caught the train into town by herself. That was when they started planning for a baby.

And by then the brand-new, character-less house had been transformed into a fine residence. A beautifully manicured garden nestled all the way around the brickwork, edging the cobble-stoned driveway and forming a mounded figure of eight around the wrought iron letterbox. Inside, tasteful furnishings were enhanced, here and there, with a nice antique piece, and gold-framed prints complemented the colours of the walls and curtains and carefully chosen knick-knacks. While wall-to-wall thick cream carpet muffled sound and aided the illusion that, when that front door closed, they were all alone.

FOUR

M onday morning they all slept in, a circumstance made worse by unfamiliar surroundings. School clothes had to be found, bags packed, lunches made. Nevertheless Mattie felt warmed by the prior evening, and fuelled by a sense of certainty that everything was going to fall into place. The twelve months of separation would be spent without losing Jake, and the distance it created would heal rather than destroy. And he seemed to feel the same way, enveloping her in a snug embrace the moment she opened her eyes so that she woke into the warmth of security and optimism.

Jake departed first, leaving behind two children made even more confused by his presence. Mattie tried to explain as they sat down for a quick breakfast of orange juice and cereal, but the incomprehension remained. And they avoided her gaze, instead concentrating fiercely on drowning cornflakes by holding them under with their spoons. Then all explanations had to be put on hold as they piled into the car for a dash to school before the 9 am bell.

Of course, children being children, what on any other morning was a fairly straightforward exercise became, that morning, a major undertaking. First it was Max, who clutched at his belly and mumbled about stomach cramps and possible appendicitis. Then, while Mattie was dealing with this, Courtney, who had exited the car quite happily, paused by the school gates to watch the car suspiciously. When her brother still hadn't emerged after a few minutes, she came running back and, upon being told to get moving, promptly burst into tears.

The end result was that neither child was ready until well after the school bell had rung. Which meant that Mattie needed to take them in via the office, where she filled out late notes and, while there, quickly changed her emergency contact number. Then she took the children to their classrooms. Max, his olive skin flushed, hung his bag on a spare hook and took his seat without even glancing at his mother again, while Courtney clung to her hand until forcibly removed by the prep teacher. It didn't matter that Mattie, peering through the window after leaving the classroom, saw the child recover quickly enough to start chatting cheerfully with the others. She still felt gut-shot with guilt.

And this morning was the worst possible time for delays because she had an appointment at 9.30 am at the district Centrelink, where she had to prove her eligibility for a parenting payment, otherwise she was going to be in serious financial trouble. The last time Mattie had visited one of these places, they hadn't even been called Centrelink, but Social Security offices. Which made a lot more sense because that was exactly what they were, a government department that supported those who needed social security, either permanently, such as the disabled, or temporarily, like the unemployed.

It had even moved since her last visit, and was now situated in a hugely busy hub attached to a shopping complex in Wantirna, as if to taunt those on restricted finances with everything that they could not afford. Pubs, billiard halls, expensive specialty shops, boutiques, restaurants, they all surrounded the Centrelink office, greedily awaiting their share of a limited bounty.

Mattie walked up the steps and past a group of male teenagers whose jeans were worn so low on their skinny hips that the crotch almost linked their knees. They ignored her as she passed, concentrating instead on gazing into the middle distance with a studied casualness. The automatic doors slid open and she entered a glass atrium with rockpool fountains and copious marbled tubs of luxurious foliage. The Centrelink door was to her left so she pushed it open and entered a world so divorced from the cool serenity of the atrium that it was almost a physical shock.

There were counters staggered over the width of the huge room, with confusing names such as 'Newstart' and 'Parenting Claims'. Each counter had a stretch of yellow tape stuck to the carpet about four or five feet back so that the person being served was separated from the line of people waiting. And there were a lot of people waiting. The Newstart line was mainly made up of younger people dressed very similarly to the group outside. The only exceptions were a girl wearing a business suit, and a black-clad youth who had so much metal on his clothing and inserted into various parts of his flesh that, whenever he moved, he glinted fairy-like in the overhead lights.

Banks of seats made up the area on either side of the doors through which Mattie had entered, and these were filled almost to capacity with people of all ages, backgrounds and styles of dress. And they, like those waiting in the queues, were relatively quiet. In fact, for an area accommodating such a large number of people, the noise level was surprisingly low. Except for the odd muffled conversation and the occasional mother telling off an errant child, most of the people waited silently, their body language speaking of lethargy as they studiously avoided eye contact.

And Mattie didn't want to be there. As she paused just inside the doorway, she was suddenly struck with a sense of alienness, of not belonging. Something had gone wrong somewhere that *she*, with her planned marriage, and planned children, and planned life, should be here, contemplating joining the ranks of the single parents dependent on government handouts for survival. This didn't happen to her. This *couldn't* happen to her.

But it had. And, after a few moments during which her sudden panic attack threatened to send her back out into the safety of the atrium, she got her breathing under control and forced herself to walk slowly past the chairs and join the queue snaking up towards the Parenting Claims counter. She stood behind a young dark-haired woman with a stroller that contained a baby suffering from a nasty cold. With red-rimmed eyes and a constantly running nose, every so often the child punctuated the silence with a loud sneeze that sprayed the air around with tiny droplets of clear mucus.

'Sorry.' The young woman mopped the baby's nose with the corner of a towelling nappy and glanced apologetically at Mattie. 'I'd have rather kept her home but I had to come and fix up a mistake. I *had* to.'

'That's okay.' Mattie tried to smile understandingly, although she really didn't. How could a mother bring out a child who was so clearly unwell? She stood back and looked away, trying to avoid further conversation. She didn't belong here.

It took twenty-five minutes, with the sick child sneezing every five minutes or so, before the young woman with the stroller was called up to the counter and Mattie's toes fronted the yellow line. There ensued a hushed conversation during which the baby's sneezes were greeted not with the nappy but with a distracted rocking of the stroller as its mother concentrated on the Centrelink representative behind the counter. This was a plump man of about forty, with a receding head of thin, sandy hair that flowed down to his shoulders at the back. Mattie glanced behind her and was not surprised to see a line of about seven people, all women, snaking back to where she had started over half an hour ago.

'Next, please!'

Mattie whipped around to see that the young mother was finished and had pushed the stroller over to the side where she was cleaning up her offspring. Neither looked happy. The man behind the counter – Brian, according to his nametag – smiled politely as Mattie walked up, feeling like a fraud. As if he would realise, immediately, that she didn't belong here and send her on her way.

'How can I help you?'

'I made an appointment last week, for nine-thirty. Um, see I've just left my – that is, my marriage has broken down and I wanted to apply for a single mother's pension.'

'It's called a parenting payment now,' said Brian cheerfully, turning towards a computer screen set slightly to one side of him. 'What's your name?'

'Matilda Anne Hampton.'

Brian pressed a few keys and turned back to her, smiling genially. 'I've let the interviewer know that you're here so it shouldn't be too long. Just take a seat over there.' He waved to the rows of seats. 'Next!'

Mattie moved away as the next person, a plump young red-haired woman, quickly took her place. She stood still for a moment, staring back at Brian as he dealt with the woman in the exact same cheerful manner that he had shown her. No difference at all. She looked away quickly before he saw her staring and turned to the seating by the glass doors. There were about twenty-five people sitting there. In the front row was the young woman with the ill child, rocking the stroller while the baby cried fretfully. Next to her was a hugely overweight woman, her bulk overflowing onto the seat either side, who glared at the young mother every time the child sneezed. Then there was a young Muslim couple, the wife with her head modestly covered, and a very well-behaved toddler. On the last chair sat a young man, his legs splayed, who had a large black-inked tattoo running down his left arm that looked very much like train station graffiti. And that was just the front row. There were another four rows behind that.

Mattie's stomach twisted and she sighed, quietly. It was going to be a long, long wait.

She had no friends.

This realisation came to Mattie as she sat at her kitchen table with the Centrelink paperwork spread out in front of her. Her interviewer had been kind and very helpful but, in the end, Mattie elected to take the paperwork home and return it the next day. So, over the past two hours, she'd filled out her details and answered the questions with a steadily growing feeling of humiliation. Not that she hadn't expected to part with a fair degree of personal information to be granted a payment, but the nature of some of the questions left her with a sense of vulnerability and dependency very similar to the one she was trying to escape. However, she was well aware that at the moment she had no room for false pride – she needed this money and she needed it soon. So she worked up and over her resentment, and forged ahead. Until she reached the end and discovered she needed third-party verification of the fact that she and Jake were no longer living under the same roof.

While one part of her was acknowledging the reasonableness of this requirement, another part was cringing as it methodically evaluated potential referees. And crossed them off. As most people do, she had a number of acquaintances meandering through her life, and they crossed paths with a smile and the occasional chat. There were several couples they'd met through Jake's work, like the Dixons and the De Silvas, whom they'd have dinner with once or twice a year. And there were the much older Carsons, next-door neighbours for the past eight years who occasionally passed some home-grown vegetables over the fence and stopped to discuss the weather. Then there were the other mothers at the primary school, with whom she exchanged pleasantries, or sat next to during extra reading each Monday morning, or did canteen with once a month, and those, such as Rachel and Ginny, who shared a humid hour with her every Monday afternoon as their children learnt to swim at the local indoor swimming centre.

But none of these people were real *friends*; rather, they gathered around the periphery of her life, giving it the appearance of fullness without the actual substance. And she paled with embarrassment at the thought of approaching any of them to verify her separation. So what did it say about her life that she didn't have a single person of whom she was comfortable enough to ask this sort of favour? *Hi, do you mind signing this for me? Let's have a coffee while you do. White and one, isn't it?* Not a single person.

Where had they gone? *When* had they gone? Because once she'd been surrounded by such people. Friends who she could drop in on unannounced, or ring for a good long chat, or meet for a leisurely lunch. *Mattie! Of* course *you can come in. In fact, I was just thinking about you!* For starters there were her three ex-flatmates, all so close at one stage that they'd shared clothing, and baths, and far too many bottles of cheap sparkling wine. Jude had married a navy guy, whose particular job kept his family up at the top end of Australia, while Paula accepted a job promotion that took her to London about six years ago. But didn't either of them ever come back for visits? Or the obligatory births, deaths and marriages? How was it that these two women, once so much a slice of her existence that she knew what brand of sanitary products they used, now just formed part of her Christmas card list rather than her life?

And there was Liz who, as far as she knew, still lived in the inner-city area, only about three-quarters of an hour away. Yet the last time they'd met was at Liz's wedding, about five years ago, when she'd wed her long-time partner, Alan, an athletic type whose life was dominated by footy in the winter and cricket in the summer. He and Jake, whose idea of a relaxing evening was bound up either with computer programs or a game of chess, had never hit it off. Perhaps that was why they had all lost contact? Or maybe it was simply because Liz was unable to have children, and Mattie felt guilty with her healthy, happy pigeon pair.

But there had been other friends too, who would cry on her shoulder over the loss of a boyfriend one minute and then drag her out to a nightclub the next. Who would turn up on a Friday night with a tear-jerker movie and a bottle of Baileys, or would sprawl across her bed and offer advice while she cleaned out her wardrobe. How had she not noticed that gradually, over the past decade, she'd drifted away from all those she could lean on and not replaced them with new friends, new confidantes, a new circle of support? So that now she sat alone, without one person who could help her even fill out a damn form.

Mattie flung the pen across the table and leant back, her head pounding with self-pity. *How had this happened?* Had marriage and children taken over her life so completely that she hadn't noticed the loss of friends? Or was this how it was meant to be – that, once married, a person was *meant* to create distance around herself, a space to be filled with family now rather than friends? But then that meant it was even harder to escape, even harder to break away and start again.

Mattie wiped her eyes roughly. It just wasn't fair. Why did everything have to be so damn *hard*? Couldn't one thing, just *one* bloody thing, come easily? She hugged herself and stared at the far wall, allowing her misery full rein. It quickly rose, greedily demanding sustenance until it became so bloated that its very wretchedness began to disgust her. So she got up to wash her hands and then shoved her chair back so that she was facing the fridge, with its confetti messages of hope. *The future depends on what you do in the present. The obstacles of your past can become the gateways that lead to new beginnings.*

She read through the sayings, and then forced herself to do so again. Because she knew, from years of close acquaintance with the malignancy of self-pity, that taking such a path led her to a place where the misery itself would render her helpless. Feeding on itself until it became a self-fulfilling prophecy that threatened to destroy her more effectively than whatever it was that had sent her there in the first place.

So, with practised determination after re-reading the motivational exhortations, Mattie dragged her focus outside of her problems and started to systematically address them. First was the issue of the paperwork and, without suitable friends, there remained only Hannah. Who would make Mattie sweat while she read it through with thin lips, and would, when finished, shake her head and sigh sadly – but she would sign it nevertheless. And then Mattie could submit the whole application and be officially on the government payroll, which meant she would have breathing space until she worked out what to do next.

But the issue of friends was still important, because Mattie knew she was going to need a support network, not so much to unburden herself but so that she could feel *connected*. A community fabric capable of weaving her a richer life. She reached across the table to retrieve her pen and started doodling on the Centrelink instructions. *We will rebuild* ☺. Shades of the six-million dollar man, back when six million actually meant something and Farrah Fawcett Majors was every young guy's pin-up dream.

The phone rang just as she was putting the finishing touches to a cartoon caricature of two little figures holding hands (*Friendship is* . . .), so she abandoned her musings and got up to answer it. No more streamlined cordless telephones networked throughout the house, just a mustard-yellow wall-phone that hung by the refrigerator with a long, tangled cord spiralling nearly down to the floor.

'Hello?'

'Hello there, sweetheart,' Jake's voice came warmly down the line. 'What's up?'

'Nothing much.' Mattie smiled, leaning against the wall and feeling a bit like a teenager as she absentmindedly coiled the telephone cord around one finger.

'Wish I could say the same. Seems everybody's left their tax returns late this year. We're flat out.'

'Poor you.'

'Yes, poor me. What I need is a hot bath, a massage, and a bit of Mattie. Not necessarily in that order. Anyway, what's for tea?'

'Tea?' repeated Mattie, the smile sliding off her face.

'Yeah – tea. You know, the meal that comes after lunch.'

'I . . . don't know.'

'That's not like you, Little Miss Organisation.'

'No.' Mattie couldn't think of what else to say. She didn't know how, or when, Jake had got the impression he was coming around to the unit tonight. She'd actually planned on taking the children out to McDonald's after their swimming lesson, as a sort of celebration and the chance for a chat without distractions. But the last thing she wanted to do was get Jake offside, again, so it looked like she would have to rethink things.

'I take it from the silence that you don't actually want me?'

'It's not that,' said Mattie quickly. 'Just that I hadn't . . . but of course you're welcome. You know that.'

'No, I don't know that. I'm beginning to think I don't know anything. But tell me, what was last night about then?'

'Last night?'

'Yeah, last night. Remember? When you were all over me like a rash?'

'A rash?'

'Christ, Mattie, I always know you're playing games when you repeat everything I say. At least have the guts to tell me where I stand.'

Mattie pulled the corkscrewed cord off her finger, leaving red indentations that numbed her knuckles. 'Look, last night I needed . . . I don't know. It's just that I –'

'Want to pull the strings. That's it, isn't it? It's all about what *you* need, what *you* want. Which is everything your own way.'

'No!' Mattie could hear the indignation in her voice, tinged with desperation.

'Yes. You want me to be there when it suits you, and away when it doesn't. And I'm expected to somehow magically know which is which. Well, life doesn't work that way, lady. You can't treat people like frigging puppets.'

'Listen, Jake.' Mattie spoke quickly, the words tumbling over each other. 'I'm *not* playing games. And I'm sorry if you . . . but how can I want everything my own way when I don't even know *what* I want? That's why I'm here – I'm *trying* to work it out!'

'Well, you'd better bloody work it out soon, because I'm fed up.'

'But you have to realise . . .' Mattie petered off as the engaged signal sounded in her ear. He'd hung up. She replaced the receiver gently and then massaged her knuckles until the blood flow throbbed painfully through her fingers. Then she washed her hands, took a deep breath and gathered together the Centrelink paperwork, aligning the edges neatly. One thing at a time and first things first. These needed to be signed and delivered, otherwise her twelve months were going to be over before they began. And, amongst everything she was confused about, one thing stood out in bold relief – if she went back now, she would never leave again.

'Do you think Daddy's sad by himself?'

Mattie looked across the scrabble board at Courtney with surprise. Because the question came totally from left field. Neither child had even mentioned their father all afternoon and Mattie had gone to great pains to make sure they'd enjoyed themselves. Although she'd given the McDonald's idea a miss, just in case Jake *did* turn up, she kept the celebratory theme going with a picnic in the lounge-room. While the two children showered after swimming, Mattie laid out the Onkaparinga blanket across the carpet for them to sit around cross-legged for dinner. Crumbed chicken pieces, thick gravy, oven-fried chips and corn on the cob. They pretended they were outside, with flies landing on the food and the sun beating down so fiercely they had to shade their eyes. At one stage Mattie made out that she had swallowed a fly, gagging and clutching her throat and finally collapsing theatrically. Even Max laughed out loud.

Then, after the picnic was cleaned up, she brought out the Scrabble things and set them up on the coffee table. All three of them were dressed in winter flannelette pyjamas, with Mattie sitting on the couch, Courtney leaning against her mother's legs and Max stretched out across the beanbag on the floor. And, with a skill born of long practice, Mattie managed to compartmentalise everything unpleasant. Like this afternoon's altercation with Jake and, later, Hannah's tight, disapproving face as she signed her sister's Centrelink forms. So both became just the faintest of sour tastes that didn't prevent her from creating a lovely evening – cosy and relaxed and compensatory.

'Well, Mummy? D'you think he is?' Courtney twisted herself around, tucking her still damp hair behind her ears as she regarded her mother quizzically.

'No way.' Mattie made herself smile. 'In fact, I wouldn't be surprised if he's having a lovely time enjoying the peace and quiet. It'll be like a little holiday.'

'You think?'

'Definitely.' Mattie glanced across at Max, who was rearranging his letters carefully. 'Don't you agree, honey?'

'About what?'

'About your father. Don't you think he'll be enjoying the peace and quiet?'

'S'pose.'

'He *said* he'd miss us.' Courtney sounded unconvinced by her mother's argument. 'He said the house was too big for just him.'

Max sat up in the beanbag, bringing his knees up and wrapping his arms around them as he looked at the other two. 'Dad said the echoes would drive him nuts.'

'If you didn't first,' added Courtney, glancing sidelong at her mother.

'Me?' Mattie stared from one child to the other, astounded. 'He actually said that? That I was driving him nuts?'

'Yep.' Courtney regarded her mother attentively, watching for a reaction. 'He said you're the reason his hair's all falling out. And that you made him cross.'

'No he didn't.' Max looked at his sister impatiently. 'He was only joking about the hair. And he said she *was* his cross, not that she *made* him cross.'

'His cross?' repeated Mattie, even more stunned. His *cross*?

'Like Jesus,' explained Max, digging his fingernails into his knees and examining the crescent-shaped moons left behind in the flannelette of his pyjamas.

Courtney frowned. 'I don't get it.'

'You don't have to,' Mattie snapped and then, as both children looked at her with surprise, took a few deep breaths. She reached forward and wrapped an arm around Courtney, giving her a brief squeeze. 'Sorry, honey. I didn't mean to take it out on you. It's just that . . . well, I'm surprised Daddy said that. And a bit hurt. Because, see – years ago, back when you were both really little, we made an agreement that we'd never criticise each other in front of you guys. That we'd be a team. And if we had something to say we'd say it to each other.'

'Some team,' muttered Max as he stared down at his knees again.

'And Daddy says you don't listen anyway,' interjected Courtney, playing with her mother's gold link bracelet.

'God.' Mattie suddenly felt tired, very tired. And angry.

'You know how you said before about Daddy being happy we're not there?' Courtney unclipped the bracelet while she spoke and laid it against her own skinny wrist, admiring the effect. 'Well, does that mean *you're* happy when we're not here too? That you don't miss us?'

'No!' Mattie shook her head emphatically. 'I miss you *dreadfully*!'

'Are we gonna play or what?' Max unfolded himself and flopped back down in front of his Scrabble letters. 'Whose turn?'

'Courtney's,' replied Mattie distractedly, her head pounding. She couldn't believe that Jake had described her as a cross to bear. And that she drove him nuts. It was so totally unfair, and so counterproductive. Because it only confused the kids and made her justifiably furious. How could he talk one minute about wanting everything to work out, and then do something like that? It was incredibly hypocritical, and made no sense.

'We're going to have special Friday nights every week.' Courtney linked two Scrabble tiles horizontally from another word to spell out

BIG. She smiled happily at the word before turning back to her mother. 'Either Max or me gets to pick what takeaway we have and then that person gets to choose a movie too. It was Max's turn last week coz of being the oldest so it's my turn this week. I can't wait.'

'Oh,' said Mattie rather faintly. She looked across at Max but he'd busied himself with his letters again.

'And we're getting pocket money now too. I'm getting six dollars because I'm six and Max's getting eight.'

'You're kidding.'

'D'you write down my points, Max?' Courtney gestured at the pad lying on the floor by her brother, her mother's gold bracelet glinting on her wrist. 'And it's your turn now.'

Rather blankly, Mattie watched Max add up Courtney's score and jot it down before turning his attention to the Scrabble board. Back when Max started school, three years ago, Mattie suggested pocket money but had been vetoed by Jake. He felt that the object of pocket money was primarily to teach children the value of money and some degree of financial responsibility, and these were not lessons that could be fully appreciated under the age of ten. Mattie reluctantly agreed and the subject of pocket money had been put on hold. Or so she'd thought.

'Are you angry about the money, Mum?'

Mattie looked across at Max quickly. 'No, no. Of course not.'

'You *looked* angry.'

'Did I? Must have been something else. No . . . I suppose I wish your father'd discussed it with me first, that's all.'

'I'm going to save up for a Baby Born doll,' announced Courtney, playing with the bracelet again. 'Daddy said if I save half the money, he'd give me the other half.'

'That's nice of him.'

'Yes. And then I'll save up for the changing centre. It's got a seat and a bath and shelves and . . . hey, Mummy, what'll I do when I get it?' Courtney twisted around again to face her mother worriedly. 'Like, where will it live? Here or at home?'

'I'm sure we'll work it out. Be careful with my bracelet, please.'

'And Dad said he'd get Max a puppy for his birthday.' Courtney frowned. 'Which is totally unfair coz I want one too.'

Mattie stared at Courtney for a few moments while she tried to digest this, her head aching even more with the effort. Then she glanced across at Max but he avoided her gaze, instead laying down three tiles from Courtney's BIG to spell the word BOOT.

'Well done.' Mattie blinked rapidly and tried to concentrate on her letters – P, O, Z, L, F – but it was difficult with so much new information demanding her attention. Takeaway food, movies, pocket money, a *puppy* – this was beginning to sound like some sort of competition in which Jake had already had several rolls of the dice. The P blurred into the smooth ivory of the scrabble tile as Mattie stared at it, and suddenly she realised that a competition was *exactly* what it was and, what's more, she should have foreseen it. Because she knew Jake, and she knew the way he operated. He was a chess player, quite capable of thinking many moves ahead and planning an approach accordingly. And also fond of advocating the methodological skills required for chess as a lucrative way of approaching life's challenges. Attack is the best form of defence.

'Mum, your turn,' said Max impatiently.

'Just a second.' Mattie put down three letters to make the word FOOL. Which, she thought, was exactly what she'd be if she tried to compete with Jake – firstly, because she didn't have enough money to match his largesse, and secondly, because she was always going to be several steps behind, like now, simply because she didn't have the same talent for tactical thinking. Manipulation didn't come easily and even when she tried it, she usually ended up only making things harder for herself. Especially against Jake.

While Max tallied up her score and Courtney started arranging her letters, Mattie closed her eyes and massaged her temples lightly, trying to alleviate her headache. But all she could think of was that if Jake was going to start playing games, she was going to be at a distinct disadvantage. And if the children were going to be used as pawns, she was going to have to guard against being dragged into the competition. The trouble was, she was beginning to suspect that was going to prove next to impossible.

*M*ax was born exactly two years after they moved into their own house. From the moment she discovered she was pregnant, Mattie read everything she could find about babies. It was like a compulsion, a thirst for knowledge that was rarely satiated. She discovered what to expect during labour, the importance of breastfeeding, the need for pelvic floor exercises. She learnt about jaundice, and nappy-rash, and how the fontanelle, that tiny stretched canvas of vulnerability, would depress if the baby was dehydrated.

The only thing she didn't discover, because words couldn't describe it, was the feeling she would experience when the baby was placed on her belly. That minute scrap of humanity, with bloody streaks across a wrinkled, marbled body.

It was contentment like nothing she had ever known. Almost spiritual in its intensity, with a liquid joy that ran through her veins, quickening her pulse and making her nerve-ends tremble. Touching the baby, stroking his damp hair and caressing his rounded belly filled her with awe. She laid a finger across his palm and his impossibly small fingers immediately wrapped themselves around it with a grip that spoke of dependence and responsibility. She smiled at him, delighted, and he gazed wetly up at her as if he, too, was struck by a sense of transcendental wonder. Of recognition.

After a while, Mattie tore her eyes away from the baby and looked up at Jake, sitting on the side of the bed with his face mirroring the same marvel. Their eyes met and tacitly acknowledged the miracle they had created. Life. An independent human being capable of loving and being loved. A member of a family, part of a team. Their son.

FIVE

Mattie walked the children to school the following morning. It was such a beautiful spring day, cool but with a crisp clarity that was invigorating, it seemed almost criminal to take the car when she was in no rush to go anywhere else. In fact, for the first time in years, the day stretched out before her with barely any demands at all. The Centrelink forms were all signed and the unit was so compact that keeping it clean took hardly any time, nor was there any need to do gardening anymore. Or repaint a wall, or file paperwork, or iron Jake's collection of business shirts. And the fact that she had only just moved in meant that there were no cupboards to be cleaned out, or linen to be reorganised, or bathrooms to be scrubbed.

It was a strange feeling, heady with indolence and intrinsic guilt. But she determined to enjoy it while she could and, after the children were safely delivered, continued her walk down towards the Mont Gully town centre. There, she window-shopped and browsed her way along the main street, going inside the pet shop and looking at the puppies that wrestled amongst the straw and leapt against their glass enclosures to attract her attention. For a moment she toyed with the idea of buying one now and pre-empting Jake, but the possible consequences of this stilled her hand. This thought allowed the altercation with Jake to filter through her defences, so she shored them up again and ignored the sick feeling that had come with it.

The shops finished at a huge intersection that guided a flood of traffic along Burwood Highway and around the town. Mattie crossed at the lights there, intending to continue her stroll back in the direction she'd come, but instead her eye was drawn to the huge pastel mural adorning the community centre that, alongside the local library, was set back from the main shopping strip behind a grassy verge with park benches and a winding gravelled path. The mural featured an array of active figures – a man with a small boy astride his shoulders, a woman pushing a pram with a happily waving baby, a builder with a ladder under his arm, a pair of schoolchildren running along hand-in-hand. The figures stretched from the entrance and around the edge of the community centre, finishing with the schoolchildren and a leg kicking back in front of them that belonged to the next character, most of which was obviously on the rear wall. Underneath the figures, rippling up and down beneath their feet, was a stream of deliberately childish red lettering that read: *It's* your *community – so come on! Get connected!*

Mattie stared at the mural, and the lettering, for quite a while. She'd been past the community centre countless times, either on her way into town or out, or when taking the children to the library, or just during her weekly shopping trips. And if someone had asked her to describe it, she would have been able to give a detailed description of the building, the mural, and probably even the message. Yet never had she *really* read it. Or perhaps, more to the point, never had it really meant anything.

Get connected. That was exactly what she needed to do. Establish roots that went a little deeper than they did at the moment so that she could thrive, blossom. With the gravel scrunching under her shoes, Mattie walked up the meandering pathway towards the community centre. Once there she pushed open the glass door before she could have second thoughts and entered the foyer. It had a crowded, busy feel, even though she was the only person there. To her right was a wall holding rack upon rack of leaflets about subjects ranging from apprenticeships to sexually transmitted diseases, while straight ahead was a huge noticeboard with glossy posters and small handmade signs thumbtacked onto every spare space. Posters about health issues (*Violence against women – Australia says no!*) and photocopies advertising local events (*St Mary's fete – be there!*) as well as laboriously printed scraps pleading for the return of family pets (*Lost! Ben, a five-year-old German Shepherd – family grieving. Reward offered*).

An exercise or dance class was in progress somewhere in the building, judging from the faint beat of music and the occasional hollow litany of foot thumps. To Mattie's right, next to the racks, was a passageway leading further into the centre and to her left was a window with a sliding glass panel set into it and a sign above reading Community Advisory Centre, with a smaller sign underneath instructing people to 'Ring if Unattended'. There was a silver bell sitting on the narrow window ledge.

As soon as she walked over, Mattie could see there was no need to use the bell as the office was occupied by a woman currently on the phone. She was large and middle-aged, with copper-tipped brown hair cut in a severe bob that contrasted oddly with the softness of her rounded features. She noticed Mattie standing at the window and smiled, rolling her eyes to indicate that she was trying to wind up the call. While waiting Mattie occupied herself by reading some of the notices on the board ahead. Next to Ben's 'missing' poster was a notice from Tamara offering her babysitting services and another from Wendy detailing her house-cleaning skills. After a minute or so, the woman in the office hung up the phone and came over to the window, sliding back the glass panel with the rattling sound of ball-bearings rolling smoothly.

'Sorry 'bout that.' She folded her arms on the inside ledge and rested her ample bosom on them, smiling cheerfully at Mattie. 'My name's Beryl. How can I help you?'

'Well, I've just, um – well, ended up with more spare time on my hands than usual and I thought I'd like to do, maybe some voluntary work or something?'

'That's excellent!' said Beryl enthusiastically. 'We always need more volunteers. And there's *heaps* of different things you can do. Did you have anything particular in mind?'

'Not really.' Mattie glanced around for inspiration. 'Um, what about what you're doing? Is that voluntary?'

'Absolutely! And you'd be more than welcome, that's for sure. Now,

you'd need to do a course in community service but it's great fun.
You'll enjoy it. And you get a diploma too! It's a proper course, y'know.
Accredited.'

'How long does it go for?' asked Mattie a bit doubtfully.

'Only a couple o' months. And you don't go every day. Here, I'll get
you the paperwork and you can have a good gander at home.' Beryl
hoisted herself away from the ledge and ambled over to a filing cabinet,
the middle drawer of which was already open with a stack of papers
piled precariously on top. Beryl rummaged through the pile, grunting
with success when she located what she was after. She came back over
to the window and passed a couple of stapled A4 pages through to
Mattie. 'There you go then. That'll tell you all you need to know. But
mind you don't give up on the idea if you don't think this is what you're
after, because there's all sorts of other things. Meals on Wheels, literacy
programs, reading to the elderly. And much more.'

'Thanks.' Mattie smiled her appreciation as she folded the paper
in half.

'But y'know, just between you and me –' Beryl leant forward con-
spiratorially – 'I reckon this here's one of the best. You get to meet some
real interesting types.'

'What sort of things do you do?' asked Mattie curiously.

'Oh, you name it! Lots of people come in off the street, like you, asking about sports around here, or clubs they can join. Stuff like that. We
also get a lot o' council queries, and complaints too! Then there's the
phone! Never stops!'

'People ring up then?' prompted Mattie, reluctant to end the
discussion.

'All the time. Some real sad cases. Lonely people – we've got a few
regulars. They know who's on when and they've got their favourites.
Then there's the shy ones. And the desperate. They're the worst of all.
No money, or food.'

'What do you do for them?'

'We put most of those onto the charities. Salvos or whatever. Every
now and then you get something unexpected.' Beryl grinned, obviously
relishing this facet. 'Like the other week this young girl walks in off

the street with a baby and a suitcase. She'd come from interstate, had nowhere to go. Just hopped on a train and split! Y'know, between you and me, I reckon she was running away from some bloke.'

'That's terrible.'

'Yeah, but gutsy too, don't you reckon?' Beryl continued without waiting for an answer. 'She wasn't saying why she shot through but I sent her over to the DV outreach anyway. They'll organise her till she finds her feet.'

'What's a DV outreach?' asked Mattie curiously.

'Well, DV's domestic violence of course. And the main centre's in town so they have outreach services for us in the suburbs. But the point is,' Beryl indicated the folded paper in Mattie's hand just as the phone rang from within the office – 'you'll have a ball. Trust me.'

'Well, thanks for your help.'

'No problem. Hopefully we'll be seeing you soon!'

Mattie moved away as Beryl slid the window closed and then made her way back to her chair where she picked up the telephone again. Hesitant to leave just yet, Mattie only went as far as the notice-board where she started perusing the signs more thoroughly. She absently straightened Ben's 'missing' poster while she wondered if he'd ever been found, or whether Tamara received any babysitting jobs, or whether Wendy actually made a living from cleaning other people's houses. And did anybody ever respond to the notices about the dangers of smoking while pregnant, and breast examinations, and domestic violence? What about requests for people to join a weight-loss support group, or help out with the community newspaper, or hold a Tupperware party?

Mattie's eyes flicked back to the little printed square extolling the virtues of a Tupperware party and, as she read it through again, a brilliant idea seeded itself in her mind. Not a Tupperware party, but something party-plan, something a bit different. The excuse to do something proactive, to ring up old friends and maybe turn those who were just acquaintances into actual friends. And it wouldn't matter if not too many came, because with party-plan it was acceptable to have any number between three and thirty. It wasn't like throwing an actual party where numbers made a statement that could be lethal. No, this was foolproof. It was perfect.

The day passed quickly. After leaving the community centre, Mattie stopped off at the library and researched party-plan options on the Internet. She left feeling even more motivated, with a list of possibilities as well as a couple of novels and a leaflet about a book club that met once a month. When she got home, she made herself a cup of coffee and got to work. First, she narrowed her list of possibilities down to three and then spent some time mulling over them before choosing her favourite. Called Whimsicalities, it offered an eclectic mix of pottery, giftware and 'whimsical knick-knacks' that were 'absolutely guaranteed to entertain you and your friends'. Mattie made the call, reaching the consultant on her mobile and booking a party for a Saturday afternoon in three weeks' time, in mid-November. The consultant, Sharon, gave her a rather breathless spiel about the range of products and promised to drop some invitations around soon. Mattie hung up, feeling an odd mix of trepidation and triumph.

She spent most of the afternoon happily making lists. A list of people to invite, a list of food to serve, a list of groceries to purchase. It was fun. And she felt invigorated, both by the knowledge that things were starting to fall into place, and by the awareness that she was helping them along. Being proactive. After the lists were more or less complete, Mattie left them on the table and started carrying the folded cardboard boxes from the laundry to the garbage bins. There, she systematically tore them into smaller pieces to fit inside the large blue-lidded recycling bin.

The weather was as pleasant as it had been that morning, and Mattie was just considering tidying her small garden when she noticed an older woman walking slowly down the main concrete driveway towards the bank of letterboxes out by the road. Mattie stood by the garbage bins and watched the woman approach, and then impetuously decided to add to her list of steadily growing accomplishments by introducing herself to her first neighbour. She ran her fingers through her hair and then walked nonchalantly across towards the letterboxes.

The woman, who was unlocking a metal flap at the rear of number two, turned as Mattie approached and watched her curiously. She was dressed casually, in a pair of black pants and a grey and black checked windcheater jacket that was buttoned up all the way to her neck. She was also older than Mattie had first thought, with a deeply lined face and light grey hair that curled softly over her head.

'Hello,' said Mattie, with a welcoming smile as she made a show of checking her own letterbox, which she already knew was empty.

The woman glanced down at the brass number adorning Mattie's letterbox and then back. 'Ah. You must be the new one,' she said, in a rather strong accent that Mattie guessed was German. 'Just moved into unit one, have you?'

'That's right. My name's Mattie.'

'Hilda.' She smiled at last, her multitude of facial lines deepening. She turned and gestured towards the unit that backed onto Mattie's. 'From just behind you.'

'Nice to meet you,' said Mattie.

Hilda's black-button eyes flicked over Mattie and settled back on her face, all in an instant. She nodded, as if in approval. 'You have nice little children. I spoke to them yesterday when they were out in your yard. Very nice. Polite.'

'Would you like a cup of coffee?' asked Mattie impulsively, astonishing even herself.

'A coffee?' Hilda pulled up a grey and black sleeve to reveal a surprisingly feminine gold watch. She studied it.

'Do you have to be somewhere?'

'No, no. Just that I don't have coffee after two. Bladder's not what it used to be.'

'Really?' Mattie paused, unsure of what to reply to this revelation.

'But it's close enough.' Hilda smiled again. 'Coffee would be most welcome, thank you. I'll just leave my mail at home. Give me five minutes.'

Mattie hurried back inside to put the kettle on, stunned that she'd even issued the invitation. It was very unlike her, and she was already doubting its wisdom. For all she knew, Hilda was a lonely old gossip who would now drop in unannounced at all hours. Or when Jake was there. Opening up her horizons was one thing, but opening up her door was another. Nevertheless, it was done. So she moved all the party-plan paperwork off the table and placed it on top of the fridge, out of sight, before putting out her crystal creamer and sugar bowl together with some shortbread biscuits on a plate. Hilda knocked on the door just as Mattie was pushing the plunger down on the brew, so she called for her to come in.

'Mirror image,' said Hilda from the lounge-room. She walked through into the kitchen, looking around with interest. 'You are exact the opposite from me. Everything. How strange.'

'Really?' said Mattie politely. She noted, with some amusement, that Hilda had obviously run a brush through her hair, which now curled up and away from her forehead in neat grey waves. Mattie poured coffee into two mugs and brought them over to the table, nodding at the sugar bowl and creamer as she put the mugs down and pulled a chair out for herself. 'Milk? Sugar?'

'No, thank you.' Hilda bent down slightly to read the sayings on the fridge. She read them silently and then sat down opposite Mattie, wrapping her hands around her mug as she continued her visual inspection. 'Only just starting out, are you?'

'Something like that.'

Hilda brought her curious gaze back. 'Mattie. What sort of name is Mattie?'

'It's short for Matilda.'

'Ah. Mine is short for Hildegarde. What a mouthful, hey? My sister was Gertrude. And my brother is called Wolfgang.'

'Are they German names?' asked Mattie.

'*Gott*, no!' Hilda looked shocked. 'Austrian! Viennese, to be exact.'

'Oh, I see. Um, sorry,' Mattie added the apology as Hilda was still looking at her askance. She realised that she probably should have guessed Hilda wasn't German; her accent didn't have that guttural depth unique to the Germans. Instead it had a melodious quality that reminded Mattie of *The Sound of Music*, with the last words of each sentence rising in an upwards inflection.

'Emigrated fifty years ago,' continued Hilda proudly. 'After the war.'

'Did you come out by yourself?'

'No. With my husband and our three children. They were only tiny then, of course.'

'How long have you been here? In the unit?'

'Let me see.' Hilda took a sip of coffee and thought about the question. 'Just after my Ernest retired. We sold the house to our eldest son and his wife, and bought the unit. Must be about twelve years now.'

'That's nice,' said Mattie, relieved that Hilda was part of a large family. 'I mean, selling your house to your son, so that it didn't pass out of the family.'

'Yes, he is a sentimental one, that boy.' Hilda smiled affectionately. 'Me, I do not much care. As long as I have somewhere to put my knick-knacks and the rain stays out, that is good enough for me.'

'Is everyone here nice?' asked Mattie curiously. 'Like, there's nobody who has noisy parties every weekend, is there?'

'No, nothing like that,' Hilda laughed. 'In fact, the only problems we have ever had was with this unit. Yours. Because it is the only rental. Before you, we had a pair of young fellows – nice to talk to but *Gott*! Did they have their music loud? Thump, thump, thump. All the time.'

'How annoying.'

'Well, there is worse,' said Hilda philosophically, taking another sip and regarding Mattie pensively over the rim of her mug. 'What about you then? Is there a husband?'

'A husband?' repeated Mattie, a bit stunned by the directness of the question.

'You think I am being nosy,' stated Hilda with a rueful nod. Then she smiled across at Mattie, her black-button eyes all but disappearing between the creases of her face. 'My husband is always saying I am. And he is right. So just tell me to keep my nose out if you like. I do not offend easily.'

'That's okay,' Mattie smiled back. 'And, yes, there's a husband, but we're having a bit of a break at the moment. Sorting out some stuff.'

'Ah.' Hilda put her head to one side and pursed her lips. 'Not good?'

Mattie was saved from answering by the phone ringing. It was Jake, it had to be. Her eyes widened slightly with this realisation and she wished fervently that she hadn't been so impulsive as to invite Hilda inside. But that wish paled against the relief that washed through her – relief that he wasn't holding a grudge, that things were back to normal and she could rid herself of the unease that framed each day whenever they weren't speaking. All this took only a second to flash through her mind and then Mattie smiled apologetically at Hilda as she stood and reached quickly for the wall-phone, leaning across the table and plucking the receiver from its cradle. 'Hello?'

'Can I speak to Mrs Hampton?'

Mattie's stomach plummeted at the sound of the unfamiliar voice. 'Speaking.'

'Hello, Mrs Hampton – or it's Matilda, isn't it? Look, this is Jan Mac-Farlane. I'm the district counsellor for your son's primary school. I was there today.'

'Oh?'

'Yes, and . . . well, I've got a few concerns that I'd like to speak to you about.'

'A few concerns?' repeated Mattie, her throat drying.

'Mattie?' hissed Hilda, levering herself up with the aid of the table.

'Excuse me one minute, will you?' Without waiting for an answer, Mattie put her hand over the mouthpiece and turned to Hilda. 'Sorry about this. It's my son's school.'

'Is everything all right?'

'Sure. They just want to chat about a few things.'

'I shall see myself out then.' Hilda picked up her mug and took it over to the sink where she rinsed it and placed it upside down on the draining board. 'Nice to meet you, and thank you for the coffee.'

'My pleasure.' Mattie watched the older woman go back out through the lounge-room and waited till she heard the front door close before removing her hand. 'Sorry about that.'

'Is this a bad time? I could call back later.'

'No, now's fine. Um, you said you had concerns?'

'Yes. Your son's teacher spoke to me about a few issues so I met with him today. Max, that is. For a little one-on-one. And I found him quite . . . closed off. Is he always like that?'

'Yes,' replied Mattie, relieved. 'Always. That's just Max.'

'But the problem is, Matilda, that I couldn't talk to him about his teacher's concerns because he was simply . . . well, uncooperative. Wouldn't discuss anything.'

'I'm not surprised.' Mattie frowned. 'Look, I don't want to be rude, but don't you need my permission to counsel my son?'

'Oh no, I wasn't counselling him. Just an initial discussion. Nothing to worry about. If I felt the need for counselling, then of course I'd get in touch with you and we'd toss a few ideas around.'

'Is that what you're doing now?' asked Mattie slowly.

'Well . . . maybe. To be honest, Matilda, I'm not sure if Max needs anything because I couldn't talk to him. That's why I thought I'd call you.'

'What were his teacher's concerns?'

'Predominantly – unnecessary aggression.'

Mattie's eyes widened. 'Aggression?'

'Yes. Apparently Max has a tendency to lash out at times. Yesterday, for example.'

'What happened yesterday?'

'You don't know?' Jan MacFarlane fell silent for a moment before continuing. 'I see. Well, perhaps you should ask Max for his detention slip when he gets home. You'll need to sign it anyway. I believe it's for Thursday afternoon.'

Mattie spoke tightly. 'Could you just tell me what happened?'

'Certainly. Apparently he got into a scuffle with another boy in the playground and a teacher had to intervene. She broke it up and sent them to opposite ends of the yard but Max wouldn't leave. The teacher had to hold him back until the other boy was out of sight. Then, when she let him go, he ran straight over to the other side and hunted this boy down. By the time the teacher got there, he had the child on the ground.'

'Oh my god.'

'Luckily the boy wasn't really hurt, otherwise the consequences could have been much worse. But, Matilda, when Max was taken inside to the principal's office, he cried so hard he had to be taken to the sick bay where he threw up.'

'Oh my god,' repeated Mattie, feeling nauseous herself.

'So you see, there're some legitimate concerns. And what I wanted to ask, if you don't mind, is whether there's anything going on at home that might be causing this behaviour?'

'Oh.'

'Like a death in the family? Maybe problems with a sibling? Anything you can tell me would help us try to get a handle on this. For Max's sake.'

'Of course.' Mattie wiped her eyes roughly with the heel of her spare hand and tried to think. 'Um, look, there *is* some stuff going on – but it's only temporary. Should be all sorted out within a month or so.'

'I see.' Jan MacFarlane sounded doubtful.

'Yes, it's just a matter of – well, we've just moved and there's the whole establishing routine and everything. It's all a bit unsettling. I'll talk to Max, make it easier.'

'Perhaps we could make an appointment? Discuss things a bit more at length?'

'Oh, that's not necessary,' replied Mattie, trying to sound breezy as she sat down again and wished that the lead weight in her belly would disappear. 'Not yet anyway. I tell you what, you give me a month or so to sort it out and then, if you still think there's a problem, we'll talk more. Okay?'

'Well, I wonder if it wouldn't be better to nip things in the bud, so to speak, try to get to the bottom –'

'There's nothing to get to the bottom *of*,' said Mattie quickly. 'Just a change in routine that Max needs to get used to. And I'm terribly grateful that you've let me know, because now I can give him a little extra attention. Help him adjust.'

'Well, Matilda, if you think that –'

'I do,' replied Mattie firmly.

'All right then. If you really feel that's all it is, we'll give it some time. And I'll speak to you again in a month. Hopefully you're right and the situation's improved.'

'Oh, it will have, I'm sure.'

'Goodbye then. Thanks for your time.'

Mattie stood again to hang up the phone and then took a deep breath, letting it out with a rush. This was all she needed. The involvement of some idealistic counsellor who learnt all her lessons from a textbook and expected them to frame real life. And then, instead of adjusting the frame when it didn't fit, she would try to mould them, or label them. But things just weren't that simple. Unfortunately.

Mattie took another deep breath and tried to think things through without emotion. Unnecessary aggression. Her Max. But did one fight make for unnecessary aggression? Wasn't that a bit of overkill? Besides, there was no point jumping to conclusions until she actually heard what had *started* the fight. And it sounded like the school had dealt with it anyway. A detention was both punishment and deterrent, and Max would have that after-school time on Thursday afternoon to think about what he'd done. But with this thought, Mattie paled and flopped limply down into her seat. Thursday was Jake's day. Which meant he would need to be told about what happened. It also meant he would dole out his own punishment. Mattie chewed her lip worriedly, because Jake's punishments varied considerably according to what sort of day he'd experienced. Sometimes they could be so lax as to be laughable, yet at other times so authoritarian that it almost verged on – well, Jan MacFarlane probably wouldn't have approved.

But that woman's interest in Max was something she certainly wouldn't be sharing with Jake, because he'd be absolutely livid to think that their son had attracted the attention of a counselling service. And he'd probably hold Mattie responsible. Definitely. This was what people like Jan MacFarlane didn't take into account – that the ramifications of their efforts could cause more difficulties than the original issue itself. But if they ever did have their meeting, Mattie knew that she would never be able to explain this, because the woman would stare at her with such lack of understanding in her eyes that Mattie herself would become flustered. All she really wanted to say was, 'Please just leave me alone. Please. I'm trying as hard as I can but it's not easy. In fact, it's like walking head-down into a strong wind. Every step is a huge effort and each time you relax, even just a trifle, you're driven backwards again. So I know you mean well and I know you think you're helping – but you're not. You're just making it harder. Giving me one more obstacle to face, one more hurdle to climb over, one more problem to keep me awake at night. And I've already got more than enough.'

Mattie stood in the kitchen doorway watching the watchers. Both Max and Courtney were so engrossed in the television that they did not look up, even though their mother had been standing there for several minutes. Courtney was lying on the couch, her legs drawn up and her pyjama top buttoned crookedly so that one side was hitched sideways, showing a triangle of bare flesh. One arm dangled over the side of the couch, her fingers trailing along the carpet, and her hair was damp from her bath and plaited neatly, so that it would brush out easily the next day.

On the floor, Max was spread across the beanbag as usual. He had pushed all the filling to one side so that he lay at an incline, with his back bowed inwardly in a manner achievable only by the young and flexible. Both elbows were bent, with his hands cupping his chin so that his neck continued the upward curve, and his hair was damp and unbrushed, cowlicking at the front and giving him a particularly vulnerable look. Mattie resisted the urge to tell him to sit straight, or brush his hair, or stay the way he was – forever. But it was hard, very hard, to reconcile what she was seeing here with the picture Jan MacFarlane had sketched this afternoon. He didn't *look* like a boy who would chase another down and then attack him. In fact, he didn't look aggressive at all. Just precious.

On the television, a cartoon cat leapt over a paling fence straight into an old-fashioned metal rubbish bin, which immediately fell to its side and rolled down the hill noisily. Max's mouth twitched sideways, as if he was amused, and then settled back into its blank absorption. Mattie grimaced to herself. She'd been postponing this talk all afternoon, using all sorts of excuses to herself. First there had been Courtney, walking home with them, talking nineteen to the dozen about her day and what it had involved. Then there'd been the possibility that Jake might turn up, and then tea to prepare, and eat, and clean up after. Now, with both children bathed and in their pyjamas, there were no excuses left. Half of her was desperate to find out more details, and the other half was equally desperate not to.

'Max? Can you come here for a minute?'

Max glanced across at his mother distractedly and then his eyes sidled back to the television.

'No, I need you away from the TV. We need to talk.'

'Talk?' repeated Max suspiciously, flicking back to Mattie. 'What about?'

'Yeah, what about?' asked Courtney with interest, sitting up on the couch.

'Just . . . things.' Mattie beckoned to Max. 'And just Max. Come into my bedroom.'

Courtney jumped up. 'Why can't I come too?'

'Because it's private between Max and me. Sometimes you have private things that you just want to talk about, don't you? Well, this is the same.'

'But Max doesn't mind if I come, do you, Max?'

'Max doesn't get a choice,' said Mattie firmly. 'Now, you go on watching TV, Courtney, and Max, you come to my room. We won't be long.'

Max stood up reluctantly while his sister threw herself back down on the couch crossly, the bulge caused by her mismatched buttons sticking out so that now it looked like she had one premature breast. Mattie left the lounge-room and, without checking to see if Max was following, took the measured steps into her bedroom. There, she sat down on the end of her bed and waited.

Max came in slowly, standing just inside the doorway with his downcast eyes even darker and more unreadable than usual.

'Close the door, Max.'

Mattie waited until he'd done so before patting the bed beside her. 'Sit down. I'm not going to bite you. Now, I think you might know what this is about. Right?'

'Maybe.' Max sat down next to her stiffly, staring at his hands as he fidgeted. 'How'd you know?'

'I was rung up at home today. By a Mrs MacFarlane. Apparently she spoke to you?'

'Yeah.'

'But you didn't want to talk to her?'

'That's right.'

'Look, I'm not angry that you didn't want to talk to the woman. In fact, I sort of sympathise. I didn't really want to talk to her either.' Mattie smiled at Max, trying to get him to relax. 'Didn't you like her?'

'Dunno,' Max shrugged, then glanced across at his mother. 'She's not family. I don't want to talk about stuff to someone who's not family.'

Mattie thought about all the 'stuff' Max could have talked about if he chose to, and paled. She had to ensure that didn't happen. 'I totally understand. I suppose you felt like you'd be, well, sort of a traitor if you spoke about family things, did you?'

'Yeah!' Max looked at her with surprise. 'Exactly!'

'Well, I think you're right.' Mattie chose her words carefully. 'It's like she's interfering, isn't it? That's how I felt too. And no-one can make you talk about things you don't want to. No-one. If they even try, you tell them to ring me, understand?'

'Okay.'

'So that's one thing. But now we need to talk about the fight.' Mattie watched his face become defensive once more. 'Look, I'm not cross. Well, actually, I *am* cross – but it's more that I want to find out what's going on. It just doesn't seem like you to be so . . . *nasty*. So let's start at the start. What happened?'

'I dunno.' Max shrugged, his eyes darting away.

'Not good enough. We can just sit here all night if you want to.'

'I hate him,' said Max vehemently.

'Okay, that's a start. Who do you hate?'

'Joshua Painter. He's a . . . a bastard.'

'You know for a fact that his parents aren't married, do you?'

'Huh?'

'His parents. Because that's what bastard means – that your parents aren't married. Pretty stupid, isn't it?' Mattie waited for Max to nod before continuing. 'But that's beside the point. The thing is, it's not a nice word and I don't want you using it. That's why we're sending you to school – to learn enough English so that you don't have to use bad words to explain yourself. Only lazy people do that. Now, tell me why you hate Joshua Painter so much.'

'Because he took my special Yu-Gi-Oh card. He really *did*, Mum, even though Mrs Gallagher doesn't believe me. He did.'

'I believe you.' Mattie tucked one leg underneath herself so that she could face Max more comfortably. 'So that's what the fight was about? Your Yu-Gi-Oh card?'

'My *special* one,' corrected Max intensely. 'And he was showing it to all these kids at lunchtime and I went over and said give it back. But he wouldn't.'

'Look, Max, I understand that you were angry, but – you hit him. Over a card.'

'He wouldn't give it back,' repeated Max in a mumble.

'And when the teacher told you to go to the other side of the play-ground you refused to. And then you chased after him and hit him again. Is that right?'

'I s'pose.'

'Max, be honest, don't you think that was a little ... extreme? Wouldn't you have been better off going to a teacher in the first place? Or even waiting till you got home and telling me? I'd have rung the school up for you, you know.'

'I s'pose.'

'And now you've got a detention after school. Your first detention. Why didn't you give me the slip yesterday for me to sign?'

'I dunno.'

'And do you realise we'll have to tell Dad so that he knows you'll be late?' Mattie, who was watching Max carefully, noted the widening of his eyes even as he kept his gaze averted. 'Would you like to ring him to explain?'

'Me?' Max finally made eye contact, with a devastated look that tore at Mattie's heart. 'Do I have to?'

'I think you need to take responsibility, yes.'

'Mum, please.' Max grabbed at her hand as the words bubbled out of him in a torrent. 'Please don't make me. I won't ever do it again, I prom-ise. You can do anything you like to me. Anything. But Dad'll be so angry, so . . . mad. Especially coz Joshua's a bit smaller than me – only a bit. But Dad always says don't hit people smaller and I did. Mummy, please. *Please?*'

Mattie waited till he wound down before picking up the small hand that had clutched at hers. 'Okay, listen. I went up to the school this afternoon and spoke to your principal before the bell. And I explained that we had a few things on and asked if he could give you the detention next Tuesday after school instead. And he agreed.'

'Mum!' Max's face lit up as he took in the implications of this.

'That's right. So your father doesn't have to know. But –' Mattie held up a hand as Max opened his mouth – 'I'm warning you, if you ever, *ever* get into another fight like this again, you're on your own. So promise me never again, understood?'

Max nodded eagerly and threw himself against her chest, wrapping his arms around her tightly. Mattie hugged him back, touched by his relief. And by her role as saviour, even though she was honest enough to acknowledge, with guilt nibbling at the edges of her pleasure, that she was playing dirty by using his fear of his father's disapproval to her own advantage. And it suddenly occurred to her that, if this was a competition, she was in the thick of it. And probably always had been.

*M*attie's second pregnancy was so entirely different from her first that it was difficult to even think of it as the same condition. Instead, it was like an illness that ravaged her body, assaulting her with new side effects at every turn. From morning sickness that lasted a full six months, to fluid retention, to pre-eclampsia. In the last three months she even developed carpal tunnel syndrome, which forced her to sleep with her arms strapped into splints, so that she lay as if crucified, arms spread, eyes staring at the ceiling, with her belly growing ever larger by the week.

She moved into the spare room halfway through the pregnancy, because the nights had become an endless stretch of restlessness during which the minutes slid past in slow motion, and Jake being next to her was just one more burden. She became slow, and dull, and depressed. Plodding through each day and doing just enough to survive. Weighted by gravity and fluid and unshed tears.

Then it was over – eight weeks before it should have been. And Mattie would have given anything to have the pregnancy back, because suddenly she learnt what unbearable really meant. It was watching a tiny baby with transparent, blue-tinged skin struggle for life. It was not being able to hold her when she was in pain. And it was knowing of the risk that she could be lost simply because she had been born too soon.

It was an accident – just one of those things. Mattie was standing on top of the kitchen step-stool, reaching awkwardly into the overhead cupboard for something or other. Max was in his highchair nearby, eating diced pears out of a yellow plastic bowl that had suction cups underneath to secure it to the tray. When she fell, catching one leg under the steps and carrying them down with her, she hit her head sharply against the stove corner and lost consciousness. And by the time she opened her eyes again, it was all over. The ambulance ride, the ruptured placenta, the emergency caesarean. She was the mother of a baby girl who was fighting for her life in the neo-natal nursery and things would never be the same again.

SIX

The next few days passed quickly and well. The only dark spot was the fact that Jake did not drop by, and nor did he ring. Mattie herself picked up the phone time and again, only to rethink making the call, then returning the handset to its cradle. Nevertheless, the lack of contact weighed in the back of her mind, shading her days with continuing disquiet and more than a touch of reproach.

But everything else went surprisingly smoothly. On Wednesday afternoon, she had returned home from collecting the children to find, on the doorstep, a neat elastic-banded bundle of lilac party-plan invitations, several colourful product brochures with fold-out order forms and a friendly note from Sharon saying that she was sorry to have missed her. Mattie spent a very pleasant evening, with Courtney's ready assistance, examining the brochures and circling the items they would have really liked if they could have afforded them.

Then Mattie had been dreading Thursday, with the knowledge that after she said goodbye at the school, she would not be seeing her children again until Sunday. But as with many things, her expectations were actually worse than the deed. First she got involved in a rather interesting discussion with some other mothers who did Monday morning reading with her, regarding the positive and negative attributes of Miss Thomson, the prep teacher. Then she handed out invitations to her Whimsicalities party and fielded the immediate, and rather curious, questions about her change of address. This was followed by a pleasant walk down to the shops where she posted off an invitation to Liz, complete with a carefully thought-out handwritten note that read: *Would love to catch up. If you can't make this, give me a ring and we'll arrange something else? Cheers, Mattie.* Before posting it Mattie had stood at the letterbox for several moments. Should she or shouldn't she? Would she look desperate after all this time? Finally, she took a deep breath and thrust the letter through the opening before she could analyse it further. And, as the letter disappeared with a flash of white, she had felt a surge of well-being, fuelled by the certainty that she had done the right thing.

Then, with that accomplished, she visited the supermarket to buy some decadent food for the weekend and dropped off the completed application at the community centre. Beryl, thrilled to see that she had followed through with her interest, had taken her on a tour of the centre and even lent her some handouts from the community service course so that Mattie could get a start on her required reading.

The smoothness of those few days were helped by a firm decision not to drink anymore while she was alone. After the ease with which she'd slipped into her maudlin state on the first night, she sensed that madness lay that way, biding its time with a sly smile. And alcohol invited it in. So she steered clear of her customary glass of scotch before tea, and her glass of wine during it, and fancied that she felt much better for it. And each night the children weren't there, Mattie went into their room to say goodnight. She touched each wall, for luck, and then kissed their pillows and closed the door. Then, in the morning, she would open the door again, just as if they were there. Even though she knew the routine was superstitious and made little sense, she was unwilling to take the risk of abandoning it, lest something happen to them.

It had rained all day Friday. Warm late October rain that was sorely needed after a rather dry winter. From the unit, it looked like a steady curtain of water that was as effective as any concrete barricade. It beat down incessantly from the skies, hammering the earth into submission. Even the bushes and trees bowed in subservience. But rather than allow it to dampen her mood, Mattie had used the rain as a ready excuse to enjoy a self-indulgent day, lying on the couch and alternating between the afternoon talk-shows and a Regency period romance from the library. And although it was obvious from page two that Sybil, the youthful heroine, would end up in the arms of the tall, swarthy and masterful Duke of Birchester, its undemanding predictability was just what Mattie wanted.

The rain eased off in the late afternoon and Hilda had dropped in unexpectedly, bringing a box of curtains that she claimed were just sitting in her shed gathering dust. Mattie was extremely touched, as well as thrilled with the difference they made when she hung them: white lace scrim for the kitchen, navy cotton tab-tops for the children's bedroom, dusky-pink velvet pinch-pleats for her bedroom and a pair of lovely green and burgundy striped drapes for the lounge-room that had only the slightest streaks of sun damage on the cream linings.

For the rest of that day, after Hilda had left, Mattie would glance at the curtains and warm herself with the goodwill that had brought them into her home. In fact it was like everything was turning around, and it was hard to believe that only a week ago she had felt crushed by confusion. Now she was making new friends and finding fresh directions. Even if others saw her progress as small and relatively petty, measured as it was by incidentals like curtains and party-plan, she knew that it was huge, leading her away from the past and illuminating the path ahead.

So when Hannah rang early on Saturday morning to inform Mattie that she was having morning tea with their mother, and she thought her sister should join them to explain her new living arrangements, Mattie agreed with only the slightest hesitation. After all, it was just another necessary step forward. She dressed herself carefully in flared denim jeans, black ankle boots and a black fitted shirt with three-quarter length sleeves, so that she could present herself with standards intact, if not actually improved.

Mattie's mother lived in Box Hill, in a neat white brick house she had purchased after her husband died and she decided to downsize from the rambling weatherboard that Mattie and Hannah had grown up in. It suited her perfectly – small, trim and rather dated. Hannah's Volvo hatchback was already in the concrete driveway so Mattie parked behind it and walked up the neatly edged pathway to the front door. It opened before she could knock.

'*There* you are.' Hannah grabbed her by the elbow and ushered her in as if Mattie had been about to attempt escape. 'I was beginning to think you'd chickened out.'

'God, I'm only five minutes late!' Mattie shook her sister off and glared up at her. Hannah looked even taller today, in high-heeled courts with a pair of pinstriped trousers and a cream shirt. Her long hair had been pulled back into a low, loose bun.

'Fifteen actually,' corrected Hannah pedantically.

'Whatever.' Mattie frowned at her back as she followed her sister into the lounge-room, where her mother was sitting on a pastel tapestry armchair and pouring tea. She was a tall woman, like Hannah, and having married relatively late, was now into her mid-seventies. Although, to Mattie, her mother had always seemed elderly, even when Mattie herself had been a child. Not just because she had been older than all the other mothers at school, but because *her* mother seemed to embrace age in a way that many other women embrace youth. So that now, when her actual age finally matched her inclinations, she seemed *right* in a way that she never had before.

And nowadays also, her frail demeanour finally seemed warranted, with her pale, powdered skin becoming more and more networked by a multitude of fine lines like treasured old parchment. Her hair, once a rich brown and her crowning glory, was now a trimmed snowy-white that was permed into crisp waves, carefully arranged to disguise its sparsity. And she wore prescription glasses all the time, a gold-rimmed pair through which her eyes were magnified, giving her a rather intense look that was largely undeserved.

Wearing dove-grey trousers and a white angora jumper, Mattie's mother presided over a circular coffee table with a pie-crust walnut top, on which was placed a tray with a trio of Royal Albert teacups, silver teapot, creamer and a small plate of chocolate biscuits. She finished pouring the tea into the third cup and then put down the teapot and beamed up at Mattie welcomingly.

'Hello, darling. My, aren't you looking well.'

'Hey, Mum.' Mattie crossed the room and brushed her lips against her mother's proffered cheek before flopping down onto the couch next to Hannah. Her mother passed her the cup of tea and Mattie took a sip. It was hot and strong, a deep honey colour through which the porcelain shimmered faintly.

'How's Jake? And the children?'

'Good thanks.' Mattie ignored the muffled cough from Hannah and put her cup and saucer down on a nearby table. 'How about you, Mum? What have you been up to?'

'Oh, you know me.' Mattie's mother waved a thin hand deprecatingly. 'I live a quiet life. Apart from the Lions Club, I don't get up to much. Although I did have a lovely lunch with Mrs DePosito yesterday. Do you remember her? Her husband used to work with your father.'

'Of course,' said Mattie, vaguely recalling a large and bossy woman.

'And Hannah's Charlotte took me for a nice drive through the mountains on the weekend with her new boyfriend. A very pleasant young man. What was his name, Hannah?'

'Nicholas,' said Hannah smugly. 'He's a lawyer.'

'How upwardly mobile of you.' Mattie leant forward and took a biscuit.

'I'll give you his card, it may come in handy.'

'I doubt that.' Mattie gave Hannah an even look and then turned back to her mother. 'I'll have to bring Max and Courtney around soon. You haven't seen them for ages.'

'That *would* be nice. How are they?'

'Good. Very good. Max is reading chapter books now and Courtney's made heaps of new friends at school. She loves it.'

'Make sure you ring me first, and I'll get some cola and sweets.'

'Okay.' Mattie picked up her tea and sat back as she drank it. Hannah began chatting to their mother about her daughter's exploits at university and Mattie relaxed, pleased at not having to contribute. It was always like this when she visited her mother, as if their worlds were so far apart it was difficult to find any middle ground. And it was a shame, especially as they'd grown quite close during the week that Mattie had spent here last year, only to fall back into established patterns as soon as she returned home.

The situation was hampered by her mother's complete inability to comprehend anything that fell too far outside her own experience. She had led a sheltered, rather privileged life, where coasters and thankyou notes assumed a disproportionate importance, and issues like crime and destitution were largely ignored. Etiquette and the 'done thing' provided a foundation that made her feel secure, and Mattie knew, without a shadow of doubt, that if she suddenly asked her mother about the latest government scandal or the war in Iraq, she would be faced with a bewildered expression as she desperately tried to dredge up something polite to say in return. It wasn't so much shallowness as a profound ignorance that led her to see everybody else as having the same opportunities, and living by the same rules, as she herself. Those who didn't make the most of these opportunities, or who failed to follow the rules, must surely then have only themselves to blame.

'So what do you think of that, Mattie?'

'What?' asked Mattie, turning to Hannah in some confusion.

'I was just *commenting*,' said Hannah pointedly, with a glance at her mother, 'that Charlotte's twenty-first is at the end of next year. Would you like me to write the date down so that you have enough notice?'

'Of course not.' Mattie gave her a level look.

'Well, I know how much you avoid family functions. *My* family functions anyway.'

'Girls,' said their mother, clicking her tongue in annoyance.

'Speaking of functions,' said Mattie smoothly, 'I'm having a little something myself a fortnight from today. Party-plan, but it'll be good – pottery and knick-knacks and stuff.'

Hannah raised her eyebrows. '*You're* having a little something?'

'Lovely,' Mattie's mother beamed. 'Such fun. Do you want me to bring anything?'

'No, all taken care of.'

'What address?' asked Hannah, with a small smile.

'You know,' replied Mattie, glowering at her sister.

'Of course she does,' said their mother, taking the lid off the teapot and peering inside. 'I think I might boil the kettle up, girls. Back in a minute.'

'No, before you go, Mum –' Mattie put up a hand to stop her mother rising – 'there's something I want to tell you.'

'Tell *me*, darling?'

'Yes. About Jake and me. It's not that big a deal – just that we've decided to take a break for a while, that's all.'

'Oh, how lovely.'

'Pardon?'

'Your break.' Mattie's mother nodded, obviously pleased. 'You deserve it, especially Jake. He works so hard.'

Hannah shook her head. 'You've got it wrong. It's not a holiday, it's a –'

'Thanks, Hannah,' Mattie interrupted crossly. 'I can take it from here.'

Hannah sniffed, leaning back in her chair pointedly. 'Only trying to help.'

'I'm afraid I don't understand.' Their mother looked from one daughter to the other. 'What are you trying to tell me, Mattie? That you're having *separate* holidays?'

'No, that's not it,' Mattie said through clenched teeth. She took a deep breath and continued before she could be interrupted again. 'It's like this. Jake and I have been having a few . . . well, *differences* lately, and we've decided to take a break from each *other*. As in, I've moved out of the house and rented a unit about ten minutes away from the kids' school. But listen,' Mattie hastened ahead as her mother's face fell, 'it's only for twelve months or so, just till we sort out stuff. It's a trial thing. To give us space.'

'To give you *space*?' repeated Mattie's mother, in a style reminiscent of Mattie's own. 'But why would you want space, darling? You're married!'

'What difference does that make?' asked Hannah rhetorically as she undid her bun and ran her fingers through her hair, examining the ends pensively.

Mattie ignored her. 'It's really not that big a deal, Mum. Just that we haven't been as *happy* lately and this will give us a chance to work it all out.'

'I don't quite understand.' Mattie's mother stared down at her wedding ring and then rotated it around her finger several times, the loose skin pouching and creasing around the gold. Finally she spoke. 'I thought you sorted everything out last year, when you came here for a week. Wasn't that what happened?'

'Well, we tried to. That is, I *thought* we had, but . . .'

'And you've rented a *unit*?' She let go of the wedding ring and looked at Mattie with incomprehension, her eyes huge behind the glasses. 'But you're *married*. Married people don't rent units apart from each other. How can you discuss anything if you're not together?'

'We can try,' said Mattie feebly.

When Mattie didn't elaborate, her mother rose stiffly to her feet and picked up the teapot. 'I can't fathom any of this, but I'm quite confident that you and Jake will work everything out. Now I'm going to put the kettle on.'

Mattie watched her leave the room and then turned to her sister furiously. 'Thanks a lot for your help.'

'What did you want *me* to say?' asked Hannah, abandoning her hair in surprise.

'I don't know! Something!'

'But, Mattie, *I* don't understand.' Hannah shook her head. 'How can I help you explain something that I don't even understand myself?'

'You could try trusting me,' said Mattie bitterly. 'That I might know what I'm doing.'

They stared at each other for a few long moments and then Hannah dropped her eyes, reaching behind and refastening her hair into a loose ponytail that she then doubled back through the hair-tie. Mattie watched, waiting for her to finish and say something, but she didn't. Instead, as soon as her hair was in place, she reached forward and picked up her cup of tea, making a show of taking a sip and then putting the cup back onto the saucer. Seconds slid into minutes as their mother stayed in the kitchen and Hannah drank her tea wordlessly. The message was clear: Mattie was on her own.

*T*hey had their first real holiday when Courtney was two years old. Although there had been brief getaways before – weekends in the snow, camping trips to the country, even a night on a houseboat once – they'd never had anything on this scale before. In his inimitable style, Jake started planning as soon as it became clear that the baby was going to pull through. Stringent budgeting, currency converters and brochures spread across the coffee table, maps Blu-tacked to the walls.

They went to Hong Kong. Ten days of living with room service and restaurants, grandiose views and heady extravagance. Their beds were made, their laundry done, their bodies massaged. Each day they piled the children into a huge double pusher and set off to explore, whether it was taking a harbour cruise, visiting the touristy destinations, or just shopping at the crowded and colourful plazas. It was a wonderful, exhilarating experience that would have been perfect but for one thing.

Stupidly standing just behind Jake as he levered the cork from a bottle of champagne to celebrate their arrival, she was struck in the eye with his elbow. And the next morning woke to find her eye swollen and rimmed by a rainbow of patchy blues. Which, over the course of a week, dulled to an ugly, dirty brown that looked like the puckered skin of a badly bruised apple.

The oddest thing about the eye was the stares it attracted. Lingering, pitying glances that then flicked across to Jake with mute accusation. It didn't seem to occur to anybody that it was an accident, just one of those things. Instead, although no-one ever said anything, it was perfectly clear what they were thinking. And from an initial sense of embarrassment, Mattie grew steadily more resentful at the very assumption.

SEVEN

The telephone was ringing when Mattie entered the unit but despite flinging her handbag aside and running into the kitchen, she was too late. The dial tone trilled in her ear, with a monotony that reminded her of Morse code. *Urgent message – stop – where were you? – stop – too late now – stop*. She hung up the phone roughly in disappointment. Maybe it'd been Jake. Maybe – probably. Definitely. Mattie clenched her fists impotently. But at least that made the decision about what to do with the remainder of the day a lot easier. She was staying home and waiting for him to try again.

Mattie kicked off her boots and lined them up neatly by the door before making a cup of coffee and a sandwich. She glanced at the phone intermittently, willing it to ring, but it remained silent. So she settled down at the table with her lists to distract herself. So far she had handed out twelve invitations to the party – eight rather casual ones at the school, two rather impulsively just now at her mother's, one to Hilda, and one posted to Liz. There was still Rachel and Ginny at the swim centre, and a few women from school that she hadn't caught up with yet, but she should be seeing all of them on Monday. Mattie estimated that about half of those invited would actually come, which still made for ten guests – more than enough for the small unit. Everybody should get on rather well, too, perhaps with the exception of her mother and Hilda. Although roughly the same age, the two women were worlds apart in every aspect. One sturdy and competent, the other embracing frailty as an accessory to life.

With this last reflection, Mattie's thoughts drifted back to the morning tea she'd just endured. Although disappointed with her mother's reaction, she was not surprised. Ignoring unpleasantness was how she always coped and she wasn't likely to change now. Certainly there was no chance that *she* would arrive at the door with a box of curtains or anything like that. Hannah, though, was a different matter. For the first time in years, Mattie actually craved the support of her older sister. Someone to lean on, to talk to. And it only made things worse that she was well aware that this support was within reach. All she had to do was break her silence, explain, admit the inadmissible, and maybe, probably, her sister would be there for her. But the simple truth was that it was harder to break the habit of years than it was to stand alone. Much harder.

Mattie spent the next few hours playing with her lists. She rewrote the menu, adjusted the shopping list, flicked through the Whimsicalities product pamphlets, and wrote out invitations for her remaining guests. Only after she'd exhausted every possibility in planning for the party did she put them away and wander into the lounge-room. There she picked her handbag off the floor and put it away before fingering the heavy material of the drapes for a few minutes to put a smile on her face. Then she curled up on the couch with Sybil and the heroic Duke.

It was nearly five o'clock before the telephone rang again. Mattie almost tripped over her feet in her eagerness to get off the couch and answer it. She ran to the kitchen and grabbed the receiver off the wall on the second ring.

'Hello?'

'Hey there. You sound breathless. Been running, have you?'

'Jake.'

'The one and only,' he laughed warmly. 'Why? Expecting someone else, were you?'

'No, of course not.' Mattie relaxed, his voice and its cheerful tone lightening her body to such an extent that she felt as if a weight had been physically removed. 'Did you ring before?'

'Yep. Couple of hours ago.'

'I answered, but you'd already hung up.'

'Well, that's what happens when you're gadding about.'

'I was only at Mum's,' said Mattie quickly.

'Ah. Fun, hey?'

'A laugh a minute. How're the kids?'

'Good. Fine. They're outside cleaning up the patio for me.' Jake's voice became businesslike. 'Listen, we're having a barbecue tea, and they wanted you to join us. What do you think?'

'A barbecue tea?'

'That's what I said.'

'Um . . .' Mattie was grinning already, but deliberately waited a moment or so before answering. 'Actually, that sounds lovely. Thank you. What time?'

'Anytime you like. Come now if you want.'

'Do you want me to bring anything?'

'Just yourself.' Jake's voice was warm. 'That's all we've ever wanted.'

An hour later and Mattie, still dressed in her jeans and black shirt, was firmly ensconced in a cedar outdoor chair, a scotch and coke in her hand, while she watched Jake fire up the barbecue. The patio, where the black chrome barbecue was situated, was set into the L shape of their house, with a sliding door leading out from the family room. Both the kitchen and dining room had windows that looked out over the area.

As Mattie and Jake were fond of outdoor relaxing, the patio had been their first major project after buying the home. It was decked to the same level as the floor plan, with three broad steps leading down into the backyard. A large circular cedar table with a revolving lazy susan set into the centre stood near the barbecue surrounded by matching chairs and a wooden slatted deckchair that Jake had given Mattie for Christmas the year before. Two hanging plants, both bushy asparagus ferns, were suspended either side of the steps, and in each corner of the patio was a ceramic-potted plant with many-fingered leaves that sprung upwards and outwards with an almost vulgar display of vitality. The overall effect was, Mattie thought, like something out of *Home Beautiful*. It was her favourite place in the entire house – neat, vibrant and incredibly relaxing.

She picked up her scotch and took a sip, closing her eyes briefly as she felt the liquid trickle down her throat, warming her from the inside out. Whilst it wasn't a cold evening, there was a lively cool breeze that made Mattie glad of the family room jutting out behind and protecting them from the vitality of the weather. The plumy smoke from the barbecue billowed upwards, until it cleared the patio area and was taken by the wind, threading apart quickly to merge with the clouds above. But it would have taken a lot more than the wind to dint Mattie's contentment. She felt full, brimmingly full, so full that her happiness could barely be contained and kept spilling over to express itself in touches and smiles and an almost ridiculous sense of all being right in her world. She was at home.

Jake turned for a second and gave her one of his lopsided smiles, picking up his own glass and gesturing a toast. Mattie smiled back. He was dressed more casually than she was, with navy Adidas tracksuit pants and a loose grey cut-off windcheater top, which made him look relaxed, and more muscly than thin. But he also looked tired, with dark shadows under his eyes, as if he hadn't been sleeping well. Or had been worrying too much. Mattie grimaced and looked away.

Courtney, dressed in her tutu once more, pushed her way through the sliding door with her arms full and came over to her mother busily. She immediately continued the conversation they'd been having earlier, regarding her pocket money purchases, as if there'd been no pause in it at all.

'And so this is what I bought at the two-dollar shop. A set of gel pens, a clickety frog thing . . .' Courtney placed each object down on the table before her mother as she spoke. 'And a little torch on a key-ring you can light up. See?'

'Very nice,' commented Mattie, watching the beam of the tiny flashlight flicker unsteadily.

'Yes. I'm going to use it in my doll's house for the torch of the people.'

'That sounds like a political tool,' commented Jake, holding his drink aloft and speaking in a sonorous voice: 'Truth, justice and liberty for all, comrade! The torch of the people!'

Courtney rolled her eyes. 'You're silly.'

Max came through the open sliding door with a plateful of meat. He stopped long enough to pull the door closed behind him with his foot before continuing over to his father and passing him the plate.

'Thanks, mate.' Jake unpeeled the cling wrap and started adding sausages to the burgers and steaks already on the barbecue.

'Can I look after them?' asked Max, his eyes on the sizzling meat.

'Sure.' Jake pierced a couple of sausages and passed the long-handled tongs over to his son, who immediately began flipping meat with concentration. With his drink in his hand, Jake leant against the brick wall of the house, keeping an eye on Max.

'Can I do it too?' Courtney stopped examining her purchases and stared at her brother with jealousy. 'What he's doing?'

Max shot a filthy look over his shoulder. 'I asked first!'

'Maybe next time,' Jake grinned. 'But you can grab the salads if you want to help.'

'I don't want to do *that*.'

'Well, you're going to. And close the door behind you this time.'

'I'll help.' Mattie started getting up.

'No you won't,' Jake said, waving her back down. 'You're a guest.'

'How lovely.' Mattie sank back into her seat and smiled across at Jake. 'I feel spoilt.'

'Good.'

Courtney pushed her toys over into a pile on the other end of the table while she glared at her father, mother and brother in turn. Then she stomped into the house, turning to ostentatiously close the sliding door before disappearing in the direction of the kitchen.

'So what have you been up to?' asked Jake of Mattie.

'Oh, nothing much. This and that.'

'Mum's going to work at the community centre,' interjected Max, glancing at his mother with shy pride. 'Helping people and all that.'

'You're what?' Jake pulled out a chair and straddled it backwards, his eyes fixed on her the entire time.

'Oh, it's nothing much. I was just thinking I was a bit bored. And I wanted to do . . .' Mattie faltered slightly under his regard. 'You know . . . something.'

'Go on.'

'Well, there isn't anything else. I'll just be helping there once in a while, that's all.'

'Don't you have to do a course?'

'Yes. A community service course.'

'Well congratulations.' Jake got back up and took the tongs from Max. 'Good to see you're moving on so quickly. Branching out and all.'

'It's not like that,' said Mattie earnestly to his back. 'Just something to do.'

'You could always try coming back. Plenty to keep you occupied here.'

Mattie flashed a glance at Max, who was standing by the barbecue staring at the busy tongs. As she thought desperately what to say to best defuse the situation, Courtney came back through the sliding door and slapped a clear plastic bowl of tossed salad down onto the table. After a quick glower at her family, she stomped inside again, the pink tulle quivering.

'I'll help her,' muttered Max to nobody in particular. He left the barbecue and walked inside without looking in his mother's direction.

'It's nothing, Jake,' said Mattie quickly. 'Really. If you think I'm moving on or whatever, you couldn't be further from the truth. It's just like volunteering for canteen or reading at the school. Only it's for the community. With a few other women, that's all.'

'Yeah.' Jake flipped some sausages in silence. Then he turned back to her. 'Don't worry about it. I'm just paranoid.'

Mattie smiled at him with relief as she felt the tension drain out of her body. As Jake returned to the barbecue, she took a deep breath and closed her eyes for just a second. Sometimes it was such hard work. Like a minefield where every now and then, quite unknowingly, you strayed too close and had to carefully negotiate the danger while praying fervently that it wouldn't blow up in your face.

Courtney came back through the sliding door with a bowl of coleslaw balanced awkwardly on top of a wicker basket of bread. Leaving the door open, she walked carefully over to the table where Mattie grabbed the coleslaw before it could topple off. Courtney put the bread down and slid back into her seat. She was followed by Max, who brought the barbecue cutlery, a stack of brightly coloured picnic plates and plastic cups, and a bottle of soft drink. He piled them onto the table and then fished in one pocket of his jeans and extracted a bottle of tomato sauce. The other pocket produced the salt and pepper shakers.

'Very innovative.' Mattie smiled at him, reaching out and touching his shoulder reassuringly.

'Anything else there?' Jake dropped the tongs suddenly and, lunging forward, grabbed Max and started to frisk him. The boy yelped with surprise and then, as his father tickled him, started laughing helplessly as he tried to protect himself, with little success. Jake stopped as suddenly as he'd started, leaving Max bent over and gasping for breath, his whole body a smile of delight.

'Grub's up!' Jake loaded a plate with sausages and burgers and steak, passing it across to the table. While he did this, Mattie filled two of the plastic cups with soft drink and gave one to each child. Then she set out the plates and cutlery and took the tongs to dole out some salad while Max and Courtney used their forks to spear meat. As they all helped themselves, Jake turned the gas off at the barbecue and, using a spatula, scraped the thick metal plate and flicked the charred crumbs over the edge of the patio onto the lawn. Then he took a small jug of water from the side of the barbecue and poured it over the hotplate, the water immediately sizzling into effervescent beads and sending hissing clouds of steam upwards. Only when that was all done did Jake sit down and pull the plate of meat towards himself.

'This is great, honey,' said Mattie appreciatively, taking a mouthful of steak and salad.

'Yeah, thanks, Dad,' Max added quickly.

'I live to serve.' Jake drained his scotch and then started filling his plate with food.

'I *love* barbecueys,' commented Courtney, shining her little torch onto her sausage and peering at the faint spot of light. 'They're my favourite. After McDonald's, of course.'

'Of course,' said Jake, smiling across the table at Mattie. Suddenly he clicked his fingers. 'The wine! I forgot the wine. I got a nice bottle of riesling –'

'I'll get it, Dad.' Max was up and through the sliding door, his half-eaten burger abandoned on his plate.

'Grab two glasses as well!' Jake called after him. '*Wine*glasses!'

Mattie chewed her steak contentedly. The evening was mild, the mood was mild, and the company consisted of her three most-preferred people in the world. If a fairy godmother suddenly appeared and granted her one wish, it wouldn't be for fame or fortune or world travel, but to have everything stay just like this forever. Was that too much to ask? Was that greedy?

Max returned, the wine and two goblets cradled against his chest, and shut the sliding door behind him before crossing to his father. Jake grinned his thanks and then levered the cork free, filling the glasses halfway before passing one across to Mattie.

'Thanks.' Mattie raised her glass. 'And cheers to all of us!'

The children enthusiastically clinked their cups against their parents' glasses and then Jake stood and leant forward, touching Mattie's wineglass with his own. He smiled at her as he sat down again and her heart soared. Just like this. Forever.

'My torch isn't working anymore,' complained Courtney, shaking it.

'The torch of the people has gone out,' said Jake in his deep voice. 'Is this the end of the world as we know it?'

'Well, how about we check it later.' Mattie reached out and took the little torch from Courtney, laying it down by the side of her plate. 'Eat your salad, honey.'

'I don't like salad.'

'It's good for you.'

'Daddy doesn't make me eat salad.' Courtney flashed a look at her father. 'And it's his weekend. Isn't it, Daddy?'

'Do what your mother says, Court.'

'But you said –'

'And now I'm saying eat it.' Jake used his no-nonsense voice, frowning at Courtney. '*All* of it.'

Courtney's mouth thinned angrily as she dropped her eyes and pushed a piece of lettuce around her plate. She speared it with her fork and then used her knife to tear it into jagged strips. Finally she looked up. 'Mummy's having a party. With all these people. And Auntie Liz who we haven't seen since we were babies.'

'Really?' said Jake evenly, glancing across the table at Mattie and rais-ing his eyebrows. 'How . . . exciting.'

'It's not a party –' Mattie waved a hand dismissively – 'it's just one of those party-plan things. Like Tupperware. Courtney, you make it sound like I'm having an orgy or something.'

'What's an orgy?'

'Nothing.' Mattie rolled her eyes and then glanced at Jake who, to her relief, was looking rather unconcerned as he refilled his goblet. The last thing she wanted was for him to start with the 'moving on' tangent again. Not when the evening was going so well.

'I wanted to go to the party too, but Mummy said she needs time to herself.' Courtney flicked her mother a fleeting look under her lashes. 'Without Max and me.'

'And me, it seems,' commented Jake, helping himself to some more coleslaw.

'Like you'd enjoy one of those,' said Mattie, striving for a light and unconcerned tone. 'A room full of women gossiping about pottery and stuff.'

'Well, Liz'll be thrilled you've gotten rid of me anyway,' Jake contin-ued as if she hadn't spoken.

Mattie's stomach immediately contracted, much like a labour pain, and she put her cutlery down, not hungry anymore. 'That's not true. You know that's not true.'

'Actually, it's perfectly true. That self-absorbed bitch never liked me and you know it.'

'Is she really a bitch?' asked Courtney of her father.

'She certainly is, sweetheart.'

'Then why does Mummy like her?'

'Courtney, shut *up*,' hissed Max, glaring across the table at his sister.

'Well, Mum's not very choosy about her friends.' Jake pushed his plate away, picked up his glass and looked at Courtney intently. 'So even though Auntie Liz makes out she's one of those feminist ball-busters, Mum still likes her because once upon a time they used to go out a lot together. Picking up blokes and all that.'

'We did *not*,' said Mattie desperately, speaking to Jake rather than her daughter. 'We were just *friends*, that's all.'

'So is she still with that idiot she married?' asked Jake, now looking Mattie full in the face. 'And won't he be thrilled you've moved out as well? You never know your luck there, Mat, they may even find you someone new. I'll keep my fingers crossed for you, shall I?'

'I don't want anyone new.' Mattie clenched her hands together under the table, her knuckles white. 'And they wouldn't do that anyway.'

'Actually, I'm quite sure they would. No wonder you don't want the kids at your shindig. They'll cramp your style, hey?'

'It's not like that.' Mattie stared at her meal and then glanced up at Jake, suddenly washed with resentment. 'And you *know* it's not like that.'

'Actually I know nothing of the sort. Sometimes I don't know you at all. It's like I try and try . . .' Jake waved a hand around the barbecue area expressively without taking his eyes off Mattie. His voice became more clipped as he continued, biting off the words and flinging them across the table at her like weapons. 'And it's never bloody enough. No matter what I do. Then you have the damned nerve to try and stab me in the back the minute I turn away.'

'I do *not*!'

'Yeah? What about your little talk the other day? I wasn't going to bring it up but what the hell. *You* know what I'm talking about. Telling the kids that I'm *happy* when they're not here. That it's like a bloody *holiday*. And that *you* miss them so much more than me. Nice try, bitch.'

Mattie flinched, as if physically struck. Then she dropped her eyes and stayed still, almost as if she felt that by doing so she would become less of a target. Less visible to the predator. But while her upper body remained motionless, her hands fidgeted incessantly, pulling her wedding ring up over her knuckle and then thrusting it back down roughly. Her stomach turned and a sour taste filled her mouth as if the steak she'd just eaten had become rancid. She opened her mouth and then closed it again, not knowing what to say to best defuse the situation. And knowing, deep down, that it probably couldn't be defused anyway. The timer had started and now it was just a matter of counting down the seconds. *Tick, tick, tick.*

Max clearly felt the same way because he suddenly pushed his chair back and mumbled something before quickly moving inside through the sliding door. He looked sidelong at his mother as he passed by, an expressionless glance that nonetheless spoke volumes.

'Where're you going, Max?' Courtney's voice was now high-pitched. When she didn't get an answer she too rose rapidly and after an apprehensive glance at her father, gathered together her toys and hurried after her brother. She dropped the little torch as she went, pausing for a moment and then obviously deciding to leave it where it was. The sliding door closed behind her with a dull thud that echoed in the silence.

With her head still down, Mattie watched the torch spin slowly on the patio decking, finally coming to a halt with the silver key-ring attachment curled like a question mark. Will it be okay? Will it blow over? What could she say to make it right?

The unit flicked into her consciousness, with its drapes waiting to be drawn. Providing warmth and security and refuge. And she wanted to be there right now, lying on the couch with Sybil and her protective paramour, or the television, or anything. Out of the corner of her eye she saw Jake drain his wineglass and then stand up with a sigh. He started to collect dishes together and then, still without saying anything, headed for the sliding door with his load. Mattie's stomach flipped as relief washed over her, leaving her light-headed. She let her breath out with a whoosh.

And suddenly from behind her she heard the plates fall to the decking with a huge clatter as an arm whipped past her face and then bent itself back, pinning her neck in the inside crook of the elbow. She stared straight ahead, wide-eyed with shock, her heart thudding so loudly it seemed to vibrate her entire body. But she barely had time to take stock of her situation before the arm rose and tightened, ribbons of taut muscle standing out as her head was pulled backwards painfully. She grunted as tears filmed her eyes.

'Could barely even wait a week, could you?' Jake's voice was so thick with emotion that it sounded like a stranger's. 'Already out there, like a fucking bitch on heat. You make me *sick*.'

Mute with terror, Mattie stared up at his face, which was distorted by the severe angle of her head. His skin looked ruddy, flushed with fury, and loose and pouchy either side of the deep lines that bracketed his mouth. But it was his eyes that were the worst. The blue-grey now forged steel, they held absolutely no compassion, or sympathy, or glint of humanity. Instead they bored into her like something so inherently hostile that it was impossible to reconcile them with the laughing, *loving* Jake of only an hour ago.

'Well, life's not that fucking easy, *sweetheart*. You'll get yours. If you think I'm going to roll over and play dead, you've got another thing coming. You fucking *whore*.'

With the last word Jake tightened his arm, breathing heavily with the effort, and bolts of pain cascaded through Mattie's skull like fireworks exploding. She grabbed the arm with both hands, clawing at it to loosen the hold. And now she couldn't speak, couldn't scream, as the force under her chin was too tight, keeping her mouth closed and her teeth firmly clamped together. With her head so far back, the weight against her jugular felt thick and heavy and life-threatening. She tried to swallow but gagged, her vision clouding as the fireworks dulled to a background roar.

And then, as suddenly as it started, it was over and Mattie was released. She fell forward against the table, choking and coughing as she tried to draw a breath that would go *all* the way down instead of just catching in her throat and spluttering out. She wheezed and gasped as the tears spilled over and her nose ran, watery mucus dribbling down to film along her lips. The pain was even more intense now that the pressure was gone. A fierce ache that burned all the way around her neck and up into the base of her skull.

At last she got her breathing under control, though it had a raspy edge that scared her. At some stage the top button of her black shirt had broken off, and the neckline plunged, exposing the lacework across the dipping curves of her white bra. Mattie wrapped her arms across her chest and then, very slowly, looked up fearfully, not knowing what to expect. But Jake had moved away to stand by the table, staring at her with his eyes still hard.

'Christ, you're pathetic.' He shook his head in disgust. 'There's something seriously wrong with you, you know. You need help.'

Mattie continued to stare at him, working hard to keep her face expressionless, though deep inside she laughed hysterically at the accuracy of his observation.

'Fucking loser.' Jake leant under the table to retrieve her handbag, which he tossed into her lap dismissively. 'Get out of here before I do something I'll regret. You're not fucking worth it.'

Mattie staggered to her feet, her legs weak and rubbery. As she rose, her head exploded again, sending waves of dizziness through her body. She stumbled slightly but then managed to right herself, with the uppermost thought now being that she had to get out of there before he changed his mind. Anger and resentment lay low, swamped by fear and an innate sense of survival. Clasping the bag to her chest, she backed away from the table, her eyes on Jake warily. But he didn't move, just watched her coldly as she somehow got down the steps and then, at last turning her back on him, ran for the side gate.

As she passed the far end of the family room with its bay window, she glanced across and was brought to a halt by the sight of Max and Courtney, their pale faces pressed against the window. Her mouth dropped open with horror that they should witness this. Their mother, a pathetic coward on the run. Filthy, disgraced, beaten. And while one part of her urged her onwards, away from their gaze, the rest of her tensed with the almost overwhelming urge to rush inside to them. To grab them and take them with her. Away from here. But she knew, and they knew also, that wasn't about to happen. There was no choice.

*O*nce, when Mattie was a child, her parents had taken her and her sister to Luna Park, in St Kilda. It had been an enormous treat as there was very little spare money in those days. She danced through the gaping Luna Park mouth at the entrance, her feet barely touching the ground in her restless excitement. They rode the scenic railway and the big dipper, screaming and clutching each other as they hurtled down the narrow tracks. They played at the sideshows and went through the mirror maze, where Mattie giggled helplessly at all the different versions of herself – fat, skinny, wobbly, curved. They ate hotdogs dripping with sauce, and fairy floss, huge sticky balls of pink fluff that stuck to the corners of Mattie's mouth.

Last of all they went on the rotor. Mattie held her mother's hand tightly as they were directed to stand around the periphery, their backs flattened against the rounded walls. And then it started. Just a slow spin at first that gradually became faster and faster. Still holding tight to her mother, Mattie turned to grin excitedly at Hannah but as the rotation sped up, her grin stretched across her face like a caricature of a manic clown. And still it went faster. Until Mattie's hand was ripped away from her mother's and she stood alone, splayed out against the wall and unable to move. Then the floor dropped away and her stomach disintegrated, bringing up half-digested pieces of hotdog and fairy floss and spreading them across the wall around her.

More striking even than the terror was the feeling of impotency. She wanted desperately for the ride to stop so that she could get off, more intensely than she had ever wanted anything before, but she knew there was nothing, absolutely nothing, she could do to make it end. It was totally out of her control and she simply had no option but to see it through. With nothing holding her up but her own momentum.

EIGHT

The flowers arrived on Monday afternoon. A huge colourful arrangement of burnt-orange and egg-yolk yellow blooms that clashed badly with the lounge-room drapes. Mattie put them in the laundry, on top of the washing machine, and closed the door. Because she simply didn't want to see them, or smell them. There was something about the aroma of florist's arrangements, perhaps from the little foam cushions as they aged, that she found unbearably depressing.

The day before, Mattie had begun with every intention of staying in bed for the duration. Just pulling the covers over herself and hibernating until the children were back. But instead, after an hour of lying there feeling sorry for herself, she began brewing a righteous anger that eventually energised her to such an extent that she was propelled out of bed to roam the unit with her fists clenched. How dare he do that to her. How *dare* he.

And, strangely, the anger pleased her. For the past few years her anger had been blunted by a dull acceptance, whereas today it felt sharp and precise, and by lunchtime she had convinced herself that what had happened last night was actually for the best, because it clearly told her how right she'd been to leave. He would never change. Never. So all the guilt and doubts that had been collecting within her about this whole bid for freedom were baseless furphies. She'd done the only thing possible, and Jake was the one who bore ultimate responsibility, not her.

But nevertheless she hurt. Physically and emotionally. Intense, stabbing pains shot through her neck from the base of her skull to her shoulders whenever she turned too quickly. And if she bent her head backwards to look up, the pain was so extreme that her vision blurred. Apart from that, a dull ache throbbed through her skull and shoulders, accentuating her anger. And because of this she told herself that she welcomed the pain. It demanded attention, prioritising itself against the emotional hurt that she refused to acknowledge, and sharpening her sense of righteousness.

In the early evening she showered, pulling an old tracksuit on and then taking more painkillers before sitting down in the lounge-room to await the arrival of the children. As if preparing for their arrival, or in fear of Jake's, her anger had begun to wear off, a wary apprehension replacing it. Much as she had on her first night in the unit, she watched the shadows lick across the walls until she was sitting in almost complete darkness. And once again she found the darkness comforting, like a cloak of invisibility, whereas the indiscriminate brightness of the overhead light was both confronting and intrusive.

It was nearly nine o'clock before the unit was flooded by headlights that were almost painful themselves. Mattie turned on the lights and listened for the sound of doors slamming – one, two. The car was already reversing as Max and Courtney ran up the path to the front door. They searched her face uneasily as they came in. Even Courtney was uncharacteristically quiet. She hugged them both, reassuring them with her presence, and being reassured by theirs. And although the events of the previous evening weren't spoken about, they hung in the air as an almost palpable entity, clearly visible in Courtney's overt affection and Max's sullen misery.

Mattie had long recognised the differing ways in which her children reacted to stress. Max became withdrawn, like a crab drawing itself slowly up into its shell; only his darting eyes, which couldn't quite meet anyone else's, indicated his internal distress. Whereas Courtney, normally ruled by the self-centredness of an extroverted six-year-old, became overly tactile, needing to touch and be touched as a form of comfort. Or, in this case, apology.

And their presence dulled Mattie's anger even further, replacing it with guilt. Guilt that they'd seen what they had. Guilt that she'd left, guilt that she'd stayed so long. Guilt at being such a failure as a wife and mother. Guilt that she loved Jake, still, and guilt that she obviously didn't love him enough. And overwhelming, gut-wrenching guilt because she couldn't think of a way out without jeopardising everything that she held dear.

She went through the next few days a bit like a Stepford mannequin. All the actions were right, but something intrinsic was missing. She cooked and cleaned, washed and ironed, hugged and kissed, did her duties at school, attended the Monday afternoon swimming lesson, chatted cheerfully with other mothers – but without really connecting. Just an animated shell, while deep down the real Mattie sat with her knees drawn up, laughing at herself hysterically because she'd been naive enough to think things would be different. That just because she had moved out, put some distance between them, that she and Jake would be able to start anew, rebuilding the foundations of their relationship so that the rest of their lives could be solid and secure, instead of constantly in danger of collapse.

The phone rang twice on Monday afternoon but she didn't bother answering. Then, when she came back after dropping the children off at school on Tuesday morning, Hilda rang the bell before knocking on the door, a brisk no-nonsense rapping that demanded an answer but didn't get one. Mattie didn't even go to the door when the flower-delivery man knocked, instead waiting until he'd gone before collecting the arrangement from the porch and carrying it straight through to the laundry.

But the flowers did achieve something the past few days hadn't. They forced her to acknowledge the pattern, of which she knew they were only the first stage. Next the phone-calls would become more insistent, then would come the face-to-face confrontation, and finally the sex to seal the deal. And after those necessary stages had been completed would come the good times. Those irresistible, intoxicating, glorious good times that always felt like they would last forever. A few weeks when everything was wonderful, and Jake would be the best husband in the world, and she the best wife, and the children would flourish in the periphery of the glow.

The trouble was that each time the pattern played itself out and she crawled blinking from the dark again, she emerged with a little less of herself. Her pride, her self-respect, her *essence*. What made her Mattie. And if she was being chipped away, slowly but surely, then there had to come a time when she would crawl out with nothing left, when the shell that she became for those few days would be permanent. She would go through the actions each day, well-trained and obedient, but with nothing flickering behind the blank eyes. Just a dull sense of once having been more. Much more.

And that scared Mattie intensely, more greatly even than the deadness of Jake's gaze when he turned. Because she knew that when he was like that, cruel and vicious and totally without heart, it wasn't the real Jake, the one she loved. No, the real Jake was there somewhere, but buried so deep down that he was powerless to do anything and was forced to watch helplessly while this alter ego, this *changeling*, took over.

So although his eyes might terrify her at those times, might make her shrivel in fear of both his words and actions, she always knew the real Jake would re-surface, given time. But if she was eventually whittled down, if a time came when she emerged without her soul, then the real Mattie would be gone forever. And nothing would ever bring her back.

The phone-calls commenced in earnest on Wednesday morning. By then the ache that ringed her neck and stabbed at her skull had begun to lessen, and the headaches at last became manageable with painkillers, but the phone-calls started the pain up again. They came every half an hour or so, and rang so incessantly that even the intervals echoed with sound. Nevertheless she didn't take the phone off the hook. That would have been too pro-active, when it was easier to remain an outsider, simply noting the number of calls and knowing, almost enjoying, the fact that they represented Jake's growing desperation.

She resisted getting changed out of her tracksuit until lunchtime, knowing that to change her outfit would be to acknowledge the importance of his opinion. But finally she gave in, shedding the old grey tracksuit in favour of a layered broderie anglaise skirt and a snug red

t-shirt. And then she took two painkillers and waited, with her book
unopened in her lap.

He arrived just before two o'clock, sitting in his car for a few minutes
before opening the door and walking slowly, heavily, up the path. He
was dressed in his work clothes, dark grey suit with a white shirt and
navy tie, but he had removed the jacket because of the growing warmth
of the day. His shirt-sleeves were rolled up, his tie was loosened and he
looked hot, and very tired. Mattie knew it was useless not to answer
his knock. Firstly, he had seen her car in the carport, and secondly, she
knew, from experience, that he would just persevere until she gave in.
So she opened the door and led the way, wordlessly, into the kitchen,
where she put on the kettle and Jake slid onto one of the chairs. The
silence deepened while Mattie made a pot of tea and carried it, with
two cups and the carton of milk, over to the table. She sat opposite Jake
and poured out the tea, still without saying a word.

Jake finally broke the silence. 'Did you get my flowers?'

'Yes, thanks. Very nice.'

'Then where are they?'

Mattie tipped some milk into her tea, avoiding his gaze. 'In the
laundry.'

'Ah, I see.' He sighed. 'Look, Mattie, I don't know what to say.'

'Don't you?'

'That is . . .' He paused, looking at her searchingly. 'I don't know
what I *can* say.'

'No, I don't suppose you do.'

'Not making this any easier, are you?'

For the first time, Mattie looked at him full on. 'Me? *I'm* not making
it easy?'

'Point taken.' Jake sighed again and stirred his tea absently. 'Mat, I
don't know why I do the things I do, I really don't. It's like I've got a
self-destruct wish.'

'But it's not *you* that you're trying to destroy,' said Mattie, with a flash
of insight.

'That's where you're wrong.' Jake leant forward earnestly. 'I *am* trying
to destroy me, because you mean everything to me. Everything.'

'They're only words.' Mattie looked at him sadly. 'Words are so easy.'

'You think this is easy?' Jake shook his head emphatically. 'Christ, Mattie, you've got no idea. This is hard. *Bloody* hard.'

Mattie looked at him, while in her head she asked whether it was as hard as seeing your children watch you creep away, thoroughly beaten in every sense of the word, with your shirt torn and tears and snot smeared across your face. Was it harder than that? Did it hurt as much as her stiff neck did every time she turned her head? Would he even ask about her pain? She already knew the answer to that.

'The thing is, Mattie, that I can't stand the thought of losing you. I just can't *stand* it. I can feel you slipping away and it feels like there's nothing I can do. It drives me mad. And stuff like you volunteering down at some centre, meeting new people, having some sort of party with friends I thought you'd left behind, well, it scares me shitless.'

'But, Jake, those aren't the things that are driving a wedge between us.' Mattie tried to speak evenly. '*You're* doing that.'

'Then come back home and I'll stop.' Jake grabbed her hand and held it tight. 'I promise. Come back home where you belong and it'll never happen again. Never.'

Mattie opened her mouth and then closed it again. She knew he was being sincere, that at this moment he really meant it, but it made little difference. There had already been too many promises, and too much sincerity.

'You don't trust me.' Jake let go of her hand slowly, and sat back. 'Either that or you don't really want to come back, and you're just using me as an excuse.'

'That's not fair.' Mattie flinched at the injustice. 'There's nothing more I'd like than to go home. To live happily ever after.'

'Then do it.' Jake looked at her challengingly. 'Come on. We'll pay the rent on this place until they find new tenants and I promise I won't hold the money against you. To tell you the truth, I'd never have agreed to this if I thought you'd actually see the whole thing through. So you can look at it as a win, okay? You did it. You've made me see how serious you are about all this. So if you come home now, we'll give it three

months and if you don't think it's working out, then we'll get counselling. I promise.'

'I asked you to get counselling last year! You refused!'

'Well, to be honest I don't see the point. I reckon it's all a crock. But
I'm trying to show you how serious I am here, that I'd even do something I don't believe in if it's what you want. C'mon, be fair, Mattie, I
can't do more than that.'

'How come suddenly I'm the one not being fair?'

Jake started to reply and then grinned instead. 'Offence is the best
form of defence.'

'Well, I suppose at least you're honest.' Mattie smiled back, relieved
that the tension was broken. They drank their tea in silence for a few
moments. She glanced up at the time, not wanting to be late collecting
Max and Courtney but also reluctant to finish things prematurely here
either. But it was only two-thirty.

Jake followed her gaze. 'Outstayed my welcome already, have I?'

'No, of course not.'

'You're not going to come home yet, are you?'

'No. I'm really sorry, but –'

'I didn't think so.' Jake looked at her ruefully. 'And unfortunately
gone are the days when I could have forced you. Damn laws.'

'Yeah.' Mattie laughed, rather flatly.

'But I've got a plan B, if you're interested. For if you wouldn't come
home. What I –'

'It's not that I don't *want* to come home,' interrupted Mattie, desperate to make him understand that she was as committed as he was.
'It's just that . . . well, I'm not sure it'll work like that. And I'm . . .' She
trailed off, unsure how to explain her fear without making him feel
defensive.

'It doesn't matter.' Jake shook his head slowly and then gave her a
half-smile. 'I'll take what I can get. As long as you can promise me that
you want this to work as much as I do. You do, don't you?'

'I do.' Mattie nodded earnestly.

'So I'm not losing you?'

Mattie shook her head, unable to say the words.

'Thank Christ.' Jake took a deep breath and then let it out in a rush. 'I don't know what I'd do without you. Even if I don't deserve you, I still couldn't let you go. No way.'

Mattie smiled automatically, but the smile didn't quite reach her eyes. Because what had once sounded romantic and flattering nowadays had an ominous ring that made her feel cornered, powerless. On the Luna Park rotor again.

'So I've got a proposition.' Jake held up his hand as if she had been about to interrupt. 'Hear me out. I'm trying to come up with a compromise, something that gives us a chance while still giving you the independence you clearly want. And don't look like that – I'm not criticising you, I'm just trying to factor everything in. What I suggest is that you stay here and spread your wings and all, but instead of this trial separation, we go backwards.'

'Backwards?'

'Yeah, backwards. To when we were going out. I know we already agreed not to see anyone else during this year, but everything else was left up in the air. And I think that's my problem – not knowing where I stand scares me. So what I thought was, we see each other a couple of times a week, have set days, and go out together every once in a while. Like before we were married. What do you think?'

Despite being quite surprised by *Jake* coming up with a compromise, Mattie was in fact thinking rapidly. On the face of it, it sounded like a good plan. And a way of keeping everything together without losing her hard-won freedom, such as it was. For a moment she thought back to when they had been dating, and how wonderful everything had seemed. How simple and straightforward. And she felt warmed by the thought.

'So?' prompted Jake eagerly. 'What do you reckon?'

'I think it's got possibilities,' said Mattie slowly. 'Definite possibilities.'

'Thank god.' Jake leant forward and grabbed her hand again, grinning at her happily. 'See? You think I don't understand but I do. I've been thinking like crazy over the past few days trying to come up with a solution. And short of you coming home, I really think this is the next best thing. It'll make me feel secure, not as shit-scared I'm losing you.'

Mattie stared at him as she grasped anxiously for the right words, knowing that this was her chance to explain herself, make him understand how she felt. 'But what about *me*, Jake? What about *me* feeling scared, or secure? I don't think you understand how – *awful* I feel after you . . . like Saturday night.'

'That's not damn fair.' Jake drew back, affronted. 'I come here waving an olive branch and you throw that in my face.'

'I'm *not* throwing it in your face!' Mattie leant forward, now desperate to make him empathise. 'It's just that I *need* to tell you how you made me feel, I *need* to make you –'

'And I don't see the point,' Jake interrupted, his smile totally gone now. 'You're trying to rub my nose in something that I've been killing myself over. You talk about how you feel, but what about how *I* feel? Do you think I'm proud of myself? Do you think I enjoyed myself?'

'No,' replied Mattie in a small voice. And she ignored the dissent deep within her because to believe Jake had enjoyed *that* was unthinkable. Unbearable.

'The fact is, you can't tell me anything I don't already know. And you can't make me feel worse than I already do. Christ, if you only knew . . . god . . . doesn't matter. Just believe me when I say I feel like shit. And I don't see how rehashing what's done is going to help us move on.'

'I suppose.'

'Do you see where I'm coming from?'

'I suppose.'

'You sound like Max.'

Mattie recognised the moment for what it was – a chance to back away and lighten up. She made herself smile. 'God, that's all I need.'

'You mean that's all *I* need.' Jake rolled his eyes. '*Two* monosyllabic family members!'

Mattie kept her smile in place, and nodded agreeably.

'So the main thing is that you're happy to give my compromise a go. And we see each other a couple of times a week, and concentrate on keeping this family together.' Jake leant forward and took one of Mattie's hands. 'And I promise you, Mat, I *absolutely* promise you, that I'll do everything in my power to make sure that happens. Okay?'

'Okay.'

'Well, then. All that's left to do is seal the deal, hey?' He lifted her hand up and kissed it on the knuckles, still looking into her eyes. Then he wiggled his eyebrows suggestively and grinned. 'If you know what I mean.'

Mattie glanced up at the clock to check the time and was surprised to see that it was only just past three. She stared at the clock for a moment or so, rather blankly, and then blinked as she forced herself to concentrate. Her neck throbbed dully as she turned back to Jake.

'Well?' He was still smiling, his eyes now warm and patient.

'Why not.'

The first time he hit her was three months after they married. He had a habit of clenching his fist when angry, but it had never been directed at her. In fact, she'd thought the habit an affectation. A rather aggressive one, but just an affectation nonetheless. And everybody had their faults, didn't they? Nobody was perfect.

Then one night she watched the fist shake in her face and saw it for what it was – an overt act of hostility. They'd been discussing feminism, of all things, when Jake became unexpectedly heated and the discussion rapidly turned into a rather one-sided argument. The fist shook in front of her to emphasise his points, or his dominance, while she sat hypnotised by its movement. Almost in shock. And he became increasingly personal, attacking her beliefs and opinions with a calculated vengeance that was even more scary than the fist.

Trying to hide the fact that she'd started crying, Mattie left the room but he came after her. He pushed past roughly and knocked her flying against the lounge-room door. So it hadn't actually been a hit, not really – more of an inadvertent shove. An accident, just one of those things.

He had been terribly apologetic, especially when he saw the elongated bruise left on her lower back by the door handle. But over the next few months it became a bit of a joke, with Mattie teasing him about being a bully and him jibing her about being a fragile little wench. His fragile little wench.

NINE

This time Mattie really thought it might work. Really. It wasn't just that the plan itself had merit, but that it was *Jake* who'd thought of it. Which meant he'd acknowledged the problems and thought things through until he came up with a compromise. And he would also be doubly committed because he himself had proposed it.

The agreement would stay the same, and they would have the children on the days already decided, but with a few added clauses. On Sundays, they would do something together as a family – a picnic, perhaps, or even just a movie. And Jake would spend the night at her unit before going to work from there the following day. Then on Thursdays, she would collect the children from school and bring them around to the house, where she would have tea with them and stay the night.

This plan had several benefits. One was that she would be able to keep the relationship that meant so much to her whilst also retaining her freedom. Another was that they would not spend two consecutive nights together which Mattie thought, but did not say aloud, was very important. Then there was the fact that she would spend additional time with her children each week, be with them at their father's house and monitor the situation. And while there wasn't much she could *do*, at least she could be there.

And maybe after a year of this cutting back, this form of almost *dating*, they would be able to rebuild those foundations that had somehow skewed, and start anew. Be the family she was convinced they could be.

Happier, healthier, stronger. Because she really did love him. Not the domineering Jake who shook his fist and stood over her with almost pathological aggression, but the Jake who held her hand and smiled that slow, lopsided smile that made her nerve-ends tingle. The Jake who massaged her feet when they were swollen, who brought her coffee in bed every Sunday, and who brushed her hair while they were watching television. She couldn't live without that Jake.

And she could not imagine doing those things with any other man. Ever. Or the other everyday, mundane things that make up two joined lives. Walking naked from the ensuite shower, chatting from the toilet, gardening side by side on a sunny weekend, waking up with mohawk hair and early-morning breath. And sex. Even the thought of sex with someone else was not just distasteful, but absolutely impossible to contemplate. So to finish this relationship, forever, was to relegate herself to a solitary life, one in which she would spend the rest of her years alone, a single mother just like those others at Centrelink. Increasingly desperate, and lonely, and unwanted.

But now it might not come to that. Now they had a workable plan, and a realistic chance. And she was going to prioritise it over everything else. She was *going* to make it work. With that in mind, Mattie put aside the acceptance letter from the community centre when it arrived. There would be time enough for the course later; for now, it was not worth upsetting the applecart. She would also have cancelled the Whimsicalities party if she'd been able but the invitations had already gone out. And, if she was honest, she was glad they had.

Thursday night she spent at the house, a nice relaxed evening during which Jake was so solicitous that even the children could see it was a tacit apology. And all she had to do to enjoy herself was to forget about the last time she had been there and not read too much into Max's sidelong glances. Then on Sunday, they drove into the hills, through Belgrave and up to Kallista, along a beautiful winding road bracketed by huge tree ferns and shady gullies. After a while, they found a picnic area and set up amongst other like-minded souls enjoying the gorgeous spring weather. Max and Courtney explored while she lay with her head in Jake's lap, staring up at the cerulean sky that was studded with a few impossibly fluffy cotton-ball clouds, and Jake slowly, tenderly, brushed her hair back from her forehead with his long, piano-player fingers. And she closed her eyes and tried to ignore the dull ache that ringed her neck.

Lunch was cold roast chicken and coleslaw, fresh rolls and potato chips, with orange juice to wash it all down. Then they went for a walk into the forest that ringed the park. A forest so dense that the sky was only occasionally visible as sparkling glints through the overhead canopy. It was the sort of day that made one glad to be alive. Absolutely perfect. And once more Mattie was able to collect together all her doubts and concerns and negative expectations, and push them to one side where they couldn't intrude. This simple achievement allowed her to enjoy the moment, and to infuse it with her natural sense of optimism. And it was far, far easier to pretend than it was to unpack all the doubts and face them head-on.

But the first cracks in the newly polished facade appeared on the following Tuesday, when Mattie was collecting Courtney from her classroom after school. Her teacher, Miss Thomson, a young and intense woman straight from teachers' college, asked her if she had a minute to spare. If it had been Max's teacher, Mattie would have approached the discussion with some premonition of what was to come. But Courtney? The girl had sailed through kindergarten and her first year of school thus far with popularity and a quickness that already had her reading and doing simple maths. So Mattie, fully expecting to be told of some minor development, perhaps an altercation with another child, waited patiently while the teacher farewelled the last of the children and dealt with a mother whose son had mislaid his school jumper.

'Courtney, perhaps you'd like to go and play outside while I chat with Mummy?' Miss Thomson stood at the door, obviously intending to close it as soon as Courtney left.

'Actually –' Mattie glanced at her watch – 'Court, could you go find Max in the playground and tell him I'll be a few minutes?'

'What're you going to talk about?' asked Courtney suspiciously.

'You,' said Mattie shortly. 'Now go.'

'Mrs Hampton, take a seat,' Miss Thomson closed the door firmly behind Courtney and gestured at one of the child-sized plastic chairs that had been placed neatly on top of a small, formica-topped table. She took one down for herself from the other side and sat, facing Mattie, with a foolscap folder in front of her.

'Comfy, aren't they?' observed Mattie with a grin as she wedged herself into the chair, her knees bent awkwardly.

'Yes,' Miss Hampton grinned back. 'But if you'd been one of my, well, larger mothers, I wouldn't even have asked you to sit there.'

'Then I'll take it as a compliment.'

'Okay.' The teacher smiled again and then, opening the folder, abruptly turned businesslike. 'I wanted to discuss something with you that –'

'Is there a problem?' interrupted Mattie, for the first time feeling a sense of foreboding. 'I thought Courtney was doing really well.'

'She *is*,' Miss Thomson said quickly. 'In fact, she's a joy to teach. Clever, well-organised, popular – she's one of my most reliable and responsible students. In that respect, I wish more were like her.'

'But in other respects?' prompted Mattie apprehensively.

'Yes, there we have it.' The teacher sighed softly and went back to her notes. After a moment she looked up again. 'And it's hard to put into words, which is why I haven't spoken to you sooner. Even though I've been aware of the, ah, problem for some time.'

'And what *is* the problem?'

'To put it bluntly, Courtney is manipulative. *Very* manipulative. At first I thought she was just getting her own way all the time because she's a natural leader rather than a follower, but it's more than that. She manipulates the others, very cleverly, and if it looks like her control is slipping, even a trifle, I'm afraid she becomes a bit of a bully.'

'A *bully?*'

'Unfortunately, yes. She seems to have an intuitive grasp of the other children's vulnerabilities and uses them to her advantage. Let me give you an example.' Miss Thomson folded her hands on top of her notes and looked at Mattie intently. 'The other day I gave the children a task in which they had to glue various pieces of material to a sheet of paper. Anyway, Courtney was particularly keen on this sequinned scrap that another girl had. Now this child is one of those shy ones who find it

difficult to mix well. So, after she refused to hand it over, Courtney simply threatened to exclude her from their lunchtime games.'

'And she got what she wanted?' asked Mattie, rather blankly.

'Yes, she got what she wanted. And I know my example sounds rather
petty, but it's actually very indicative. Mind you, Courtney's quite willing to get more personal too. I've heard her pick on the other children's
weight, or glasses, or what-have-you, simply to achieve her own ends.'

'You don't like her,' stated Mattie suddenly.

'What? Oh, no.' For the first time, Miss Thomson seemed flustered.
'That's not true at all. Besides, I wouldn't let personal feelings intrude
on my professionalism. I'm telling you this because I want to *help*
Courtney, not attack her.'

'Whatever.' Mattie looked at her rather narrowly and then, with a
sigh, broke eye contact. What did it matter if the teacher didn't like
the child when the issue was Courtney herself? Then she thought of
something even worse and looked up quickly. 'Is she violent? I mean,
this bullying, does she get aggressive?'

'No, no.' Miss Thomson shook her head, obviously pleased to report
something positive. 'Never. I mean she *can* get verbally aggressive, but
never physical.'

'Good,' said Mattie with relief. She smoothed down her jeans and
stood up, pushing the small chair down. 'Was there anything else, or
was that it?'

'Ah, that's it.' Miss Thomson looked up at her with some surprise.

'Well, thank you very much for bringing it to my attention.' Mattie
smiled politely. 'I'll speak to my husband and we'll deal with it.'

'I don't think it's as simple as that.'

'Well, we'll soon find out. And please don't hesitate to contact me
should any other problems arise.' Mattie picked up the chair and placed
it neatly on top of the table as Miss Thomson rose from the other side,
staring down at her notes as if it contained hints on how to deal with
parents who end interviews too soon.

Mattie washed her hands briskly at one of the drinking tap fountains and then shook them dry as she went to find her children. They
were in the far playground, where both were clambering over the

climbing frame with the agility of small monkeys. There were few other children around by now. Most were probably already home, sitting at a kitchen counter eating afternoon tea. Happy, healthy, and secure. Mattie stood watching her two pensively. She thought about what she had just been told, and realised she wasn't all that surprised. Only the words had come as a jolt – manipulative, bully, verbally aggressive. And she wished she'd thought to ask Miss Thomson whether Courtney's behaviour had worsened over the past couple of weeks. But, then again, maybe it was just as well she hadn't, because she didn't really want to know the answer.

The next crack in the facade appeared in her bank account sometime in the early hours of Thursday morning. Her first complete Centrelink payment. The week before she had received a partial payment so, while the money had been handy, she'd ignored the actual amount as irrelevant. But Thursday's mail brought confirmation of exactly what she would be receiving each week, and it quite simply wasn't enough. After paying her rent she would have very little left to pay for groceries, electricity, gas, phone, prescriptions, swimming lessons, petrol and all the other incidentals that laid claim to her purse each week. Heaven help her if the car broke down, or they had a run of ill-health.

And there were only two things she could do about it. One was to start looking for a job immediately but, for many reasons, Mattie cringed at the thought. The children, child care, fear of the unknown, lack of suitable clothing, doubts regarding her ability to cope and, last but by no means least, Jake's reaction should she contemplate such a step. He would hate it. Mattie took a deep breath and shook her head. Maybe in a few months, when she was stronger, and their relationship was more secure.

The other, and more realistic option was to ask Jake for some child support. A month ago she'd been eager to agree to almost anything to clear the road and, given the fact they would be sharing custody, it seemed to make sense to simply ignore any extra financial support, either way. But the reality was that she was the one who would have to buy them clothing, and pay for their activities, and schooling – and all the other myriad expenses that came with young children. It made perfect sense that he contribute something to these expenses, because simply feeding them and keeping them entertained for a few days a week just didn't measure up.

The necessity to speak to Jake about this was uppermost in her mind as she collected the children on Thursday afternoon and drove them to the house. Jake wasn't expected for another hour so she fixed a snack for Max and Courtney and then wandered around, tidying an ornament here and a cushion there. It was strange how out of place she felt, so quickly. After all, only three weeks ago this had been her home and now she felt almost intrusive, like a visitor passing through.

The house was very open plan, with a wide, virtually wall-less passage leading from the front door all the way to the kitchen, with rooms jutting off it. The family room and then kitchen to the right, and the study, lounge-room and meals area to the left. Then, down at the far end of the house were the bedrooms and bathroom. Mattie already knew that the passage was exactly fifteen measured steps from the entrance to the kitchen, and also how many steps divided each room from the other.

Max and Courtney settled down in front of the television in the lounge-room to play video games, so Mattie watched them silently for a while. Then she wandered off again, pausing at the family room sliding door to look out at the patio, where the cedar setting sat neatly, all the chairs pushed in, and the barbecue gleamed with a pewter sheen. A slight breeze ruffled through the pot-plants and caused the nearest hanging plant to brush its spiky tendrils against the glass with an irritating scratchy sound. Mattie stared out expressionlessly and then turned to glance at the double window set in the other wall, where her two children had stood, faces pressed against the glass and eyes wide.

Mattie shook herself quickly before she became maudlin. It didn't pay to dwell on what couldn't be undone, because there was no benefit at all. On her way out of the room, she stopped to gaze at the Margaret Olley print that hung on the wall by the door. They had purchased the limited edition still life, of oranges overflowing a wicker basket, early in

their marriage, as an investment. And Mattie loved it. It had a tranquil-
lity that brought comfort, while still possessing an intensity that was
compelling. And it was the coexistence of these two seeming opposites, this placid vibrancy, that she loved the most, because it offered
visual proof that conflicting traits could actually enhance rather than
detract.

Mattie ran a finger gently over one corner of the painting, feeling the
textured surface of the print. Then she sighed and turned away, heading back to the lounge-room and intending to settle on the couch until
Jake returned. On the way she passed the linen cupboard and, hit with
a sudden idea, opened it to look for the box containing an embroidered
tablecloth given to them by one of her elderly aunts for their wedding.
It would be perfect to cover her old pine table for the Whimsicalities
party next weekend. Mattie found the flattish, oblong box easily, sliding
it out and removing the lid to ensure the cloth was still within. The deep
crimson of its embroidered roses and the coral-pink of one scalloped
edge were visible through the white tissue paper that protected it.

She closed the box again and took it down to the kitchen bench,
placing it next to her handbag, and then wandered back into the
lounge-room. But no sooner had she sat down than Jake's burgundy
Commodore pulled smoothly into the driveway and coasted past her
car into the carport. Mattie smoothed down her jeans and then looked
up and saw Courtney watching her, almost appraisingly. Just as their
eyes met, Jake's key could be heard scraping in the lock and the girl
jumped up as her father appeared in the passage.

'Daddy!' Courtney launched herself at her father as if it had been
weeks since she'd seen him rather than just days. He lifted her up and
kissed her heartily.

Max waved. 'Hey, Dad.'

'Hey to you too, mate.' Jake put Courtney down and turned to Mattie. 'And hello there, good-looking. Want to come and give me a hand
with tea?'

'Sure.' Mattie got up and followed him down to the kitchen, where
he stopped long enough to grab her by the shoulders and give her a
slow kiss.

'Ah, that's better.' Jake smiled at her, his eyes crinkling.

'I'd have to agree.' Mattie grinned back, feeling light and loved. 'Now, what do you need?'

'Nothing, actually. It's all under control. I just wanted your company.'

'Easily done.' Mattie sat up on one of the stools lining the bench and settled down to watch Jake produce the meal.

'Now, first a wine for the lady.' Jake took a bottle from the fridge and uncorked it with a hollow pop. He half filled two glasses and passed one to her. 'And now for some dinner magic.'

Mattie watched Jake as he opened the fridge and removed some foil-wrapped garlic bread and then her large cast-iron saucepan. He turned on the oven and put the saucepan on a hotplate at a simmer. The thought that he'd already prepared this meal, probably last night, made Mattie feel soft with pleasure.

'Spaghetti bolognaise?' she hazarded.

'Yes, ma'am.' Jake filled another saucepan with water and put it on an adjoining hotplate.

'Lovely.' Mattie took a sip of wine. 'How was your day anyway?'

'Pretty shitty, actually.' Jake stopped long enough to drink some of his own wine. He smacked his lips appreciatively. 'But I'm making a valiant attempt to rise above that.'

'Good,' said Mattie with sincerity.

'How's your week been then?'

'Good,' said Mattie again. 'Quiet.'

'Same here.' Jake put a lid on the saucepan and turned its handle out, away from the hotplates. 'But it did give me a chance to get some gardening done. I've turned over the earth down at that far corner. Thought I might make a vegetable patch. What do you think?'

'That's a great idea!' said Mattie enthusiastically. 'Do you need any help?'

'I wouldn't say no. I'll take you down there after tea and show you what I've done so far.' Jake moved Mattie's bag to the far end of the island bench-top and then frowned at the oblong box. 'What's that tablecloth doing out?'

'Oh, I was just going to borrow it. For my thing next weekend.'

Jake paused, looking across at her. 'I thought we agreed the wedding presents stayed here. Except for the blanket, that is.'

'Oh, yes,' said Mattie quickly, 'I just wanted to borrow it, that's all.'

'Well, no offence but I'd rather you waited till I was home. It gives me the creeps to think of you rifling through all the cupboards while I'm not here.'

'I did *not* rifle,' exclaimed Mattie, stung by the injustice. 'I just wanted to borrow it! For one day!'

'I'd still rather you waited, if you don't mind.' Jake ran his hand over the box and then looked at her expressionlessly. 'After all, for this year it's my house. That was the deal, wasn't it? *Your* deal?'

'Yes,' said Mattie flatly, sliding down off her stool. 'I'll put it back.'

'No, don't be stupid.' Jake put his hand back on the box so that she couldn't take it. 'Next time, just wait till I'm home, okay? Otherwise I'll have to take your key off you.'

Mattie stared at him, trying to work out whether he was joking. After a long moment, he smiled, his face transforming in an instant, and she let her breath out with some relief. She climbed back onto her stool. 'Sorry.'

'No problem. But do you see my point?'

'I think . . . yes, of course I do.'

'Well, that's the main thing.' Jake lifted the lid off the saucepan with the water and frowned at it. 'Come on, you bugger, boil already.'

'I think you need to turn it on,' offered Mattie.

Jake stared at the dial and burst out laughing. 'I think you're right. Christ I'm good at this, aren't I?'

'I think you've done a great job,' protested Mattie as she watched him turn the gas on.

'Wait till you taste it!'

'Well, it smells good anyway.' Mattie took an appreciative sniff.

'Oh, I've got something for you.' Jake abandoned his saucepans to pluck an envelope off the bench and hand it across to her. 'Came home with Max last Friday and I forgot about it.'

The envelope had been opened so Mattie just slid the folded paper out. It was a school notice advising of an excursion to be held in early December, at a cost of twenty-three dollars. Scienceworks, in South Melbourne. Bring a packed lunch and a packet drink. Mattie sighed and then looked across at Jake. This seemed as good a time as any.

'Listen, I've been meaning to talk to you about these things. I know we left a lot of the financial side of the kids up in the air, but don't you think we should be going halves? Not just this –' Mattie waved the paper in the air – 'but also swimming and stuff like that?'

'No.' Jake frowned, not in an unfriendly way but as though he was confused.

'Why not?'

'Because you get the family allowance from the government, of course.' Jake looked at her as if she had suggested something totally outlandish. 'You can't seriously expect me to pay for stuff when *you're* the one who's getting paid to look after them?'

'But, Jake, do you know how much I get?'

'That's not the point. You should have researched all that before you left.'

Mattie stared at the school notice dumbly. 'I simply don't have enough for these. Half my money goes in rent alone. There'll be nothing left after I pay for groceries. I don't even know how I'm going to pay the bills.'

'Well, once again, you should have thought of that, shouldn't you?'

'But, Jake, be fair . . .'

'*You're* the one who's not being fair, Mattie! I mean, let me get this straight.' Jake picked up the wooden spoon and stirred inside the large cast-iron pot. Then he turned back to Mattie. 'You want me to pay for them even when I don't have them? So, apart from paying for them when they're here, you want me to pay you money for when you've got them as well. Swimming is on a Monday, that's *your* day. And if you check that notice, you'll see the excursion is on a Wednesday. Your day also. If something comes up on *my* day, then I'll pay for it.'

'But I –'

'And you're damn lucky I'm even willing to do that. For Christ sake, Mattie, that's what the frigging family allowance is for, isn't it? I should be asking *you* for money!'

'*Me?*'

'Yes, you! But am I asking for half the family allowance? No, I'm not. Because *I'm* trying to be fair. Your problem is you've had it too easy. Always had a good wage coming in here, didn't you?'

'Yes, but –'

'Well, now you need to learn to budget, that's all.' Jake turned his back on her and stirred the bolognaise with obvious annoyance.

'Then I'll have to get a job,' said Mattie, frowning at his back. 'I'll have no choice.'

Jake stirred for a few more seconds and then turned to her, his eyes hardening even as he spoke. 'Are you trying to blackmail me?'

'No, I'm just trying to be honest!'

'Honest?' Jake laughed, but his eyes remained cold. 'Don't give me that. You're trying to give me an ultimatum. You fucking amaze me, Mattie, you really do. Doesn't matter how much I try –' Jake paused as he waved his spare hand at the saucepans on the stove – 'you just want more.'

'That's not what –'

'Well, I tell you what, you can have it.' Jake flung the wooden spoon in the direction of the sink, spatters of thick red bolognaise sauce marking its passage. Then he pulled his wallet out of his pocket and threw it down on the bench, where it flipped open and lay with its contents exposed before her. 'There you go. Take the lot. I'm going to get changed.'

As Jake strode past her, Mattie stared at the wallet blankly. In the upper section a fifty dollar note sat sandwiched between two twenties and, underneath, was a small, colour photo of her with Courtney on her lap and Max leaning against her shoulder. They were each smiling, a normal, happy family. Mattie blinked and looked away, towards the red spray left behind by the wooden spoon. One fat droplet hung on the edge of the counter-top, a piece of onion in its centre like a pallid eye. The droplet slowly elongated and then fell to the floor, splattering on the slate like blood. Mattie shook her head, trying to focus. If anything, she'd just made things worse. Ruined the evening at the outset. And the worst of it was that she was no longer even sure she had been right in the first place. She *did* get all the family allowance, despite only having the kids half the time. So now she just felt greedy and grasping.

'Why d'you *always* make Daddy angry?'

Mattie whipped around to face Courtney with surprise. 'What?'

'You!' Courtney stood by the bench with her fists clenched. 'You ruin everything!'

'*I* do?'

'Yes, you *know* you do! Daddy was in a really good mood until *you* started at him.'

'Courtney, I *had* to talk to him.' Mattie bent down and took her daughter by the arms to try and make her understand. 'It was about important things. I *had* to.'

'No you didn't.' Courtney shook her off angrily. 'You *like* making him angry. Why can't you just be nice?'

'Oh god.'

'I hate you here.' Courtney stamped her foot and then, after glaring at her mother fiercely with over-bright eyes, ran back into the lounge-room. Dumbly, Mattie watched her go. Is that how she really saw it? Max too? She rubbed her neck, which had started throbbing again, and stared down at the bench-top, willing herself not to cry.

Then, after a few moments in which a mix of emotions churned nauseously in her gut, Mattie took a deep breath and resolutely pushed the Courtney business to the back of her mind. She would deal with that later. For now, there were more immediate things to do. And first and foremost was rescuing this evening before it became a disaster. And she knew, from long experience, there was only one thing that could accomplish that at this point.

'Dinner'll be ready in about ten minutes. I just need to see Daddy for a bit,' Mattie called into the lounge-room as she slid down off the stool. She took the dishcloth and quickly cleaned up the spilt bolognaise, wiping down the tiles and mopping the splattered droplet off the floor. She watched the small piece of onion circle the plughole slowly as she rinsed the cloth off and then turned the tap on full, jabbing it through the holes with her finger. The top of a fingernail split across as it hit the plughole at an angle so she pulled that off and washed it down as well.

That done, she washed her hands thoroughly and took a last gulp of wine before walking deliberately down towards the master bedroom. At the door she paused, running her fingers through her hair and then undoing the top few buttons of her cheerful, raspberry-coloured shirt before pushing the door open and entering the room.

*T*he second time was almost a year later. They'd been to a New Year's Eve party hosted by Liz and Alan, her soon-to-be husband, who erected a huge marquee in their backyard for the occasion. It was a windy evening, and the white canvas rippled around them like a boat's sail, sometimes flapping with such force that it cracked like a whip.

When the countdown began for midnight, Mattie was at a table with some friends she hadn't seen for ages, chatting about marriage, and work, and catching up on gossip. She grabbed her champagne and set off in search of Jake as the crowd joyfully yelled down the seconds – ten, nine, eight, seven . . . Weaving in and out, she had laughingly given up, trusting they would find each other sooner or later. Instead she joined in with Liz and her group as they raised their glasses and yelled out the last moments of the year. Three, two, one.

Everybody cheered as midnight struck and kisses rained all round. Paula had run past, kissing Mattie on the top of the head, and then Liz kissed her, on the cheek, before Alan lifted her up and planted one on her lips. Then, while Liz and Alan shared a longer embrace with each other, Mattie exchanged kisses and 'Happy New Years' with the others before she turned away, looking for Jake again. And saw him almost immediately, standing not far away and staring straight at her. At first she hadn't realised that anything was wrong and just made her way, grinning hugely, towards him. Even when she got closer and saw that his face was frozen in a mask of anger, her smile had stayed in place. Just more uncertain, and confused by the juxtaposition of celebration and flat fury.

He grabbed her by the arm, roughly, and steered her through the throng of people towards the exit. Friends called out as they passed and she tried to answer, playing down her embarrassment. 'Sorry, gotta go. Left the iron on. Ha, ha.' But Jake hadn't paused, not even when she stumbled over an abandoned chair. He just dug his fingers in deeper, dragging her upright as he went. And there had been no reply to her exclamations or questions as to what was wrong either. Not until they got home.

TEN

Hilda visited on Friday afternoon, bringing a large, round tin with snowy Christmas scenes decorating the sides. Her short, square frame was dressed in a navy skirt with a rather pretty coral ribbed top. She was also wearing a quantity of gold jewellery – several bracelets, a chain and earrings studded with a large round pearl. The overall effect made her look far more like a cultured European than she had previously. Almost like a different person, especially since her hair had obviously been set recently; it was brushed up and back from her forehead in firmly lacquered waves the same soft colour as a dolphin's belly. She carefully sat the tin down on the kitchen table, opening it to reveal a mound of small, horseshoe-shaped homemade biscuits that were generously dusted with icing sugar.

'Vanilla *Kipferl*,' explained Hilda rather proudly, taking one out and offering it to Mattie. 'Christmas biscuits. Delicious.'

'Thanks.' Mattie, who wasn't in the least hungry, took a bite to be polite. And it *was* delicious. With a distinctly almond taste, it almost melted in her mouth. She ate the rest of the biscuit, and then dusted her t-shirt, icing sugar sprinkling down to the floor like snow. The fresh-baked smell of the biscuits brought back vague memories of her mother baking when she and Hannah were young. Nothing as nice as these, though.

'Good, hey?'

'Yes. *Really* good.' Mattie rinsed her hands off and went over to the stove to put the kettle on. 'Are they all for me?'

'Tch, tch.' Hilda shook her head with mock disappointment. '*And the children.*'

Mattie grinned. 'If they're lucky.'

'I shall have to ask them, make sure they got some.' Hilda's smile faded as she regarded Mattie pensively. 'You look tired. Something happened?'

'Pardon?' Mattie gaped at her, startled by the abruptness of the question.

'I asked if anything has happened.'

'Um . . . no.' Mattie turned her back, stalling, hoping Hilda would have focused on something else by the time she got two mugs out of the cupboard and over to the table. But when she finally faced her she found that Hilda was still regarding her searchingly.

'Thank you,' Hilda gestured at the coffee and then returned her black-button gaze to Mattie's face. 'Actually, you look even worse close up.'

'Thanks a lot,' Mattie laughed as she sat down, trying to lighten the mood.

Hilda didn't even smile. 'So what is it?'

'Nothing.' Mattie shrugged noncommittally. 'Probably just things on my mind. Like we're going up to Yea on Sunday to visit my in-laws, and you know what they say about in-laws!'

'Hmm . . . bad night sleep?'

'That too.'

'But you were not here, were you? Your car was gone.'

'Um, yes, that's right.' Mattie began to feel like she was being cross-examined. She took another biscuit. 'These really are wonderful, Hilda. You must give me the recipe.'

'Certainly. So stay with a friend, did you?'

'If you must know –' Mattie let some of her annoyance seep into her tone – 'I stayed with my husband. We've decided to stay together twice a week. To talk things through.'

'Did it work?' Hilda ploughed on relentlessly, her eyes fixed on Mattie's like ebony interrogation lamps. 'Talking things through, I mean.'

Mattie got up to rinse the icing sugar off her hands again and then sat down again, looking at Hilda narrowly while she finished formulating a cutting reply to the woman's nosiness. She opened her mouth to deliver it but what came out instead, in a whisper, was: 'No. No it didn't.'

'I did not think so.' Hilda passed her another biscuit. 'Eat up. Everything is always worse on an empty stomach.'

Mattie chewed in silence, while she juggled with the sudden temptation to open up, just a trifle. The thought of being able to discuss *anything* was incredibly appealing, but smacked of a disloyalty that made her gut clench. And then there was the possibility, the *probability*, of being told things she didn't want to hear. This biscuit had now lost all taste, forming instead into a congealed lump that refused to go down.

'Have another,' Hilda pushed the tin over. 'And tell me about it.'

Mattie nodded her thanks but looked away from the tin as she forced herself to swallow the biscuit already in her mouth. It travelled slowly down her gullet, carrying with it a wave of pain. Mattie closed her eyes until it had almost dissipated and then brushed the white dusting on her fingers against her pants. 'It's just . . . well, I'm sure it'll get better. I'm probably having one of those days. You know, when it all just seems so *hard*.'

'That is because it probably *is*,' said Hilda practically.

'I suppose.'

'And you said the talking was not helping?'

'Yes. I don't know.' Mattie rubbed her fingers against her sleeve. 'I'm sure everyone else has the same problems. And sometimes they just seem a bit much.'

'Men.' Hilda rolled her eyes sympathetically. 'They never listen.'

Mattie frowned. 'Yes . . . or they listen *too* much. And you have to watch what you say, because it's like a minefield. And you have to be so careful that you feel *drained* afterwards. Even when things go well.'

'Because you have been tense.'

'*Yes*,' said Mattie, nodding eagerly. 'That's *exactly* it.'

'I know what you mean.'

'Do you? Do you really?' Mattie stared at Hilda. 'Do you find sometimes you have to *force* yourself to relax? Like physically make yourself loosen up? God, I get such bad headaches.'

'I am not surprised.'

'And like, you know what you want to say, but somehow it never comes out quite right, so you end up being defensive. Like you're always in the wrong. *Always.*'

'*Always?*'

'Yes, just about.' Mattie stared at her fingers, and the faint smudges of white that remained. 'Even when I know I'm not. And afterwards, I feel almost sick.'

'That does not sound good.'

Mattie glanced at Hilda and flinched at the concern in her face. She got up and went to the sink, washing her hands thoroughly.

'Perhaps you need to look at this marriage.'

Mattie didn't turn around. 'We are. But maybe I just need to relax more. Learn meditation or something.'

'Bull-crap.'

Mattie turned around and faced Hilda with surprise. 'Pardon?'

'Tell me if I am interfering –' Hilda gave her a long look that dared her to, and then when Mattie didn't answer, continued on – 'but this is not normal, Mattie. Not normal at all. To feel like that *sometimes* is one thing, but I think you feel like that often. Am I right?' Hilda took Mattie's continued silence as agreement and went on. 'And if that is so, you need to make some changes. Because it is not good for you, not good for the children. You need to make some changes.'

'But I *have*. That's why I moved out. That's why I'm here!' Mattie sat down again, wiping her hands down her tracksuit pants. She knew she had to stop this conversation before it went any further, but she couldn't summon the energy to do so. Mainly because she didn't want to.

'No, not really. I mean, you put some distance between you and your husband, but has anything else really changed?'

'Well . . . I suppose not.'

'There you go.' Hilda took a sip of coffee and then looked across at Mattie thoughtfully. 'You need to ask yourself some hard questions, girl.'

'What sort of questions?' whispered Mattie, not sure she wanted to hear.

'Not *dumbkopf* questions, like –' Hilda put on an exaggerated high-pitched voice – 'Do I love him? Can I imagine living without him?'

'But those questions –'

'Are stupid.' Hilda waved her hand dismissively and then leant forward. 'What you need to ask yourself is: can I imagine life *with* him?'

'Oh.'

'*Ja.* Close your eyes.' Hilda frowned at her when she didn't immediately obey. 'Close them! Good. Now imagine this. It is the end of the day and the house is all tidy, you have prepared a lovely meal, and the children are bathed and quiet. You hear your husband opening the front door, home from work. How do you feel? And I am not asking whether you are *happy* to see him, I am asking if you're *content*. Comfortable, serene, at ease. See the difference? Now imagine another day – it has been a shocker. You had to be out all day, and the hot water is on the fritz. And the house is still messy, dinner has not even been started and the children are all grubby and bickering. And there is that front door. Now how do you feel?'

Mattie's eyes popped open and she stared at Hilda, her face speaking volumes. Hilda nodded sagely and then drank her coffee quietly, giving Mattie a chance to digest this. But what Mattie wasn't game to tell her was that her feelings in the first scenario, when everything had been perfect, weren't that positive either. Because although Jake made her happy, he rarely made her serene. Ever.

'Have another biscuit.' Hilda passed her the tin but Mattie shook her head. 'See, women are stupidly designed. Proof that the Lord is a man. We choose the men who make our hearts sing the loudest, not the ones who are going to make them sing the longest. Often we are lucky and they are one and the same, but sometimes . . . sometimes they are not.'

'No,' said Mattie softly, staring down at the wet tracks left by her hands across her pants.

'You have people who say you make your bed, you lie in it,' continued Hilda, still staring fixedly at Mattie. 'But they are the ones who have either never had a badly made bed, or the fools who want everyone else to be martyrs too.'

'Martyrs?'

'Yes. Don't be a martyr.' Hilda stood up and stretched. 'And now I am off home. Ernest and I are going to Heidelberg this evening, for tea.'

Mattie rose also and led the way to the front door. Hilda walked outside and then paused on the porch before turning back to face Mattie. 'You think I am an old busybody, I know. But I had a sister with a bad marriage. And you look like she did. Like a mouse.'

'A mouse?'

'Yes, a mouse. And he is the cat.'

Mattie couldn't think of a response to this but Hilda didn't seem to expect one. She gave Mattie a rather humourless smile, her black eyes without their customary sheen, and then turned again and walked around the corner towards her own unit. Mattie watched her go, and wished suddenly that she'd asked what had happened to the sister. The one who looked liked a mouse.

After a few minutes, she closed the door and walked into the bathroom where she washed her hands, dried them on the towel and then stared at her reflection in the mirror. To her, she looked the same as always – same eyes, same mouth, same complexion. And she wondered what it was that Hilda had seen, and whether other people saw it too. So maybe all her efforts to present a cheerful front, a *normal* front, were really for nothing when her face said what she wouldn't – that she was deeply, deeply unhappy and didn't have any idea what to do.

On Saturday morning, Mattie took Sybil and company back to the library. From deriving a sense of enjoyment from the young heroine's romantic adventures, she'd begun to find them annoying, and vaguely depressing. Instead she chose a few non-fiction books – two on relationships and one on budgeting tips for those on low incomes. Then, just as she got to the counter with her load, she saw a new book on display entitled *Bringing Up Happy, Healthy Children* and grabbed that as well.

When she got home, Mattie made herself coffee and settled down at the kitchen table with her reading material. She started with the book about children and very quickly found the author irritatingly sanctimonious. Nevertheless, drawn by the jacket photo of glowingly happy children, Mattie persevered for nearly an hour. But at that point she slapped the book shut and sent it sliding across the table in disgust.

She sat staring blankly at the window. The author's primary message was to listen to your children, *really* listen, because apparently it was often the questions you dismissed that held the actual answers. And Mattie clearly saw her daughter, standing before her with clenched fists and tear-filmed eyes, her face flushed with anger. *Why d'you always make Daddy angry? You ruin everything. I hate you being here.*

Where had Max been during this encounter? There was no doubt he'd have been able to hear Courtney from the lounge-room. So why hadn't he intervened? *Don't be stupid, Courtney. It's not Mum's fault. And we do want her here.* Unless, that is, he agreed with her. Unless he thought it was his mother's fault as well, and he didn't want her there either. And maybe they had a point. Because she *did* appear to be the catalyst for Jake's temper. There didn't seem to be a problem when she wasn't there. So rather than helping things by being around more when they were with their father, perhaps she was simply making things worse. Ruining everything.

Mattie sipped her coffee, ignoring the fact that it had long gone cold. She followed through with her train of thought and suddenly arrived at a rather unexpectedly congratulatory conclusion. If she *did* make things worse by being there, then moving out had actually been the best thing she could have done. For herself, for the children, even for Jake. And while this conclusion didn't solve anything, it let through a glimmer of light that illuminated the situation, and the possibilities.

But it didn't do anything to lessen her concerns about the next day. Because on Thursday evening, Jake had come up with the brilliant plan of interpreting this week's 'family day' as exactly that: driving up to Yea to visit his parents and sisters and their extended family of aunts, uncles, cousins, boisterous brothers-in-law and numerous children, who enjoyed a family life so utterly divorced from her own quiet, placid upbringing that Mattie always felt utterly overwhelmed. And she would struggle through the visits with a smile so fixed that afterwards, back at home, her jaw muscles would ache with the strain.

Was he punishing her? As soon as this thought formulated, Mattie dismissed it as paranoia. Besides, she had enough problems without excavating more. Apart from being unsure whether her children wanted her with them, there was the fact that she had no idea how Jake's family were going to treat her in light of the separation. In spite of their unruly household, they were a very traditional family with definitive gender roles for the males and females. With only a few exceptions, the men worked and the women kept house and, as far as she knew, there had never been a divorce in the Hampton family – no single parents, broken homes or dysfunctional children. They would find the whole idea as bewildering as her own mother did, and Mattie already knew who they would hold responsible. And it wasn't Jake. No, he was their only son, who could do no wrong.

With two older sisters and one younger, Jake spent his early child-hood years on a farm halfway between Yea and Seymour. But, before he even started school, his father suffered a farming accident (still referred to within the family as 'the accident'), which left him with a bad leg, and necessitated the move to a hardware store in town. The rest was history, and told over and over again at the least opportunity. At the start, the store had been tiny and rundown, with the family living in three rooms overhead. But by dint of hard work, they slowly expanded the original shop into a sprawling business, including a lumberyard and farm machinery showroom, which employed about twenty people, most of them relatives. This was the business that Jake had been destined to take over, until he got a taste of city living and found it more to his liking. And Mattie had a distinct feeling that, although his choice had been made before he even met her, they laid much of the blame at her door.

So tomorrow would be an interesting day. As well as long, tedious and tiring. And if there was any way she could have gotten out of it, she would have. But that would be really pushing it. Mattie sighed and pulled over the two library books on relationships. One was called *Enriched: How to Build and Maintain a Healthy Relationship*, and the other *How to Construct a Marriage Made of Brick,* the cover of which featured a colourful cartoon of two little pigs holding hands at the window of their solid house while, outside, the wolf huffed and puffed to no avail.

Mattie started with the brick one, figuring that if this was a yardstick, then her marital house was currently built of straw, on a foundation of sand – and with no floor. She smiled wryly to herself at this analogy and flicked the book open. Because if it was possible to rebuild, and strengthen, and shore up the foundations, then she was going to give it all she could, so that nobody, ever, could truthfully say that she was the one who was ruining anything.

The drive to Yea was always an attractive one, past Coldstream and up the Melba Highway through Kinglake National Park with its towering trees and steep, winding roads. On this particular day, the weather was lovely too. Early showers had given way to a cloudless sky with barely a breeze, the air still smelling faintly of the damp crispness of morning rain. Along the way, the children played 'spotto', in which the aim was to see a variety of objects: a Mack truck, a man with a hat, a caravan, a bicycle. In between enthusiastic cries of 'Spotto!', there were the inevitable arguments about who saw it first and whether, if only one had seen it, he or she was trustworthy.

When they'd arrived to collect her, Mattie was relieved to see that Jake had paid some attention to what the children were wearing today. Courtney, for once divested of her tutu, was in neatly pressed jeans and a pink Barbie t-shirt, while Max was in mud-brown cargo pants and a red t-shirt that featured a pop-eyed monster flexing his muscles. Jake was also in jeans, with a lightweight black suede shirt and black runners. With Mattie in her boots, flared jeans and black three-quarter shirt again, they looked like they'd dressed to coordinate, a fact that had made them both laugh when they first noticed.

They arrived in Yea just before noon, letting the rest of the traffic continue on towards Seymour and the Hume Highway while they turned right and drove down the main street and into the outskirts of the town, where Jake's parents now lived. They had moved from the rooms over the hardware store as soon as circumstances allowed. It was a ranch-style house, with a long gravel driveway and a four-car carport off to the side. Not only was the carport full, but another three cars were parked diagonally in the grass beside the driveway under the shade of a huge willow tree. As Jake pulled in neatly beside a red 4WD, Mattie looked around at the other cars, her heart sinking as she realised this was going to be an all-out gathering.

'Now remember your manners,' Jake instructed Max and Courtney, who were already scrambling out of the back seat. They nodded impatiently, without really listening, and took off towards the house at a run.

'Who's here today?' Mattie slammed her door shut, still eyeing the row of cars.

'Let's see –' Jake grabbed her hand and started walking as he glanced at the cars. 'Mark and Sandy are here. And you remember my cousin Garth, Aunt Dolly's eldest? And Frank and Dana. I told you they've moved back home while they're building, didn't I?'

'I think so . . .' Mattie's voice trailed off as they reached the veranda that spanned the wide frontage of the house. Numerous voices could now be heard coming from within. Max and Courtney had already gone inside, slamming the wooden screen door behind them. The force of the slam had bounced it open again and Jake stepped forward to grab it, putting one hand on the small of Mattie's back so that she preceded him into the house. Immediately, a small blond boy came racing through an archway to the right and cannoned straight into her knees, the force of the impact sending him sprawling backwards. He immediately began to howl noisily and Mattie, rather embarrassed, bobbed down to try and comfort him.

'Are you okay?'

'Of *course* he's okay. Aren't you, mate?' said Jake jovially as the boy ignored them both, knuckling his eyes roughly as his sobs increased in intensity. A young woman with long blonde hair hooked up in an elaborate waterfall hairdo came bustling in, giving them both an accusatory glance before she gathered the boy up into her arms.

'What's all the commotion?' Jake's eldest sister, Dana, leant around the doorway and examined the scene. 'Are you two beating up on the children already?'

'Something like that.' Jake gave the small boy, who was now sobbing wetly against his mother's shoulder, a rather disparaging look and then dismissed him, turning to his sister. 'How's things, Dana? How's your tribe?'

'Surviving. Saw your two burst through here a minute ago. Hey, Mattie. How're you? Love the matching outfits.'

'I'm fine, thanks.' Mattie smiled at her sister-in-law distractedly, being more concerned with any damage the boy might have sustained. She put a hand on his mother's arm. 'Is he all right?'

'Obviously not,' snapped the young woman, pulling away crossly.

'Calm down, Tracey,' said Dana with some amusement. 'It was just an accident.'

'Well, people should look where they're going,' muttered Tracey as she carried her son up the passage towards the kitchen.

'And other people should be watching their kids,' Jake called after her. He glanced at Dana. 'Who the hell's she?'

'Garth's latest. A proper pain. But apparently they're engaged. Come on in, you two.'

Mattie followed Jake into the lounge-room, an enormous rectangular room that ran along the front of the house, looking out over the driveway. In typical Hampton fashion, the room was full of men watching an Australian Rules football match on television, with the volume turned up loud, and Mattie immediately felt intimidated by the overwhelming *maleness* of the atmosphere. Several of them called out raucous greetings as she and Jake entered. Mattie smiled and gave a general wave as Jake did the rounds, pumping hands and clapping some of the men on the back.

Mattie recognised Dana's husband, Frank, a large bear of a man with frizzy ginger hair that sprang up and away from his head as if permanently charged with static electricity. He was leaning back in the corner of the L-shaped modular lounge-suite, both arms stretched across the top of the couch. Next to him was Mark, a thin, sharp-featured young man who had been living with Jake's youngest sister, Sandy, for the past five or six years. On the other side was cousin Garth, tall, dark-haired and rather good-looking, like the rest of the Hamptons.

Behind the couch and leaning across next to his father was Dana's eldest son Mitchell, a lanky teenager who, whenever Mattie saw him anyway, never seemed to utter a word. And sprawled across the floor in front of the television was a younger teenager who Mattie identified as Joshua, the son of Lisa, the second eldest sister.

The last occupant of the room was also the one who drew the most attention, even without speaking. Sitting regally in his Jason recliner, which was positioned so that he could see the television and both doors leading from the lounge-room, Jake's father always reminded Mattie of an aging but still dominant lion, regally surveying his pride. He was a man who revelled in his patriarchal role, which was enhanced by the fact that most of his family also worked for him. He looked much like Jake would in another forty years, with sparse dark grey hair carefully combed over his bald pate and grooves either side of his mouth so deep that they gave his cheeks the loose, jowly look of an aging bulldog.

'Good to see you, son,' Bill Hampton rose slightly as he shook his son's hand and grasped his shoulder affectionately.

'You too, Dad. How are you?'

'Fit as a Mallee bull.' Bill let go of Jake and turned to Mattie with a smile. 'And how's your beautiful wife? You're certainly looking lovely, dear.'

'Thanks, Bill.' Mattie leant forward and kissed her father-in-law on the cheek.

'We're watching the exhibition match – 'pies against the Blues. Find a seat.' Bill waved towards the couch and Frank drew himself in a bit to make room. At the same time the voice of the commentator rose excitedly and everybody's eyes automatically focused on the unfolding action, even the teenagers becoming somewhat animated. On the television, a knot of football players fought furiously over the ball in front of the goalposts and then suddenly one player broke free and swivel-kicked the ball towards the goal. The commentator became almost hysterical as it sailed through the posts.

'You little beauty!' Garth jumped up, pumping his fist in the air.

'How'd you like *that*?' Frank chortled happily.

'I'd have liked it even better if I could've seen it,' complained Mark, frowning crossly at Jake. 'Your father wasn't a glassblower, mate, so sit down!'

'I'll just say hi to Mum first.' Jake, not fazed in the least by the criticism, grinned genially at his relatives and, grabbing Mattie's hand, crossed the room towards the kitchen doorway. On the way, he squeezed her fingers and smiled down at her. Mattie felt soothed by the certain knowledge that he was trying to reassure her, as he knew full well how out of place she felt here. He probably also realised how nervous she was in light of their separation. How would his family take it? How would they treat her? Although so far, judging by the reactions of Dana and Jake's father, things would go on as normal. Mattie fervently hoped so.

She preceded him into the kitchen and moved to the side so that he could enter as well. And it was like intruding into a different world, one that always reminded Mattie of the Chinese yin and yang symbol, the curled quotation marks that represented the female and male forces of life. Here, in the kitchen, was the yin that complemented the yang of the lounge-room, and together the two made up the Hamptons' existence.

The kitchen, a huge square room, was wholly female. Cooking, cleaning, preparing, bustling, with a steady humming conversation that was picked up by one the instant it was dropped by another. Like a continual game of Chinese whispers, but without the secrecy. Dana stood at the stove, stirring a huge saucepan of thick brown gravy, and Sandy, the youngest sister, sat at the table, using a pair of long-handled tongs to turn dozens of roast potatoes and pumpkin and parsnip wedges in two large electric frypans that had been set up there, no doubt to make space on the benches. The vegetables sizzled fitfully as they were turned, spitting hot bubbles of frying oil into the air. Next to her was Dana's daughter Jessica, who was rather desultorily slicing thick slivers off a cob loaf of white bread. All of the Hamptons were very similar. Deep brown hair that greyed darkly over time, dark eyes, olive skin and a slim build that, on the females, thickened as they aged. But not in an overweight way, more like a steadily reliable progression from nubility to maternity.

Tracey, having shed herself of her offspring at some stage, stood out with her blue eyes and blonde hair, albeit with an expanse of dark roots. She was positioned at the far end of the kitchen bench, counting cutlery as she took it out of a drawer and piled it on the counter. And everywhere at once, but seemingly without any rush, was Jake's mother, a sturdy woman in her mid-sixties whose pewter-grey hair was the colour, and texture, of steel wool.

'Hey there, Mum.' Jake let go of Mattie and crossed the room to his mother, enveloping her in an expansive hug and lifting her off the ground.

'Put me down, you horrible boy!' Lorna Hampton flapped a tea-towel at him, her pretence of crossness doing nothing to disguise her obvious delight.

'As soon as I get a kiss.' Jake, still holding his mother aloft, offered his cheek.

'If I have to.' Lorna rolled her eyes and then kissed her son, lightly, on the cheek. 'Now put me down!'

'If you insist.' Jake lowered her gently and grinned down at her. 'Have you lost weight? You're as light as a feather.'

'Maybe a bit.' Lorna, flushed with pleasure, whipped him around the legs with the tea-towel. 'Now get out of here, you big nuisance, or lunch'll be spoiled.'

'Okay, okay.' Jake turned to Mattie. 'Do you want to stay here, or . . .'

'Mattie, love!' Lorna came over to where Mattie was still standing, against the wall, and kissed her as well. 'I didn't see you hiding over here!'

'Hi, Mattie,' called Sandy, waving the tongs cheerfully.

'Hello, Mattie,' said Jessica, rather shyly.

'Hi, everyone.' Mattie smiled with relief as her knot of nervousness started to break up at their wholehearted welcome. She turned to speak to Jake. 'I'll stay here and help. You go watch TV.'

He nodded appreciatively and grabbed her hand briefly, squeezing it again before making his escape back to the lounge-room where, judging by the noisy celebration, another goal had just been scored. Mattie looked over at Lorna, who'd already returned to her preparations and was pulling on a pair of chequered oven mitts.

'What can I do, Lorna?'

'Um, let's see . . .' Lorna bobbed down by Dana, opening the stove and pulling out a roasting pan that held an enormous piece of deep-brown roast beef. Steam curled upwards and the rich smell of the meat filled the room.

'You can do this gravy,' offered Dana. 'My damn hand's about to fall off.'

'No, no.' Lorna slid the roasting pan onto the sink draining board. 'She can help Tracey set the table. We're almost ready to go. Have you met Tracey, Mattie?'

'Yeah, they met at the front door.' Dana grinned.

Mattie went obediently over to Tracey, who was just gathering the cutlery up into a spare tea-towel. 'What would you like me to do?'

'You can take these.' Tracey thrust the bundle at her. 'We're setting up in the games room.'

Mattie hugged the cutlery against her chest and went through into the Hamptons' games room, a flat-roofed extension that jutted out from the rear of the house with a sliding door that led into the backyard. The billiard table, a huge walnut affair with six elaborately turned legs, had been covered by its table-tennis top and then two white double bed sheets to serve as tablecloths. Each side housed five places, and there were another two at either end. Nearby, two card tables had been placed end-to-end and covered with a floral plastic tablecloth for the younger children.

Mattie moved around the billiard table, setting out the cutlery neatly. Through the sliding door she could see Max and Courtney, playing with several other children on a swing set that Bill Hampton had installed many years ago for his growing number of grandchildren. Apart from the swing set, the yard itself was rather empty. Just a few trees, a couple of overgrown shrubs and, up at the far end, a set of cricket stumps. Neither Bill nor Lorna were fond of gardening, preferring an expanse of lawn that was easy to mow and maintain.

While Mattie set the table, Tracey came in and out several times, delivering salt and pepper shakers, bread plates, water jugs and glasses. Then, with Dana's help, the hot vegetables started arriving and by the time Mattie was finished, the table was covered with steaming platters of roast potatoes, pumpkin and parsnip, and blue and white Corning-ware bowls of peas, carrots and corn.

Dana pushed open the sliding door and put her head out. 'Lunch is ready! Go get washed up, all of you, and move it!'

Tracey brought in two large crystal gravy boats and placed them carefully on the table, using a finger to dab up a thick droplet dribbling down the outside of one gravy boat and then licking it. Mattie folded the cutlery tea-towel and took it through to the kitchen.

'Back, back!' Lorna met her in the doorway, carrying a large platter on which the beef sat, deep brown and shiny with juices, alongside an electric carving knife and fork. 'Nothing to do in there now, so grab a seat, love!'

Mattie waited till she passed and then put her tea-towel down on the bench and washed her hands before going back through to the games room. She was followed by the men, who were still discussing the football match.

'They're lost without Buckley, though.'

'Ought to clone the man.'

'I dunno. Reckon some of those young guns are gonna make a fair difference.'

'True. True.'

The children's table was already full by the time Mattie got back to the games room. Having obviously washed rather cursorily under the garden tap, they sat and flicked water off their hands at each other, shrieking merrily. Max and Courtney were flanked by Dana's youngest son, Sam, who was just a little older than Max, and Sandy's four-year-old twins, an almost identical pair of brown-haired girls clad in matching pinafore dresses and red-chequered ribbons. A place was also set for the small boy who had cannoned into Mattie earlier, but he was currently leaning against his mother's chair at the larger table and whining fretfully.

Mattie hung back until Jake came in and then pulled out a chair next to him. On her left was Dana, then Frank and Mitchell, with Lorna and Sandy sitting at the end. On the other side of the table, from Sandy up, were Mark, Garth, Tracey, and then her son, who had now taken an adult's seat, with Joshua at the far corner. And, at the head of the table and already expertly carving the beef, was Bill, in his element. Jessica came in last, looking around for a spare seat and realising that the only empty one was next to her grandfather.

'Come sit next to me, love,' Bill said jovially as he concentrated on the beef. 'We'll be beauty and the beast.'

'Sure, Grandad.' Jessica pulled out the chair and sat down, rolling her eyes expressively as she and her cousin Joshua exchanged glances.

'Not too bad so far?' asked Jake in a low voice, smiling at Mattie.

'No.' Mattie looked around quickly to make sure nobody was listening. 'I'll live.'

'Glad to hear it.'

'Hey, Jake, Mattie. Have you heard our news?' asked Sandy, passing a water jug across to Mark.

'You've won Tattslotto?'

'Not that good,' Sandy grinned. 'No, Mark and I are getting married!'

'Well, it's about time!' Jake beamed at them both. 'Good on you!'

'Yes, congratulations,' added Mattie. 'That's wonderful.'

'Thought I'd better make an honest woman of her,' said Mark, with mock resignation.

'Better late than never,' said Bill, without humour. The carving knife whirred as he sliced thick segments of beef and angled them neatly atop each other on the platter as well as on two separate dinner plates.

Sandy ignored her father. 'And I'm expecting again!'

'Not another set of twins?'

'Christ, don't jinx us!' Mark rolled his eyes.

'When are you due?' asked Mattie curiously. 'And when's the wedding?'

'The baby – note the *singular* –' Sandy grinned at her brother before continuing – 'is due in March and we've set the wedding for May. The girls are going to be bridesmaids. Mum's making them matching outfits.'

'They'll look gorgeous,' said Dana, with a fond glance at her twin nieces, who were giggling at Sam and Max. Both boys had laid their serviettes on top of their heads and were blowing energetically at each other, trying to dislodge the paper hats.

'Help yourselves!' announced Bill grandly, flicking the carving knife off and laying it down by his plate after it had stuttered to a stop. He passed one dinner plate of sliced beef to Jake and the other to Joshua. Then he proceeded to help himself off the platter, which held several slices as well as the leftover knob of roast beef, a deep brownish-red in the centre.

The vegetables were also being passed around and Mattie was just taking some roast potatoes when Lisa, Joshua's mother, came into the room. Although younger than Dana, she looked by far the oldest of the sisters. She was the only one, apart from Jake, to have inherited her father's deep grooves on either side of her mouth and, on her, they were emphasised by a matching furrow between the eyes and a somewhat sallow complexion instead of the standard Hampton glow. Today her dark brown hair was pulled back into a low ponytail and she had obviously come straight from work as she was still wearing a pea-green tunic top with *Hampton Hardware* embroidered in red cotton on one breast pocket.

'Hey, all.' Lisa leant against the back of her son's chair and ruffled his hair. 'And hello, Jake, Mattie. Long time, no see.'

'It hasn't been *that* long,' protested Jake.

'Almost three months,' said his mother placidly, turning so that she could hold one of the dinner plates of beef by the children's table while they helped themselves.

'So where's your better half?' asked Jake.

'John's not feeling well,' replied Lisa, staring down at her son's head.

'Busy?' asked Bill, fixing Lisa with a firm eye.

'Off and on. Had a bit of a rush around ten-ish. A bloke came in to see you about his chainsaw. I told him to come back Monday.' Lisa glanced around. 'What, no seat for me?'

'Certainly there is,' said her mother with a frown. 'I counted them out . . . oh, that's why. Tracey's youngster is at the table. Tracey, would you mind moving him, dear? There's a space down at the children's table. I'm sure he'll enjoy himself more there.'

'Don't want to!' The boy, who was about three or four years of age and a sturdy child, slid to the end of his chair so that he could grab the side of the table.

'Can't we get another chair in for Lisa?' pleaded Tracey.

'No,' replied Bill shortly, looking expressionlessly at her son. 'There's no room.'

'But he's shy, aren't you, sweetheart?' Tracey looked down at the boy who answered by clutching on to the table even more firmly.

'Garth?' Bill glanced over at his nephew and raised his eyebrows questioningly.

Garth, who had been happily eating his meal, looked at his fiancée with irritation. 'Come on, Trace. Move the kid.'

Tracey, her mouth set in a thin line, attempted to pry her son loose from the table, but as soon as she freed one hand and went to work on the other, the freed hand simply latched on once more. By this time everybody else, except Garth, was watching with fascination. Even Courtney had come over from the children's table and was standing behind her mother's chair, enthralled by the proceedings.

'Is he spoilt?' Courtney whispered to Mattie, rather loudly.

'Certainly is,' Dana answered instead. 'Absolutely rotten.'

Finally Tracey gave up and slapped the boy's hands hard with embarrassed frustration. He immediately let out a howl of indignation and, releasing the table at last, slapped his mother right back, straight across the face. There was an almost communal drawing in of breath from the watchers. Then Garth, laying down his cutlery with visible annoyance, rose from his chair and strode over to the boy, grasping him under each arm and hauling him upwards. The boy, shocked into silence, hung with his mouth open as Garth carried him out in front, as if he were contagious, over to the children's table. There he held the child over the spare seat and then let him go. The boy fell onto the chair, hard, and then toppled off onto the floor where he sprawled, crying loudly.

'*Garth*!' exclaimed Tracey, who had stood up on the other side of the table to watch, horrified.

'Enough!' Garth turned from her to the boy and pointed his finger at him. 'As for *you*, you can get up onto that chair and eat your lunch. And I don't want to hear another peep out of you, understand?'

The boy, still sitting on the floor, drew a ragged breath but didn't answer.

'*Understand?*'

Mattie turned away so she couldn't see the boy's final capitulation, although it was inevitable. She stared down at her meal rather miserably. Although she agreed that the child's behaviour was disgraceful, she didn't condone Garth's actions at all. How could the boy ever learn not to use aggression when that was the very tool used to discipline him?

'Needs a good clip around the ears,' commented Bill, without bothering to lower his voice.

Garth returned to the table and sat down heavily in his chair, picking up his cutlery and turning to Tracey, who had tears in her own eyes. '*Now* can I eat my meal?'

'Please yourself,' she replied sulkily.

'Next time I think I'll bring my own chair,' said Lisa brightly as she pulled out the now spare seat and sat down. She turned to Tracey, who was staring at her plate. 'Sorry, Trace, I didn't mean to cause such a fuss.'

'S'okay,' replied Tracey, without looking up.

Courtney, still standing behind her mother, leant forward and gave Mattie a hug, as if she sensed her mother needed one. Mattie smiled at her daughter appreciatively and watched as she went back over to the children's table, sitting down in her seat between the twins.

Lorna passed Tracey's son his plate of food and he sat on his chair before it, poking at the meat miserably. A bubble of yellowy mucus formed in one nostril as he breathed, popping and then reforming again with the next breath. Mattie grimaced and turned away, wiping her hands down her jeans automatically. The conversation at the larger table was now revolving around the benefits of advertising at an upcoming tractor pull, so Mattie concentrated on eating her meal. The sooner they were all finished here, the sooner this whole day could end.

When she'd first met the extended Hampton clan and was enveloped in their sense of family, Mattie had been overjoyed. They were vastly different to anything she'd known and, it seemed to her at the time, vastly superior. Demonstrative, tactile and generous to a fault, they immediately and wholeheartedly embraced her as one of their own, despite their disappointment in Jake's choices. Blood ties were all important. And although Mattie found their gregarious gatherings rather overwhelming, she rejoiced to be included amongst them, feeling a deep sense of appreciation that when she and Jake had children, they would enjoy such a sense of belonging also.

But over time she came to realise that the family, for all its inclusiveness and overt affection, had stringent rules in place that were non-negotiable – and that she found difficult to adhere to, or even witness. The fundamental rule that underpinned all others was that the structure of their lives revolved around their gender. It was not only the strict division of labour, but a sense of expectations that fortified their relationships with each other. Men were allowed certain liberties and were awarded a position within the household not on merit, but purely on the basis of their maleness. Men 'worked', while women 'kept house'. And even those who did work outside the home, like Lisa, would still be expected to clear the table and wash the dishes after this lunch, while the men retired to the lounge-room to drink beer and watch a rerun of the footy.

Mattie's own mother had also done the lion's share of the housework, but there had been a major difference. It was perceived, without ever being formally verbalised, that such work was a *job*, rather than a role in life. It was simply part of her contract with her husband – he worked outside the home and she worked within it, thus creating a functional environment within which to raise their family. And when they took their annual holiday to Rosebud, to set up home in a seaside caravan for a fortnight, her father would immediately pitch in and do dishes, or cook meals, or take the two girls down to the beach to let their mother have a rest. It was seen as shared labour, rather than innate characteristics.

Whereas the Hampton women did all the cooking and cleaning and childminding no matter whether their husbands were working or not.

Lisa's deadbeat husband John hadn't worked for the past five years, yet Lisa was always complaining, with increasing bitterness, that she would rush home from work to cook the entire evening meal, tidy the house and even prepare a lunch for him to heat up at midday the following day. It was, quite simply, women's work, and no self-respecting male would ever voluntarily participate. Mattie knew, from long experience, that after lunch today, the women would congregate in the kitchen to wash dishes and chatter and put away the leftovers. Children's faces would be washed, babies fed, and advice offered on everything from infant colic to sex appeal. And any male over the age of twelve who entered, for whatever reason, would be teased mercilessly before retreating quickly to the sanctity of the lounge-room where, similarly, any female who made herself comfortable amongst the men whilst the others toiled was viewed with uniform disapproval by both sexes.

And Mattie found it all extremely unfair, and restrictive, and hypocritical – and she didn't want her own children raised that way. She wanted Courtney to see the sky as her limit, and Max to have an equal partnership with his own wife one day. She didn't want them to act like Jake did. At home he was known to change nappies and wash dishes and perform a range of household chores, but he reverted the minute he walked through the Hampton front door. And made jokes about the 'little woman', and being 'henpecked' and about who 'wore the trousers in *this* family'.

Mattie glanced over at the children's table and was pleased to see Max cutting up the little boy's beef for him. The child sat staring at him dully, both nostrils now clogged, as Max laid down the cutlery and looked at him expectantly. When nothing happened, Courtney reached across with an adult sigh and pushed the fork into the boy's hand, pressing his fingers closed around the handle. But he still didn't seem to get the message, picking up a piece of meat with his other hand and pushing it into his mouth instead. Courtney sighed again, crossly.

'She's a dear little girl,' commented Lorna, following Mattie's gaze.

'Yes, she is,' agreed Mattie, nodding even while Courtney's face flashed into her mind, flushed with anger. *I hate you being here. You ruin everything.*

'I know she's great with the twins,' said Sandy, reaching past Mark for some more beef. 'A real little mum.'

'Maybe she'll go into child care,' suggested Dana. 'It's a booming industry now.'

'So's paediatrics,' said Mattie, a little more sharply than she intended.

'For god's sake, don't start,' hissed Jake as his mother and sisters looked at Mattie with some surprise.

'Does Courtney *want* to be a doctor?' asked Lorna. Then, before Mattie could answer, she twisted around to face the children's table directly. 'I hear you want to be a doctor, Courtney love?'

'Christ, don't call her Courtney love,' called Lisa, with a laugh. 'That's the name of that flaky American singer.'

'Oh, yeah.' Frank, who had already finished his meal, clicked his fingers. 'The blonde who was married to Kurt Cobain.'

'They had a daughter called something Bean,' added Sandy.

'Something bean what?' asked Lorna, looking confused.

'Frances Bean,' said Dana. 'That was it. Frances Bean.'

'Damn fool woman.' Bill frowned, pausing with a laden fork halfway to his mouth. 'Saddling the poor kid with a moniker like that. Oughta be a law against it.'

'Mummy?' whispered Courtney, who was standing behind her mother's chair again. 'Why'd Gran ask me if I want to be a doctor?'

'She was just showing an interest, honey.'

'Hey, Jake. Mattie.' Sandy put down her cutlery and leant forward. 'I've been meaning to ask you if it's okay for us to stay with you guys for a night next month. Mark and I thought we'd take the girls to town for a day. See the Myer Christmas windows and do some shopping. Would that be okay?'

Mattie's mouth dropped open slightly as she stared at her sister-in-law, realising with a rush of panic that Sandy didn't know they'd separated. And if she didn't know, probably none of the others knew either. Jake hadn't told them.

'Absolutely,' said Jake smoothly. 'You know you're always welcome. Mattie and I'd love to have you.'

Courtney, who was still leaning over the back of her mother's chair, frowned at her father. 'But, Daddy, Mummy's still –'

'Court –' Jake twisted around to face his daughter – 'remember what we spoke about last night? Besides, have you finished your meal?'

'Nearly. But –'

'Then finish it.' Jake used his no-nonsense voice and Courtney, pouting crossly, sidled over to the smaller table and slid into her seat. She folded her arms and glared at her father's back.

'Mattie doesn't look that sure about having visitors,' commented Dana, staring at Mattie with amusement. 'In fact, she looks like she's in shock.'

'Mattie?' Sandy frowned at her. 'If it's a problem, we can stay at a motel or something.'

'No way.' Jake grabbed Mattie's hand and squeezed it. 'You'll stay with us. Just let us know the day and we'll order in some good steak. Have a barbecue. Actually, you should stay a couple of days. Get all your shopping done at once.'

Sandy was still focused on her sister-in-law. 'Is that okay, Mattie?'

'Sure it is.' Jake stretched and laid an arm along the back of Mattie's chair. 'I think Mattie's just flummoxed by the talk of Christmas, aren't you, sweetheart?'

'That's right.' Mattie nodded slowly and then stretched out a smile. 'It feels like we've only just got through last Christmas, and here it is again.'

'I know what you mean.' Lorna sighed. 'This year's just flown past.'

The talk turned to Christmas and several conversations broke out around the table. Lorna and Sandy started discussing the merits of a family Kris Kringle while Bill, at the far end of the table, and Frank, up towards the other end, began working out several staffing issues for the Christmas period. As various people up and down the table called out contributions to both conversations, the talk flowed loudly. Mattie laid down her cutlery and let the noise surge around her as she faced the fact that Jake hadn't told his family yet. Not about anything. And while she now realised why she hadn't been inundated with searching questions and disapproving glances, she was more concerned with what this said about Jake's attitude than the Hamptons' probable reactions. She glanced at him automatically and met his eyes. He grinned at her, totally unconcerned, and suddenly she knew, with a flash of insight, that he didn't intend telling his family at all. Not now, not ever.

Mattie's skin felt clammy as she faced this understanding head-on and realised that it fitted perfectly. Of *course* he wouldn't tell his family, not when he was so confident about her eventual return. It would be far easier, to Jake's way of thinking, for his family to simply never know. Clearly he had even talked to the children about keeping this quiet – *Remember what we spoke about last night?* – so that when Mattie regained her senses and came slinking back, life could simply go on as normal, and none of his relatives would ever be aware of the temporary hiccup in their lives. In his life.

And, what's more, he would probably use Sandy's visit as leverage. Persuade Mattie to come back for a few days to present a smooth facade of happily married life. Mattie's stomach knotted at the thought. Because that was why she had left in the first place. She had been so tired, so *very* tired, of continually having to polish the veneer so that it would be presentable. Yet it didn't matter what she tried, however frantically she worked, the tarnish remained, slowly eroding the gloss so that her work was constant, and futile.

'Penny for your thoughts?' Jake grinned down at her, daring her to speak and knowing that she wouldn't.

'Christ, mate, *never* ask a woman what she's thinking!' Frank leant forward to look at Jake with mock disgust. 'Haven't you learnt that yet?'

'It's like opening up a beehive,' grinned Bill, jabbing towards his son with his fork. 'You're bound to get stung.'

Lisa snorted and shook her head. 'Whereas asking a *man* what he's thinking is like opening up the pantry after you've forgotten to do the grocery shopping. Lots of stuff in there, but nothing you can really use.'

'Good one!' Sandy clapped gleefully and the table erupted into an affectionately bantering male versus female debate. Mattie stared down at her lap, twisting her serviette and trying to muster the energy to join in before someone noticed her silence, but she was unable to. She felt like she was weighted down with rocks.

'It'll be okay.' Jake spoke in a low voice, squeezing her shoulder and giving his crooked smile. 'Trust me.'

Mattie looked at him, the grey eyes crinkling with his smile, the slim features that she knew as well as her own, the slight five o'clock shadow that coloured his jawline. And she knew that, as heart-wrenchingly tempting as the offer was, unfortunately it was the one thing she most certainly couldn't do.

*B*ecause the violence was so infrequent and because, afterwards, Jake was just as devastated as she was, Mattie never actually thought of it as violence per se. Instead she viewed it as a bad temper that, the vast majority of the time, Jake kept under strict, even admirable, control. And although she did recognise it as a problem, she didn't see it as something that undermined their lives. While it was happening, of course, it was a hugely horrible experience, but this was so infrequent that it was easy to push to the back of her mind during the months where everything was fine. And to convince herself that it would never happen again.

But then she fell pregnant with Courtney and it seemed that suddenly it raised its ugly head and forced itself, snarling and biting, into their lives as a regular entity. It was there, all the time, either just below the surface, biding its time, or in full attack, driving her backwards until there was nowhere to go. It was as if, with her pregnancy, she had brought something ugly into their house, something that would spend most of its time hiding just around the corner, only to emerge every now and again to run riot. And it didn't matter what she tried – bribery, placating, pleading, or just trying to stay out of its way – things would still come to a head and she would have to confront it. After which it would retreat for a while, but she always knew it was there – skulking, snarling, listening, waiting . . .

In hindsight she could see that it had actually been a slower escalation, both in severity and frequency, than it seemed at the time. And that, whether she'd fallen pregnant or not, it was always going to become part of their lives. Because it was part of Jake. Maybe she had just been in denial. Maybe she still was.

ELEVEN

The morning of Mattie's Whimsicalities party came with a dawn shower that quickly cleared to herald a beautiful day. Near enough to summer to be brushed with a touch of humidity, but still retaining enough spring to balance it out with a fresh, brisk breeze that filled the unit with a lovely airy smell. The sky was a perfect cobalt blue with scattered cotton-ball clouds that, if they'd been faithfully reproduced in a painting, would not have looked 'real'.

The past week had flown. Although she'd been concerned that problems might arise on Sunday evening after the Yea visit, it passed without incident. Helped, no doubt, by her decision to stay quiet on the matter of Jake not telling his family she'd moved out. Mattie knew it would have to be discussed sooner or later, but she pushed it to the back of her mind where it lay, only partially buried, amongst everything else. For now, she just wanted to get the party over and done with.

The first few days of the week Mattie had spent fixing up the unit. She enlarged two small photographs of the children, bought matching frames and put them up in the lounge-room where they immediately injected a more homely, settled look. In addition, she bought a large framed print from the local bargain shop, a striking abstract with overlapping squares of burgundy, forest green and bright, shimmery gold, and put it up on the long blank wall by the lounge-suite. It might not have been a Margaret Olley, but it made a huge difference. Even Max commented on the effect.

Thursday night was difficult, as Jake was extraordinarily touchy and critical. Several times Mattie had to bite her tongue for fear of starting something, and negotiating the evening was like walking on eggshells, the strain leaving her headachey and depleted. The situation was made worse, or perhaps even started, by Courtney's campaign to attend the Whimsicalities party on Saturday, which involved wrapping herself around her father's legs for the first half of the evening and then, for the second half, sitting in the lounge-room angrily staring at the wall with her arms folded. Mattie, trying to placate her, offered to swap with Jake – two nights for the one day, but this just seemed to make the mood more tense. In the end Mattie pleaded stomach cramps and escaped. And the incredible relief she felt as she drove home was scary in itself.

Friday was spent shopping, cleaning and baking, so that on Saturday morning she woke to a sparkling clean home and a fridge full of assorted delicacies – meatballs, vol-au-vents filled with mustardy cheese and tiny slivers of bacon, toothpicks stabbed through curls of ham and vintage cheese, platters of kabana, celery, carrots and French onion dip, Philadelphia cheesecake, meringues, miniature pikelets with jam and cream, and the pièce de résistance – a double-layered chocolate sponge cake with lashings of rum and chocolate cream.

Mattie had a lovely morning. All she needed to do was add some crackers to the dip platter, put it out in the lounge-room and cover the kitchen table with the lovely embroidered tablecloth that she'd borrowed. And the knowledge that in the afternoon the unit would be full of the warmth of friends and family filled her with a sense of relaxed, contented anticipation – so much so that she willed the time to go more slowly, because the anticipation might well be more enjoyable than the experience. To heighten her sense of indulgence, she ran herself a frothy bubble-bath and luxuriated in there for nearly an hour. Finally, at about one o'clock, she started getting ready, blow-drying her hair so that it fluffed out and became even more feathery than usual, and dressing in low-heeled sandals, jeans and a spaghetti-strapped nut-brown silky top that fitted snugly over her breasts and then flowed out and down, finishing with a jagged hemline around her hips. Lastly she carried the burgundy beanbag through to the children's room, because she felt it lowered the tone, and curled up on the couch to wait.

Sharon, the party-plan consultant, arrived at a quarter to two. She was a slim, breathless woman with very pale skin and long, flat black hair worn loose, so that it continually flopped forward and she would scoop it up with one hand and toss it back again in one deft movement. She was dressed in a pair of black slacks and a lilac polo top that was emblazoned with silver stars and the word *Whimsicalities* across the chest.

After introducing herself, Sharon took over a corner of the lounge-room, setting up two card tables, one of which had about ten inches of its legs sawn off. By placing the shorter table in front of the other, and covering them both with a large purple cloth, she was able to quickly construct a very effective layered display unit. Next, with Mattie's help, Sharon brought in three huge striped canvas bags from the boot of her car and started removing the Whimsicalities wares, arranging them neatly on the tables. To enhance the display, she threaded lengths of artificial ivy up and amongst the goods and scattered around a few large pieces of autumn-coloured pot pourri.

Hilda arrived as Sharon was halfway through the last bag. She was wearing a pair of navy slacks and the coral ribbed top from the other day, together with her gold jewellery, and she brought with her a tea-towel covered platter.

'Strudel.' Hilda placed the platter down on the kitchen table and removed the tea-towel with a flourish to reveal a flaky-pastry log on a crystal plate.

'Thanks, Hilda. It looks delicious.'

'My pleasure. Lovely tablecloth.' Hilda fingered the embroidered table-cloth briefly and then walked over to the lounge-room doorway to peer at Sharon's display curiously. 'Thank you for inviting me. Very interesting.'

Rachel from the swimming centre arrived next, rather embarrassed to be one of the first and also because she had brought her young daughter, thinking that Courtney would be there. While Mattie was reassuring her, two women from the preps reading group arrived together, both of them blonde, plump, expansive and extroverted. Their large personalities immediately filled the room and broke any tension as they settled themselves on the couch, eating kabana and providing a cheerful running commentary on the Whimsicalities goods.

After that, everybody seemed to arrive together and the noise level rose even further. Ginny from swimming, tall and cool with her ice-blonde hair, Anne, Sally and Gina from canteen, Jo from reading group and Marianne and Jenny, two of the mothers that Mattie chatted with while waiting for the children after school. Fortunately Jo also brought her daughter, Georgia, one of Courtney's friends, so Mattie was able to introduce her to the other child and usher the pair into the bedroom to play.

As people kept arriving, Mattie hurriedly brought out the four kitchen chairs and then the desk chair from the children's room. But the chairs filled as soon as she put them down and still some were sitting on the armrests of the couch. Avid eyes glanced curiously around the unit as greetings were exchanged, if the women knew each other, or introductions were made, if they didn't. The two plump blondes, Marie and Helen, squeezed themselves up on the couch and called out 'the more the merrier' every time somebody else came through the door. Hilda, who had settled herself on one of the chairs by the kitchen doorway, gestured for Mattie to come over.

'Have you got many more coming?'

'I think so.' Mattie looked around the crowded lounge-room worriedly. 'At least two. Maybe more.'

'You need extra chairs?'

'Oh yes.' Mattie looked at Hilda with relief. 'Could you? Do you need a hand?'

'No, I will just use your phone. And get Ernest to bring them over.' Hilda hoisted herself up and headed over to the kitchen as the front door opened again to reveal Hannah, their mother and Hannah's daughter Charlotte, a tall, very thin young woman who wore a pair of tiny rectangular glasses perched low on the bridge of her nose. All three looked rather astounded to see how many people were crowded into the lounge-room, which now seemed extremely small.

'Charlotte, how lovely to see you.' Mattie smiled rather distractedly at her niece, and gestured for them to come in. 'Mum, Hannah. Thanks for coming. There'll be more chairs in a minute.'

Sharon sidled through the lounge-room crowd towards Mattie and asked, with some concern, how many more were expected.

'I think that's it now. We're just waiting on some chairs.'

'Well, while you're organising that, I'll hand out order forms and pencils, shall I?' Sharon gathered up her errant hair and flipped it neatly behind her. 'Then we'll get started.'

Hilda returned from the kitchen to find her chair already taken so she went over to the front door and opened it, obviously waiting for her husband. But instead of him, or the chairs, Courtney, dressed in her pink tutu with white, rather grubby tights and red sneakers, came running through the doorway and stood just inside, beaming around at the company happily. Mattie looked at her with amazement.

'Courtney!'

'I'm here,' Courtney announced smugly. 'Daddy said he couldn't put up with my whining anymore.'

Mattie's eyes widened. 'Where is he?'

'Gone.' Courtney glanced around at the guests, smiling at the mothers she knew. Her gaze did a full circle and finished with her grandmother and Hannah. 'Grandma! Auntie Hannah! Mummy didn't tell me *you* were coming!'

'Hello, Courtney. My, haven't you grown!'

'Lovely to see you, Court.' Hannah gave her a hug and then stood back, gesturing towards Charlotte. 'You remember your cousin Charlotte, don't you?'

'Hello,' said Courtney shyly, pleating the tulle of her tutu between her fingers. 'I like your glasses.'

Sharon had finished handing out pamphlets with the order forms attached, so while Courtney reacquainted herself with her much older cousin, Mattie went over to the front door to see if the chairs had arrived. Hilda was out on the porch, impatiently watching a rather short, very bow-legged, elderly man stagger up the pathway with a stack of white plastic outdoor chairs. He lowered them with a groan and looked up at his wife.

'Where d'you want them, Hilde?'

'This is Mattie,' Hilda said instead of answering him, pointing towards Mattie.

'Pleased to meet you,' said Ernest with a strong Austrian accent, smiling cheerfully.

'Likewise. And thank you very, *very* much for bringing these over.' Mattie slipped the two uppermost chairs out of the stack. 'I'll take them from here. And thanks again.'

'Some more coming.' Ernest turned and, with an ambling gait that reminded Mattie of old-time sailors, headed back towards his unit at the back.

'Now that we've got plenty of chairs, I'll get someone to put your other ones back in the kitchen for later,' said Hilda, taking the two chairs from Mattie and passing them inside the unit.

Mattie nodded her thanks as she lifted up the remaining two and brought them in. As the chairs were quickly occupied, one by Hilda herself, Mattie did a rapid calculation and worked out that, with the ones Ernest was now bringing over, the seating arrangements should end up fine. Definitely crowded, but at least everybody, including herself, would have a seat. The noise level inside was high, as half a dozen conversations ebbed and flowed into and around each other, and Mattie noticed that Courtney had made her way over to the display tables where she was studiously examining some ceramic animals one by one, her tutu brushing against the lower table. Sharon hovered nearby, watching her with concern. Mattie frowned and then suddenly remembered the two little girls who'd arrived earlier.

'Hey, Courtney, there's a surprise for you in your bedroom.'

'A surprise? For *me*?'

'Yep.' Mattie pointed towards the passage doorway. 'So you go in there while we do this and then you can come out later and look at everything.'

Courtney put down the blue glazed owl that she had been holding and, to Sharon's evident relief, made her way eagerly through the maze of occupied chairs, disappearing up the passage. Mattie watched her go and then looked outside just as Ernest ambled around the corner and deposited the next load of chairs by the front door.

'Thank you so much,' Mattie said with sincerity.

'Tell you what –' Ernest grinned and winked at her – 'you can thank me by keeping the wife here for the afternoon. Then I can put my feet up.'

'It's a deal.' Mattie smiled back and, as Ernest left, she took the top two chairs and passed them to Charlotte, who'd come over to the doorway to help.

'Shall we get started?' called Sharon, over by the display tables.

'Absolutely.' Mattie passed Charlotte another chair and motioned for her to take that one for herself. 'Just ignore me. And I'll make coffee and everything after you've finished.'

As Sharon introduced herself to the rapidly quietening women, Mattie went outside to fetch the remaining chair. She paused, while there, to take in a deep breath of fresh air and just enjoy the moment. As she did, a metallic blue hatchback turned into the communal driveway and paused for a second before executing a neat three-point turn and then coasting to a halt behind Hannah's Volvo. Mattie watched curiously as the driver-side door opened and a slim woman emerged, beautifully dressed in strappy sandals, black hipsters and a cream vest that hung loosely over a snug black singlet. She had short dark hair that spiked with burgundy highlights and a pair of gold-beaded earrings that dangled almost down to her shoulders. It was Liz.

Half an hour later, Sharon finished the introduction and her pitch about the benefits of hosting a Whimsicalities party and moved on to a brief spiel about the products on display, but Mattie missed it all. Instead she spent the entire time in the kitchen, with Liz, barely able to stop smiling because her friend was really there, in the flesh.

'And Jude's in Cairns now. We were up there on holiday last year and caught up. They've got a lovely house. Two storey, with a built-in pool that's got lights set into it so at night it looks fantastic. We went there for dinner. Got out all the old photos and all.'

'That must have been good.' Mattie's smile froze for a second, immobilised by a twinge of jealousy. Then she shook it off impatiently.

'It was. And Jude's looking really good too, although she's put on a fair bit of weight.' Liz smoothed her vest down, unconsciously demonstrating how flat her own belly was.

'Well, she's always been a bit plump.' Mattie pictured Jude as she'd last seen her, with a jolly nature almost too stereotypical of her rounded features. 'And now that she's had children . . . how many does she have anyway?'

'Four.' Liz pushed Hilda's strudel to one side and leaned forward confidingly. 'And they're real shockers too. The eldest is only ten but she's already giving them hell, and the others aren't much better. Temper tantrums, foul language – and the way they lay into each other! Some people shouldn't have kids. Seriously.'

'That bad?'

'Worse. Trust me.'

'That's a shame,' said Mattie ineffectually, suspecting that Liz's rather harsh assessment stemmed from her own history of infertility. She searched for a change of subject. 'What about Paula? Do you ever hear from her?'

'All the time!' Liz sat back again and raised her eyes to the ceiling briefly. 'Did you know she married a Pom? God, Mats, you should *hear* his accent! Not that hers is much better nowadays. They both sound like they've got their mouths full whenever they speak. It's hysterical.'

'And how is she?'

'Oh, good. Great actually. I believe she's doing really well over there. They say they don't want any kids, but lots of people *say* that, don't they? They soon change their minds.' Liz looked at Mattie, rather expectantly.

'How often do you see her?' Mattie deliberately steered the conversation away from children once more.

'Oh, only every other year when she comes back to visit her parents. Same as Jude.' Liz looked at Mattie intently. '*You're* the only one who fell off the radar.'

'Not really,' protested Mattie, stilling an undercurrent of guilt. 'You always knew where I was.'

'Yeah, just not whether I'd be welcome. Remember when Alan and I dropped around about five years ago? Just before we got married?'

Mattie nodded slowly, remembering the occasion well.

'It was probably the most uncomfortable afternoon I've ever spent. Jake hardly said two words and you were all jittery, jumping up and down to get us cups of tea and check on the baby and whatever. Do you know what I said to Alan afterwards?'

'What?' asked Mattie, not really wanting to know.

'I said you looked squished. It was the only word I could think of that described it.'

'Squished,' repeated Mattie slowly, running a finger over the ridges of a crimson embroidered rose on the tablecloth.

'Yes. So when I got this invite and I looked at the address and saw that you'd moved . . . And as it was a unit, I guessed you'd moved *away* from Jake. I thought – well, I thought . . .' Liz petered off, staring at Mattie and willing her to ask her what she meant.

'Go on.'

'I thought you'd come to your senses,' said Liz quickly.

Mattie grinned wryly. 'Not quite. As I said before, there's every chance we'll work it out. We just need some time.'

'Yeah.' Liz picked at a fingernail absently, then looked back up at Mattie. 'How're your kids?'

'Good. They're good.'

'Well? Aren't you going to ask me?'

Mattie sighed inwardly as she accepted the unavoidability of opening that particular door. She looked across the table sadly, and suddenly realised that rather than appearing despondent, Liz was quite literally glowing with news. Mattie's eyes widened. 'You haven't?'

'I have.'

'Oh my god!' Mattie grinned, washed by a wave of happiness for her friend. 'I'm *so* glad for you! That's fantastic! When?'

'Two years ago.' Liz smiled smugly, but her eyes shone. 'His name's Thomas and he's the most beautiful, wonderful, cute, talented . . . and everything else. We love him to death.'

'I'm *so* pleased for you.' Mattie grabbed Liz's hand impulsively.

'Believe me, so are we. If only because the cost of IVF was sending us broke.' Liz rolled her eyes. 'And the bloody injections, and waiting, and timing. Alan said he got so he'd forgotten what sex was like without a beaker.'

Mattie laughed. 'Poor thing.'

'Poor thing nothing!' Liz shook her head. 'What about me? I felt like a womb on legs, with a flashing vacancy sign. Took us four tries, you know.'

'I should have guessed, the way you kept bringing the conversation back to kids all the time.'

'I know!' Liz smiled. 'And you kept changing the subject!'

'I was trying to be sensitive.' Mattie shook her head and then grinned back. 'But I'm so happy for you both. I can't wait to meet him. Why didn't you bring him along?'

'Oh, you know what two-year-olds are like. It's nice to have a break.'

Mattie smiled back and nodded understandingly. But she wondered, fleetingly, if this was the only reason Liz hadn't brought the boy along. Could it also have been because she had no idea of the situation Mattie was in? She was saved from dwelling on this by Hannah, who poked her head around the corner and raised her eyebrows questioningly when she saw Mattie and Liz sitting at the kitchen table.

'Good on you. So we have to sit through a lecture on ceramics while you two sit in here and have a gossip?' Hannah smiled at Liz. 'Hello there, it's Liz, isn't it?'

'That's right,' said Liz with some surprise. 'And I know you're Mattie's sister, but I'm afraid . . .'

'Hannah,' interjected Mattie.

'Of course.' Liz clicked her fingers. 'Hannah. You had a little girl, didn't you?'

'Not so little now,' said Hannah ruefully. 'But it's nice to see you again. Have you two stayed in touch all this time?'

'No.' Liz shook her head and her earrings glittered as they swung. 'Actually we haven't spoken for years, but we're making up for it now.'

'That's really good.' Hannah nodded to give her words emphasis. 'I'm glad. Mattie needs her friends right now.'

'Enough, Hannah,' said Mattie shortly, embarrassed by her sister's intensity. 'I'm fine. Now, has Sharon finished in there?'

'Yes, thank goodness. Everybody's looking at the products and she's helping with order forms. Maybe now's a good time for coffee?'

Mattie got up quickly and crossed to the stove where she lit the gas under the kettle. While it was coming to the boil she got a stack of bread and butter plates out of the cupboard and some dessert forks out of the cutlery drawer. She put them on the table next to the strudel and started bringing the afternoon tea out of the fridge.

'Do you want me to pass some of these around?' asked Hannah, picking up the plate of meatballs, each with a little cocktail stick skewering its centre.

'Yes thanks.'

'I'll take some too.' Liz got up, smoothing down her hipsters, and took the vol-au-vents through to the lounge-room.

After they left, Mattie brought out her plunger, spooned coffee into it and then got out the teapot and readied that too. By then the water was boiling so she filled both and got everything else ready before refilling the kettle and putting it back on the flame. She walked over to the doorway. Most of the chairs were now empty, with nearly everyone crowded around the display tables asking questions of Sharon, who answered breathlessly, flipping her hair back every time she bent down to point to something. Those women who were still sitting down had clipboarded order forms balanced on their knees and were filling them out. Liz, minus the vol-au-vent plate, had bobbed down by the shorter table and was holding up a set of terracotta pottery wind-chimes and examining them. Mattie smiled, pleased that the Whimsicalities goods appeared to be popular.

'There's coffee and tea and cakes out here on the table if you'd like to help yourselves,' she called cheerfully before going back into the kitchen. Once there, she took her large knife and carefully sliced the sponge cake into triangular wedges and the strudel into slices. She got some cream out of the fridge and spooned it into a crystal bowl, which she placed on the table with a serving spoon.

Hilda came in, carrying one of the pamphlets with her finger holding a page open. 'Can you look at this for me, Mattie? I am thinking of getting it for Christmas for my eldest granddaughter. She is about your age. What do you think?'

Mattie turned off the gas under the boiling kettle and then looked at a picture of a pottery herb urn with green glazed leaves etched around each of the openings. 'Does she like gardening?'

'Very much.'

'Then it's perfect,' said Mattie decisively. 'Now, coffee or tea?'

'Coffee. But I can get it. You go and have a look at the things. Some are lovely.'

Mattie smiled appreciatively and came into the lounge-room just as Rachel and Ginny passed by on their way into the kitchen. The area around the display had now started to clear, with most of the other women filling out order forms on available surfaces and, in the case of Sally, on someone's back. Liz held up the wind-chimes, causing them to tinkle lightly, and gestured towards Mattie.

'What do you think?'

Mattie looked at the delicate bell-shaped chimes. 'Gorgeous.'

Courtney, with her two friends, came in from the passage and stood inside the doorway, gazing across the room hopefully. 'Can we look at stuff now?'

'Not yet,' replied Mattie. 'Just play for a little while longer.'

'There's nothing here to play with,' complained Courtney petulantly.

'Well, whose fault is . . .' Mattie petered off as she noticed several of the reading group mothers listening in curiously. 'Doesn't matter. Look, there're cakes and meringues out in the kitchen. Why don't the three of you go and help yourselves? But only take what you're going to eat. You can come back for more later.'

As they left, Mattie pulled a chair up next to her mother, who was sitting on one of Hilda's plastic chairs by the couch. 'I haven't had a chance to thank you for coming, Mum. What do you think of the unit?'

'Very nice. Ah – a bit small though, isn't it?'

'It doesn't seem small when it's not so crowded,' said Mattie, smiling. 'Just cosy.'

'As long as you're happy.'

'I am.' Mattie paused, hating the fact that she couldn't think of what to say next.

'I noticed you're using Auntie Vera's tablecloth. She'd be very pleased.'

'Yes. It's lovely.'

'You're looking after it? Keeping it in tissue paper?'

'Yes. Absolutely.'

'I meant that, before,' said her mother suddenly, staring at Mattie with the faded blue of her eyes magnified through her gold-rimmed glasses.

'What?'

'About being happy. Life's too short to be unhappy, Mattie. All I ask is that you think carefully before you decide what it is that *makes* you happy. And consider everyone that it might affect.'

'I will. I promise.' On impulse Mattie took her mother's hand and watched the skin crumple inwards as she held it, mottled brown age spots punctuating the thready veins that stood out amongst the folds. So fragile.

'Good. Ah, here's Charlotte with my tea. Thank you, dear.'

Mattie let go of her mother's hand so that she could take the cup of tea from Charlotte, who also passed over a small plate with a slice of strudel and a dessert fork. Mattie got up quickly.

'I've taken your chair.'

'That's fine. I'll just grab another.'

'No, I've got to look at the things anyway. I'll be back later, Mum.' Mattie smiled at her mother, her hand already feeling strangely empty. Then she headed towards the display tables but was stopped several times by women who wanted to show her something in the pamphlet or just to say how much they were enjoying themselves and what a lovely unit she had. Mattie smiled and nodded noncommittally, know-ing full well that they were avid for gossip, especially those whose daughters had come to Courtney's birthday party earlier in the year and knew that it had been held in a house, with a husband. Finally she made it to the display, where Sharon, with her long hair draped around her neck and down across one shoulder, was tallying up some figures on a calculator.

'Mattie, just in time. You've done very well, you know.'

'I have?'

'You most certainly have.' Sharon, her breathy voice making the proclamation sound even more exciting, showed Mattie an invoice covered with names and numbers. 'You get ten percent of these sales plus a bonus because I've picked up two party bookings here. That means you have one hundred and twenty dollars to spend.'

'Seriously?'

'Seriously. On whatever you want.'

'That's terrific!' Mattie grinned with pleasure and turned to the tables, on which was arranged a wide variety of merchandise: lots of pottery, ceramics, novelty gifts, feathered dream-catchers, wind-chimes, planters, a range of vases and bowls, little resin gargoyles and dragons, plaques, and much more. The scattered pot pourri gave off a heady, incense-like smell and the artificial ivy set off the preponderance of pottery beautifully, giving it an outdoor, rustic appearance. Behind Mattie, her guests were coming back into the lounge-room slowly, each carrying a coffee or a tea and a plate of afternoon tea. The noise level started to rise again but it was pleasant, and friendly, and resonated with a relaxed camaraderie that was heart-warming.

Mattie stood up and turned around. 'Charlotte? Could you stick your head in the kitchen and call Courtney for me?'

'No problem.'

Mattie had now looked everything over and kept coming back to a finely crafted ceramic frog that was glazed with a gorgeous pattern of earthy browns and greens and each of its splayed feet were tipped with deep, rich gold. It was lovely, expensive, and absolutely useless.

'Can I look now?' Courtney gazed over her mother's shoulder at the goods, the corners of her mouth etched with cream.

'What do you think of him?' Mattie pointed to the frog. 'Shall we get him?'

'Oh! He's *beautiful*.' Courtney clapped her hands. Then she dropped to her knees beside her mother. 'Anything else?'

'Well, we can pick a couple of other things. I thought we might get some Christmas presents for people. What about these wind-chimes for Auntie Dana and Uncle Frank's new house?'

'And a dream-catcher for Max! He's *always* having bad dreams.'

Mattie looked at her, surprised. 'Is he?'

'Yes. And, Mummy, can I have one of those little pink and gold frames? I want to put a picture of my friends in it.'

'Why not?' said Mattie expansively. She tallied up what they wanted and then selected a set of pottery herb signs for Sandy, who was an avid kitchen gardener. Sharon wrote it all down and then gave her a copy of the invoice along with a list of who owed what and instructions to collect all the money over the next fortnight before delivery.

By the time Mattie had finished, the lounge-room was crowded once more and several conversations were in full swing. As Sharon started to pack her goods carefully into the striped canvas bags, Mattie sat down on one of the couch's armrests, next to Liz, and helped herself to a piece of celery, generously loaded with French onion dip.

'So I told him if you're so keen on showing everyone who wears the pants, mate, *you* can wash them. And iron them too.' Marie nodded emphatically to press her point.

'I know what you mean,' said Ginny from across the room. 'It's like suddenly they have to prove something.'

'But mainly when there're other guys around,' added Rachel, stirring a cup of tea that she had balanced on her knee.

'My husband does his own washing and ironing anyway,' commented Marianne, causing everyone within earshot to stare at her in amazement. 'And he often does the other stuff too.'

'Are you kidding?' Anne shook her head. 'How did you manage that?'

'I don't know. We've just always done it that way.'

'Send him round to my place,' said Marie, finishing her coffee and placing the cup on the floor by her foot. 'I'll swap you.'

'Did you make this cheesecake, Mattie?' asked Gina, who was sitting over by the front door between Jenny and Anne.

'That depends whether you like it or not,' replied Mattie, smiling as she licked some dip off her finger.

'*Love* it. Can you write the recipe down and give it to me Monday?'

'No problem.'

Liz, who had been sitting quietly eating a large piece of cream-filled sponge-cake, put her dessert fork down and sighed happily. 'I may have to spend an hour on the treadmill tomorrow, but it was worth it.'

'What are you worried about, you skinny thing?' asked Helen, slapping a plump pantyhosed thigh and then pinching the trembling flesh between thumb and finger. 'Look at this! What do you think? Five weeks on the treadmill?'

'No.' Marie prodded the thigh critically. 'At least eight.'

'Cow,' said Helen, laughing.

Anne pointed over towards the framed abstract. 'Love that print, Mattie. Gorgeous colours.'

'Yes,' agreed Rachel with a nod. 'Goes beautifully with your drapes.'

'Well, I have to thank Hilda for the drapes.' Mattie glanced around the room. 'Actually, where *is* Hilda?'

'Is that the older woman with the pink top?' asked Rachel. 'If so, she's in the kitchen.'

Mattie got up, stretching, and went out into the kitchen to wash her dip-sticky hands and see if Hilda was all right. Or if she needed to be introduced to some people. To her surprise, she was sitting at the kitchen table with Mattie's mother and Hannah, having an animated conversation.

'So Geoffrey Withers ended up marrying Sophie, after all that,' said Hilda in her melodious accent, shaking her head grimly. 'He soon found out there *was* something worse than being widowed.'

'Someone should have warned him.' Mattie's mother shook her head, rather sadly.

'I went to school with his daughter,' put in Hannah, stirring a cup of tea. 'Mary. We were quite good friends once. You don't know what happened to her, do you?'

'Mary Withers, hmm . . .' Hilda paused, thinking. 'Yes, I remember. She married, quite young, this absolute fool of a man. Ended up leaving him though and put herself through university. Last I heard she had married again and was living down at Mt Eliza.'

'Hello,' interrupted Mattie, as she dried her hands on the tea-towel. 'Having fun?'

'Absolutely.' Mattie's mother smiled contentedly. 'Did you know that Hilda here and your father used to belong to the same bowls club?'

'Small world, yes?' said Hilda. 'I remember him well. Lovely man.'

Mattie's mother nodded in agreement as she poured some more tea into the teacups in front of each of them. Mattie grinned happily. Everything was going so well, so much better than she'd even hoped. She watched them continue their conversation for a while and then left, returning to the lounge-room where the conversations were still flowing and Sharon was just taking her last bag to the door, negotiating her way awkwardly through the scattered chairs. Mattie smiled again and continued on up the short passage to the children's bedroom, where the door was closed with no light showing beneath it.

Mattie opened it slowly, peering through into the semi-darkness. The light from the passage illuminated a broad strip down the centre of the room and the three girls could be seen sitting cross-legged on the floor, facing the corner.

'Mum!' Courtney's voice was shrill. 'Close the door! Quick!'

'What on earth are you doing?' Mattie still held the door open, so that she could see.

Charlotte's voice came from the corner of the room which was bathed in shadows. 'I'm telling them a scary story. We're pretending that we're at a campfire, aren't we?'

'Yes,' replied Courtney, frowning crossly. 'And now you've let the light in and ruined it.'

'Well, why don't you just pretend that it was the moon coming out for a few minutes, and now it's gone back behind the thundery clouds.'

'Okay!' Courtney's frown vanished as she nodded enthusiastically, turning to her friends. 'That was the moon there.'

'And you know what?' Mattie used her scary voice, drawing out the words. 'It's a *full* moon too. You know what *that* means.'

The three little girls all shivered happily as Mattie slowly closed the door. She leant against the wall, taking a deep breath and trying to wipe the smile off her face before taking the three small steps to the lounge-room. But it was a stubborn smile and, try as she might, all she succeeded in doing was flattening it out so that it looked like she was hugging a private joke to herself. And in a way, Mattie supposed she was.

*

Rachel left first, rather reluctantly, and only because she had to collect her other two children from her mother-in-law's house. But her departure acted as a trigger for the others to cast startled glances at their watches (*Are you kidding? It can't be five-thirty already! My god! I'm supposed to be doing a roast!*) and start gathering cups and mugs and plates together. Mattie cut short the tidal wave of movement towards the kitchen by insisting that everything be left where it was, so instead her guests fished handbags out from under chairs and behind cushions, and children from the bedroom, before, almost as a single mass, departing. Declarations of how much they had enjoyed themselves, and let's do this again sometime, hung cheerfully in the air behind them so that the warmth they brought into the unit was still there even when they no longer were.

Mattie's mother, Hannah and Charlotte were almost the last to depart, leaving only Hilda and Liz still there. Then it was just a matter of stacking Hilda's plastic chairs on the porch for Ernest to collect later and waving goodbye to Hilda, who left with her empty strudel plate hugged against her chest.

'I'm going to ring Alan and tell him I'll be home in about an hour and a half,' said Liz, removing a small silver mobile phone from her bag and flipping it open. 'That'll give us a chance for one more coffee before I go. And a chat.'

'Won't he be annoyed?' asked Mattie, worriedly.

'Annoyed?' Liz paused in the midst of pressing numbers and looked at Mattie, surprised. 'No, why would he be? I'll just explain we're catching up. He'll understand.'

Mattie left Liz to make her phone-call and went into the kitchen, where Courtney was eating another slice of cake in lieu of dinner. 'Did you enjoy yourself?'

'Did I *ever*,' Courtney said with sincerity, separating the icing carefully from the top of her cake with a sticky finger. Then she glanced up at her mother accusingly. 'You didn't tell me Katie and Georgia were coming.'

'I didn't know.' Mattie slid Courtney's plate over to the other side of the table. 'And you can have that later. Now I want you to have a bath. You get your 'jamas ready while I run it.'

Courtney opened her mouth to argue but her mother was already leaving the room, so she quickly reached over to grab the icing layer before following. Mattie held up two fingers to Liz, who was still talking on her phone in the lounge-room and mouthed *two minutes* as she passed. She hurried into the bathroom, shortening her steps automatically, and turned the taps on full, sitting on the side of the bath while it filled.

By the time Courtney was organised in the bath, with several Polly dolls and their blue plastic waterslide, Liz had refilled the plunger and made them both a fresh cup of coffee. Mattie cleared a space at the kitchen table, stacking the dirty dishes in the sink, and sat down opposite her friend. She grinned at her.

'I can't believe you came.'

'I tried to ring you to RSVP,' said Liz, wrapping her hands around her coffee mug and blowing at the steam. 'Twice. But you weren't home, and you obviously don't have an answering machine.'

'No. Not yet.'

'You should have seen my face when I got the invite. I couldn't believe it. And then when I looked at the address –'

'Yes, you said.'

'So what's the story? I know you said before that you're having a break, but that must mean you've been having problems?'

Mattie remembered Liz well enough to know that the concern on her face, although genuine, also masked a fervent desire to discover the details of Mattie's marital problems. And she would not hesitate to pass them on to others, not so much in a malicious way, but as a trump card in an exchange of information. Knowledge is power.

'Well, 'fess up. Maybe I can help.'

'There's nothing *to* help,' Mattie replied confidently. 'Just a temporary separation. Breathing space.'

Liz looked doubtful. 'Your idea or his idea?'

'Both.'

'So let me get this straight. You've separated but you're still together?'

'That's right. He even stays here one night a week and I stay there, and we all spend Sundays together, going on a picnic or whatever. And that was *his* idea.'

'Hmm . . .' Liz chewed her lip pensively. 'How come he got to stay in the house then?'

Mattie paused, brushing some crumbs off the tablecloth. 'Look, I know you never really liked him –'

'It's not that I didn't *like* him,' corrected Liz, 'just that he always seemed so, well, high maintenance.'

'High maintenance?'

'Yes.' Liz paused as she searched for the right words. 'You know, hard work.'

'The thing is, you've never seen the Jake *I* see,' protested Mattie defensively. 'The private one. Who *is* easygoing. And gives me massages, or plays with his kids, or brings me breakfast in bed.'

'True. But I did see the Jake who dragged you out of a party by the arm just because you kissed a couple of other guys, on the bloody *cheek*, for New Year's Eve.'

A shaft of remembrance twisted in Mattie's gut but she ploughed on regardless. 'See? It's easy to look at *that* Jake and think the worst. But it's not the *real* Jake.'

'How do you know?' Liz leant forward and looked at Mattie intently. 'Maybe the Jake who gives you massages and breakfast in bed isn't the real Jake. Have you ever thought of that?'

'No, because it's not true.'

'But, Mats, listen. It's not so much a choice of which is the *real* Jake and which isn't. They're *all* Jake. The one who does the nice things and the one who's just plain bad-tempered. You act like there's two different people, like a Jekyll and Hyde type set-up, but it's still all him. That's Jake – the good *and* the bad.'

Mattie looked at her friend wordlessly. She knew what Liz was saying made sense, but she also knew that it was a reality that did not, *could* not, be reconciled with her ability to look at Jake as a fundamentally good man. How could she explain that, if she allowed herself to accept this, she would have to question everything that held her marriage together? And how could she have hope for the future if she believed that the *bad* side of Jake had as much permanence as the good side? It was too depressing to even contemplate.

'Can I ask you something?' Liz dropped her gaze, a sure sign that she was about to ask something quite personal.

'It depends,' replied Mattie, her voice coming out hoarsely.

'You remember that New Year's Eve when he dragged you out?' Liz paused and then continued again, even though Mattie just looked at her without nodding. 'Well, afterwards Paula and I were talking and we thought, well . . . does he hit you?'

'Hit me?' repeated Mattie, her eyes widening.

'Yes. Hit you. Only . . . because the way he dragged you out was so – *vicious*. I'll never forget the look on his face.'

Mattie took a sip of her coffee and then looked across at Liz. 'So you thought he hit me?'

'Well, yes . . . does he?'

'Do you really think I'd have stayed as long as I did if he hit me?'

'I suppose not,' said Liz doubtfully.

'And that I'd still be trying to make a go of it now?'

'No . . .' Liz grimaced again. 'Sorry, Mats. It was just we talked and . . . forget it.'

'You'd have to be nuts, wouldn't you?' asked Mattie, shaking her head.

'Absolutely crackers,' agreed Liz, breaking a piece of shell off an abandoned meringue and putting it in her mouth, not looking at Mattie.

'See, that's what I mean,' said Mattie grimly. 'You make assumptions about the Jake you think you know, or knew, but you don't see –'

'The real Jake,' finished Liz, with a derisive edge to her voice. Then she looked back across at Mattie expressionlessly. 'Yeah, I know. So you said. But the thing is, when you two got together, I stopped seeing the real Mattie too.'

Mattie stared at her, trying to digest this, not wanting it to make sense. Wanting the conversation to change, or Liz to leave – anything rather than this dance along the precipice.

'But it's none of my business.' Liz wiped her fingers, flecks of meringue falling onto the tablecloth. 'It's your choice.'

'Yes, it is.'

Liz nodded, dropping her gaze to the tablecloth as she started brushing the crumbs off it. Several remained stuck within the ridged needlework of the embroidered roses so she began to pluck them loose one by one and flick them onto the floor.

Mattie broke the silence first. 'What about you, anyway? You've hardly told me anything. Like, are you still working? How's Alan?'

'He's good.' Liz looked up again, a smile transforming her face. 'And I'm working part-time, as a special ed teacher. I job-share with this other woman and it works really well. Means Thomas only goes to creche two days a week and Alan's Mum has him the other day. Which she loves.'

'That sounds perfect.'

'It is.' Liz took another sip of coffee and then stood up, grabbing her handbag off the spare seat. 'Look, I'd better get going. Long drive home.'

'Absolutely.' Mattie stood also. 'And thanks so much for coming. It's been great.'

They walked to the front door, the gurgling sound of draining bath-water coming from the bathroom. Mattie opened the door and preceded Liz onto the porch. She noticed that the chairs were gone and absently made a mental note to thank Ernest tomorrow.

'Nice neighbourhood,' commented Liz, standing on the porch and looking around.

'Yes.' Mattie nodded, following her gaze. 'It is.'

'And I've really enjoyed myself.' Liz looked back at Mattie and hesi-tated, then took one of her hands and held it. Mattie dropped her gaze to her hand, now nestled within Liz's, and for a second saw her mother's juxtaposed over the top, with its age spots and raised blue veins amongst the loose folds of skin. Then it was gone and there was just hers again, with a gold wedding band as smooth as the skin beneath it.

Mattie shook her head to clear it before smiling up at Liz. 'Me too. And we must do it again sometime. So I can meet your Thomas.'

'Definitely.' Liz squeezed Mattie's hand and then let it go. 'And we won't wait so long before the next time either.'

'No way.'

Liz walked down the path towards her car, which Mattie could now see housed a cumbersome baby seat in the rear. As the engine fired, the window rolled down smoothly and Liz turned to blow a kiss before the car jerked forward and continued to the end of the driveway where it paused for a second before accelerating quickly down the road. Within moments, it crested a rise and was lost to sight.

Mattie stood on the porch long after it had gone, pleating the jagged hemline of her silky top between her fingers. Her eyes, which at first had filmed over so that the hatchback blurred slightly before it vanished, dried quickly and her vision returned.

'No way indeed,' she whispered to herself with a wry, self-deprecating smile as she finally went back into the unit, closing the door firmly behind her.

*M*any years ago, sitting in a beer garden with a group of girlfriends on a hot Saturday afternoon, the talk turned to good and bad attributes in a boyfriend. Mattie, sipping sugar-crested blue lagoons, made a comment that if any boyfriend/husband/partner of hers played around, she would end the relationship without a second thought. And one of the others, a small, freckle-faced girl called Jeanette, started to cry, slowly but miserably. It emerged that her fiancé had cheated on her about two years before, and although they decided to stay together and she didn't regret this decision, the hurt still remained.

Years later, Mattie was reminded of this when, after a committee meeting at Max's kindergarten, one of the other mothers breathlessly told them of a mutual acquaintance who was beaten on a regular basis by her husband, a nasty bully of a man. The women collectively drew back, horrified, and then plunged into discussing the situation with an expertise that none of them, probably, actually possessed. And the favourite comment was: 'If my husband hit me, why, he'd be out of there so quickly his head would still be spinning.'

Mattie sat, silently listening, and thinking of Jeanette. How she had lowered her head onto her arms and sobbed wretchedly. And how they had all disregarded their own ignorance in their eagerness to press advice and guidance on the poor girl, none of them really knowing what it was like to be in her shoes. Just like none of the kindergarten women knew what it was like to be that poor soul who was attacked each week, but that didn't stop them having all the answers.

TWELVE

Not knowing what time Jake would arrive, Mattie and Courtney got ready early the following morning. Mattie finished cleaning the unit the night before, washing all the dishes and storing the leftovers in the fridge. She even sponged down the embroidered tablecloth, dried it off and then re-boxed it, putting it on the table for Jake to collect. So the unit now bore few visible reminders of the wonderful day they'd enjoyed. But the invisible reminders remained, permeating the walls and furniture with a sense of cosy complacency that put a smile on Mattie's face from the moment she woke, and stretched, staring at the ceiling as she happily relived the events of the previous day.

It had all gone so perfectly, so smoothly, that Mattie couldn't quite believe it. She'd never imagined that her mother would strike up a friendship with Hilda, or that Liz would come, or Courtney, or that Charlotte would enjoy entertaining the children, or that so many of the school mothers would turn up, *and* they would all stay so long and enjoy themselves so much. And it didn't really matter if Liz had misunderstood what was going on, or failed to appreciate the real Jake, because by the time they caught up again, no doubt everything would have sorted itself out. Life, at the moment, was damn good. And so Mattie spent much of the morning pausing in whatever she was doing to shake her head with pleasure and smile again.

But the smiles started to falter around eleven o'clock, when Jake still hadn't turned up to collect them for the 'family day'. Finally, at twelve,

Mattie rang him, first on the home phone and then on the mobile. But there was no answer from either. She made Courtney a peanut butter sandwich and sat her in front of the television, where a movie matinee was beginning. Mattie herself just picked at a few leftover meatballs before getting changed, shedding her jeans and heels in favour of a pair of navy tracksuit pants and a white Adidas t-shirt. Then she clock-watched, her pleasure at yesterday doing battle with her growing concern about today.

And as the afternoon slid by, it was like watching a pair of scales slowly but surely tilt, more and more heavily, in one direction. The overwhelming ascendancy of the morning's contentment gradually faded until it was matched by trepidation. Then, in the face of the shifting scales, the contentment began to capitulate, to surrender, until, by early evening, it had leached from the walls and retreated, shrinking, into the background. Earlier, Mattie thought that this shift was within her, a personal battle, until Courtney asked haltingly if his absence meant that her father was angry. And when she saw her own fears reflected in her daughter's face, Mattie realised that it wasn't just her. It was everywhere. And the more time that went by without word, the more readily the apprehension, and sense of dull foreboding, mounted within the unit, radiating outwards like a malignant cancer.

They finally arrived at eight o'clock that evening, and from the moment Mattie opened the front door she knew there was going to be trouble. For starters, Jake's flushed face and glittering eyes indicated that he had been drinking. And then there was Max's silent wariness, and the long look he exchanged with his sister. And, if these clues weren't enough, confirmation came from Jake's face which, although politely smiling, also wore the closed, impenetrable look that she feared more than any other. And Mattie knew she would respond as she always did, because even though it seldom worked, it was automatic. She'd become overly bright, bubbly and conciliatory as she desperately tried – by refusing to take offence and glossing up and over each barbed comment – to defuse the situation before it escalated. Like a mechanical Barbie doll. While behind the stupidly upbeat smile, she would be a bundle of panicky nerves.

Jake, dressed very casually in a pair of old jeans and a cut-off grey windcheater, came in, slowly. He looked around the lounge-room, almost as if he thought it would bear evidence of yesterday's party, and paused at the abstract print, staring at it for so long that Mattie felt compelled to fill the silence.

'Do you like it? I bought it last week. At a bargain store.'

'Nice.' Jake nodded. 'Looks good there.'

'Yes it does, doesn't it?' Mattie knew she was babbling but couldn't stop. 'I'm really happy with it.'

'Thought you were struggling for money?'

'It was cheap. Hardly anything. Have you eaten?'

'We had Subway earlier.' Jake turned to Max and grinned, at last. 'Didn't we, mate?'

'Yes.' Max's eyes flicked from his father to his mother and then back again.

'But I wouldn't say no to a glass of wine.'

'Coming right up!'

Mattie escaped into the kitchen where she took a slim cask of riesling out of the fridge and half-filled a fluted glass. She hesitated, unsure whether she should join him, and then decided that it would be more companionable to do so. Maybe it would slow the drinking down. She pushed the cask back into the fridge, taking the two glasses into the lounge-room. Jake was sitting on the couch, watching television, and both children had vanished.

'Where are the kids?' Mattie asked as she put the wine down on the side table.

'In their room, I suppose.' Jake picked up his glass and examined the level. 'Tide's out, is it? Thanks anyway.'

'Pleasure. Um, I'll just go and see if they want anything.' Mattie left the lounge-room and took the three short steps into the children's bedroom. Both were sitting on Courtney's bed talking but they stopped as soon as their mother came in and looked at her expectantly.

'Hey, Mum,' said Max, picking at the sole of one of his runners.

'Everything okay?'

'Sure.'

'Would you like a hot chocolate or anything?'

'Nah. Thanks.'

'Courtney?'

'No thanks, Mum.' Courtney paused, looking at her mother questioningly. 'Is Daddy all right?'

'Of course he is,' replied Mattie brightly. 'Just a bit tired probably. Now, you two can get changed into your pyjamas and come out and say goodnight, okay?'

'But it's only quarter past eight!' Max looked at his mother with surprise.

'Yes, but you both need an early night.' Mattie held up her hand as Courtney opened her mouth. 'No arguments for once, Court. Just do it.'

'Not fair,' mumbled Courtney crossly.

Mattie left the room without bothering to answer. One step into the passage she paused to rake her hands through her hair and take a deep breath before going the other two and entering the lounge-room, a smile plastered on her face. Jake didn't even glance across from a travel program on the television, which showed a man hiking through a red-wood forest, dwarfed by towering firs. Mattie went over to the couch and sat down next to him, slipping her runners off and tucking her legs underneath her to appear relaxed, at least.

After about five minutes of silence, long minutes that hung awkwardly between them, Mattie glanced at Jake. 'Did you have a good weekend?'

'Fine, thanks.'

'Good. That's good.' Mattie turned back to the television, where the trekker, fully laden with knapsack and sleeping bag strapped beneath, was now perched on the edge of a ravine. With a wry smile, Mattie decided that their situation was very similar, but did not share this insight with Jake.

Max came into the lounge-room dressed in a pair of last season's summer pyjamas that were now too small for him. He crossed the room and stood before his father, waiting till Jake looked at him before ducking forward and giving him a kiss on the cheek. 'G'night, Dad.'

'Night, Max. Sleep well.'

Max came over to his mother and repeated the performance. 'G'night, Mum.'

'Goodnight, honey.' Mattie reached forward and hugged him. 'Look at you. You're getting so tall. We'll have to get you a whole new wardrobe at this rate.'

'Well, stop spending money on art and you'll be able to afford it,' commented Jake, without looking at her.

Courtney bounced into the room, wearing silky pink boxers and a matching cotton t-shirt. She came straight over to her father and threw herself at him. 'Night, Daddy. Love you.'

'Love you too, pumpkin.' Jake grinned at her affectionately.

'Are you coming in, Mummy?'

'Okay.' Mattie got back up heavily and followed the two children to the bedroom, waiting while they clambered into their beds. She kissed Courtney first and then stood on tiptoes to reach Max, on the top bunk.

'Story?' asked Courtney questioningly.

'Not tonight. How about I read you two stories tomorrow night to make up, hey?' Mattie kissed Max, wanting to say something reassuring but unable to think of what. So instead she left the room, closing the door behind her, and returned to the lounge-room. Jake hadn't moved.

'Anything on tonight?' asked Mattie conversationally as she settled back on the couch, tucking her legs up again.

'Dunno.' Jake shrugged.

Mattie stared at his profile, so familiar yet so alien. And so close. She wondered what would happen if she just reached out and trailed her fingers, ever so gently, from the point where his hair had started to recede, all the way down the side of his face. The urge to do so was so strong that Mattie even raised her hand slightly, letting it hover between the two of them, and then she dropped it again. On the television, the hiker had left the ravine behind and was now abseiling down a cliff, swinging in towards the face and then bouncing out again as he lowered himself down. All the while a voice-over gave a running commentary but Mattie couldn't concentrate on the details, being far too aware of Jake's stiff silence to relax. Maybe he *was* just tired, and she was simply reading too much into his attitude. Maybe everything would be fine.

'How did your shindig go yesterday?'

Mattie jerked, instantly alert. 'Good! It went really good!'

'Many turn up?'

'A few. Just mothers from school, you know. Oh, and thank you very much for letting Courtney come. She had a ball. Two of her friends came as well so they played together all afternoon. I really appreciate you dropping her off.'

'Like I had a choice.' Jake shifted slightly on the couch, but continued to stare at the television. 'So did Liz come?'

Mattie's first instinct was to prevaricate, but then she quickly realised that things would get a whole lot worse if he questioned Courtney as well. And she couldn't ask the girl to lie – how could she explain the necessity? In the few seconds it took her to reason this through, Jake turned to look at her, at last, so she replied rapidly, 'Yes, yes she did. She said to say hello. And guess what? She and Alan have finally managed to have a baby! A little boy called Thomas.'

'Good for them.' Jake continued to stare at her. 'So – what'd you two talk about?'

'Oh, nothing much. Stuff. The baby.'

'What did you tell her about us? About you living here?'

'Jake, you've got to realise it was so busy we hardly had a chance to talk at all. There were people – women – everywhere. And I bought the most gorgeous little frog! Wait till you see it. And I got some wind-chimes for Dana, and something for Sandy too. I just can't remember what it was. Let me think . . .'

'Who the fuck cares?'

Mattie tensed, every nerve on alert. Staring at him watchfully.

'Tell me what you talked about.'

Mattie decided to face the issue head-on, as perhaps then there would still be a chance to avoid the collision. 'Jake, you obviously think we talked about you, but we *didn't*. You've got to understand that it was so crowded, and then the consultant woman talked for nearly an hour, then everyone looked at the stuff, and then I served afternoon tea. It never stopped.'

'But you had a chance to find out about her baby, didn't you?' Jake had now turned side on and was no longer paying any attention to the television. Just staring at her. 'Yet you really expect me to believe that she showed up here and never even asked why you were living here and not at home, and what'd happened between us?'

'Of *course* she asked.' Mattie changed tack, thinking quickly. 'But I just said we had a few things we were working out, that we were still *together*. Naturally. And then when Courtney got dropped off, it just reinforced everything. Our *cooperation*. And that was it.'

'What a load of shit,' said Jake conversationally. He picked up his glass, drained his wine and then stood. 'I'm getting a refill. You?'

'No thanks,' replied Mattie in a small voice. As Jake left the room, she stared at the man on the screen, now at the bottom of the cliff holding a handful of sandy-coloured dirt which he was showing to the camera. He made a fist and the dirt crumbled out between his fingers and fell to the ground.

Jake came back into the room, and stood just inside the doorway, holding his glass of wine out in front. The newly enlarged and framed photos of Max and Courtney were on the wall to his left, and his face was in perfect alignment with theirs. The three of them in a row. Her family. Jake stayed there, staring at Mattie with a pensive look. She could see him in her peripheral vision but didn't turn, pretending instead to be enthralled by the television. After a few minutes her eyes started to hurt with the effort required to concentrate on the periphery without changing focus.

'I'm not sure what's the most insulting,' said Jake suddenly, still in the friendly, conversational tone he'd used earlier. 'That you talk about me behind my back or that you treat me like a fucking idiot.'

Mattie turned to him, beseechingly. 'I *didn't*. You *have* to believe me.'

'Well, I don't. Sorry.'

'Then I don't know how I can convince you.' Mattie shook her head miserably, knowing that the collision was now inevitable. Her organs knotted with dread and the little wine she'd drunk surged in her gullet sickeningly.

'You can't,' Jake drained his wine and then held the empty flute up and let it go. It fell straight to the carpet, where it rolled to the side of one of his runners but didn't break. Mattie watched, as if hypnotised, as he lifted his foot up and brought the runner down on the glass, hard. It broke with a sharp crack and Jake ground down on the pieces, crushing them into the carpet.

When only the stem remained intact amongst the finely ground shards, Jake walked slowly over to the couch and stood in front of her, looking down. Mattie stared ahead, at eye-level, at his crotch, and was suddenly filled with the urge to reach out and grab his genitals viciously through the denim and pull, twist, tear, with all her might. And not let go even when he fell to the ground, writhing in agony and begging her to stop. *Please, please, Mattie. I'll do anything. Anything.*

But she didn't. Instead, Jake reached down, wound his fingers through her hair and then clenched his fist, bringing the strands of hair together and stretching them out painfully. Mattie gasped and grabbed upwards automatically with both hands, trying to prise his fingers loose. But the grip was tight, and absolutely inflexible.

Jake waited a few moments while she tried ineffectually to tug his hand loose, and then started to walk backwards away from the couch. Mattie first fell to her knees, now batting at his hand desperately, and then scrabbled alongside him, trying to keep her head as close to his hand as possible so that the pain was not as intense. Once in motion, Jake turned quickly, twisting her hair even more savagely, and walked determinedly across the carpet towards the kitchen doorway, dragging Mattie alongside him.

By the time they got there, she was crying and pleading in one long low litany without pause. 'No no please Jake no don't do it please no don't don't please.'

Jake stopped just before the doorway and, with one decisive downward thrust, pushed her towards the broken glass with the hand still entwined through her hair. Mattie was now sprawled full-length on the carpet, finally letting go of his fist so that she could use both hands to push against the carpet with all her might, desperately trying to keep her face away from the glass. Jake pushed harder as she strained hopelessly against his hand, and the shards came closer and closer until they were only an inch away, magnified by the proximity and glistening sharply amongst the brown carpet threads.

Then suddenly he stopped his pressure and her head immediately shot upwards with the momentum. But when it hit his hand, which was still clenched within her hair, he punched his fist down at an angle into her skull and propelled her sideways, just clear of the glass but still onto the carpet. The pain was intense, an exploding nucleus which, for just a few moments, took over her entire consciousness and coloured it crimson. While it lasted, she simply lay there, unable to respond or even to move. Then, just as the crimson tide started to abate, she felt his hand again as it pushed down and almost immediately her face was being ground into the carpet with an implacable strength that seemed almost inhuman. Mattie spluttered and gagged against the overwhelming musty smell of the old carpet, even while she felt its fibres embed themselves into her flesh. She tried to jackknife herself enough to turn her head and draw breath, just one breath, but only her body moved, flailing, while her head remained rigidly held, with her face squashed so hard against the carpet that it seemed her only hope was for the floor to break apart with the pressure. Then he kicked her once, in the side, and finally let go.

Mattie rolled, still gagging, and curled into a foetal position. Her skull throbbed and when she put a hand up to touch it, her fingers came away with strands of dark brown hair clinging to them. She knew that Jake was still standing over her, and she knew that he was waiting for her to look at him. But she refused to give him that pleasure. It wasn't much, but at least it was something.

The whole episode had probably only taken a few minutes, at most, although it felt like hours. A few minutes in which Jake had said not one thing, not even in answer to her pleas. But Mattie knew that would change, very shortly, and she didn't know what was worse – the physical pain and humiliation, or the emotional beating that was about to commence.

'Look at you. You're *pathetic*. Absolutely *pathetic*.' Jake's voice was thick, viscous – a stranger's. Not her Jake, her husband, her friend – just some stranger who, once started, couldn't stop. Firing broadsides one after the other and knowing that at least some of them would hit home.

'Piece of *scum*. *Gar*bage.'

'You don't *deserve* those kids.'

'I should get them up to see you like this. Show them what you're *really* like.'

'Or better still, I should take them *away* from you. Give them a fucking chance.'

'World's worst mother. World's worst *wife*.'

'Selfish *bitch*. Liar, whore. Pathetic *scum*.'

Mattie flinched each time his voice rose, but she stayed where she was, with her eyes open just enough to get some warning if he moved. His runners were about ten inches away from her face and she had her hands ready to protect it in case he kicked out. Then the verbal tirade stopped suddenly, with the last *scum*, and Mattie tensed even more. Waiting. She knew he was staring at her. She could feel his eyes burning into her flesh.

Then he started again, and this time he emphasised his point every few words with a kick to her leg and stomach region. 'You know what you are?' *Kick*. 'A leech.' *Kick*. 'A fucking leech.' *Kick*. 'First off me, now off the government.' *Kick*. 'So you sit here and reckon you're independent.' *Kick*. 'But in the end I'm still paying for you, aren't I?' *Kick*. 'Me and all the other taxpayers trying to do the right thing.' *Kick*. 'But instead we're supporting whores like you.' *Kick*. 'Who want their fucking cake and eat it too.' *Kick, kick, kick*.

By now Mattie had curled up even more tightly, with her hands pressed against her face and her elbows in front of her stomach, warding off the blows. She grunted each time Jake's foot connected but did not cry out, very conscious of the children only a few metres away behind their bedroom door. The smell of the carpet was growing even more disgusting, a dusty suffocating stink that only added to her misery.

For the second time the verbal flow stopped and, as seconds slid by, Mattie started to pray that it was over. Finally she heard his footsteps move away, into the kitchen, and she opened her eyes, quickly, to see if he was standing in the doorway. He wasn't, so Mattie scrambled to her feet, and backed away until she was standing against the front door. Her head throbbed painfully and her arms and knees ached from the

force of the kicks. She took a deep lungful of the clean air and saw, by
the kitchen doorway, clumps of her hair scattered over the carpet, near
the glass shards and the wineglass stem. When she noticed the stem,
Mattie dived forward and, in one rapid movement, picked it up and
threw it behind the couch before jumping back into position.

Jake came in just as she was straightening up and stared at her suspiciously. He glanced around and then narrowed his eyes at her. 'What
did you do?'

'Got up,' said Mattie in an unfamiliar croak.

'And?'

'And nothing else.'

'Come here.'

'No.'

'I said come here.'

'Jake, I really –'

'I didn't ask for a fucking conversation.' Jake's eyes no longer glittered
but were flat, like dulled marbles. 'I said come here.'

Mattie moved forward, hesitantly, maintaining eye contact as she
came across the carpet. She stopped when she was about three feet
away and stood still, swaying slightly with apprehension. He put his
head on one side and regarded her thoughtfully. Then he slowly nodded as if he had seen something that provided confirmation of whatever
he was thinking.

'I'm going to do something I should've done a long time ago,' Jake
announced, his voice not as thick as it had been, but still not normal.
'I'm going to do my kids a favour.'

'A favour?' repeated Mattie, the words drying up in her throat.

'Yes. A *huge* favour.' Jake smiled at her, a smile that stretched his
mouth but went nowhere near the non-negotiable eyes. Then he reached
out, quickly, and grabbed her by both shoulders, pulling her across the
kitchen doorway at the same time as he thrust her backwards, so that
she ended up flat against the short wall between the kitchen and the
passage, staring at him, terrified.

'Jake,' Mattie shook her head rapidly. 'We can work this out. We
can –'

'We can work this out,' Jake mimicked her voice, with an exaggeratedly high pitch.

'We *can*. Remember what we spoke about the other day?'

'All lies.' Jake looked at her, and real hate flashed in his eyes. 'You never intended coming back. Not from the moment you left. It was all lies. All fucking lies.'

'No, it *wasn't*. It –' But Mattie didn't get to finish. Instead Jake, still holding on to her shoulders, whipped her forward and, sliding his hands quickly around her throat, lifted her and slammed her back against the wall at the same time, so that her feet left the ground and the back of her head smashed against the framed portrait of Max, cracking the glass. She screamed, involuntarily, and then all sound was cut off as he started to choke her.

Mattie struggled fiercely, ripping at his hands and clawing them with her nails. Her feet drummed against the wall, making the plaster vibrate all the way up to her head, and her eyes protruded with a fear so pure and intense that it throbbed through her temples, pushing against her skin and threatening to explode. And Jake's face hung only a foot away, grim with concentration as his hands squeezed, and her throat constricted. And then everything started to blur and she got double vision – two Jakes, four eyes, twice the pain, twice the fear. Her mouth gaped, trying to get air, and suddenly, in amongst the pulsations within her head came the astounding thought that this could be it. Who would have thought he was capable of *this*? It could all end here, at Jake's hands, and the children would be alone. And as this last thought winged its way behind her bulging eyes, she mustered the last of her strength and, using the wall for leverage, she kicked out, with all her might. And connected.

She was free. Falling to the floor in a heap, gasping for breath, her muscles now flaccid with relief. So flaccid that she felt a warm rush of urine course down the inside of her tracksuit pants and realised, foggily, that she'd actually wet herself. With a huge effort, Mattie forced her head up to see what was happening. And there, in front of her, crouching over and clutching his crotch, was Jake. He staggered to one knee and dry-retched.

Bullseye, thought Mattie, but with no sense of victory. She wondered, vaguely, how much time she had before he recovered and killed her for this. Fear shot through her and brought with it a determination to escape, so she reached out, using the wall as support to get to her feet. Once up, she started edging towards the front door and, when she was nearly there, she looked back to see Jake staring straight at her, his gaze so venomous that she stumbled and almost fell. But she grabbed out, snagged the doorknob and held herself up, still looking back into the room. Watching Jake take a deep breath and straighten, slowly. This gave her the drive she needed, and she turned, scrabbling at the doorknob urgently to try and make it turn. But her very desperation made her clumsy and the knob slipped within her sweat-slicked hands.

'You bitch. You fucking bitch. I'm going to fucking *kill* you.'

The stranger's voice was back. Mattie whimpered, taking her hands from the knob and wiping them down her tracksuit pants quickly. *Should wash them. Need to wash them.* Then wrapping them back around the knob and twisting, frantically, until it turned and the door came open, the night air rushing towards her and giving her strength. She felt, or thought she felt, Jake's hand brush against her back as she flung herself through the doorway and jumped over the edge of the porch, falling onto her knees on the grass. But she didn't stay there, instead leaping up quickly and running, in her socks, to the side fence that divided the block of units from the house next door. Once there, Mattie bobbed down in the shadows against the fence and looked back, breathing rapidly. But there was no-one behind her and the door of her unit stood open, and empty. An illuminated rectangle of light, the doorway to another world.

She stayed where she was, watching warily, until, after about six or seven minutes, Jake appeared in the doorway, still slightly bent. He looked outside and then took a step onto the porch, peering to the right and left. At one stage he looked straight at her and Mattie held her breath, sure that he would be able to see her chest rise and fall. But then his gaze moved on and she let her breath out, quietly. After a while, Jake stepped back into the unit and closed the door behind him. Mattie listened carefully and heard him engage the inside lock. Even though she had no intention of returning inside, the finality of the sound filled her with fresh despair.

She crawled along the fence-line towards the side of her unit until she reached the huge rhododendron bush that edged her short back-yard fence, next to the wheelie bins. The bush reached along almost the entire six feet of this fence, forming a lustrous semi-circle that, at its deepest point, sprung about seven foot away from the fence as well. Mattie crawled underneath it, all the way to the back, with the branches jabbing and scraping along her skin. When she got to the fence, she leant against it and drew her knees up, wrapping her arms around them.

It was cold out here, and a brisk night breeze rustled through the bush, raising goose-bumps on her bare arms. Her tracksuit pants, damp where she'd wet herself, stuck to her legs with a cold heaviness. Her head throbbed, her arms and legs hurt, her sides ached, and her throat burnt with a slow fire that scorched with each gulp of air. Mattie took a deep even breath to regain control, and started to weep. Soundless tears, fat and heavy and gravid with frustrated misery, stung her eyes and then limped down her cheeks to pool against her lips. And, in between the misery, a furious resentment started to build. This was *her* unit that she had worked so hard for. *Her* refuge. He had no *right* to take it from her. Enough was enough. No more.

The truth was, Mattie had very few accidents. She was not particularly clumsy, or accident-prone. Just one of those things, to Mattie, really meant just one of those things. Those troughs in the cycle by which she lived, when Jake would lash out, not at the nearest object, but at her. Always her. So that she worked out long ago that it was not about lack of control, but about perfect control. Because he didn't hit anybody else. Not his work colleagues, or his family, or his children. Just her.

At the same time, these little truths that occasionally revealed themselves could not be reconciled with the image she clung to. Of the good Jake, bad Jake. The man she loved and the violent stranger. And it was easier to tell herself that the cycles, with the troughs of despair and the wonderful heights of happiness that came after, were actually better than most people's lives, with their even keel of mundane existence. But the reality was that she would have traded her peaks and valleys in an instant just to know where she stood. Day by day and hour by hour. To feel safe and secure and content, all the time. To know that her children did not hear the yelling, and screaming, and violence. And their mother crying and pleading and hurting.

Sometimes she wondered if it was something weak in her that he reacted to, and that if she changed somehow, tried harder, explained herself better – then everything would be okay. Or maybe she just didn't love him enough. After all, to change the aggressive beast into the handsome prince, all that was necessary was love. True love.

And then there was her addiction. To Jake and their life together, their past and their future. And there was so much baggage there, not just the shared finances and furniture and children, but the memories and the years and a deep, deep sense of commitment. But as the children got older, it was harder to face them the morning after and know that the damage was not limited to her. And the truths she tried to ignore became so obvious it was hard to build defences against them. All the while, more and more, her sense of commitment was coming head to head against her sense of survival. And something had to give.

THIRTEEN

Mattie woke early, and stared at the crumbly brown earth next to her face with sick confusion. But remembrance, along with awakened pain, came flooding back in an instant. And as she recalled the events of last night, and the fact that everything had fallen apart – again – her spirits sank so that it felt like her insides solidified into one heavy, deadened mass. In fact, last night had been the worst violence that she had ever experienced. The most unreachable Jake had ever seemed. The closest he had come to doing real, permanent damage. Never before had she thought that he actually wanted to kill her, but then again, never before had she defended herself to such a degree. Actually hurt him. Was there any going back after something like that? She felt a depression that was so overwhelming, and so debilitating, that she could not muster the strength to move. Instead, she just lay there, curled on her side and staring blankly at the ground.

An ant came stumbling across her line of sight, going straight up and over a few broken twigs rather than around them. It lurched away, dislodging minute pieces of crumbly earth as it went but never pausing. At first Mattie's body felt like one giant ache but the longer she lay awake, the more diverse the pain became, until she could isolate the more severe pain and match it with what she'd endured. And lying down was not helping, so at last she forced herself to sit up, stiffly and slowly, being careful to avoid the network of lower branches that caged her.

The morning was still tinged with the greyish light that indicated the sun had not long risen, and the trees sent elongated shadows across the lawn. Mattie automatically went to stretch and then stopped, wincing as streaks of pain shot across her upper body. Her throat also hurt, a harsh but dull ache that sharpened itself whenever she tried to take a deep breath. Mattie closed her eyes, and with all of her might wished that last night hadn't happened, and that she was just now waking in her bed, in her unit. In her home.

The sudden shrieking laughter of a kookaburra made her open her eyes again. It was sitting on one of the power-lines that flanked the road, looking in her direction and probably even laughing *at* her. Another kookaburra flew down to join it and they both stared over at her. *Can you see her, mate? She's a fool. A naive, stupid fool.* Both kookaburras burst out laughing hysterically, vying with each other to achieve the most raucous noise, and then flew off down the road.

Over the next hour or so, the neighbourhood slowly came to life. A teenage girl came down the road on a bike, thrusting newspapers into a few letterboxes as she rode past. The woman across the road let out her cat, with instructions to behave, and then a silver Holden Vectra reversed out from the units, swinging backwards into the road before accelerating off with a muffled roar. The couple from the house next door emerged together, chatting about a dinner party tonight, before getting into separate cars and leaving. Then finally came the sound Mattie was waiting for, the sound of the shower in her unit. A spluttering that quickly settled into a steady flow. As soon as it did, she crawled out from under the rhododendron bush, every part of her body screaming in protest. Once free, she straightened stiffly and then hurried around the front of the unit and onto the porch. She tried the door and, not terribly surprised to find it unlocked, let herself in and closed it gently behind her.

Even though she remembered exactly what had happened the night before, the evidence still came as a jolt. She could see the photo frame with its broken glass segregating Max's smiling face, the shards of glass across the carpet, even the wiry tufts of her hair by the kitchen doorway. She stared for a few moments and then shook herself into action.

The rushing of the shower was still coming from the bathroom so Mattie took the time to go to the toilet, as fast as she could. But her bladder was aching so much that she had little choice. When she finished, she didn't pull her pants back up again. She couldn't bear to. Instead she shrugged them off and, with a sense of urgency dulling her pain, ran into the kitchen to wash her hands. She stood at the sink, rubbing in the soap viciously until the sound of the shower ceasing stilled her, and instead she stared at the window, trying to fight the rising panic.

Within a few moments, a new noise started up, the whirring sound of an electric razor, and Mattie let her breath out in a rush. She threw the soap into the sink and ran lightly up to her bedroom where she stripped off quickly, throwing the dirty clothing into a corner. Then she pulled on the oversized t-shirt she usually slept in and a clean pair of knickers before racing to the children's bedroom door and slipping inside, her heart beating loudly and painfully.

Mattie took a few measured breaths to calm herself and peered around the semi-darkness of the room. Soon she could clearly see Courtney was sitting up in bed, the covers still over her legs and Max sitting on the edge of the upper bunk with his legs dangling over the side. Both children were looking at her with surprise.

'Good morning, guys,' Mattie whispered, trying to smile but failing.

'Are you . . . okay?' asked Courtney hesitantly.

'I'm fine.' Mattie left the door ajar and went over to the bunks where she hugged Max fiercely and then clambered awkwardly into bed with Courtney who, although obviously astounded, willingly made room.

'Are you sure?' Max slipped down off the top bunk, landing neatly on his feet.

'Absolutely. But keep your voice down.' Mattie put her finger to her lips for emphasis. 'We'll talk later.'

'Mummy!' Courtney was peering behind her mother's head. 'You've got blood in your hair!'

'Oh.' Mattie put her hand up to touch the back of her head gingerly and felt the stiffness of dried blood matted amongst her hair. Not much, but enough.

Max looked at her, aghast. 'Mummy?'

'It's okay, I'm fine.' Mattie waved a hand dismissively. 'Nothing to worry about.'

Both children would probably have argued this point, but at that moment the sound of the electric razor abruptly halted. Courtney immediately wiggled closer to her mother and Mattie put an arm around her reassuringly, trying not to wince. Max, his eyes wide, sat down on the end of Courtney's bed and stared at the door. And Mattie waited, tensely, trying to take regular breaths to calm her stomach. After a few minutes, she heard the bathroom door open and felt Courtney stiffen against her. Jake's footsteps came past and went into the bedroom next door. Then he could be heard getting dressed and, last of all, the squeak of the bed as he sat down to pull on his runners. Soon the footsteps started again, this time pausing at the children's bedroom door. Then, as Mattie squeezed Courtney's shoulder for comfort, the door was pushed all the way open and Jake was silhouetted in the doorway.

Nothing was said and if Jake was surprised to see Mattie in bed with Courtney, he didn't show it. In fact, he didn't show anything. Just stared expressionlessly at them for a few long moments and then left. Mattie let out a breath that she hadn't been aware she was holding as she heard him walk towards the front door, open it, and leave. And she looked at the children wordlessly and saw the relief she felt reflected back at her.

Mattie jumped up and hurried into the lounge-room where she saw the front door had been left half open. Automatically dodging the area with the broken glass, she went to the side of the window and peered out through the drapes, just in time to see Jake's burgundy Commodore take off down the road with a squeal of tyres. Mattie watched until it disappeared and only then did she let the relief truly wash through her, cleansing her fear. She closed the front door quietly, making sure the lock engaged, and then leant against it, taking another deep breath and letting it out. It hurt her throat, but was worth it.

Max came into the lounge-room hesitantly, with Courtney just behind him. Mattie smiled at them and then suddenly realised they were both barefoot.

'Don't move!' She held up a hand commandingly. 'Glass!'

As the two children peered at the floor around them, Mattie took a huge step over the kitchen doorway and then hurried into the laundry where she grabbed the vacuum cleaner. Dragging it back out into the lounge-room she plugged it in, turned it on and ran it over the carpet. The tiny shards of glass made a crackling, tinkly noise as they were sucked up, while the strands of her hair disappeared smoothly and silently.

When she was sure no glass remained, Mattie switched it off and backed it against the wall. Then she turned to the children. 'I'm going to have a shower and then I'm making you both a huge hot chocolate. Okay?'

Both nodded so Mattie left them there and went into the bathroom. It still smelt of Jake, his shower and his aftershave. Mattie closed her eyes and put her head back, but this caused sharp points of pain to stab into the base of her skull. She straightened quickly and then shed her clothing, standing in front of the mirror to stare at herself. There were red marks and bruises on her thighs and arms, and a dark pear-shaped bruise on one hip. But the worst damage was around her neck, where deep blue blotches stretched around her throat like macabre jewellery. Mattie closed her eyes and then opened them again, but the bruises were still there. And so was the strain on her face, and the dark grey semicircles beneath her eyes.

Mattie shook her head in denial but knew, at the same time, that what was done was done. Trying to pretend it hadn't happened just wasn't an option. Not anymore. She turned the shower on and stepped under-neath the spray before it had even heated up. Because it was cleansing, washing away the fear and disgust, and the dirt and the urine. Mattie washed her hair gently, wincing at the tenderness of her scalp, and then scrubbed her body hard, even over the bruises, despite the pain. She got out, drying herself with a towel that smelt strongly of Jake, and then threw the towel into the laundry hamper and dressed again. But when she started to brush her hair the pain was so intense that she had to stop, running her fingers through it lightly instead, and bringing them away with fine strands of damp hair stuck to them in clumps.

The children were already in the kitchen when she got there, sitting at the table and waiting. Courtney's plaits had feathered out during the night and tendrils of hair frizzed around her head like a darkened halo. Both children were silent when she entered, and they remained silent while she fixed their drinks. Mattie found their quietness disturbing, but understandable. She herself was just so relieved that Jake had now left that even her injuries felt more bearable. When she'd finished making the two hot chocolates, Mattie put them on the table in front of the children, and suddenly realised that the box with the embroidered tablecloth was gone. She shrugged to herself and then took a tub of vanilla ice-cream from the freezer and spooned a scoop into each of the mugs. The ice-cream plopped deliciously and sank, only to resurface and float along the top, its edges frothing as they melted.

'Yum!' said Courtney, pushing at the ice-cream with a finger. 'Can I have a spoon?'

'Sure.' Mattie fetched two teaspoons and passed them over. Then she took some painkillers and fixed herself a coffee with the remaining hot water. She sat down next to Courtney, opposite Max.

'I hate him,' said Max suddenly, stabbing viciously at his ice-cream with his spoon.

Mattie opened her mouth to give her standard spiel, about how he didn't *really* hate him, and about how much *pressure* their father was under, and how he didn't really *mean* it – but she closed her mouth again without saying anything. Because, right now, she hated him too. Max stabbed at the ice-cream again, holding it under with his spoon.

'Did you make Daddy angry?' asked Courtney in a small voice, her eyes flicking down to her mother's neck briefly.

Mattie looked at her. 'You heard us last night?'

'Yes.' Courtney chewed her lip. 'You screamed. And cried.'

'I *hate* him,' said Max again.

'Court, you know how you think it's my fault? That I make Daddy angry?'

'I don't think it's *all* your fault, just that . . .' Courtney frowned, unable to express what she meant. 'I don't know.'

'Remember when you told me about that little girl at kinder last year? The one who never stood up for herself?'

'Oh, yeah. Jasmine. She had curly hair.'

'Well, would you like me to be like Jasmine, and never stand up for myself?' Mattie held Courtney's gaze. 'Sometimes you *have* to stand up for yourself. And if someone else behaves badly because of it, then *they're* the one at fault, not you. Understand?'

'Then you're saying Dad behaves badly?' asked Max, obviously expecting her to come back with the speech about pressures, and intent, and the usual excuses.

Mattie looked at him evenly. 'How much did you hear last night?'

'Um . . .' Max glanced across at Courtney and then looked back at his mother. 'I don't want to get in trouble.'

'Why would you get in trouble?'

'Because we sneaked out,' answered Courtney, looking at her brother. 'And saw it.'

'Saw what?' asked Mattie, her stomach knotting again.

'Saw Dad choking you,' whispered Max, staring down at his hot chocolate. 'Against the wall. And you were kicking and all.'

'I thought you were killed!' Courtney threw herself against her mother and wrapped her arms around her waist.

'Oh god.' Mattie held her daughter, stroking her long dark hair back while she stared across at her son. 'Hell.'

'I wanted to save you.' Max still couldn't meet her eyes. 'But I . . . I –'

'He was scared,' finished Courtney, still holding her mother tight. 'And so was I.'

'Oh, Max.' Mattie felt her throat tighten even more. 'It's all *right* to be scared.'

'No it's not,' muttered Max. 'You could've died. And I did nothing.'

'Listen to me –' Mattie kept one arm around Courtney and reached the other across to put a finger under Max's chin and forced it up, so that he was looking at her – 'it *is* all right to be scared. *Anyone* would have been scared.'

Max stared at her, even though she had now let go of his chin. His eyes shone with unshed tears. 'Were *you* scared?'

'You have to realise –' Mattie paused. 'Yes. I was terrified.'

'I'm a *coward*,' blurted Max, the tears spilling over. 'A dirty stinking *coward*.'

'Oh, Max.' Mattie grabbed one of his hands and held it tight. 'You're *not* a coward. You're the bravest boy I know. Just sneaking out to see what was happening is brave. It really is.'

'Really?' Max looked up at her, his brown hair spiking across his head and his eyes huge. He looked so young, and so defenceless.

'Absolutely.' Mattie nodded emphatically and then, taking Courtney by the shoulders, pulled her upright. 'Now listen, you two. I'm going to tell you some things I maybe should have told you a long time ago. Okay?'

'Okay.'

'I'm not going to lie to you either, and you can ask me any questions you want.' Mattie let go of Courtney and took a sip of coffee before continuing. 'First of all, your dad loves you both. Max, don't look like that. You know it's true. But the thing is, parenting isn't just about love. It's about showing by example. And your dad sometimes makes big mistakes there. Like last night. You know how I was saying before about sticking up for yourself? Well, if someone says something you don't like, or don't agree with, you have two choices. You can choose to talk about it reasonably, or you can walk away. Unfortunately, your Dad doesn't choose either of those.' Mattie took a deep breath. 'He chooses violence.'

'Why?' asked Max, looking her full in the face.

'I don't know the answer to that.' Mattie sighed. 'I wish I did. But I think it's got something to do with power. Violence makes him feel powerful, and it makes him feel like he wins every argument. But that's no way to argue, is it?'

'Then he's a bully,' said Max decisively.

'Daddy's *not* a bully.' Courtney glared at her brother, outraged.

Mattie took another sip of coffee, thinking this over. There was no doubt that Jake *could* be a bully, but was it right for her to say this to their children? She was already going further than she ever had before, and felt flickers of guilt both about not having done it before, and about doing it now. She was stabbing him in the back, playing dirty. Then there was the chance that this conversation might get back to him, and the thought of the repercussions that would cause terrified her.

'But, Mum?' Max looked at her, then dropped his gaze to stare at her mug of coffee. 'You know how you said Dad has a choice? Well, so do you, don't you?'

'Yes, of course. But what do you mean?'

'Well, when Dad gets . . . angry. Then why don't *you* walk away?'

'You mean, during an argument? Or altogether?'

'Both.'

Mattie smiled at Max grimly. 'During an argument I'd walk away if I could, honey. But your Dad likes to . . . *finish* arguments. As for altogether, well, you know how Dad's not always like that? How sometimes he's really nice?'

'Yeah. Sometimes.' Max stared at her while Courtney nodded emphatically.

'Well, I love that person. Very much. And I never wanted to lose him. Or our family.' Mattie suddenly realised that she had spoken in the past tense.

'Oh.' Max looked back down at his hot chocolate.

'Is there anything else you'd like to ask me?'

Max picked up his spoon and watched some hot chocolate dribble down the outside of his mug and pool against it on the table. 'Don't we have to get ready for school?'

'No.' Mattie smiled at them both. 'Because you're not going. I declare today a holiday. We're going to lie around all day and relax. How does that sound?'

'Great!' Courtney beamed happily while Max, still with his head down, sneaked a look at his mother and smiled.

'Thought you'd both like that.' Mattie stood up, her body groaning. 'So why don't you go watch the morning cartoons and I'll make some scrambled eggs for breakfast?'

'With more hot chocolate!' Courtney leapt up and skipped into the lounge-room to turn the television on.

Max stayed at the table for a while longer, playing with his spoon and dabbing at the puddle of hot chocolate with his finger. Mattie left him alone while she went to the fridge to get some eggs. But there she paused, frowning. Something was missing, and it took her several

moments to realise what it was. The inspirational sayings were gone,
every single one of them. All that was left were bits of sticky-tape with
tiny scraps of paper caught under them. Mattie went to the rubbish bin
and opened it. And there they were, all torn to shreds.

She stared at them for a moment and then took a deep breath. It
could have been worse, much worse. Mattie let the lid close and then
got six eggs out of the fridge and broke them into a bowl, adding milk
and then beating them briskly with a fork. She thought about her sayings for a while. *The future depends on what you do in the present. It is
hard to fail, but it is worse never to have tried to succeed.* Then she filed
them away where they couldn't be destroyed and glanced across at her
silent son. He had the sort of face that always made her want to ask
'What are you thinking?', but for once she held back, reasoning that if
he had questions, she would just allow him to ask in his own time and
space. Instead, as she poured the egg mixture into the frypan, Mattie
tried to read his expression. But it told her nothing. And she suddenly
realised that he was very much like his father in that. The same ability
to shut down, to become impenetrable. To build a wall that isolated
him, while keeping all those who cared at a distance. With this insight,
Mattie stared blankly at the now bubbling egg mixture. And felt a cold
shiver tiptoe up her spine.

Mattie didn't expect any phone-calls until at least Tuesday, and flowers
or something probably Wednesday or Thursday. The fight had been a
particularly bad one, and if the pattern continued to follow past form,
Jake would probably take a few days to wind down. She knew, from
experience, that if she was to see him now, the chances were that he
would remain impassive, and the violence might even flare again.

But whereas this pattern, when she had been living with Jake, had
been so horribly soul-wrenching on those days when she tiptoed around,
always tense and always watchful, in the unit it was almost like a form
of release. A gift of at least two days that she could count on being alone
and undisturbed. Two days to think, get her head together, decide what
to do. And a new element began to creep into her consciousness. Until

lately, she'd been able to convince herself that because Jake had never touched the children, they weren't *really* affected. In fact, she was doing the right thing by them, keeping the family together, giving them a father. But it was becoming harder and harder to believe this. The fallout, on them, was becoming obvious. And it was clear that, whether or not they were actually ever the objects of their father's aggression, they still experienced the repercussions. And they were very damaging.

Nevertheless she felt that, if given the choice, they would stick with what they knew. But this was one thing that she didn't discuss with them. In fact, after the initial talk on Monday morning, they didn't speak of Jake again for the next few days. They enjoyed a day in front of the television, and playing board games, on Monday, and even skipped swimming for the first time that term. Mattie simply didn't feel up to it. In the afternoon, reaching for her notepad on top of the fridge to write absent notes for Max and Courtney, she found the note that had been pinned to the Onkaparinga blanket that very first night. *Mattie – I'll always be here. Love you, Jake.* It made her cringe, and she wondered whether, back when he wrote it, Jake had been aware that it read not just as an avowal of love, but as an implicit threat. And she decided that he probably had, as it was all part of the game. So she threw it away.

On Tuesday the children returned to school, and Mattie wrapped her neck in a scarf despite the mild weather. She was greeted cheerfully by those who'd attended the Whimsicalities party, with congratulations on hosting such a lovely afternoon, and promises that the money would soon be forthcoming. To Mattie, though, the party seemed so long ago that the joy it brought her had long faded, and so she nodded and smiled politely, and made her escape as soon as possible.

After dropping off Max and Courtney, she spent the entire day inside the unit, just sitting and thinking. And she planned to do exactly the same on Wednesday, and Thursday, and Friday. Postponing life until this *situation* was resolved, one way or the other. But matters were taken out of her hands on Wednesday afternoon when Hilda marched past the lounge-room window and knocked on the door with a vigour that demanded an answer.

Mattie got up from the couch reluctantly, and wrapped her scarf loosely around her neck. Then she fixed a polite smile on her face before opening the front door. 'Hilda, how are you?'

'Fine, fine.' Hilda looked at Mattie's face searchingly. 'And you?'

'Oh, good. Thanks.'

'Too busy for a coffee?'

'Coffee?' repeated Mattie, before giving in to the inevitable and standing back. 'No, of course not. Come in.'

Hilda followed her through to the kitchen and sat down in her usual place while Mattie put the kettle on and prepared the plunger. In her old grey tracksuit with its oversized windcheater and loose pants, she felt like a slob next to Hilda, who was impeccably dressed in her navy slacks and a crisp white ribbed top. Mattie ran her fingers through her hair surreptitiously, avoiding the tender spots.

'Your party went well,' said Hilda, breaking the silence. 'Very enjoyable.'

'Yes, it was, wasn't it? And thanks again for the strudel.'

'My pleasure.'

'Here we go.' Mattie put a mug of coffee in front of Hilda and then, putting hers down on the table opposite, slid into a chair. She wrapped her hands around the mug and smiled across at her guest. 'You're looking very dressy. Are you off somewhere?'

'I was supposed to be,' answered Hilda obliquely, 'but I am here instead.'

'Oh?'

'Yes. See, my Ernest is a good man, but very protective. And very . . . private to other people's business.' Hilda frowned momentarily. 'Maybe that is not the right word.'

'Oh?' repeated Mattie, unsure of where the conversation was going, and not really caring.

'He does not believe in interfering. *That* is what I mean.'

'Oh,' said Mattie, yet again, as a frisson of premonition sharpened her senses.

'We heard you on Sunday night,' Hilda stated, looking closely at Mattie to gauge her reaction to this. 'You and your husband. Fighting.'

Mattie stared back, unable to answer.

'He was yelling, a lot. Then you screamed. And I think he threw you against the wall, because I heard a thump. Then more thumping.'

Mattie still didn't know what to say, but she felt like crying with embarrassment.

'My guess is that he choked you or something too,' continued Hilda matter-of-factly, 'because I can see a bit of bruising under your scarf.'

'God.' Mattie's hand flew up to the scarf in a belated but automatic attempt to adjust it. She felt exposed, mortified, and wished fervently that she could disappear. Shrink until she could slip through the cracks in the linoleum, and vanish.

'I wanted to come over but Ernest said it was none of our business. Then we argued about calling the police but the noises stopped, so Ernest said that was that. It was over. He forbade me to come over the next morning. In fact, to be truthful, he has forbidden me to visit at all. He does not wish for us to be involved.'

'Then why are you here?' asked Mattie in a small voice.

'Because he can be a fool sometimes and I know better. And I am very ashamed for not coming over until now but I have to try and keep the peace. So Ernest has gone to the bowls and I said I was going to visit our son.'

'But you'll get found out!'

'No matter.' Hilda shrugged. 'He is wrong and he even knows he is wrong. Deep down.'

Mattie took an even breath. 'Look, Hilda, I'm very grateful for your concern but it's not as bad as you seem to think. Yes, we *did* have an argument but there was no throwing against the wall or anything. And the bruises are . . . from something else.'

'Fiddlesticks,' said Hilda, sounding annoyed for the first time. 'Bull-crap.'

'It's *true*.' Mattie frowned. 'Why would I say it if it wasn't true?'

'Because you are a fool also.' Hilda shook a finger at Mattie. 'And trying to protect him. And probably also because you feel embarrassed.'

'No, you're wrong. I just –'

'Listen to me,' Hilda thinned her lips at Mattie angrily. 'You remember I told you about my sister? Gertrude? Well, she had a husband like yours. He liked to emphasise his points with his fist. No, not all the time. Sometimes he was Prince Charming himself, and people would say, "Is that Bert not a nice fellow? Gertrude is *so* lucky to have him". And even that stupid Gertrude thought she was lucky to have him, and that she would never get another man if she left. Not one so charming, and educated, and well-paid. And he continued to be charming, and educated, and well-paid, and my sister became a frightened little mouse. And people started to say, "Why does he put up with her?" and, can you believe it, she was frightened she would lose him?'

'What happened to her?' asked Mattie, rather reluctantly.

'She died about twenty years ago. He killed her. No, not directly, he just wore her down until there was no fight left. She died of cancer, but it was his fault.'

'Didn't you say anything? To her?'

'Oh, yes. Over and over. Every time I saw the marks. And all the while Ernest was saying, "This is none of our business, Hilde. You have a family of your own, Hilde". And finally I told Gertrude that it was too hard for me to see her like this, that it was killing me. Can you believe that? Killing *me*!' Hilda snorted with disgust at herself. 'So I hardly saw her for the last ten years she was alive. My only sister.'

'Oh.'

'Yes. I kept telling myself that it was her choice to put up with it, and that if she ever left, *then* I could help her. By staying away, I thought I was putting pressure on her to leave, but really I was just isolating her. I was her *only* relative over here. Her only one. And all I did was make it even easier for him to treat her exactly how he wanted. I did not even know she was sick until it was too late.'

'I'm so sorry, Hilda, I really am.' Mattie reached out and held the older woman's hand, and felt it tremble. But only for an instant, because Hilda clasped Mattie's hand back, tightly, and then wrapped her other one around it also, so there was no escape. And she looked across at Mattie with her black-button eyes shiny with emotion.

'So do *not* lie to me. I will not have it. Lie to yourself if you want to, but not to me.'

Mattie stared back, unsure of what to say.

'If you do not wish for my help, that is your choice. But I shall still come over, and I am not going to ignore what I see.'

'Okay,' replied Mattie softly.

'Good.' Hilda let go of her hand abruptly and Mattie pulled it back, rubbing it.

'But you have to understand that it's much more complicated than –'

'Of course it is.' Hilda shook her head derisively. 'It always is.'

'And there's the children . . .'

'Does he hit them too?'

'Of course not!' replied Mattie, horrified at the thought.

'Just you, yes? Well, that's okay then.'

Mattie looked away from the sarcasm and into her coffee mug, as if searching for answers. Then she picked it up and took a sip, buying time instead. She had never been in this situation and didn't know how to react. What went on between Jake and her had always remained strictly that, between them, and even the discussion she'd had with Max and Courtney on Monday morning had been further than she'd ever strayed before. This, now, was totally uncharted territory.

Hilda drank her coffee, watching Mattie carefully as if waiting for her cue on how to proceed. But Mattie had no cues to give, no ideas. The silence started to grow uncomfortable, and tense, and Mattie decided that the best thing she could do was to ask Hilda to leave. Now, before it went even further. But as she tried to find the right words to accomplish this without sounding too dismissive, the doorbell rang, a shrill buzz that broke the silence and widened the eyes of both of them. A moment later, it rang again, even more insistently, and Mattie got up to answer it.

'Excuse me,' she said to Hilda, in a more or less even tone. She left the kitchen and walked steadily towards the front door, on the way adjusting the scarf so that it covered her whole neck. *Please don't let it be Jake. Please don't let it be Jake*. And it wasn't. It was Hannah.

'Jesus, what *are* you wearing?' Hannah looked her up and down, pausing at the silky, Aztec-patterned scarf. She herself was dressed very smartly, in heels, black slacks and a frothy paisley shirt. Her hair was done in its customary plait, hanging neatly down the centre of her back.

'I'm not going anywhere,' said Mattie, defensively. 'So it doesn't matter, does it?'

'I suppose not,' replied Hannah doubtfully. 'Got time for a cuppa?'

'No, not really –'

'Of course she has.' Hilda suddenly appeared in the kitchen doorway, smiling welcomingly. 'We were just about to put on the kettle again, yes?'

Hannah looked at her sister huffily. 'Well if you'd rather I didn't stay . . .'

'No, no. Of course not. Come in.' Mattie stood back and then closed the door behind Hannah. She felt like screaming. Nothing was going right. Nothing. She followed Hannah into the kitchen where she washed her hands and put the kettle on while Hannah sat down, looking rather ill-at-ease. Mattie collected the empty mugs from the table and rinsed them. Then she set up the plunger again and, when the kettle had boiled, filled it.

'I only dropped around to give you the money,' said Hannah, watching her. 'Mum's and mine. From your party. I didn't know when it was due.'

'Thanks,' said Mattie shortly. 'Just pop it on the table.'

Hannah took an envelope out of her bag and placed it carefully on the table. She looked at Mattie again and then across at Hilda, who hadn't said a word since inviting Hannah to stay.

'There we go.' Mattie put a mug of coffee in front of Hilda and Hannah and sat down next to Hannah with her own.

'Remember I don't drink coffee?' Hannah stared into her mug disapprovingly and then looked across at her sister. She frowned. 'What's going on? Did I interrupt something?'

'Of course not,' said Mattie.

'Yes,' said Hilda.

'Hilda!' Mattie looked at her, absolutely aghast. '*No!*'

'Yes,' said Hilda again, staring straight at Mattie. 'I am going to do you a huge favour here. And you will probably hate me for it, but I know it is the right thing.'

'Don't you *dare!*' Mattie got up again, pushing her chair back roughly, and pointed a shaking finger at Hilda. 'Don't you bloody dare!'

'I *have* to. Can you not see that?'

Mattie changed tack abruptly. Desperately. 'Please? *Please* don't. I'm begging you.'

'What on earth is going on?' Hannah, who had been looking from one to the other, now stared at Hilda in confusion. 'Tell me what's going on!'

'Did you know your brother-in-law hits your sister?' asked Hilda conversationally, much like she would have asked, 'Did you know your brother-in-law plays golf?'

'*What?*'

'He hits your sister. Regularly, I think.'

'He does not.' Hannah looked at Mattie. 'What's she talking about?'

'So you did not know.' Hilda nodded to herself. 'I thought not.'

'Mattie?' Hannah kept her gaze on her sister. 'What's going on?'

Mattie, who was still standing, opened her mouth but her throat was frozen and no words came out. They were trapped.

'He hit her Sunday night. And choked her.'

'You're mad,' said Hannah flatly, staring now at Hilda.

'Am I? Look at her neck. Go on, have a look under the scarf.'

Mattie shot a hand to her neck to hold the scarf in place and Hannah, seeing this, started to look doubtful for the first time. As if there might have been some truth in what she was hearing. She reached out a tentative hand, and Mattie drew back.

'Mattie, let me see,' said Hannah, her confusion making her cross.

'No.' Mattie shook her head.

Hannah stared at her for a moment and then patted the chair beside her and spoke as she used to years ago, when Mattie was small. 'Come on, sit down next to me. Let me see. Come on now.'

Part of Mattie wanted to do exactly that, to sit down next to her older sister and show her the bruises. And tell her everything so that she could bask in the sympathy and the advice and the knowledge that she was not alone. But that part was no match for the other, honed over the years, that refused to share this facet of her life. It was not just her loyalty to Jake and their marriage, and a disinclination to listen to him being criticised, but her pride, which could not bear to let her admit the extent of the problem. And the length of time it had been happening. So instead of moving towards Hannah, she moved away to stand behind the chair and glare at them both.

'Come along, Mattie,' said Hilda, but without any exasperation. 'This is for your own good.'

'How dare you presume to know what's for my own good?' asked Mattie tightly. 'Who are you to sit in judgement on me?'

'But I am not sitting on –'

'Oh yes you are. With your assumption that *you* know what's best.'

'Mattie, can you just tell me if it's the truth?' pleaded Hannah.

'No,' said Mattie, shaking her head to emphasise her refusal. 'Because it's none of your business.'

'I'm your sister!'

'So what? Do I interfere in your life?'

'But this is different!' Hannah stood up too, as if her height might give her an advantage. 'I'm your older sister! If something's wrong between you and Jake, then it *is* my business!'

'This is *your* fault.' Mattie turned to Hilda and stared at her narrowly. 'Who asked you to interfere anyway?'

'My conscience,' replied Hilda, her black eyes fathomless.

Hannah, who hadn't taken her eyes off Mattie, suddenly dived forward and pulled at the scarf, which fell open enough to expose a blotchy dark purple section of bruised flesh.

'Oh my god. Oh Jesus.'

'Get off,' hissed Mattie, stepping back quickly.

'Jesus,' repeated Hannah, sitting down hard on her chair.

'You must help,' Hilda said to her. 'You must stand by her.'

'That's enough.' Mattie pointed first at Hilda and then Hannah. 'You, and you. Get out. Both of you. Out now.'

'This is your pride talking,' said Hilda, not moving. 'Push it to one side and talk with your brain instead.'

'Who are you to talk?' spat Mattie viciously, wanting to injure someone, anyone. 'You've got the damn gall to drag my sister into *my* business but where were *you* when *your* sister needed you? Well? Where were *you?*'

Hilda went pale, her eyes standing out even more darkly.

'Yes, that's right. You're a hypocrite, aren't you? And what's more –' Mattie stopped abruptly and stared at Hilda. Her pale, rigid face looked much more lined than usual and even though she hadn't dropped her gaze, her hands were clenched at the table edge, the whitened knuckles sharply delineating ridges of bone that rose from the wrinkled flesh. Mattie walked forward slowly and then flopped down onto her chair. What was she doing? What had she become?

'I don't understand any of this,' said Hannah despairingly.

Mattie glanced at her sister and then back to Hilda. 'I'm so sorry. God, I am so *so* sorry.'

'That is all right. You were just lashing out.'

'But that's unforgivable,' whispered Mattie. 'You were only trying to help. Even if I think it's misguided . . . that's no excuse.'

'I understand.'

Mattie felt the tears well up in her eyes and could not muster the will-power required to keep them at bay. Instead, they spilt over and then suddenly everything, all the emotion of the past few days, maybe even the past ten years, spewed up to the surface and gushed forth. And she buried her head in her arms on the table and started to cry. Not the soundless tears she usually cried, but huge gulping sobs that shook her body and throbbed through her aching head. Even so she felt Hannah draw the scarf all the way off, and she heard her quick intake of breath.

'Jesus Christ.'

'Yes,' said Hilda shortly. 'He did it.'

That made Mattie cry even harder, and she felt she'd never be able to stop. She cried because she felt betrayed, and vulnerable, and humili-ated, but most of all she cried because she simply couldn't help it. It was like a dam wall had broken and all her restraint was pouring out with the torrent. And after years of smiles and shrugs and subterfuge, it was suddenly out in the open and there was no way she could rein it back in again. They wouldn't let her, and besides, it probably wouldn't fit. Not anymore.

'How did you know?' Hannah asked Hilda in a shocked whisper.

'I suspected, from her face sometimes. I have seen it before, you see. But I did not know, not for sure, until Sunday night. I heard him yelling at her – yelling and yelling. And throwing her against the wall. And her screaming.'

'Jesus.'

'Stick by her,' said Hilda forcefully. 'No matter if she stays with him or not.'

'What do you mean? Of *course* she won't stay with him.'

'Ah, you're thinking this was the first time, hey? But men like that do not wait ten years and then lash out. He is a cat, and she is his toy. This was not the first time, and it probably will not be the last.'

'Are you saying that he hits her regularly?' asked Hannah disbelievingly. She shook Mattie's shoulder roughly. 'Mattie, stop it. Stop it now. Tell me this never happened before.'

Mattie heard her, but only from a distance. It was as though Hannah was talking at the end of a tunnel, so that while her voice floated through the words made little sense. Her sobbing had started to abate but as it did, pain started to come. Pain in her throat, which had already been dry and sore, pain in her swollen eyes, pain in her head, which felt as thick and heavy as if she had the flu, and pain in her mind, which flinched away from the knowledge that Hannah and Hilda now knew.

'Mattie? Tell me this was the first time. *Tell* me. What about the children? Does he hit the children?'

Mattie stood up, pushing the chair back so roughly that it toppled over and fell with a crash. The scarf slid off her shoulders to the floor but she ignored it. Because she had to get out of here, get away from the questions and the attention, escape. She folded her arms across her chest and started backing away. 'Excuse me.'

Hannah turned on her chair to watch her. 'Where are you going?'

'Just – away.' Mattie reached the lounge-room door.

'Let her go,' said Hilda. 'Give her a few minutes alone.'

Mattie fled to the bathroom. She stood before the vanity unit and then suddenly realised that she hadn't measured out her three steps to get there. She laughed at herself scornfully for even noticing. *Forget it.*

It doesn't matter, it's only steps – it means nothing. She stared at herself in the mirror but couldn't concentrate. *It does matter.* Quickly and quietly she backtracked to the lounge-room doorway and started again, this time doing it properly. Then she closed the door behind her and returned to the vanity, now seeing her reflection clearly.

She was a mess. Hair damp and tangled, nose running, eyes tiny and red under swollen, puffy lids, her face blotched and shiny. Mattie took a facecloth from the side of the bath and wet it thoroughly before laying it flat against her face. She couldn't tilt her head back because her neck was still too sore, so she stood straight and felt the facecloth leak water that dripped steadily down the front of her windcheater.

After a few minutes she took the facecloth off and threw it into the bath where it slapped against the enamel, sounding very much like the back of her skull when it had hit Max's picture. Mattie stared at the facecloth for a second and then shook her head. What was happening to her? Why was she falling apart like this? She took a deep breath, and another. Then she dried her face off with a towel, dabbed it against her chest, and ran a brush gently through her hair. It didn't make a huge difference, but it did make her look a bit more presentable. Last of all she washed her hands, hard, and mustered up every ounce of her energy in order to walk back out into the kitchen and try to minimise the mushroom cloud that was spreading over her exposure.

Hilda and Hannah stopped talking as soon as she came back into the kitchen, and both turned immediately to look at her. Hannah, now with a cup of tea in front of her, had been playing with the end of her plait, a sure sign she was distressed. As she sat down, Mattie tried to give them a reassuring smile but it folded in on itself and collapsed. She took a deep breath instead.

'It's okay. I'm fine. And I'm sorry about before. All that crying. I don't know what came over me, I really don't.'

'Maybe it all just caught up with you,' said Hilda. 'But I shall leave you to discuss it with your sister. I am sorry if you think I stuck my nose in, Mattie. But I would do it again. And I will stop by either tomorrow or the next day. See how you are.' Hilda bent forward suddenly and gave her a hug, which Mattie returned stiffly. She waited until she heard the front door close before turning back to Hannah.

'Well, I'm sorry anyway. You know I don't usually act like that.'

'Whatever,' said Hannah dismissively. 'Perfectly understandable. I just can't believe that . . . no, doesn't matter. But we need to get organised. Hilda's been telling me some background, about your type of . . . situation. And I think –'

'Before you go any further –' Mattie held up a hand as she interrupted – 'you need to know that this isn't as bad as it looks. Yes, I admit we had a fight, and I admit that Jake hurt me – but I hurt him too. I left him for starters, and he's absolutely terrified that our marriage is falling apart. So he's been drinking more than he should and naturally that hasn't helped matters. But these conclusions that Hilda's been jumping to are simply not –'

'She said you'd say all that,' said Hannah, glancing down at Mattie's neck and visibly flinching.

Mattie put a hand up to her throat self-consciously. She opened her mouth but it dried before she could speak so she closed it again and swallowed painfully.

'She also said that it'll only get worse.' Hannah sat back and looked at Mattie with angry bewilderment. 'So for god's sake, Mattie, don't start making excuses for him. If he's so worried about your marriage, why is he doing *that*?' She pointed at the bruises and then let her hand fall as she shook her head. 'No, there's *no* excuses. That's abuse. And we need to call the police.'

Mattie drew back, horrified. 'The police!'

'Yes, the police. Of course.'

'I don't want to call the police!'

'Mattie, he *assaulted* you. What, are you just going to let him get *away* with it?'

'It's not like that.' Mattie shook her head. Her eyes felt sore and heavy and her head throbbed. She got up and took two painkillers from the medicine cabinet, swallowing them with water. Then she rinsed her hands off and stood against the bench, putting distance between herself and her sister. And her sister's suggestion.

'Look, I understand you probably feel loyal to him. In fact, I understand a lot more now than I have before. Like why you moved out and took this unit. Why you went to Mum's last year. What I *don't* understand is – why didn't you tell me?'

'It's not as simple as that.'

'Didn't you trust me?'

'It's not about trust.' Mattie shook her head. 'This is *my* marriage. You don't tell me the personal stuff that goes on in your marriage, do you? So why would I tell you?'

'But this is different.' Hannah looked upset. 'This goes way beyond privacy. Look at you! He *hit* you. He's a *wife*-beater.'

'Don't be ridiculous,' said Mattie derisively. 'He may have a problem with his temper, but you're acting like he's some sort of criminal.'

'Well, he *is*!'

Mattie folded her arms across her chest. 'We're not going to get anywhere if you keep talking like that. Look, I admit there's a problem here and, yes, that's why I went to Mum's last year and that's also why I'm now living in this unit. But let's not make a huge deal of it.' Mattie paused when she saw her sister's expression. 'Okay, that wasn't put very well. What I meant was that it's under control.'

'Under control!'

'Yes. I'm handling things the best I know how.'

'Mattie, you've got huge bruises around your neck. And goodness knows what other bruises you've got that are hidden. You're not *handling* it, you're just *surviving* it.'

'I know what I'm doing,' replied Mattie stubbornly.

'Does Mum know?'

'No, and you must promise not to tell her!' Mattie jumped forward and grabbed Hannah's arm. 'Promise you won't tell her! Or Stuart either. No-one!'

'Mattie, if you think I can just go home and pretend this didn't happen, you're nuts. In fact, I've got a good mind to go straight over to Jake's office now and –'

'*No!*' Mattie screamed into her sister's face. Wide-eyed, Hannah recoiled and her obvious shock jolted Mattie, who took a step backwards.

They stared at each other for a few long moments and then Hannah's eyes flicked down to the bruises that ringed her sister's neck. Mattie slid into Hilda's vacated seat and put her head in her hands.

'Mattie, look at me.' Hannah gently tried to pry one of her hands loose.

Mattie took her sister's hand and stared down as she covered it. 'I'm sorry. I didn't mean to do that. It's just you don't understand.'

'You always say that. But then you never try to explain either.'

'It's just so hard *to* explain.' Mattie took a deep breath. 'Like, if I say it out loud, it doesn't even make sense to me.'

Hannah looked at her steadily. 'Well, try anyway. Please?'

'First, you have to know I really am doing the best I can. I'm not saying I haven't made mistakes here, but maybe they're mistakes I had to make to get to where I am now.'

'And where are you now?' asked Hannah softly.

Mattie looked down at her hand as it held her sister's. She let her mind flit to the other night, when she had fled the unit and had watched Jake stand in the doorway as he searched the darkness for her. There had been none of the loving, laughing Jake there – just the silhouette of a menace so petrifying that her breath caught in her throat for fear of being heard. From there she moved straight to the visual image of her two children, faces pressed against the glass as they watched their mother scurry away, beaten and humiliated. And then, barely a week later, they heard her screams and then peered down a dark passageway to see her being choked by their father. And had to run back to bed not knowing whether she was alive or dead.

Mattie blinked, and the images faded. What was it that Hannah had asked her? *Where are you now?* She looked back up at her sister's face and flinched from the pity that she saw there, immediately letting go of her sister's hand and folding her arms across her chest protectively. She didn't want pity, not at all, it only made the humiliation worse.

'Mattie?' prompted Hannah softly.

'At the end,' replied Mattie before she could think it through any further, and as she spoke she realised that it was the truth. She pushed all the repercussions and ramifications to one side and stared at Hannah earnestly. 'And that's why you have to let me handle this. If I go to the police or whatever, it'll make things just so much worse. It'll force Jake into a corner, and he'll become vindictive. I *know* him. And think of the kids. It'll be much better to handle this without the police. For me, for them. So I really need you to just keep it to yourself for a while and let me deal with it. Finish it properly. Safely.'

Hannah looked at her sister's intense face thoughtfully. Then she undid the hair-tie at the end of her plait and started running her fingers through the strands, separating them. 'I understand what you're saying, but I just feel like I should at least let him know that *I* know. That you're not alone.'

'It won't help,' said Mattie, shaking her head to add emphasis.

Hannah fell silent for a few moments as she examined the ends of her hair. 'I can't believe that I acted the way I did when you left. Tried to talk you into going back. Told you that you were a fool for throwing it all away.'

'You weren't to know.'

Hannah looked back up at Mattie. 'I just can't understand why you didn't tell me.'

'Would you have told me? If the positions were reversed?' Mattie watched Hannah as she thought about this, and then continued: 'If you really want to help me, you'll just keep it to yourself for a while. Don't tell Stuart, or Mum, or anyone. Give me a while to sort it out.'

Hannah started redoing her plait. 'All right, I'll give you a chance to sort things out yourself. But, mind you, this isn't a long-term promise. I'll tell all and sundry if I think you're putting yourself at risk again. Including Mum, even though I don't think she'd understand. At all. I mean, *I'm* having trouble getting my head around it. Bastard. I can't believe that he . . . bastard.'

Feeling reprieved, Mattie sat back. Her stomach ached with the mix of emotions that churned within. Embarrassment, resentment, guilt, fear, and a deep sense of loss. But surging through this turmoil was also a profound relief that the decision had been taken out of her hands. That there was no turning back now. She ran her finger lightly over a dark-ringed knot in the stained pine table and felt a sudden urge to explain this to Hannah, make her understand that she was not trying to put her off, not burying her head in the sand. She looked up. 'Do you know, if I had a choice I'd far rather you not know, but at the same time, I'm sort of relieved.'

'What? Why?'

'Because I'm embarrassed. *Horribly* embarrassed. I mean, I can't even do something simple like hold a marriage together, and I look like such a fool. Taking him back. Believing all his promises.'

Hannah flicked her plait over her shoulder. 'Don't start blaming yourself – that's ridiculous. But what do you mean about being relieved?'

'Well, this is hard to explain.' Mattie jabbed her fingernail into the darkest part of the knot as she searched for the right words. 'What you have to understand is that it's like Jake is two different people. There's the one *you* know, and that's the one I love, and then there's the other. And he's . . . horrible. So after one of these – episodes, well, when he comes to me absolutely stricken with guilt, and brings flowers, and makes all these promises – I *want* to believe him. Desperately. Because I don't want to lose the other Jake, and I don't want my kids to grow up without a father, and I don't want to be a single mother. So I ignore the part of me that says he's not going to change, that it's all part of a pattern, and I start again. And again.'

'Jesus. How long has this been going on?'

'A while. But let me finish. See, the part of me that's been saying this stuff has been getting louder and louder. That's why I'm here, in this unit. And that part isn't alone anymore. Now that you know, there's one more voice – and it's not a voice I can tell to shut up and go away. I can't even bear to think of the look on your face if I gave in again. The disappointment, the contempt.'

'And you're right.' Hannah shook her head. 'I'm not going to shut up either. If this is part of a pattern, then it's part of Jake. And that won't change without professional help. If then.'

'I know.' Mattie abandoned the knot and stared down into her coffee mug, where the surface of the liquid had congealed into a thin film. She thought of what Liz had said after the Whimsicalities party, about the good and the bad Jake both being the same person. One Jake. Not that this came as a huge surprise, because deep down she'd known it all along – it had always just made it easier to think of him as two people. Mattie pushed the coffee mug handle to the left just a touch so that it was lined up over the swirled knot in the table surface. And she suddenly realised that, for the first time in three days, she felt like she had some energy. Lighter.

'Listen, Mattie, I don't want to make threats, but I will say that if you take him back, after this, then I'll tell Mum, and Stuart, and the police, and anyone else I happen to see.'

Mattie smiled bleakly. 'Fair enough.'

'It's going to be all I can do to go home tonight and keep this to myself.' Hannah held up a hand at Mattie's frown. 'I know, I promised. And I won't say anything. But I'm just saying, well, this is *huge*. And I can't share it, do anything, discuss it with anyone. Can I ask you something?'

Mattie fidgeted apprehensively. 'Depends.'

'Well, how often did it happen?'

'Oh, I don't know.' Mattie shrugged. 'And I don't really want to talk about it.'

'Lord!' Hannah looked at her sister with horror. 'That broken arm you had when Max was a baby! That was *him*, wasn't it?'

'Actually, no.' Mattie laughed, and felt a surge of amazement that she could. 'That really *was* the rollerblading. No, this –' she indicated her neck – 'is the worst it's ever been. But it's always where I can hide it.'

'So he thinks about it then?'

'I suppose.' Mattie put her head on the side and thought about this. 'Yeah, probably.' She looked back up at Hannah and felt an urge to explain. 'See, I've worked out that it's about power. It's like every so often he feels he has to rein me in.'

'Bastard,' said Hannah, almost spitting out the word.

Mattie, although still feeling lighter, was uncomfortable. It was one thing to discuss her plans and the violence as an entity, but it was another talking about Jake like this. It made her feel intensely disloyal, as if she was stabbing him in the back. Betraying him, and their marriage. Even if it was over. She glanced up at the clock and jumped up. 'Hannah, it's twenty past three! I've got to get the kids!'

Hannah stood up too. 'Then you'd better run.'

Mattie left the dirty mugs where they were, picked up the scarf and then grabbed her handbag from the lounge-room on the way out. She waited for Hannah to follow and slammed the front door shut. They walked down to Hannah's car in the driveway.

'I'm going to drop in again, either tomorrow or the next day.' Hannah unlocked the car door. 'Your choice.'

'Make it Friday,' said Mattie. 'And Hannah – thanks.'

'No problem.' Hannah turned suddenly and hugged Mattie. 'I can't believe I never knew this. That I didn't guess or something. And there I was when you moved in here saying *you* need help. That *bastard*.'

'Okay, let's leave it for now.' Mattie patted Hannah's back lightly and then stepped away.

'Until Friday anyway.' Hannah gave her a level look. 'And for heaven's sake, look after yourself. Ring if you need me. For *anything*.'

'I will.' Mattie watched her sister clamber into the Volvo and then waved as she hurried over to her own car. She jumped in and started the engine quickly. As she reversed out, she was buoyed by a rush of what almost felt like exhilaration. Someone once said that 'a problem shared was a problem halved', and while Mattie's problem certainly hadn't halved, its edges had been whittled and it no longer felt as sharp. Suddenly things were looking clearer. Her options had decreased dramatically, but this had clearly revealed the way forward for the first time in years.

After tea, while Max and Courtney watched a cartoon on television, Mattie sat down at the kitchen table with a notebook and pen and prepared to write one of her lists. It was to be a 'to do' list, which covered the preliminary steps she'd need to take now that a decision had been made. And even the thought that a decision *had* been made brought a mix of feelings that both complemented and contradicted each other. On the one hand, she felt deeply bereft – as if about to undergo an amputation of sorts. But on the other hand, she felt an almost buoyant sense of relief, which fed off her underlying bitterness and resentment while overshadowing, for now, a deep-seated fear of what her decision would mean.

Tell Jake. Mattie stared at this number one priority for a few moments and decided that for the time being all she would say was that she needed the weekend to think things through. Then, when he dropped the children off on Sunday, she would tell him it was over. And that meant he had a few days to get used to the idea before any of them saw him again.

Tell Max and Courtney. She'd buy something really nice for tea on Sunday night and break the news to them then. That their parents were splitting up for good. She would have to remember to stress the fact that it wouldn't mean they'd miss out on either parent. The shared care arrangement would stay in place. But it would mean no more arguments, no more fights – no more sneaking out at night to watch their mother being choked against the lounge-room wall.

Visit library. To access the Internet and get some information on marital separation. Legally, what did she need to do? How could she best protect her interests? At present, the vast majority of their possessions were at the house, with Jake. So, if he proved unreasonable about a fair share, what could she do? What about the house itself? Did she need a lawyer?

Go down to the community centre. Definitely. As soon as possible.

Visit bank. They'd emptied their joint account before she left and added the principal to their existing term deposit, signing it up for twelve months. The remaining money had been split between them and put into new, individual accounts. So the term deposit represented a substantial sum of money and, although safely tucked away for another ten months, that period would probably have to be terminated early. Apart from needing some of her half to live, the very fact that it was sitting there in both their names made her feel financially linked to Jake. And even if it meant losing some of the interest, she no longer wanted that. At all.

Mattie rubbed her sore neck gently and then got up to get a drink of water. She stood at the sink, staring out of the window. It had been raining again, and the wooden paling fence was transformed from a dirty, faded concrete colour to a crisp fresh steel-grey. The small grassy patch was puddled with water and the part of the rhododendron she could see had hung its head, dripping. On impulse, Mattie went to the back door and opened it, standing at the top of the steps. The air had that wonderful smell of warm rain, slightly musty but incredibly invigorating. Mattie breathed deeply, letting it permeate her lungs.

The smell and feel of the world after a good downpour had always delighted Mattie. It made her feel that anything was possible, that the rain had washed away the sins of the past and created a blank slate for her to write on. *Tabula rasa* – heady with possibilities. Like Max's little handheld computer console that said, whenever a game was finished: *Game com*-plete, *be*-gin *again*. *Game com*-plete, *be*-gin *again*. With the emphasis on 'be' weighted with expectations.

'Mum, what're you doing?' Max stood inside the laundry, looking at her, puzzled.

'Just smelling the air,' said Mattie, smiling. 'Come here. Smell it for yourself.'

Max came closer and took a noisy sniff. 'Mmm. Nice.'

'Lovely, you mean.'

'Uh-huh. Can I have a couple of biscuits?'

'Okay.' Mattie ushered him inside and closed the laundry door, locking it securely. While Max was helping himself to the biscuit barrel, she saw her 'to do' list lying on the table for anyone to read so she picked it up and shoved it on top of the fridge, out of the way. Then, as she stood back, Mattie noticed an edge of paper poking out from under the fridge and bent down to pick it up. It was one of her cut-outs, the motivational sayings: *The obstacles of your past can become the gateways that lead to new beginnings.* Mattie read it again and then worked a piece of the sticky-tape on the fridge up with her fingernail and pressed down to secure it.

The doorbell rang just as she finished this and she smiled to herself. Hilda, most likely, come to check up on her. Grabbing her scarf from the back of the chair, Mattie wound it around her neck loosely and went to answer the door. Courtney was already there, struggling with the lock. Mattie frowned at her.

'What have I told you about answering the door?'

'You said if I *didn't* know who it is.'

'And you do?'

'Sure! I looked through the curtains. It's Daddy.'

As Courtney made this announcement, she also succeeded in turning the lock and the door swung open. It was indeed Jake, and he didn't look happy. Mattie stared at him apprehensively, her stomach twisting as the relief that had been propelling her dissipated in a moment.

'Daddy!' Courtney hopped forward.

'You bitch.' Jake stepped inside, staring straight at Mattie, and slammed the door shut behind him. It sounded like a cannon, and the unit shook with its force. Courtney stopped, her eyes widening. She flicked a nervous glance at her mother and then back to her father.

'Kids, into the bedroom.' Mattie waved a hand at them urgently as, despite herself, she retreated a step. Out of the corner of her eye she saw Courtney back away and she guessed – hoped – that Max had also left with her.

'You bitch,' repeated Jake, without taking his eyes off her. 'You told your sister, didn't you?'

'My sister?' Mattie stared back, confused.

'Yes, your fucking sister. You remember? The tall nosy one?' Jake leant forward as he spoke and his voice shook with barely suppressed fury. 'The one who rang me tonight and gave me a lecture on criminal fucking behaviour!'

Mattie felt a surge of anger at Hannah for putting her in this position, and then the anger was almost immediately displaced by fear as Jake thrust his face at her. She recoiled, staring at his eyes which, although his face was blurred by close proximity, stood out darkly. Deep pools of cold implacable rancour. She dropped her gaze and noticed, at the corner of his mouth, a bead of spittle that stretched as he spoke and then condensed when he paused. She watched it, hypnotised.

'How *dare* you, you conniving piece of *shit*. How the hell do you think I felt getting lectured to like that? Especially when I thought we were . . . *Christ!* What a fool I've been! All this time I thought you were on my side! When you've been running around backstabbing me every chance you get! How long's this been going on, hey? How long?' Jake's hand whipped out and grabbed Mattie by the upper arm, shaking her. 'Well? Answer me!'

'It hasn't,' whispered Mattie jerkily. 'It hasn't at all.'

'Don't give me that.' Jake stopped shaking her and instead dragged her a few inches towards him and then thrust her away hard and let go, so that she tumbled backwards, landing on her behind by the passage doorway. She stared up at Jake and, as he started towards her, she attempted to crawl away, crab-like.

'Leave me alone,' Mattie said, but it came out so low that she barely heard it herself.

'Do you know what you've done?' Jake shook his head, almost as if he was bewildered. 'Do you have *any idea* what you've done?'

Mattie stared up at him and, through her fear, felt a rush of guilt, and pity. 'I didn't —'

'Oh, yes you did. You've fucked everything up. *Everything.*'

'No I didn't.' Mattie shook her head fiercely as she swallowed the guilt and tried to resurrect the resentment that had helped her justify telling Hannah and Hilda. 'It was *you*, not me. *You* fucked everything up with your insults, and your fists, and your chokings. So leave me alone. It's over.'

Jake frowned at her as if he didn't quite believe what he had just heard. A tic appeared under his left eye, pulsating softly beneath the skin. Then, after several moments of silence, he took a step backwards and pointed at her contemptuously. 'What did you say? It's over? Is *that* what you want? Christ, look at you. On your back as usual. You're *pathetic*. You need help. *Serious* help. So, sure, I'll leave you alone. But I'm taking my kids with me. Max! Courtney!'

'No!' Mattie found her voice and, using the doorway frame as leverage, got to her feet rapidly. She shook her head with determination. 'You can't take them!'

'Watch me, bitch. Now I'm going to go get their schoolbags and if you know what's good for you, you'll just go hide somewhere. You're good at that.'

Mattie stared at him as he strode away through the kitchen to the laundry, where the schoolbags were kept. Her legs were trembling so hard that she thought the floor should have been shaking too. She couldn't believe what was happening, just couldn't believe it. He *couldn't* take the children. It was so *wrong*, so *unjust*, that it seemed impossible.

Within what seemed like seconds, Jake was back. He placed the two schoolbags at the front door. With amazement, Mattie saw that he had also thought to collect the two clean polo tops that had been hanging on the drying rack waiting to be ironed. She dragged her eyes away and was then brought up short by something else. While getting the bags, Jake had pulled his windcheater sleeves up to his elbows, revealing his forearms, which were covered with long, livid scratches all the way down to the back of his hands. The scratches had clearly been treated with ointment at some stage because each was bedded among smudges of faded red, which made them seem even angrier.

It looked like he had been caught in barbed wire, or had to force his way through some type of prickly bush, although Mattie knew neither of those was the truth. She blinked, to break her gaze, and then looked up at Jake's face. He was waiting patiently, watching her stare at his arms and take in the damage. And even though he was displaying no emotion, Mattie thought she saw his eyes smirk, and suddenly she recalled Hilda, and her cat and mouse analogy. It was all deliberate. He was playing with her.

The instant her face set, Jake took a step forward. 'Max! Courtney! Get out here!'

'No! *No!*' Mattie instinctively jumped into the centre of the doorway to stop him getting past. 'It's *my* day! Mine!'

'Who gives a fuck?' asked Jake, almost politely.

'Get out,' she hissed, her voice tripping over her emotions. 'Get out of *my* house.'

Jake paused for a second, looking at her with astonishment. Then he laughed again. '*Your* house? That *I* paid for, you mean. Now move it, you fucking backstabber. Move it or I won't be responsible for what happens.'

Mattie stood her ground, her growing rage not quite masking her fear. She shook her head. 'No. You're not taking them.'

'Have it that way then.' Jake reached out in an instant and grabbed her by the hair, dragging her towards him quickly and up, off the ground. Her hands automatically shot up to rip at his, trying to loosen the hold, but the pain was unbelievably excruciating. It actually felt as if she were about to have her entire scalp torn off. As her eyes teared up, blurring her vision, Mattie whimpered even while she kicked and clawed at him with every bit of strength she could muster. *Go for the balls, that worked last time. Or go for the arms, they're already damaged.* Then the doorbell rang.

Jake let her go, quickly, and she fell against the wall with both hands on her head. He stared at her narrowly. 'Don't answer that.'

'I will,' said Mattie in a croak, although she didn't move. Couldn't move.

'Police!' came a deep, masculine voice from outside the door. 'Open up!'

Mattie's mouth gaped as she stared back at Jake and was suddenly, and strangely, pleased to see that he looked equally shocked. It gave them something in common. He took a step towards the door and then stopped.

'Police!'

Jake started moving again, walking purposefully over to the door and opening it wide. 'What can we do for you?'

'We've had a report that there was a disturbance here, sir.'

Mattie leant against the wall and straightened her scarf automatically as she peered past Jake and saw two police officers, a male and a female, at the door. They were both exactly the same height but the male was older, and more heavy-set. The female had wispy blonde hair pulled back severely under her hat. Both exuded confidence, and authority, and purpose. And Mattie's heart flipped with intense relief. And humiliation.

'I can't imagine why,' replied Jake, with his charming-Jake voice.

'You haven't been having an argument with your wife then?'

'No, not at all. That is, we were discussing some things, but it *wasn't* an argument.'

'Ma'am?' The policeman leant to the side so that he could see Mattie clearly. 'Can you verify that?'

Mattie came forward, thinking quickly even though her head was throbbing so hard it felt like it might explode. She made her face smile, just slightly, from one police officer to the other. 'That's right, only a discussion. And my husband was just leaving anyway.'

'I see.' The policeman glanced at Jake's arms and then looked at him expectantly.

'That's right,' said Jake tightly.

'Well, in that case, we'll walk you out to your car. Thanks for your time, ma'am.'

The policeman stepped back so that Jake could leave the unit, and then walked with him down the path. The policewoman, though, hung back and looked at Mattie.

'I have some pamphlets on —'

'Oh no.' Mattie smiled tightly. 'It's nothing like that. And I'm sure it'll be fine.'

'Okay.' The policewoman shrugged slightly, gazing at Mattie expressionlessly. 'Your choice. If you have any more problems, just call.'

Mattie nodded, and watched her join her colleague by the police car. They spoke to Jake there for a few moments and waited while he climbed into his Commodore and drove away. Then they left too. Mattie watched their tail-lights disappear over the rise and then closed the door, leaning against it while she tried to come to grips with what had just happened. And the price she might have to pay for it.

Max appeared in the passage doorway, staring at her wide-eyed. 'Was that the *police?*'

'Did they take Daddy away?' Courtney was crying, and plucking at the hem of her pyjama top in agitation. 'Will we ever see him again?'

'Oh god.' Mattie felt ill, and weak. She sat down where she was, on the carpet, and held out her arms wordlessly. Both children ran over, Courtney folding herself neatly onto her mother's lap and Max kneeling by her side. He reached out a hand and tentatively ran it down her arm, as if he were trying to console her.

'Did they put handcuffs on him?' asked Courtney, her face still crumpled.

'No, of course not.' Mattie started to shake her head but her headache intensified so she stopped. 'No, someone rang them to say there had been yelling here, so they just stopped by to make sure everything was okay.'

'Aren't you allowed to yell?' asked Courtney, her brown eyes huge.

'You're allowed to yell, but sometimes when people yell, they also get nasty, so the police just check to make sure everyone's okay.'

'Then why'd Dad leave?' Max shifted himself to get more comfortable.

'Because I asked him to.'

'Oh.'

'And there's something else.' Mattie took a deep breath, reluctant to continue but knowing that she had to. Things had changed. 'Did you hear Dad call you?'

'Yes.' Courtney flashed a look at her brother. 'Max said to hide, so we did. In the wardrobe.'

'And we heard you tell him he couldn't have us,' said Max, admiration creeping into his voice.

'He was very upset, otherwise I'm sure he wouldn't have done that. The last thing either Dad or I want is for you two to be caught in between everything. But what I need to tell you is the reason he was upset.'

'Why?' Courtney twisted around, curiosity overtaking concern.

'Because he's a bully,' said Max quietly.

'No, well, that's something different. The reason he was upset was that Hilda from next door heard us on Sunday night, and she saw the –' Mattie hesitated and then ploughed ahead – 'the bruises on my neck today. And she told Auntie Hannah, and Auntie Hannah rang Dad and told him off. So Dad is upset because other people know that he . . . well, that he didn't behave very well.'

'Did Auntie Hannah call the police too?' asked Max, his eyes fixed on her.

'No, that must have been someone from around here who heard us.'

'Oh.' Max fell silent for a moment. 'Are you going to Dad's tomorrow night?'

'No. Definitely not.'

'I don't want to either. Do I have to?'

'I'm afraid so.' Mattie reached out and ran her fingers through his thick, messy hair. 'You have to realise that Dad misses you heaps when you're with me. Just like I do when you're over there. We *both* want you. So it wouldn't be fair for you to stay the whole time with me, or with him.'

'What about what's fair for me?' asked Max, frowning.

'Look, honey, I know it's hard. The thing is, we're trying to do the best we can by everybody. And children need their father as well as their mother. That way you get balance. And without me there, there won't be any fighting. That'll be good, won't it?'

'Yeah.' said Courtney, slipping the scarf off her mother's neck and draping it around her own. 'I'm *sick* of the fighting.'

'Me too.' Mattie rolled her eyes.

'Mummy, is your hair falling out?' Courtney held up several strands of dark brown hair. 'It was on your shoulders.'

'And there's some on your back too.' Max peered behind her.

'Must be stress,' said Mattie lightly. 'And now it's bedtime.'

'What about hot chocolate?' Courtney wrapped her arms around her mother and peered up at her winsomely.

'With ice-cream!' added Max.

'Hot chocolate?' Mattie laughed, surprising herself. 'It's bedtime, you monsters!'

'But we're upset.' Courtney kissed her on the cheek. 'And you *always* make us hot chocolate when we're upset.'

Mattie lifted Courtney off her and stood up, groaning theatrically with the effort. Then she narrowed her eyes at the two children. 'You two are a pair of opportunists. But all right, I'll make you a hot chocolate. Then bed!'

'Okay,' said Courtney agreeably as her brother nodded.

Mattie grinned at them. Then she went through into the kitchen and put the kettle on. While she waited for it to boil, she ran her fingers gently through her hair and freed the loose strands, putting them in the rubbish bin. At this rate, she thought grimly, she'd have to get a wig soon. Next she gingerly checked her scalp for any tears in the flesh itself.

The pain had been so intense, and the throbbing was still so severe, that she felt sure something must be there to show for it. But she could find no abrasions and, when she brought her hand down, it was free of blood. So there was no visible damage.

Mattie took a couple of painkillers and then leant against the kitchen cupboards, trying to get her head around what had just happened. But she couldn't. It wasn't so much the violence, although the cycle itself seemed to have escalated frighteningly, but the fact that Jake had been going to take the children with him. By force if necessary. And if it hadn't been for the police, it would have happened.

She knew that it was naive of her to be shocked by this, but she was. Shocked, and deeply angry. But she also knew this didn't stem from surprise at his actions but because those actions had so clearly exposed her vulnerability. *That* was terrifying. Infuriating. And she wasn't at all sure she had done the right thing by not involving the police. It had been a self-protective instinct but one that left her with some unease.

Mattie looked out through the window at the rapidly darkening backyard. It was hard to believe that not long ago she'd stood here look-ing at the rain-washed shrubbery and thinking everything could be rinsed away. A clean slate. Game com-*plete,* be-*gin again*. But instead of the game being over, it seemed all that had happened was that the rules had changed. And now they were being played out on a totally new level.

For a man, Jake had a strong nurturing streak. Once, the day after a particularly nasty fight, he had even made up a bed on the couch for Mattie. Covered her with blankets, brought her cups of tea, kept the children amused. In the evening, he sat stroking her hair and, at one stage, she glanced up quickly and caught him staring at her with the most amazingly gentle, almost wistful expression.

She liked to think that this expression was born of regret, of self-loathing, for what he had put her through. But she couldn't ask him, because the subject was taboo. He would be willing to do almost anything for her during the conciliatory period except talk about what happened. So she had to use her imagination to fill the gaps, and her imagination was born of a hundred fairytales, and romance books, and women's magazines. It told her that true love was all-conquering and there was always an answer, if only she did not give up. On him. On them.

At other times, when he was not quite so cherishing or the pain was really severe, she allowed resentment to guide her thoughts. Then she would suspect that her imagination was doing her more harm than good, and that she was projecting positive emotions onto Jake that he did not really possess. In her weaker moments, when she started thinking this way, she would even start to imagine that Jake enjoyed it all. The violence because it made him feel powerful, and the nurturing because it made him feel like her saviour. And it was only his own inherent narcissism that sheltered him from the irony that what she really needed to be saved from, to be protected from, was Jake himself.

FOURTEEN

The next four days were the slowest that Mattie had ever experienced in her life. They dragged more than they had when, as a child, something special was going to happen, and the days and hours and minutes leading up to it tiptoed past with a sluggishness that drove her to a hyperactive frustration. But now it wasn't so much that she was looking forward to something, apart from the return of Max and Courtney, but that she was consumed with concern for them, and what was happening at the house.

Because of this concern, Mattie had spent a good part of Thursday composing a message to leave on Jake's answering machine, so that he would get it when he returned from work that day. Then, in a voice that she tried to keep as expressionless as possible, she read into the phone from her notes: 'Hi, Jake, this is Mattie. First, I would like to tell you that I *didn't* tell Hannah. My next-door neighbour did, after she heard us on Sunday night. But the real reason for my call is that I am very concerned that the children are getting dragged into this. Any problems we have are between you and me, not them. So surely we can both be adults and discuss our situation rationally, and keep them out of it. If we can at least agree on one thing, let's make it that their welfare comes first. Thank you.'

After she hung up, it suddenly occurred to Mattie that Jake might think *she* was collecting the kids today and taking them to his place. After all they had never formally changed plans. This possibility worried at her all afternoon, until she finally gave in and rang Jake on his mobile. The conversation was short and terse and finished with Jake hanging up on her in the middle of her garbled explanation. Then, after she'd calmed down somewhat, she realised that he would probably think she'd left the answering machine message *after* this last phone-call, and that she was having a deliberate dig at his attitude. This made her feel ill again, and she spent an hour walking through the unit with her fists clenched, trying to think of ways to improve matters. But there were none.

To make herself feel better, she tried to blame Hannah – if she hadn't taken it upon herself to call Jake, none of this would have happened. But deep down she knew that Hannah's call had not *caused* the inferno, all it had done was fuel the flames. Certainly Hannah was guilty of thinking she knew best, but her actions had arisen from concern and from an impotency that Mattie understood only too well. So although she didn't call Hannah, she gradually ceased to see her sister's actions as a betrayal and instead began to use them to give her a sense of solidarity. But although this approach lessened her feeling of isolation, it did not diminish the horribly powerless feeling she carried with her as she waited till Sunday, to see what would happen next, with the days stretching out before her like a prison sentence.

So she began following through on her 'to do' list as much as a defence against this frustration as a genuine desire to get the ball rolling. She started with the Internet, and spent a large part of Friday ensconced in a small cubicle at the local library facing a computer screen. She discovered that custody and access were no longer called that, but were now known as residence and contact. She also found out that they were laid out in what were called 'parenting orders', which separating couples could write up themselves and then have formalised by the courts. Mattie hoped fervently that it wouldn't come to that; instead, after he had accepted the fact that it was over, Jake would agree to continue following the shared care arrangement they had already established.

She visited a couple of sites where separated couples aired their issues and problems that arose as time went by. There were some triumphant stories, but the vast majority were terribly sad considering these had

once been committed families that were now imploding. Others were
nothing short of tragic: people spoke of vendettas carried out against
them, of petty revenge, and of a life led amidst bitterness and spite. By
using keywords related to separation and child contact, Mattie ended
up in a few men's group sites, where the level of nastiness rose so much
that she exited quickly and remained in the mainstream. That was
depressing enough.

Last of all she explored property splits and this area, too, seemed
to be a minefield of recriminations. Finally, she left the personal
accounts behind and just tried to get the facts. And they didn't bode
too well. Property settlement, it appeared, could drag on for a long
time. The push was for both parties to agree without going to court,
which seemed reasonable, but Mattie was doubtful about her ability
to negotiate with Jake from a position of strength. However, what concerned her most was the minor property – furniture, personal effects
and suchlike. While the courts could easily track the sale of a house,
for instance, it would be more difficult to trace the other items. And
she had left an entire house full of them behind. Would she ever see
her share?

By the time Mattie left the library, her neck and back aching from
sitting so long, it was too late to go to the bank and get some information on withdrawing the term deposit early. So she walked home slowly,
taking the time to think about what she had discovered and what her
next steps should be. She was just beginning a mental list of household
effects when she turned into her road and saw Hannah's car parked outside the unit. Mattie stepped up her pace and turned into the driveway
just as Hannah was coming away from the front door, looking rather
concerned. Her face cleared when she saw her sister.

'*There* you are. I saw your car in the driveway and couldn't work out
what'd happened to you!'

'Just gone for a walk.' Mattie looked at her sister curiously. 'Hey, you
were really worried, weren't you?'

'Of course I was!' said Hannah crossly as she followed Mattie onto
the porch.

Mattie unlocked the door and opened it for Hannah to go through first. 'He's not going to do away with me and bury my body in the linen closet, you know.'

'Don't bet on it,' replied Hannah grimly, walking straight into the kitchen and sitting down in the same seat she'd occupied on Wednesday.

'Cup of tea?'

'No, I haven't got time. But a glass of water would be nice.'

Mattie filled a glass from the water jug in the fridge. She passed it to Hannah before sitting down and watching her sister with interest. She couldn't remember Hannah paying so much attention to her since, as a teenager, she was paid to babysit. It was an odd feeling to be looked after again, at her age, but not entirely unpleasant. She suspected Hannah had even dressed down today, just in case Mattie was wearing her old grey tracksuit again. But now the roles were reversed. Mattie was looking quite smart, in low-heeled sandals, black pinstripe pants and a fitted white shirt, while Hannah was wearing runners, black tracksuit pants and a sleeveless lemon windcheater vest with a hood. Her long hair was caught up in a ponytail.

'Have I smeared my mascara or something?' asked Hannah, frowning slightly at the attention.

'No,' Mattie smiled.

'So where have you been?' asked Hannah suspiciously.

'Researching actually. They say knowledge is power, so I'm going to get powerful.'

'What sort of research?'

'Divorce, child residence, property. All that sort of stuff.'

'So you're going through with it?'

'Yes.'

'Thank god!' Hannah sat back in her chair and stared at her sister with relief. 'You don't know how worried I've been. See, I did my own bit of research and discovered most women in your situation go back and back and back. And that they even tend to cut off those who know about what's happening. Mainly because of what you said – that it's embarrassing. Shameful.'

'Yeah, but don't forget I've already been back and back and back.'

'You mean more than just that time you stayed at Mum's?'

Mattie nodded grimly. 'I like to think that this time I'd have made it permanent even if you hadn't found out, but I can't swear to it. Sooner or later, though, I think I would have.'

'So I made a difference?'

'Absolutely.' Mattie smiled at her sister. 'You were like the straw that broke the camel's back. Hilda next door made a difference, but not a major one. You're family. And I suppose that was just enough to tip me totally. You know what it was? Not your threats or anything like that. It was seeing the look on your face when you found out.'

'I was gobsmacked.'

'Yes. And, well, when you live with it you sort of normalise it so when you see someone with a *real* response – horror, shock and all that – it's like seeing it clearly.'

'Seeing it through someone else's eyes.'

'That's right.'

'I didn't tell Stuart.' Hannah rolled her eyes. 'Although, boy, was it tempting. And I still think we should.'

'You promised.' Mattie looked at her evenly. 'Besides, you already did enough damage ringing Jake. I *asked* you not to. So why'd you do that?'

'Did I do damage?' Hannah looked upset. 'Did I really? But I just had to do *something*. And he had it coming!'

'He might have had it coming but I didn't.' Mattie grimaced and swallowed a surge of annoyance that Hannah just didn't understand. 'All it meant was that he marched straight around here and did a lot of yelling and screaming.'

Hannah's eyes widened. 'Did he hurt you?'

'Oh no.' Mattie shook her head. Even though it was tempting to tell Hannah about the consequences of her phone-call and emphasise her ignorance, Mattie had already decided that would be counterproductive. She was dealing with it and there was a fair chance that things would quickly settle anyway. 'Nothing like that. It's just I wanted to have a discussion with him and there'll be no chance of that for a few days now. Till he calms down.'

'Sorry.'

'That's okay.' Mattie grinned even as her stomach clenched. 'I gather you really got stuck into him?'

'Oh, I gave him both barrels.' Hannah grinned back. 'I called him a bully, a thug, asked him if he enjoyed torturing small animals as well. Told him what he'd done was criminal, and if he ever tried it again he'd be going to jail.'

Mattie continued to smile, but one small scared part of her was sneering at Hannah and snidely commenting on the fact that her threat had deterred him for precisely fifteen minutes. As long as it had taken for him to drive over. She got up to give her hands a wash.

Hannah took a deep breath. 'To be honest, I think the real reason I rang him was to alleviate some of my own guilt.'

'*Your* guilt?'

'Yes.' Hannah flicked her plait forward and started to separate the strands at the end. 'See, I was thinking last night about how I reacted when I found out you'd left him. How I gave you a hard time at Mum's and all.'

'Yes?' prompted Mattie, interested.

'And I think a part of me *wanted* it to be your fault. Which is why I was so eager to believe it was. And don't ask me why –' Hannah finally looked at her sister and grimaced – 'because I'm no Freud. It's probably a sister thing.'

'You told me I needed help.' Mattie smiled to take the accusing edge off her words, but the smile did not quite reach her eyes.

'Don't remind me. Although . . .' Hannah grinned back. 'I probably did have a point. Just not in the way I meant. Which reminds me, has Liz rung?'

'No, why?'

'Just thinking about your friends.' Hannah shrugged. 'So what's the game-plan?'

Mattie's smile vanished and she wiped her hands down her pants. 'Well, first I need to talk to him. Reiterate that it's over, work out some property details, money. Stuff like that.'

'What about the kids? Are you going to stick with this shared care arrangement?'

'For now.'

Hannah finished her water and got up, putting the empty glass by the sink. She looked out the window. 'Do you think you'll end up with enough money to be able to move out of this dump?'

'Excuse me!' Mattie pretended to take offence. 'This dump is my *home!*'

'I didn't mean it like that,' Hannah turned around and leant against the sink. 'In fact, I think you've done wonders with the place while you've been here. But you have to admit it's a bit cramped. And that carpet . . .'

'True.'

'So if you're able to buy after it's all sorted, then that'll set you up nicely. Hey, have you still got that money Mum gave us after she sold the house?'

'Yes.' Mattie nodded. 'It's in a term deposit with the rest of our savings. So when we go halves, I should have enough to put a good-sized deposit down anyway, and some to back me up till I get a job. Probably next year when everything's been sorted.'

'Then there's the sale of the house too.'

'Yes, but I'm not counting on that for a while. I think Jake'll probably try to keep it and pay me out. And that'll take some time.'

Hannah looked thoughtful and then pointed at her. 'Why don't *you* keep it? Then you don't have to worry about house-hunting or anything. And the kids are already settled there.'

'No,' Mattie answered without hesitation. 'I want to start again. Not there.'

Hannah nodded slowly. 'Okay, I understand.'

Mattie's snide little voice popped up again to say: *Oh no you don't, you've got* no *idea*. But she smiled even more to hide the fact that she was even listening to it. Hannah gave her a strange look and then plucked her handbag off the floor.

'I'm really glad you've been thinking about all this stuff. I know it sounds mercenary, but you've got two kids to consider. And your future.'

'I know.' Mattie got up from her chair and pushed it in under the table.

'Good.' Hannah nodded approvingly. 'And now I'd better get moving. I just wanted to see how things were going.'

'Check up on me, you mean.'

'Well – yes.' Hannah leant forward as if she was going to kiss Mattie, but then drew back again and smiled, slightly embarrassed. 'But only in the nicest possible way.'

Mattie followed Hannah through to the front door. She opened it and walked out onto the porch, staring at the blue cloud-studded sky.

'Your bruises are just about gone anyway,' said Hannah, looking at Mattie's neck.

'Yes. Doesn't take long.' Mattie turned to her sister. 'Look, thanks for dropping by. I really appreciate it.'

'No problem. Now we're going away this weekend but if you need me, just ring on my mobile. And I'll drop in on Monday. See how you're going.'

'Okay.' Mattie smiled at her concern. Then Hilda rounded the corner at the end of the unit and headed towards them. She too was very casually dressed, back in the slacks and grey-checked windcheater jacket that she had been wearing the first day Mattie had met her.

'Hello, Hannah. Lovely to see you here.'

'I was just leaving.'

'And I was just visiting.' Hilda smiled genially at both of them. 'Got time for a coffee, Mattie?'

Mattie nodded, amused. 'This is like the changing of the guards, isn't it?'

Both Hannah and Hilda laughed, and then Hannah went over to her car, unlocking the driver-side door and climbing in. The electric window on the passenger seat wound down and Hannah leant over. 'Look after yourself. And ring if you need me!'

'I will.' Mattie waved, and watched as Hannah reversed out of the driveway. After her sister had driven off down the road, Mattie turned and followed Hilda into the unit. One down, one to go. But at least it passed the time.

*

Saturday limped past like an old man with a walking frame, but Sunday finally arrived and Mattie woke with a buoyancy born of the knowledge that today her children were being returned. Today she would be able to shake off that feeling of vague, impotent anxiety that she felt whenever they were not with her, and she *knew* they were safe and secure.

Motivated by her anticipation, after breakfast Mattie cleaned the unit from top to bottom, spending much of her time in the children's bedroom where she tidied, changed sheets and rearranged the bookshelves. In the lounge-room she straightened the framed photographs, with Max's now minus the glass, and vacuumed. It was only when she moved the couch out from the wall and saw the glass stem from the wineglass that she remembered throwing it behind there the previous Sunday night. She smiled grimly when she recalled how she'd thought she might be protecting herself, in case Jake got any ideas of using it as a weapon. But he didn't need weapons, not when he had his hands, and his feet.

It was mid-afternoon by the time she finished, and getting close to the earliest she could expect the children home. So Mattie took the library book on budgeting and curled up on the couch to read until they arrived. At teatime, she tossed a salad together and left it in a bowl on the bench. Then she defrosted a couple of chicken fillets and marinated them in honey, mustard and wine. She herself wasn't hungry although she was sure the children would be when they arrived. She returned to the lounge-room but left the budgeting book lying on the floor and turned on the television instead. And every time she heard a car approach, she glanced quickly towards the window and waited, tensely, to see if it pulled into the driveway. None did.

As the evening crept by, Mattie started reminding herself about how late they had been dropped off the week before. And she recognised this was probably even deliberate, to string her out as long as possible and disrupt her life. Finally, she covered the salad and the marinating chicken and put them both in the fridge. Then she made herself a bowl of cereal and ate it standing up by the window, counting cars.

At nine o'clock, headlights lit the room as a car pulled into the driveway and Mattie breathed a huge sigh of relief, finally admitting to herself that she'd been starting to suspect they weren't coming back at all. But instead of stopping, the car continued on towards one of the rear units where the engine was switched off and, in the ensuing silence, Mattie was left with her now acknowledged fear. She sat down on the couch armrest and stared blankly at the floor, feeling sick. Where were they?

Fifteen minutes later, she stood up and walked stiffly into the kitchen to dial Jake's home number. It answered on the third ring.

'Hello?'

'Jake. This is Mattie.'

'Yes?'

'Where are the kids?'

'In bed.'

Mattie was struck dumb. Even though this was the exact suspicion she had been wrestling with, confirmation still came as a shock. She stared at the wall near the phone blankly, trying to compute and move on from what he'd said. They were in bed. There.

'Was that it?'

'No, hang on,' Mattie said in a high-pitched rush. '*Why* are they in bed? They're supposed to be here! You were dropping them off!'

'I changed my mind,' replied Jake smoothly, politely. 'Now, if that's it?'

'No!' cried Mattie. But he had hung up.

She cradled the phone in her hand and tried to think. But it was hard, very hard. Her face seemed to have frozen, and something hurt dully at the back of her eyes. As well as that her stomach was surging so that her throat actually felt obstructed, and for the first time in days started to hurt again. *Think*, her mind said urgently, *you must think. Quickly*. But it was like the message lines had been severed, and her body was partially paralysed. It could move and it could breathe, but it couldn't react.

Mattie fumbled behind her back and pulled out a chair, letting herself fold backwards until she was sitting down. She was still holding the phone and the cord stretched from the wall, the spirals extended. Then, suddenly, anger started to seep in and this seemed to act as a stimulant. *How dare he! How* dare *he!* Mattie jumped up again, slapped the phone back into its cradle and then jerked it out once more. Then, fired by adrenalin, she dialled the same number.

'Hello?'

'I'm coming around to get them. Now.'

'You're going to wake two children up from their sleep just to make yourself happy?' Jake chuckled, almost cheerfully. 'This is a new low, even for you.'

'I'm still doing it.'

'I wouldn't bother, sweetheart, because remember our friendly police? I'll ring them the moment you pull into the driveway.'

'You wouldn't.'

'Try me. And if you're thinking you'd still have time to get in before they came, think again, because you don't have any keys. Now, have a lovely night, you hear?'

And then Mattie was listening to the engaged signal again. She wrenched the phone away from her ear and threw it at the wall, where it bounced off the plaster, leaving a crescent-shaped dint, and then swung to-and-fro on its stretched lead, just above the floor. But Mattie had already left the room, running into the lounge-room to grab her hand-bag. She unzipped it and then scrabbled inside it, swearing futilely as she searched until she finally just upended all the contents onto the couch. Her purse, some spare coins, a tiny vial of perfume, a packet of mints, a few tissues, and finally her key-ring with the rectangular gold tag that read *Matilda* in raised silver lettering. Mattie snatched it up and started fumbling through the different keys. The unit front door key, back door key, her car keys – no house keys. Both the copper front door key and the elongated silver back door key were gone. And so was the small security door key. All gone.

Mattie dropped the keys on the carpet and sat down on the couch, staring blankly ahead. He had taken her keys. Not that she cared about them per se – in fact she didn't much care if she never had access to their house again – but she *did* care about the children and she *did* care about what he'd done. Deeply. She also cared about the fact that he was probably sitting there, right now, having a smug, self-satisfied laugh at her expense. *Christ, she's a fool. Too easy. Sucker.* And it just wasn't bloody fair. She felt robbed, cheated, violated. Bereft. And now she had to spend the evening alone, worrying about them until she saw them tomorrow. Conjuring up questions that couldn't be answered. Were they upset? What had he told them? Had he washed their uniforms? Made their lunches?

And why had it never occurred to her that he might try something like this? In retrospect, it was so very like him. Checkmate with a twist. The trouble was that she kept allowing her fervent desire for a happy resolution to colour her thinking. She had to stop that, right now, because it wasn't doing her any favours. She had to think like him and play like him, otherwise it wasn't just the house or the property or even the marriage on the line, but the children. Because he was going to go for what would hurt her most and he was going to go for it with a vengeance. She had to keep up, or give up. Simple as that.

Strangely, when Max was a baby, Jake never used him as a pawn against Mattie during an argument. Maybe that was because the arguments were still fairly rare then, or maybe the potency of such a weapon simply never occurred to him. But all that changed when Courtney came along. During her first year, Jake discovered and then steadily improved on the perfect punishment. Often, after a few drinks, he would draw a line halfway down the passage and demand Mattie stay on one side, where she had free run of the dining room, the family room and the sliding door through to the backyard if she needed to go to the toilet. The rest of the house was his. And the baby was out of bounds.

On the occasions that he did this, he would justify his behaviour by asserting that she monopolised Courtney, spending all day with her and often all night. That she was deliberately robbing him of a chance to bond so he had no choice but to force the issue. And this, now, was his turn.

So he would parade through the house with the baby in his arms, and lecture her about her mother's faults. And Mattie would sit against a wall, out of sight, and have to bide her time. Wait until he got bored or ran out of steam and went to bed. And then wait until she was absolutely, one hundred percent sure he was asleep before she crossed the line as quietly as possible and went to satisfy herself that the baby was all right. Only then could she curl up on the family room couch and go to sleep herself. Once she misjudged her timing and he was still awake, patting the baby's nappy-thick bottom rhythmically to send her off to sleep. She never did that again.

FIFTEEN

Monday morning at 9 am sharp, Mattie was at the children's school nervously waiting to start reading groups in Courtney's classroom. She pretended to be engrossed in the brightly painted pictures stuck up on the walls, all the while glancing at the door anxiously awaiting Courtney's arrival. And, as the school bell pealed and echoed through the classroom, Mattie had a horrible feeling that the child wasn't even going to arrive, that Jake wasn't going to send them to school. But finally her daughter walked through the doorway, the last one to come in. And if Mattie had been expecting, even half hoping, to see a dishevelled, miserable-looking child, she was disappointed. Because Courtney was freshly washed and ironed, and bounced in with her hair neatly pulled back in two pigtails and a huge smile on her face. When she saw her mother, the smile stretched even further and she dropped her bag and flung herself at her.

The other mothers, standing around and idly chatting, looked at them with interest, but Mattie didn't care. She wrapped her arms around Courtney and lifted her off the ground, then put her back down and cupped the girl's face in her hands, looking at her closely. 'Are you okay? Everything all right?'

'Sure!' replied Courtney brightly. 'Why not?'

'Okay, children!' Miss Thomson clapped her hands briskly and the tardy children, including Courtney, hung their bags up quickly and sat down cross-legged before the teacher. While she called the roll, Mattie stood at the back of the room with the other mothers, waiting to start the reading.

'You and Courtney look like you haven't seen each other for months,' commented Marie, in a low voice.

'She spent the weekend with her father.' Mattie kept her voice light and noncommittal.

'Oh.' Marie exchanged glances with Helen and Jo and the other woman there, a slim redhead named Stacey. Mattie pretended not to notice.

'I've got your money for you,' whispered Helen, leaning forward so that she could see Mattie. 'From the party the other Sunday.'

'God!' Mattie looked at her with surprise. 'I'd forgotten all about that!'

Helen grinned. 'Does that mean you don't want it?'

'No, bad luck.' Mattie shook her head. 'Can't believe I forgot about it. I must check when the delivery's due.'

'Next week I think,' said Jo, pulling her purse out of her bag and removing a few folded notes. 'Here's mine anyway.'

'Nice to know you've got such a busy life that you forget about things like this,' said Marie curiously. 'Wish mine was.'

'So, children!' Miss Thomson clapped her hands again, a habit that Mattie found particularly irritating. 'If you'd like to break into groups around one of our lovely mothers over there, you can start your reading time.'

The children who had mothers in attendance made a beeline for them, dragging friends along behind. Courtney fronted up with three other little girls, all blonde, all pigtailed, and all blue-eyed. Courtney thrust a large picture book at her mother.

'This is about Duncan the railway cat,' she announced, quite obviously in charge. 'It's very good. We'll start with that.'

Mattie took the book and sat down on the edge of one of the low tables, Courtney leaning against her and the other little girls keeping a little more distance. She opened the book, took a deep breath and began to read. This once-a-week foray into the classroom for reading groups was by no means Mattie's favourite time of the week, but

Courtney loved it, just as Max had done before her. And on that particular Monday it was even more important, a way of reassuring herself
that they were all right. So, after the reading hour was finished and
she'd kissed Courtney goodbye, Mattie went over to Max's classroom at
the other end of the school and knocked softly on the door. His teacher,
a middle-aged woman called Mrs Hope, opened the door and smiled
at Mattie.

'Mrs Hampton. Were you after Max?'

'Yes. I just wanted to have a quick word if that's okay.'

'Sure, but first –' Mrs Hope glanced at the class, all busily writing in
exercise books, and slipped outside the door – 'I wondered if you'd been
contacted? By a Jan MacFarlane, the district counsellor?'

'Yes, we spoke,' said Mattie shortly.

'Oh. Good. Um, I'll just get Max, shall I?' The teacher glanced at
Mattie again, but when nothing else was forthcoming, she slipped back
inside and called Max's name.

Mattie stared at the rows of pegs and schoolbags, and the wooden
shelves of reading materials that were jammed down the corridor. Next
to her was the lost property cupboard, overflowing with school jumpers and jackets and even, strangely, one school dress. Max came out
of the classroom and looked at her, then at his feet. Mattie, filled with
pleasure at the sight of him, bobbed down and hugged him. But it only
took her a second to realise that he wasn't hugging her back.

Mattie pulled away. 'Max? What's the matter?'

'Nothing.'

'Tell me.'

He glanced at her again, briefly, and then stared down at his shoes.
'Where did you go yesterday?'

'What do you mean, where did I go?'

'Dad said you were too busy to have us.'

'*What?*' Mattie rocked back on her haunches and then stood up, still
staring down at Max. '*What* did he say?'

'He said you were too busy to have us.'

'Oh, Max.' Mattie put a hand on Max's shoulder and pulled him
towards her. A teacher walked past up the corridor towards the office,

a small boy trudging behind her. Their footsteps thudded loudly in the heavy silence. Mattie waited till they'd passed before bobbing down again. 'I was *not* too busy for you. I am *never* too busy for you. Are you listening?'

'Yes.' Max stared at her, finally.

'In fact I was waiting for you all day, and all night. And I rang Dad twice to find out where you were. He said you were staying with him and that you were already asleep.'

'I heard the phone,' whispered Max. 'I hoped it was you saying you weren't busy after all. That you were coming instead. So I stayed awake for ages.'

'Oh my god.' Mattie swallowed, pushing away the image of her eight-year-old son lying in bed, waiting and waiting for her.

'But you didn't come.'

'No, Dad said you were already asleep. Max, I don't know what's going on. I think Dad's angry because I moved out, and he's trying to make me angry too.'

'Are you?'

'At the moment, yes. Very angry.'

'Me too.' Max plucked idly at the collar of her shirt. 'Are we going with you today? After school?'

'I will be here at three-thirty exactly. Don't worry about that.'

'Good.'

'I'd better let you get to class.' Mattie glanced towards the doorway and then back at Max. He was still playing with her collar. She rocked forward on her toes and hugged him, fiercely, and this time he hugged her back. After a moment, he broke the embrace and stepped away, smiling at her and then disappearing through the doorway.

Mattie stood up and watched him through the high, long windows set along the corridor. He threaded his way through the rows of desks to the second front row, where he slid into his seat and picked up his pen. But before he started writing he glanced back at the doorway and then quickly scanned the windows. And when he saw Mattie he smiled, almost with relief, and then hunched over to continue his work.

*

Fifteen minutes later, Mattie was standing in the queue at the bank, waiting grimly for her turn. After driving down to the shops on the verge of frustrated, angry tears, she had managed to focus on the task at hand and push Max and Jake and the whole ghastly mess to the back of her mind to be mulled over later. Years of defensive compartmentalisation helped here, as did the certain knowledge that the only way she was going to survive this was to keep up, and not let her emotions cloud her judgement. Instead she needed to harness her bitterness and use it to her advantage. Maybe *she* needed to be on the offensive too.

A square black metal box propped on the railing at the front of the line lit up with a glowing red arrow every few minutes, pointing either left or right to a free teller. And the queue shuffled forward slowly, listening for the *ping* that would advance them further along the line. When it was her turn, Mattie walked up to the teller whose light was flashing and stood before a vertical gap in the frosted glass window.

'Can I help you?' The teller, Mary, according to her nametag, smiled professionally. She was a young, groomed blonde with eyebrows and eyelashes so faint as to be almost invisible, giving her a rather surprised look even when she smiled.

'Yes. I wanted to make a few enquiries about a term deposit, please.'

'Certainly.'

'It's a joint one that my husband and I set up nearly two months ago, but now it looks like we'll have to close it early. So what I need to know is how we go about this, and how much interest we lose depending on when we close it. And I also want to get the paperwork needed to close it, so that I can get him to sign.'

'Not a problem. Do you have the account number?'

'No, but I've got my driver's licence as ID.' Mattie slid the laminated card out of her purse and across the counter. 'Will that do?'

'Oh, sure.' Mary smiled reassuringly and took the licence, glancing at it briefly before starting to tap away at her keyboard. She watched the computer screen as she did so, her fingers flying over the keys, before turning back to Mattie questioningly. 'Was the joint account in your name?'

'Yes. And my husband's – Jacob Francis Hampton. Of Mont Gully.'

Mary's fingers started typing again and, a minute later, she stopped and glanced across at Mattie and then back at the computer screen.

Mattie told herself that it was only the faint eyebrows that made Mary looked surprised. 'Is something the matter?'

'Well, maybe.' Mary kept her eyes on the screen. 'Um, I only have one active account registered for you here, Mrs Hampton. It's a standard savings account.'

'The term deposit is under both our names.'

Mary turned to Mattie, almost reluctantly. 'Yes. And the records show that there *was* a term deposit, but it was closed down last Thursday.'

'Last Thursday?' repeated Mattie, her throat drying.

'Yes.' Mary nodded, and her face spoke louder than her words. For the first time, her professionalism receded, overshadowed by a visible pity that made Mattie's diaphragm compress painfully.

She took a breath. 'That can't be. We're joint signatories.'

'I'm afraid it can,' said Mary slowly, as if she thought Mattie was having trouble taking it in. 'It's like a joint account. Either party can access it.'

Mattie looked down at her driver's licence, which was still lying on the counter. It was a terrible photo that made her look like a member of the mafia. She shook her head and tried to focus on what was happening.

'I'm sorry, Mrs Hampton.'

'Can you check again?' asked Mattie, her voice coming out so strangely that the customer at the next stall glanced across curiously.

'Certainly.' Mary turned back to the computer and went through the process again, even though both of them already knew it was pointless. After a moment, she paused and looked at Mattie sympathetically, shaking her head.

Mattie swallowed. 'Can you tell me where it went?'

'I can tell you it was transferred, as a whole, but I'm afraid I can't tell you where.'

Mattie stared at her, her dread giving way to a desperate fury. She swallowed again, painfully, and then spoke in a low voice that throbbed angrily. 'This isn't fair. That money was in a *joint* term deposit. And for *twelve* months. So now you're telling me it's all gone, and you won't even tell me where? That's *my* damn money!'

'Mrs Hampton, I'm really sorry.' Mary leant forward to encourage Mattie to keep her voice down. 'I can see you're upset but the bank hasn't done anything wrong. A joint term deposit *can* be accessed by either party. That's standard practice. And it's also standard practice to allow early closure if a client wishes. All that means is that they forgo some of the interest payable. And I can't give you information relating to another person's account. I just can't.'

'I don't bloody well believe this.'

'Would you like to speak to the manager?'

A large elderly man with a cane knocked Mattie as he passed by on his way to a nearby teller. He continued on without apologising and Mattie glared at his back. Then, as she watched him settle himself awkwardly at the teller's window, her anger dissipated as quickly as it had surfaced, to be replaced by the sick certainty of defeat. She turned back to Mary. 'Would it do any good?'

'Not really. No.'

'Then what's the point?'

'I really am very sorry, Mrs Hampton.' Mary slid the driver's licence back across the counter. 'Perhaps you could discuss it with your husband?'

'Yeah, sure.' Mattie didn't even bother to laugh. It wasn't funny.

'Um, is there anything else I can help you with?'

'No,' said Mattie dully. 'Nothing else.'

She left the row of teller windows the wrong way, and had to manoeuvre herself along the queue of waiting clients with some difficulty. Then she left the bank and walked towards her car, unlocking the door and climbing in automatically. She sat in the car park for a while, staring at the rows of parked cars. He had taken her children temporarily to flex his muscles, and he had taken their money to show her his strength. Every step of the way he had been ahead of her, way ahead of her. While she was still organising her responses, he was busily putting the next move into play. Attack is the best form of defence. But what else could he do now? Surely there was nothing left?

*

But there was. As she found when the school bell rang at three-thirty and the children began pouring out from their classes. Mattie was standing outside Courtney's classroom, trying to sound natural as she chatted with Jo and Helen, when the prep classroom door opened and the mothers started to file in to collect their children. It only took a moment for Mattie to see that Courtney was not sitting with the other children and, even though she looked again, and then glanced around the classroom quickly, she already knew where she was.

'Mrs Hampton?' Miss Thomson looked her with surprise. 'I thought – that is, didn't you know Courtney's gone? Her father collected her about an hour ago.'

Mattie was aware of the other mothers turning to stare at her with avid curiosity. She forced herself to smile. 'Of course! I totally forgot. God, I'm forgetting everything at the moment, aren't I?' She turned to smile at Marie and shake her head at her own stupidity. 'Here I am with the whole afternoon off and I come down here! It must be automatic.'

'Wish someone'd give *me* the afternoon off!' laughed Marie, her small son poking her in the thigh and whining about being hungry.

Mattie smiled at them all, and then made her escape. Although she felt like running, she made herself slow down as she walked through the school, past the excited children and swerving bicycles and clusters of mothers and the occasional father. She already knew it was useless checking the playground for Max, but nevertheless she went straight there, scanning the play equipment and benches for any sign of her son. Without reward.

For a brief few minutes, as Mattie was rocked by the realisation that her children were gone, she felt numbed by her anguish. And as she continued to stare at the playground, it seemed like everything else sped up around her. Children clambering, and running, and screaming. Mothers talking, and hustling, and rushing. Everything in fast motion except her. And she was reminded, strangely, of a commercial she'd once seen, in which a man stood in a city street while, around him, life sped by in a blur. Peak hour in double-quick time while he froze, staring straight ahead, isolated by his immobility.

Mattie blinked, and the world slowed down again, back to a

manageable speed that could include her. Before she could attract any attention, she made straight for her car. Her mind was churning with impotent anger and an underlying fear: *I promised him I'd pick him up. I promised him. Bastard. Bastard. Bastard.* She drove around to the swimming centre, thinking all the way about how she could avoid a confrontation but still reclaim her children. No answers had occurred to her by the time she parked the car but nevertheless she strode into the centre without hesitation, deliberately not allowing herself to become more nervous. Once through the glass doors, the centre was hot and humid, and filled with echoing high-pitched voices and the sound of splashing. Mattie walked down the ramp and rounded the corner to where she usually sat with Ginny and Rachel each week. Rachel was already there, getting young Katie ready for her lesson, but Ginny was obviously yet to arrive. Mattie sat down next to them, feeling out of breath.

'Are you okay?' asked Rachel, looking at her with concern.

Mattie nodded and forced herself to smile. Surreptitiously she took a deep breath and stilled her hands, folding them neatly on her lap.

'Where's Courtney?' asked Katie, escaping from her mother, who was now folding her daughter's school clothes.

'She's coming with her dad.' Mattie glanced across at Rachel and managed a laugh. 'That is, if he remembers.'

'Men!' said Rachel dismissively, diving under her chair to pull out her bag. 'Here, Mattie, I've got your money. And where were you last week?'

'I wasn't feeling well,' replied Mattie blithely, fidgeting again while she stared towards the swimming pool entrance. 'So we had the day off.'

'Lucky you.'

'Can I go in, Mummy?' Katie ran to the edge of the pool where the water lapped up and over the concreted edge, draining into a narrow grating that ran all the way around the huge pool.

'Okay, but stay near the side.'

'Hi, guys.' Ginny appeared from the direction of the change-rooms, with both her sons already in their bathers. While the boys jumped straight into the pool with whoops of joy, she put a large bag containing their school gear down by a chair on the other side of Mattie and sank down with a sigh. 'I'm stuffed.'

'You and me both,' said Rachel, watching Katie carefully.

'What happened to you last week, Mattie?'

'She wasn't well,' said Rachel.

'Was it that bug that's going around?' asked Ginny with interest.

'Don't know,' said Mattie, trying to keep her hands still. 'It only lasted a day.'

'Probably the bug,' decided Ginny with a nod. 'Jack had that two weeks ago, and then David had it the very next day. Thought I'd get it too, but I was lucky.'

Mattie didn't say anything.

'Now – money.' Ginny pulled an envelope out of her pocket and passed it over. 'There you go. Had a lovely time. And I'm looking forward to getting my stuff.'

Mattie slipped the envelope into her jeans pocket with Rachel's money, still watching the entrance. There was a continual stream of parents and children, but no Max or Courtney. After a few minutes the young swimming instructor, a plump, broad-shouldered girl with cropped red hair, came from the office with her clipboard. She sat down on the edge of the pool with her legs in the water and started calling out names. 'David? Yep. Jack? Yep. Katie? Yep. Max? Courtney?'

'Not here yet,' called Mattie quickly. 'In fact I'm beginning to suspect their father's forgotten to bring them.'

'And they missed last week too,' commented the swimming instructor, glancing down at her clipboard.

'Mattie was sick,' offered Rachel.

'I'll go outside and give him a call on his mobile.' Mattie stood up and smoothed her jeans down. 'But if he's forgotten, they probably won't get here in time now.'

'Well, see me next week and I'll arrange some make-up lessons.' The swimming teacher smiled dismissively and turned back to the children, clapping her hands much like Miss Thomson.

'Okay then, I'll see you two next week.' Mattie waved at Ginny and Rachel cheerfully. 'And I'll bring your things from the party.'

'Excellent! See you then!'

'Lucky you, escaping from this damn sauna! Bye now!'

Mattie strode down the outside of the swimming pool, in between the classes now in progress and the plastic chairs full of watching parents. What with the heat and the noise, she felt incredibly nauseous. She went up the ramp quickly and pushed open the glass doors, taking in a huge lungful of cold, fresh air as she did so. But it didn't seem to make much difference.

By the time she got to the car, Mattie really thought she was going to vomit. She stood by the car and bent over as she felt bile surge towards her throat. She gagged several times, but nothing else happened so after a few minutes she straightened and opened the car door to slide in, out of sight. Then she took a series of measured breaths – one, two, three, four, five – and turned over the ignition, put the car into gear and drove around to Jake's house before she could change her mind. But from the moment she turned into the court, she could tell that this was also a dead end. There was no car in the driveway, the curtains were drawn and mail stuck out from the letterbox. Nobody had been home since this morning.

Mattie turned at the bottom of the court and drove down to the shops, where she went straight to the local McDonald's and cruised slowly through the car-park. Children screamed joyfully as they clambered over the play equipment and a line of cars backed up behind the drive-thru window. But Jake's car wasn't there. By now, for Mattie, nausea and concern were vying with the return of her anger. How *could* he do this to her? She would never, *never* have done this to him.

Mattie gunned the car out of the McDonald's parking lot and drove around to the police station. There she parked the car and sat staring through the windscreen at the huge mesh fence that divided the police station from the back of the railway station. A train came through, rattling noisily over the tracks as it decelerated into the station. Mattie watched a tardy passenger run past the fence but while he was still in sight the train could be heard moving off, and then tooting loudly as it approached the far intersection. With the clatter of the train receding into the distance, Mattie took a deep breath and got out of her car, locking it and then marching towards the police station. She couldn't believe she was doing this and was numbed by a very real fear that she might even be making things worse. But she also knew, without a shadow of a doubt, that she couldn't let Jake get away with this. She had to meet strength with strength.

The front door was an automatic sliding one which slithered back with a metallic hum as she approached. There was a small foyer with closed glass doors to the right and left and, straight ahead, a passage into the main room. Mattie walked in and was rather surprised to find herself alone. No people waiting, and no people serving either. A row of chairs stood against one long wall, with posters and flyers tacked to the noticeboard behind. Opposite was the counter, a shiny black affair that ran the length of the room, with mirrors all the way along the wall behind it. Mattie guessed they were two-way mirrors, from the telltale stripes, so she stood at the counter and waited impatiently to be seen. She put a hand up on the counter but, when she saw the way it trembled, she dropped it again and clasped it within the other for protection.

Within a minute or so, a policeman came through a door at the far end of the wall and approached her with a smile. He was young, blonde and very good-looking, with a clean-shaven face but for a meticulous tuft of beard in the cleft of his chin.

'Can I help you?'

'I hope so.' Mattie kept her voice controlled and unemotional. 'My husband – my *ex*-husband has kidnapped our children.'

'I see.' The young policeman frowned sympathetically. 'Well, that's no good. Can you give me some details?'

'He has the children from Thursday till Sunday, and I have them the rest of the time. Now he didn't bring them home yesterday, and when I rang he'd already put them to bed, so I left it. But today when I went to get them from school, he'd already collected them. Early.'

'And you have parenting papers written up? For this arrangement?'

'No, we don't.' Mattie's heart sank as she watched his expression. 'But it's *still* an agreement. And he's *still* broken it.'

'Yes, that's right,' the young policeman said patiently, 'but without legal papers, there's nothing we can enforce. They are his children, just as they are yours, and you both have a legal right to them. So it's not kidnapping, see.'

Mattie stared at him, dumbfounded. Her throat tightened and she blinked. *I will not cry, I will not cry.*

'Ma'am? Do you understand?'

'Yes, but . . . then what *can* I do?' Mattie leant forward desperately. 'Just give up?'

'No, not at all. My advice would be to get down to the Dandenong Family Court first thing tomorrow and apply for interim residency orders. You'll need to go for your final orders first but they can take up to twelve months to be heard. If you apply for an interim one as well, then that'll get heard quicker and you'll have legal orders in place pending the final version. They'll explain it all to you down there.'

'Okay,' said Mattie slowly. 'Interim residency orders?'

'That's the ticket,' said the policeman cheerfully. 'Then if he goes against the orders, we can do something. But as it stands, unless the kids are in danger – they're not in danger, are they?'

'No, they're not,' replied Mattie reluctantly. She stared down at her hands for a moment and then looked up again. 'He took our money too.'

'Sounds like you really need some legal advice. Go sort out the orders and then see a lawyer, that's what I'd do. Or contact legal aid. Speak to them at the courts tomorrow and get some information.'

'Okay.' Mattie nodded politely. 'Thank you.'

'No worries. Good luck!'

Mattie walked back down the passage and the automatic doors slid open at her approach. Suddenly a thought popped into her head – however many steps it takes me to get to my car is the length of time I'll be without my children. She set off, taking long strides, and reached the car in sixteen steps. Sixteen minutes without them. Maybe they would be home by the time she got there. Or maybe it was sixteen hours, or sixteen days. She wiped at her eyes roughly, started the car and drove home. And it came as no surprise to find that Jake's car was not there either so, as soon as she turned off the ignition, Mattie leant her head against the wheel. Then, at last, she started to cry.

Mattie might have stayed there, in the car, for the rest of the day had it not been for Hilda. Inside the double carport that serviced the two front units, she couldn't really be seen by anyone just passing by and, even once she'd finished crying, Mattie quite simply lacked the motivation to move. Instead she sat with her head resting against the steering-wheel and alternated between a deep despondency and an almost mind-numbing anger. Her head throbbed and her limbs felt weak, drained. And although she dearly wanted to be inside her unit, closed off, the thought of physically getting out of the car and crossing the driveway was overwhelming.

It was about three-quarters of an hour after she'd parked that Mattie heard the sharp knocking on the window just by her left ear. She jerked in surprise and turned to stare into Hilda's black-button eyes, peering at her through the glass with concern. Embarrassment flooded Mattie immediately and with it came the motivation she needed to get moving again. She grabbed her handbag and leapt out of the car, slamming the door behind her as she wiped her face quickly and tried to look relatively normal. That was when she noticed that standing behind Hilda was her husband, Ernest, holding his car keys and looking ill-at-ease.

'Mattie!' Hilda took a step towards her and then stopped. She looked at her searchingly. 'Are you all right? What happened?'

'Nothing. I'm fine, really. Hello, Ernest.'

'Hello, dear.' Ernest looked at her rather sadly.

'You go on inside, Mattie,' said Hilda. 'I shall be there in a minute.'

'What?' asked Ernest, frowning as he took his wife by the arm.

Mattie didn't really want Hilda's company, especially if it meant she would get into trouble with her husband, but she didn't have the strength to argue either. She just nodded and started walking towards her unit. One foot in front of the other. Behind her she could hear Hilda and Ernest arguing, but not loudly or aggressively – just disagreeing. She got out her keys and unlocked the front door, walked inside and threw her keys and handbag onto the couch. Then she dug Ginny and Rachel's money out of her pocket and threw that down too. One of the coins bounced off the couch and rolled along the carpet towards the beanbag. Mattie ran her fingers through her hair. Her scalp still hurt, along with the rest of her.

'Okay then.' Hilda came bustling in and closed the door. She put her hand on the small of Mattie's back and ushered her into the kitchen, guiding her towards a chair. Then she went over to the stove, filled the kettle and lit the gas underneath it. She didn't say anything while she made the coffee, and neither did Mattie, who just sat at the table and stared at her hands. She needed to wash them but couldn't summon the energy. Finally Hilda placed a steaming mug of coffee in front of her and sat down on the other side of the table.

'Thanks,' said Mattie quietly.

'Now tell me what happened. And start at the beginning.'

Mattie took a deep breath. Part of her wanted to spill everything but another part just wanted to curl up and cry. It was all just so embarrassing, so mortifying to be in this situation.

'Come along.' Hilda took a sip of coffee and regarded Mattie patiently. 'I am not leaving till you tell me. And you never know, I might be able to help.'

'You can't help.' Mattie shook her head without hesitation. 'I don't think anyone can. It's all happening so fast. This time last week I was thinking maybe there was a chance that my marriage might work after all, and now I don't even know where my kids are.'

'The children are missing?'

'They're with their father.'

'But I thought they were with you during the week?'

'So did I.' Mattie laughed shortly. 'But it seems the rules have changed.'

'Okay. How about you start with last Wednesday night. What happened?'

'How did . . . oh. *You* were the one who rang the police.' Mattie looked at Hilda for confirmation. 'I suppose I should thank you then. That was all because Hannah rang him and told him off. But that's also when things went really bad too. He wanted to take the kids with him but the police arrived then and he left. So now he's having his revenge.'

'How so?'

'He didn't return them on Sunday. And he picked them up early from school today, before I even got there. I've gone everywhere, but I can't find them.'

'Did you go to the police?'

'Yes.' Mattie looked at Hilda hopelessly. 'But he's not doing anything illegal. It's not kidnapping when he's their father and we've got nothing written on paper.'

'But did they at least give you some advice?' Hilda frowned. 'There must be something you can do.'

'There is. I can go to the Dandenong Family Court tomorrow and file for what's called interim residency orders. But god knows how long they'll take.'

'I am so sorry, Mattie.'

'Me too.' Mattie sighed, the breath of air making rippling brown circles in her coffee mug. She stared at them as they faded.

'But at least you will be doing something tomorrow.' Hilda tried to sound upbeat. 'And as soon as you have these orders, then you have the law on your side.'

'I suppose so.' Mattie looked up grimly. 'But there's more.'

'More?'

'Yes. Just before I left, we put all our money into a term deposit for the year. So that . . . well, so that it'd be safe.' Mattie laughed flatly. 'Safe! I thought nothing could happen without both our signatures, but I was wrong. Stupid. He's closed it down, transferred the money into his own account. It's gone.'

'Oh, Mattie.'

Mattie shook herself. 'I shouldn't be telling you all this. It's not your problem.'

'You need to tell someone,' said Hilda matter-of-factly. 'And I really do not mind. But would you like me to call Hannah, yes?'

'God no,' replied Mattie with feeling. 'She was coming around today but she probably dropped in while I wasn't home. It doesn't matter anyway because I just don't want to see anyone at the moment. I mean that, Hilda, please.'

Hilda looked at her doubtfully. 'You should not be alone.'

'If you think I'm going to do something stupid – don't. And to be honest, I think being alone will help me think things through rationally. Plan my next move.'

'You make it sound like a –'

'A game?' finished Mattie derisively. 'That's exactly what it is. To Jake anyway. And I've got to stop feeling sorry for myself and start thinking one step ahead.'

'That is the spirit!' Hilda got up and rinsed her cup under the sink. Then she turned and faced Mattie. 'And what is more, you can take a leaf out of his book. Pick up the kids early tomorrow. Make *sure* you get them.'

Mattie stared at her, surprised. 'Do you know . . . that's a good idea! Why didn't I think of that?'

'Because you are a nice person who does not think that way.' Hilda pointed to Mattie's mug. 'Now you drink that coffee up and then make yourself something to eat. And I shall leave you alone.'

'Thanks, Hilda.' Mattie smiled at her sincerely. 'You're a truly good neighbour.'

After Hilda left, Mattie got up and washed her hands and then stayed at the table for a while mulling over the conversation, and the events of the afternoon. There were no more tears, simply because she felt cried out. Besides, the thought of action – that there was *something* she could do to stem this flood she seemed to be caught up in, or at least help turn it a bit more to her advantage – revitalised her to some extent. As far as the money was concerned, she had to face the fact that it was as good as gone. At least until the property settlement anyway, where she should be able to regain her portion. But until then she couldn't bank on it, and was probably better off not even thinking about it.

The children were another matter. There was absolutely no way she was going to lose them. Mattie's mouth set grimly at the thought. And it was not just a case of her missing them and wanting them and needing them, but that she knew in her heart of hearts that she was by far the better parent. More even-tempered, less selfish, more interested, more in tune, more willing to listen. And more willing to see past the circle of her own life, with its hopes and dreams and desires, to the circle around them. To see them as separate entities, and not merely extensions of herself. She'd long known that Jake had problems in this area, but if there was one thing that was certain, his actions over the past few weeks had cemented this in stone.

It was this that was still uppermost in Mattie's mind when she arrived at the primary school at two o'clock the following day. She deliberately kept it at the forefront because it had helped her do what she needed to do today, which was front the Dandenong Family Court and apply for orders against Jake. It was an overwhelming morning. A lot of waiting, a lot of paperwork, a lot of new information. She ended up applying for both final orders and interim orders but also collected a kit that allowed for parents to do their own orders and then file them. This was by far Mattie's most preferred option, but she didn't have a great deal of confidence that it could be accomplished. But then again, faced with a lengthy and potentially expensive legal process, Jake might prefer it too.

The good news was that the paperwork had gone through relatively smoothly and her brand new concession card meant that the fee, which she quite simply didn't have the money to pay, had been waived. The bad news was that, as the children weren't in danger, the interim order could take up to twenty-eight days to be heard. But Mattie kept telling herself that at least she was finally doing something. Playing the game, and even wielding a pre-emptive strike.

She arrived home to find a rather worried note from Hannah under the door so she rang her to set her sister's mind at rest. She didn't tell her about the children, or the money, deciding that these were things better left to a face-to-face meeting. Then she raced down to the school where she was now. About to collect Max and Courtney and take them home. Where they belonged.

Mattie went to the office first where she asked for two early slips, which she filled out for Max and Courtney Hampton with the time and a reason that she made up on the spur of the moment – *Doctor's appointment.* That would do. When Mattie passed the slips back to the lady in the office, she glanced at the names and then looked up at Mattie, puzzled.

'Didn't these two finish early yesterday too?'

Mattie smiled reassuringly. 'Been one of those weeks.'

'And it's only just started,' the lady laughed, making a notation on the slips and then passing them back to Mattie. 'Do you know which classrooms they're in?'

'Yep. Thanks.' Mattie took the slips and began the long trek down the corridor, past the hanging bags and long high windows through which she could see the occasional teacher and the tops of the student's heads. There was a certain sound that walking down a school corridor made, a sort of hollow linoleum thud that was unique. It was impossible to walk quietly and all the way Mattie fancied that Jake would suddenly appear behind her. *And just what do you think you're doing, sweetheart?*

She went to Max's room first, simply because it was the closest, and stood on tiptoes to peer through the window, struck by a sudden dread that they'd already gone and she had lost, again. But almost immediately she saw the top of Max's brown head, bent laboriously over an exercise book. She let her breath out in a rush, and then went to the door and knocked on it softly. After a moment it was opened by a young boy and Mattie slid inside, smiling at Mrs Hope even as she walked between the desks to hand her the early slip.

'*Another* early day, Max,' Mrs Hope said after reading the slip. 'Aren't you lucky?'

There was a general muttering through the class as the majority agreed with her and jealously watched Max get up and fetch his bag. Mattie went back over to the door and waited till Max joined her.

'Thanks,' she said to Mrs Hope as she backed out. As soon as the door was closed, she smiled down at Max. 'Well?'

'Are you getting us early coz of Dad?'

'Absolutely. And I'm so sorry about yesterday. I know I promised you that I'd be here and, Max, I was. But you'd already left.'

'He said you had other things to do. That you asked him to get us. But I didn't believe it.'

'Quite right,' replied Mattie shortly. Then she glanced nervously up the corridor. 'Come on, let's get Courtney and go home.'

They walked down to the end of the corridor where the prep class-room was situated next to the outside doors. Mattie knocked on the door and, after a long minute, it was opened by Miss Thomson.

'Ah, Mrs Hampton. Can I help you?'

Mattie handed her the early slip. 'I'm picking up Courtney early.'

'Oh, what a shame. She's just having a lovely time cutting out magazines.'

'Sorry,' said Mattie ineffectually.

'Courtney!' Miss Thomson called from the door, without moving. 'Mummy's here to collect you.'

'Don't wanna go!' Courtney could be heard clearly from within the classroom.

'I'm afraid you have to. You have a doctor's appointment. Now get your bag. Georgia can put away your material as well when she tidies.' Miss Thomson gave Mattie a tight smile. 'She'll be out in a minute.'

Mattie watched the door close in her face. 'I hate that woman.'

'Me too.' Max smiled up at her.

'God! I forgot you were there,' Mattie grimaced. 'Forget I said anything.'

The door opened and Courtney came out with a huge frown on her face. 'I don't *wanna* go! I was having fun! Why do I need to go to the doctor's anyway?'

'Sorry.' Mattie bent and kissed the top of her head. 'Now come on, let's get home. I'll explain later.'

She quickly led the two children through the outside doors near Courtney's classroom and across the school grounds, with Courtney running to catch up. Once at the car, Mattie made herself slow down, aware that she was infecting Max with her nervousness. But she didn't start to relax until they had driven away from the school, and she refused to let herself embrace her victory until she had ushered both children through the front door and locked it behind them. She'd done it. She had them.

'So why'd we have to come home?' Courtney was still frowning.

'Can we have hot chocolate?' asked Max.

'Certainly.' Mattie grinned at him, feeling almost weightless with relief. 'And I'll explain while I'm making it. Put your bags away and then come in the kitchen.'

Mattie put the kettle on. While she was waiting, she looked outside and remembered, with a shake of her head, how simple everything had seemed only a few days ago, when she'd looked at the rain-drenched yard and fancied she could just rinse everything clean and start again. How deluded she'd been.

Max and Courtney came into the kitchen just as the kettle boiled so Mattie put together their hot chocolates while they sat at the table expectantly. She passed them across and then leant with her back against the bench, chewing her lip pensively. How much should she tell them? How should she start?

'Why were you so busy you couldn't have us this week?' asked Courtney, hot chocolate beaded along her upper lip. 'That was a bit mean, you know.'

'I wasn't,' said Mattie, glad that Courtney had started the ball rolling. 'And that's what I wanted to talk to you about.'

'Daddy said you was.'

'Well, I wasn't. Now, look, your Dad and I are going through some things right now that aren't very pleasant. And I'm really sorry but it looks like you two are going to be dragged in the middle for a while. All I can say is that it *will* get better.'

'How d'you know?' asked Max.

'Um, well, things like this always start off rocky and then calm down.'

'Dad says things'll always be crappy till you come to your senses,' commented Courtney, staring into her hot chocolate. 'How come we don't have ice-cream?'

'Ice-cream?' repeated Mattie, still stuck on the comment about her senses. 'Hang on, I'll get you some. Did he say anything else?'

'No. Can I have a big scoop?'

Mattie plopped a large scoop of ice-cream into Courtney's mug and then did the same with Max's. She put the ice-cream away in the freezer and turned back to the children. 'Do you know what he meant by coming to my senses?'

'He means when you come back home,' said Max softly, staring at his mother.

'Oh, I see.'

'Are you gonna go back home?' asked Courtney curiously.

Mattie looked from her to Max. 'No. Definitely not.'

'Good,' said Courtney. 'I hate it when you fight.'

'Me too.' Mattie smiled at her gently. 'Which is why that's all finished. And what's more, you know how I've been staying with Dad on Thursday nights and he was staying here on Sundays? Well, that won't be happening either. We're breaking up for good.'

Both children greeted this announcement with silence. They stared at her as if waiting for more. After a few moments of this, Mattie started to feel uncomfortable. 'It'll be okay, you know.'

'Will you get another husband?' asked Max suddenly, staring down into his drink.

'No.' Mattie was rather stunned at the question. She tried to imagine herself with someone else and failed. 'I want to be by myself. And I promise that even if I did *meet* someone, which I don't think I will, that I'll make sure you both like him before I go out with him. Okay?'

'I won't like him,' announced Courtney decisively.

'No problem.' Mattie smiled. 'I'll keep that in mind.'

'So will we be going home early again tomorrow?' Max looked up at her.

'To be honest, I haven't even thought past today.' Mattie scratched her head tiredly. 'But it'll sort itself out in time, because what I did today was go down to the family court – that's where a judge works out what's best for families who break up – and I applied for the judge to put down on paper what days you're with me and what days you're with Dad. And then it'll all be legal, and can't be changed.'

'So Dad won't be able to pick us up on your days?' asked Max hopefully.

'That's right. Unless I've agreed, like we've made a swap or something.'

'Good.'

'Yeah.' Courtney frowned. 'I'm sick of getting picked up early. I hate it.'

Max grinned. 'I like *that* bit.'

'Now, one last thing,' Mattie said, looking at them sternly, 'until this all sorts itself out, I don't want either of you to answer the door. If someone knocks, just call me. Okay?'

'Why? Do you think Dad'll come?' Max's eyes widened and he glanced towards the kitchen doorway.

'Of course not . . . well, maybe. I'm just playing it safe.'

The two children fell silent, concentrating on their hot chocolates. They reached the bottom of the mugs and started slurping so Mattie passed them a spoon each, which they used to scoop up the remaining ice-cream.

When she finished, Courtney sighed happily. 'Can I go watch TV?'

'Sure.' Mattie nodded as she put the empty mug in the sink. Max stood up too, glancing across at his mother. Concern darkened his eyes and Mattie's heart tightened. She put her arms around him and gave him a hug. 'It'll be fine. I promise.'

'Okay.' Max pulled back just as Courtney flung herself into the hug. Mattie squeezed her fiercely, lifting her up high and then putting her back down again.

'So you two go watch some TV and I'll see if I can find something for tea later.'

Mattie watched them leave. Two such different children, but both equally vulnerable in their own way. Why couldn't Jake see that? Why couldn't he recognise the damage he was doing to the two people that he probably loved most in the whole world? And what was she to do now? She'd only thought up to the point where she got them home, with her, and not about what might happen afterwards. What would happen tomorrow? Would she need to collect them early again? Then Thursday became Jake's day, again, but seeing as she'd only had them twice for her turn, fairness dictated she should have them the next two nights as well. But she already knew that, although he might let today go without responding, there was no way he would sit back and let her keep them. The whole point had been to flex his muscles, so any sudden show of strength by her would be met with stiff, aggressive opposition.

A car could be heard turning into the driveway and Mattie's eyes widened. She ran over to the kitchen doorway and peered around the corner, through the open curtains. But the car was a red Subaru 4WD and it continued on past her unit towards the rear. Mattie let her breath out, and then glanced down at the children, who were lying on the carpet by the television. Max met her eyes, and she knew he had been thinking the same thing. With the same fear.

Mattie gave him a reassuring smile and returned to the kitchen where she sat down at the table, staring blankly towards the window. A possible twenty-eight days until the interim order was heard. Almost a month. And one thing was for sure, they couldn't go on like this. But, then again, she couldn't see any choice.

*M*attie often thought it odd that even severe physical trauma, like the time she broke two ribs and bruised her kidneys, paled as it aged within her memory, while the emotional stuff seemed to stay fresh forever. All the name-calling, the derision, the humiliation and degradation were like whips across her soul, leaving open wounds that festered continually and never seemed to heal.

So while the bruises faded, the hair regrew and the ribs mended, the psychological damage permanently scarred her, making her question her decisions, her abilities, her reactions, and her choices. Everything. And knowing that most of the accusations levelled at her – like whore, or bad mother, or lousy lay – were untrue made little difference. Because, over time, they still undermined her confidence and her self-esteem, so that when she was at a function and another man approached her, or when she was called upon to settle something with the kids, or when she and Jake were making love, her insecurities made her awkward. And she would end up looking guilty, or inefficient, or inept, and the next time they had an argument, Jake would have substantiation for his venom.

At other times he'd tell her, in a voice almost solicitous, that she was not quite sane: 'Don't you feel that you're just a little unstable? Other people sense it, you know. I think you need help. Professional help.' And it was like Chinese water torture, where if it was said often enough, or sympathetically enough, it would start to shadow her confidence and make her second-guess the most simple decisions. And then he would hold her and sigh regretfully as he said, 'See what I mean, Mattie? But never mind, I'm here for you. I'll always be here for you.'

SIXTEEN

Mattie woke early the following morning, after a bad night's sleep in which she'd spent a great deal of time staring at the darkened ceiling and trying, desperately, to switch her mind off. The strange thing, to Mattie, was that for the two nights the children were at Jake's when they should have been here, she'd slept reasonably well. Yet the night she had them back and knew they were safely tucked up in the next room, she couldn't sleep. Like everything else that was happening, it made little sense.

So when she woke at six o'clock and glanced at the bedside clock, Mattie was frustrated to see that she'd only slept for a few hours overall, and she would have to drag herself through the day feeling tired on top of everything else. But she also knew that there was no chance of her going back to sleep. She was instantly wide awake, with her mind already churning.

By seven o'clock, Mattie decided the game they were playing was more like trying to solve Max's horrid Rubik's cube – you had to twist everything in order to make one side come out right, only to turn it over and find every other facet was still a confused jumble. And the side you'd worked on for so long would have to be destroyed in order to concentrate on the other ones. Everything affected everything else, and nothing came easily. She was quite pleased with that analogy, and thought perhaps it would help her see things clearly. Instead of an impossible task, it would simply take practice to master. Mattie rolled over, wrapping her arms around her spare pillow, and then Courtney screamed.

'Mummy! *Mummy!*'

Mattie leapt from the bed and flew out of the room in her oversized t-shirt and bare feet, racing down the passage into the lounge-room. Even in her panic she adjusted her feet to take the three steps and, for some reason, that angered her. She burst into the kitchen, expecting to see – something. But Courtney seemed fine. She was standing by the bench wide-eyed and pointing at a dark mound on the table.

'Mummy! *Look!*'

Mattie, her heart already regulating itself with relief, followed Courtney's finger and looked towards the object. She took a step closer, frowning.

'It's a yucky dead bird!'

It *was* a dead bird. A magpie by the looks of it, with one black and white wing tucked underneath itself and the other spread out, as if pointing towards the phone. There was no blood but the head was bent back at an angle that suggested its neck had been broken. One dull black eye gazing sightlessly up towards the ceiling. Mattie gaped at it, absolutely dumbfounded.

Max came in and walked up to the table, staring. 'Is it dead?'

'Yes.' Mattie felt hypnotised by the eye, absolutely lifeless yet filled with warning.

'How'd it get here?'

'I don't know. Don't touch!' Mattie slapped Max's hand away as it crept towards the feathered pile. 'Don't go *near* it.'

'It's totally yuck,' commented Courtney, grimacing.

Mattie, still trying to get her head around its presence on her kitchen table, suddenly became aware of a cool draft coming from over the sink. She glanced across and was stunned to see the window wide open, with the lacy scrim undulating in the early morning breeze.

'Did it come in the window?' asked Max, following her gaze.

'It must have,' replied Mattie slowly, going over to the window and winding it closed. She looked back towards the bird, and then at the children. 'Yes, it must have. Poor thing has flown inside by accident and then broken its neck against the wall.'

Max frowned. 'But you never leave the window open.'

'I probably did last night, because it's getting warmer. Well, I won't do that again!' Mattie forced a smile on her face and clapped her hands, regretting it as soon as she did because she sounded like Miss Thomson. 'Okay, show's over! Both of you get in your school clothes and then we'll have breakfast. In the meantime, I'll get rid of the bird.'

'Can we have a funeral?' asked Courtney enthusiastically.

'Definitely not.'

'What are these then?' Max approached the table and picked up a slip of paper. For the first time Mattie noticed that there were several, all identical, laid out in a fan on the table behind the bird. She took the one from Max's hand and examined it.

'It's an early slip. From your school.'

'Yeah, I know.' Max picked up another one. 'There's about twenty of them here.'

Mattie dragged her eyes from the one she was holding to those spread across the table. She blinked rapidly while she thought. 'Oh, now I remember! I got some from your school yesterday and must have left them here. Wow! For a minute I thought the magpie had brought them!'

'Silly Mummy,' said Courtney fondly.

'Okay, off you go. Get dressed.'

Mattie watched the children leave the room and then turned back to the table. She dropped the early slip she was holding, letting it flutter back to join the others. Her insides hurt like someone had taken them and tied them into knots, and she felt distinctly ill. Because although everything she wanted to believe strained against the suspicion, she could see only one way that this tableau had evolved, and that was if Jake had done it.

The chances of her leaving a window open were nonexistent. Mattie had a compulsion about windows, and didn't like *any* to be open, especially at night. She had a habit of checking each window in a certain order every evening before bed. And this was not a simple matter of glancing at them – she needed to physically place her hand on the glass, to check that it was closed, and then on the window winder-knob, to check that it was tight. Every night, without fail. And she hadn't taken any spare early slips yesterday. Why would she?

Mattie rubbed her temples tiredly as her stomach roiled with agitation. He had keys. Of *course* he had keys – how could she have forgotten? She lent him a set when she was moving in, and never thought to ask for them back. But to accept something so bizarre as Jake *killing* a bird, and then leaving it as a message or warning or whatever, was to also accept other conclusions about him. Scary conclusions. And her mind skittered away from these fearfully. Instead she stalled on the thought, bad enough in itself, of him quietly walking through her house while she slept, totally unaware of his presence. Bringing in his macabre gift and then bending over the table to set up his little display before leaving. Or did he perhaps walk up the passage before leaving, and lean in her bedroom doorway to watch her – maybe that was why she had had such a bad night. Maybe she had sensed him, in her sleep.

Mattie's knees felt weak. She pulled out a chair and sat down, not caring that she was right next to the dead bird. Now she could not shake the mental image of Jake watching her while she lay in bed, tossing and turning, ignorant of even his presence, let alone the message he was leaving. A rather dramatic message, and one that was having a far stronger impact than a simple note would have. Either a dare to go ahead and use the early slips, or a threat if she ever did such a thing again. Or perhaps a mixture of the two.

Mattie took the children to school and delivered them right on time. She kissed Max goodbye at the top of the corridor and then walked Courtney down to her classroom door and watched her hang up her bag. Other mothers also said their goodbyes, lingering afterwards outside the school gates to talk. And Mattie smiled, exchanging greetings and wondering, almost surreally, whether any one of them had ever had their husband give them the gift of a dead bird. One that he had killed himself, just for them. *Love is* . . .

Mattie drove home quickly, still undecided about how to react to the events of the morning. Should she confront him? Or should she maybe just ignore it, treat it as if it had never happened? Would that be more effective? These options, as well as the events themselves, were still swirling around in her head as she pulled into her driveway and saw Hannah's car. And the thankfulness she felt surprised her.

Hannah came over to the car and opened Mattie's door as she turned off the ignition. 'Hey there. Keep missing you.'

'I know.' Mattie got out of the car and kissed her on the cheek, resisting the urge to throw her arms around Hannah and start crying. But if she started, she would never stop.

'I brought morning tea.' Hannah held up a brown paper bag. 'Muffins.'

'Excellent.' Mattie looked at her sister thoughtfully, then said, 'First, though, come with me.'

Hannah followed Mattie as she walked purposefully around to the other side of the unit, beside the big rhododendron bush where the wheelie bins were kept. She lifted up the lid of the smaller one, with the yellow lid.

'What *are* you doing?' Hannah stared at her, perplexed.

'Just look in here. On the top.'

Hannah frowned at Mattie but stepped forward obediently and peered into the bin. She recoiled immediately. 'Jesus, Mattie! Thanks a bloody lot!'

'It was on my table this morning.'

'It was *what?*'

'On my table,' repeated Mattie, closing the bin and walking back around the unit towards the porch. She got her keys out of her bag and unlocked the door. Then, without moving, she let it swing open as she peered into the lounge-room.

'What on *earth* is going on?' asked Hannah, standing behind her.

'I'll tell you in a minute.' Mattie stepped inside, still checking everything, and then walked into the kitchen. The table was clear. She put her bag down and went to put the kettle on.

Hannah followed, staring at her sister with confusion. She placed her handbag next to Mattie's and then slid into a chair, putting the paper bag down on the table. 'All right. Tell me.'

'When I got up this morning, it was on the table, right there,' Mattie pointed with a teaspoon. 'Dead.'

Hannah, who had just rested her elbows on the table, removed them quickly. She grimaced. 'Ah, you did –'

'Clean it? Yeah.' Mattie smiled, without any humour, as she poured boiling water over the tea-bag in Hannah's mug. 'Scrubbed it with disinfectant as well. Twice.'

'Good.' Hannah put her elbows back, gingerly. 'Go on.'

'Courtney found it. She screamed and I came running. The window was open too.'

Hannah looked immensely relieved. 'Oh, so it came in the –'

'No. It didn't. I rarely open the windows, and besides, I check them every night. There was no way that window was open. And there's more anyway. Behind the bird was a pile of early slips from the children's school. You know, the slips you fill out to collect them early.'

'*Early* slips? Why on earth would there be early slips?'

'Because it's a message.' Mattie put Hannah's tea down in front of her and sat opposite. She leant forward intently. 'I'd better start with what's happened over the past few days.'

'Before you do, I should tell you that Hilda rang me last night and told me about the money, and Jake taking the kids.'

'I see.' Mattie sat back, expecting to feel resentment, and was surprised by its absence. In fact, she was almost relieved, and touched by the concern.

'Hope you don't mind. She said she'd been going to ring me Monday night, after she saw you, but you'd wanted to be alone. So she waited. But she told me you got the kids yesterday.'

'I'm glad,' said Mattie. 'Glad she waited, and glad she told you as well.'

'That bastard.' Hannah looked at Mattie grimly. 'To think I used to like him.'

'Me too.'

'How much?'

Mattie knew exactly what she meant. 'About twenty-eight thousand altogether. And that includes the ten thousand that Mum gave us after Dad died, when she sold the house.'

'But that's *your* money!'

'I don't think Jake sees it that way.' Mattie smiled bleakly. 'Or cares.'

'Christ.'

'Look, the money's one thing, and I don't deny it hurts, but that's only the half of it. It's everything else! One thing after another! He's gone *mad*.' Mattie took a deep breath and slowed down. 'I've never seen him like this.'

'You've never crossed him to this extent, either,' said Hannah, shaking her head. 'Maybe this is the real Jake. Showing his true colours.'

'Well, I'll tell you what I've done too. I've applied for final residency orders, and also interim ones. That means that the case will be heard any time within the next twenty-eight days.'

'Well done!' said Hannah approvingly. 'But still – twenty-eight days.'

'I know.' Mattie sipped her coffee silently.

Hannah undid her hair and shook it out, a flowing dark brown mass that covered her shoulders and softened her features. Then she ran her fingers through it while she thought. 'Well, we need to ring the police. About the bird.'

'No point,' replied Mattie, shortly. 'I already thought it through.'

'Of *course* there's a point! It's breaking and entering, for starters!'

'No, it's not. He has keys.'

'You're kidding.' Hannah stared at her. 'He has *keys*?'

'Yep. He kept a set when I moved in. I'd forgotten.' Mattie moved her mug slightly and then dabbed with her finger at the damp ring left behind. 'Besides, leaving the window open was quite smart. The police are never going to believe I didn't just forget to close it.'

'And you're certain –'

'No doubt at all.'

'Well, first things first,' Hannah tried to sound hearty. 'We need to get your locks changed.'

'I can't.' Mattie looked up, her eyes shining. 'I have to get permission from the landlord, and besides, I can't afford it. I'm near broke.'

Hannah shook her head decisively. 'Stuff the landlord. We'll tell him later. And I'll pay for the locksmith. Think of it as an early Christmas present.'

'I can't accept –'

'Either that or you have to come and stay with me.' Hannah smiled. 'And believe me, I think we'd both rather the first option.'

'Hannah, you're being . . . I mean –'

'Forget about it. But, I'm sorry, I have to insist that I tell Stuart.' Hannah looked at Mattie, expecting an argument.

'Okay.' Mattie nodded, and wiped at her eyes. Her head throbbed with tiredness. She stood up and went to the sink to wash her hands. 'Because I'm beginning to realise that, much as I hate the thought, the more people who know, the better. Me keeping everything quiet is playing right into his hands.'

'I think you're right.' Hannah suddenly shook her head crossly. 'Do you know, we've been doing this all wrong. We've been waiting for him to act, then we *react*. And not even doing that well. I mean, do you still have those bruises?'

Mattie sat down and pulled at her tracksuit top to show her neck clearly, even though she knew the answer. 'No. All gone.'

'We should've taken photos. Are you *sure* there's none left? Anywhere?'

'None. Sorry.'

Hannah smiled ruefully. 'I'll forgive you this once. But try to keep them longer next time, will you?'

Mattie was saved from answering this rather weak attempt at humour by the phone. She got up to answer it as Hannah, remembering her muffins, went to get a plate.

'Hello?'

'Hello. Is that Matilda Hampton?'

'Yes. Speaking.'

'Hello. My name is Ronald De Sousa, from Centrelink. Now, can I ask you a couple of quick questions for identification purposes?'

'Certainly.' Mattie frowned. Why would Centrelink be ringing her?

'Okay then. Date of birth please?'

'Nineteenth July seventy-five.'

'Full name?'

'Matilda Anne Hampton.'

'Mother's maiden name?'

'Um, Ford.'

'Okay then. No problem. Now, you recently applied for a parenting payment, didn't you?'

'Yes, is there a problem?'

'Not necessarily, no. What's happening is that you're just having a review done.'

'A review?' repeated Mattie, glancing across at Hannah, who was watching her curiously.

'Yes, nothing to worry about. We'll just be sending you some questions in the mail to be answered, that's all. You need to fill them out and send the form back.'

'What sort of questions?'

'Oh, regarding your living arrangements, things like that. Whether you have any other adults staying with you.'

'I see.' Mattie twisted the cord. 'Is this normal procedure? I mean, I've only been on the parenting payment a few weeks. Isn't this a bit early for a review?'

'Not necessarily. It's just –'

'Did someone ring you?' interrupted Mattie. 'About me?'

There was a silence and then he spoke again, rather stiffly. 'I wouldn't know. But if that were the case, I wouldn't be at liberty to tell you anyway. Now really, it's quite simple and this is just a courtesy call. Okay?'

'Okay.' Mattie hung up the phone slowly and turned to face Hannah. 'Well, at least I now know what his next step was. He's going to strike at me from every angle.' She looked down at her hands, which she was surprised to see were trembling visibly. 'Every bloody angle. Until there's nothing left.'

The locksmith arrived just after lunch, a friendly middle-aged man wearing a pair of bone-coloured bib and brace overalls. He worked quickly and efficiently, installing deadbolts over the standard locks on both front and back doors, and also installing window locks throughout the unit. Mattie filled out Hannah's blank cheque with the total amount and paid him. But as she closed the door on him, and engaged the deadbolt, Mattie was surprised to find that she still didn't feel safe or secure. Instead she had a deep-seated belief that if Jake wanted to get in, he would, regardless of shiny new deadbolts and double-sided window locks. When it came down to it, they might slow him slightly but they wouldn't stop him.

She left for school at twenty past three, having decided not to attempt the early pick-up again. And although she tried to tell herself this was because she didn't want to disrupt the children's routine more than she had to, she knew the real reason was fear. Simple fear, curled down deep in her gut where every now and again it sent out trembly tentacles to remind her of what she was up against.

Mattie smiled at a few women she knew as she walked through the school grounds but did not stop for any conversation. With her hands shoved deep into her windcheater jacket pockets so that nobody would see her nervousness, she strode purposefully towards the prep classroom and did not pause until she got there. Then she took a deep breath and peered through the long window over the room to see if Courtney was there. And she was. Sitting cross-legged on the floor beside her friend Georgia and listening to her teacher. Mattie stared at her for a few more seconds. She'd been so convinced the child would *not* be there, it took a while to persuade herself otherwise.

'Not picking the kids up early today?'

Mattie turned to smile at Marie, who was watching her curiously. 'No, not today.'

'So everything's okay now then? With the kids, I mean?'

'Oh, absolutely. It was just a couple of doctor appointments. One after another, you know how it is.'

'Tell me about it!'

The bell rang, a strident clanging that was immediately followed by the shuffling of chairs and the rushing of feet as children ran to fetch their bags. Then doors up and down the corridor burst open and they swarmed from every room. Except from the prep room, where they had to be physically collected. Mattie stood in line and edged forward as mothers squeezed out with children in tow.

'Courtney Hampton!' announced Miss Thomson with a brisk clap on seeing Mattie in the doorway. 'You may go now.'

'Mummy!' Courtney ran towards her mother and thrust her school-bag into her hands as she ducked past. 'Can I play on the playground for a bit?'

'If you're quick,' replied Mattie, picking up the bag that had tumbled to the floor. 'Just till I get there, then we're going straight home.'

Courtney was already gone, running out of the double doors and around the corner. Mattie followed in a more leisurely fashion. By the time she got to the playground, Courtney was nowhere in sight, but Max stood by the crowded climbing frame with his schoolbag by his side.

'Not playing today?' asked Mattie.

'Just wanna go home.' Max scuffed his shoe in the pine chips and watched the dust fly up. 'I feel sick.'

'Do you?' Mattie bent down and put her spare hand on his forehead, concerned. 'You don't *feel* hot.'

Max shrugged. 'But I feel sick.'

'Okay then, we'll head home. I'll just find your sister.' Mattie straightened, shading her eyes to search the multitude of scrambling children for her daughter. 'Did you see her come past?'

'Yeah.'

'Where?' Mattie looked down at Max, rather impatiently.

'Over there.' Max pointed towards the fence. 'With Dad.'

Mattie's heart seemed to leap into her throat, strangling her. Her fingers opened involuntarily and Courtney's bag fell to the ground as Mattie followed Max's pointing finger until she saw, over by the school fence, Courtney chatting happily with her father. Jake, dressed in his work suit, was leaning against the low fence and laughing. He saw Mattie looking over and waved cheerfully.

'My god . . .' Mattie stared, trying to comprehend the fact that he was there. She'd really thought that when the children were still in their classrooms at three-thirty, he was going to leave it for now. Let her have them tonight.

'Can we go?' Max kicked at the pine chips again.

'In a minute.' Mattie was still staring at the fence. Jake leant over it and kissed Courtney on the top of her head and then, suddenly, turned and walked away. Mattie blinked nervously, unwilling to feel any relief just yet. She watched as Courtney came running back across the school-yard, her pigtails flying behind her.

'Can I play now?'

'What was Daddy doing here?' Mattie asked in a strangled voice.

'Oh, he just came to say hello. And Max was rude and wouldn't come over.'

'Don't care,' mumbled Max.

'Did he say anything? For me?' asked Mattie, trying to keep her voice normal.

'No, why? Can I play now?'

'Definitely not.' Mattie shook her head emphatically and picked up both bags. 'We're going home. Max isn't feeling well.'

'Unfair! I didn't get to play at all!'

Mattie didn't bother answering, just set off at a steady pace towards the back of the school where she'd parked the car. She only just prevented herself from breaking into a run and concentrated on keeping her breathing even, trying to remain calm. Or become calm. But all the time she half expected a hand to suddenly fall on her shoulder. *Why hello there, sweetheart, fancy seeing you here!* They reached the car without incident and Mattie threw the bags into the back seat.

'My turn to sit in the front!' yelled Courtney.

'I don't care,' replied Mattie, scanning the other parked cars. 'Just get in.'

Courtney pulled open the front door and leapt in, Max climbing into the back a little more sedately. After Mattie had reassured herself that Jake's car was not in the vicinity, she got in and slammed the door, locking it quickly, which automatically locked all the other doors with a loud click. Courtney looked at her, surprised, but Mattie ignored her, instead starting the engine and watching her hands shake against the steering-wheel.

They drove home in silence, even Courtney picking up on the tense vibe that emanated from her mother. Mattie pulled into the carport, still nervously glancing around even as she walked up to the front door and unlocked it. When it didn't open straight away, Mattie experienced a frisson of panic but then remembered the new deadlocks. She fiddled with her key-ring, isolating the shiny brass key and pushing it shakily into the new lock. Finally the door swung open and she ushered the children in, pulling the door closed behind her and listening to the double click as both locks engaged.

The evening went fairly slowly after that. Mattie fed the children baked beans on toast for tea as she suddenly remembered she hadn't prepared anything else. Nor was there much food in the cupboards as a grocery shop was well overdue. Mattie herself settled for a weak scotch and coke, an uneasy compromise between hitting the bottle with a vengeance and total abstinence. She made a huge effort to act normal, to appear unflustered and in control, but she didn't think she was fooling anyone. Least of all Max, who sat on the beanbag with his arms wrapped around his knees, his eyes deep pools of discontent. Every now and again he half-heartedly complained of a stomach-ache, although without a great deal of conviction.

But things came to a head after Mattie read them both a story and kissed them goodnight. About ten minutes later, as she was standing in the kitchen trying to decide whether to have another scotch, Max emerged and promptly burst into tears. He felt sick, he didn't want to go to school tomorrow and he didn't want to go to his father's. At all.

Mattie had never felt worse than when she had to tell him he had no choice. That *she* had no choice. She felt as if she'd stabbed the child in the heart, or that she'd let him down so badly that he would never forgive her, even if she ever forgave herself. Finally she took him to bed and tucked him in again, while Courtney snored softly in the bed below. She tried to kiss him but he turned away, facing the wall.

So, with such an evening behind her, Mattie sat on the couch at about nine o'clock feeling frustrated and deeply unhappy. The television was on low in the background but she wasn't really watching. Instead she sat and tried to think, while drinking scotch so weak that it provided no answers, or even temporary relief. The rawness of her earlier fear had abated during the evening but its ongoing proximity was evidenced by its rapid return as soon as a car drove slowly down the driveway and came to a stop right outside her unit. Mattie jerked upright and listened intently as the car door opened, then slammed shut, and the footsteps started towards her front door. Now frozen, she stared straight ahead with her hand wrapped tightly around her glass to stop it from trembling. And when the sound of a key came, trying to fit into the lock, she leapt up and backed away to the other side of the room, staring at the front door and almost expecting it to magically open. The sound of the scrabbling key paused and shortly afterwards came a brisk knock.

'Mattie? You there?'

It was Jake, sounding friendly and cheerful. *Her* Jake. And for one wild moment, Mattie was tempted to fling the door open and throw herself at him with relief. *Jake, I'm so glad to see you! I've had such a dreadful week and I've needed you so much!* And this idea was so ludicrous that it made her hiccup a giggle that surprised her. She put her drink down on top of the television and walked quietly across the room towards the door, watching it intently.

'I see you've got new locks. Very nice. Did you like my little present this morning? Found it by the side of the road and knew you *had* to have it. You barracking for Collingwood and that.'

It wasn't her Jake after all. And the realisation brought a deep shaft of loss.

'And I see you didn't use one of the early slips I dropped off. Wise choice, sweetheart. After all, you've stuffed those kids around enough, don't you think?'

'I haven't – *you* have!' Mattie burst out, clenching her fists.

'Ah, she lives! But no, don't you try to pin this on me, you little minx, *you're* the one who left and started the whole thing. I'm just trying to get my family back together and let me tell you something, sweetheart.' Jake's voice suddenly dropped the friendly bantering tone and became deadly serious. 'I'll stop at nothing to get you back where you belong. And the sooner you accept that, the sooner all this can stop.'

'Go away,' croaked Mattie, but it came out more as a plea than a demand.

'Certainly.' Jake's banter was back. 'Far be it from me to stay where I'm not wanted. Just dropped by to deliver some papers for you.'

'Papers?' repeated Mattie, thinking of the interim orders. Why would he have them?

'Yes, just some information I believe you're after. Save you spending the day at the library having to track it down. See, I'm always thinking of you. Now, pay particular attention to page five. I think you'll find that most pertinent. Bye now, sleep tight.'

She heard Jake's footsteps walking away from the door and down the path towards the car. Then came the sound of the car door opening and, a few seconds later, shutting again. But Mattie stayed where she was until she heard the engine start and the high-pitched whirr as the car reversed out of the driveway and into the road. Then it roared off until its noise faded into the distance.

Only then did she move, walking slowly to the door and undoing both locks before pulling it open. On the porch was a manilla folder containing a thick wad of papers. Mattie picked it up quickly and shut the door with more force than she'd intended so that it slammed noisily and she jumped, her heart galloping. For a moment she stayed where she was, certain the noise would have woken the children, but the unit remained silent except for the murmuring of the television in the background.

Mattie sat down on the couch and picked up the folder as gingerly as if she were picking up a venomous spider. She opened it and several computer printed sheets slid smoothly into her lap. There were ten altogether, and they seemed to be information regarding the subjects Mattie had researched at the library earlier that week. Child support, divorce, property issues, child residence and contact. How had he known? Mattie chewed her lip as she flicked through the pages and tried to work out the purpose behind delivering these to her. There *had* to be a purpose. Or did he simply want her to know that he was aware of her every move?

Then she remembered that he'd made particular mention of page five so she pulled that one out and let the others slide, with the folder, onto the couch next to her. Page five, at first glance, was just like the rest. It started off with a paragraph about divorce, how the decree nisi was not absolute until twelve months after the divorce was granted. But after this paragraph was a story written in first person. And this, Mattie knew without any doubt, was what he wanted her to see.

I don't call the cops anymore now. It doesn't do no good and makes me feel worse. One time, the cop knew him and says 'hey mate, how's it hanging?' And he's going to listen to my side? Anyway, if he's round giving me a hard time, he's gone before they get there. And they go 'oh, you again. What now?' We've been apart seven years and it never ends. Always looking over my shoulder, always wondering if the kids are going to be brought back, always wondering if I'm going to be killed. One time, we were in a car park and he just goes nuts. Left me almost unconscious by the car. And the kids saw all this! They are so damaged. He uses them to get at me and says it's all my fault because I left. I'm the bitch. And they repeat the stuff he says when they're angry with me. He takes me back to court again and again, and makes up all this stuff. Once he even accused me of sexually abusing our daughter. One time he rang up my boss, where I worked, and told him all these lies. I was let go a few weeks later. God, I've had early menopause, my mother had it at 58 and I had it at 35. I know it's because of all this shit. I get headaches all the time, I'm on depression medicine, I cry a lot, I abuse alcohol when things get bad. But it never stops. Sometimes I think I would have been better off if I'd stayed. Because I don't think it'll ever stop. Not until I'm dead.

Mattie put it down and stared at her lap, where the sheet of paper balanced on one knee and then slowly slid off and wafted down to the floor. She wondered when the story had been written and what had happened to the woman since. And she wondered where Jake had found this story and then realised it didn't much matter. Because the implications were clear. This would be her future if she didn't come to her senses and return. *All my fault because I left.*

But what Mattie couldn't get her head around was how quickly everything had deteriorated. It was less than three weeks ago that she'd held hands with him as they visited his family, and he'd squeezed her fingers to let her know he appreciated her feelings. Anybody watching them would have thought they were just any other normal couple. A normal *loving* couple. And even though she'd known deep down that her marriage wasn't really salvageable, and that Jake wouldn't change, she'd been able to fool herself into occasionally being happy. And from that she had been thrown into hell, where everything kept happening so quickly she barely had time to react before she was hit with something else. An ongoing nightmare that showed no signs of abating.

And now this message, hand-delivered to her door, telling her a parable with a definitive moral. A threat. The game would never stop, and he would never call it quits. They would always be linked through the children and he would always be there. Watching, waiting and winning.

*A*nd of all the emotional bruisings she took during their marriage, none were as bad as the time she lost their third child. It had not been a planned pregnancy, not like with both Max and Courtney, and she barely had time to get used to the idea before it was gone. But it still hurt. And what hurt almost as badly was that with the loss came her final acceptance of her husband's deep self-absorption.

Mattie had been experiencing stomach-cramps all day and by the evening had become truly concerned. As she'd suspected for several weeks that she was pregnant, she thought it was maybe an impending miscarriage. By nine o'clock the pains were fierce, emanating out from her back and clenching around her belly like a metal vice. But it was during one of their 'down' times, when the cycle was entering its final phase, and she could not convince Jake of the magnitude of her pain. Eventually she broke down and pleaded with him to help her, but he still insisted she was exaggerating. So she hobbled to the door, determined to reach a hospital emergency room herself. And he watched her go.

She told herself they had no choice anyway, someone had to stay home with the children, and that when she didn't return immediately he would realise how serious she had been. But to make matters worse, her car was low on petrol and she had to fill it up during her journey. Staggering up to the cashier with her face pale and hands clasped across her belly, he must have thought she was drunk or mad. Or both. She finally made it to the hospital just after ten and, seeing her stumble from the car, an orderly brought out a wheelchair. She was rushed straight into the emergency department and the diagnosis was equally rapid. Ectopic pregnancy, in which the egg lodges in the tube and threatens implosion. Immediate surgery.

And while being injected with a blissful mix of pethidine and morphine, Mattie begged the nurses to let her ring home before she was taken to the operating theatre, because her husband would be so worried about her. And as the drugs took the edge off the pain, she clutched the phone to her ear and listened to it ring and ring and ring. Finally he answered, yawning heavily. He'd been asleep.

SEVENTEEN

Thursday was a day of phone-calls, which was just as well, otherwise Mattie might have crawled back into bed after dropping the children off and simply stayed there. She'd experienced another shocking night's sleep, waking up every hour or so convinced that Jake was in the house, and then having to get up and check. Walking quietly through the unit with her heart pounding, half expecting him to materialise at every turn. And even after she'd convinced herself no-one was there, Mattie would feel compelled to inspect every window once more and go through her nightly ritual with the children, kissing them on both cheeks, forehead and chin. Then she would fall back into bed only to wake, again, an hour or so later.

By the morning, Mattie was exhausted, physically as well as emotionally. And things didn't improve. Max, his face pale and eyes averted, started crying again as she parked the car at the school, sitting in the back seat and sobbing miserably while pleading to be allowed to stay home. Then, embarrassed by his own behaviour, using his own tears as an inducement: 'What will the other kids say?' But Mattie had no choice. If it had just been for the day, she would have been tempted but she knew it wasn't school Max was trying to avoid, it was his father. And she tried to explain how much worse things would become if it seemed like she was encouraging him in this avoidance. Not just for her, but for Max also.

So instead she used a handkerchief to clean his face and slipped him a dollar to buy himself something at the canteen. And then drove home with guilt and misery rasping against her throat and making it difficult to breathe without pain. When she engaged the deadbolts, it was with the uncomfortable feeling that she was only protecting herself. However, tiredness numbed the guilt and made it so difficult to reason that she decided to go back to bed and seek temporary oblivion. But the first phone-call came through then, so instead of bed, Mattie walked tiredly into the kitchen to answer it.

'Hello?'

'Mattie! It's Hannah. How are you?'

'Oh Hannah.' Mattie took a deep breath so that she wouldn't start crying.

'What is it?'

'Just – everything. I'm sorry, I know I sound all whiny, but god, Hannah, this is just so damn hard.'

'Well, no-one said it was going to be easy,' replied Hannah briskly. 'Now, tell me, has something else happened?'

'He was at the school yesterday, but only chatted with Courtney. Didn't come near me. Then he came around last night.'

'Are you okay?' Hannah's voice went brittle with concern.

'He didn't get in if that's what you mean.'

'Good. But what did he say?'

'Just that he was never going to give up. That this . . . harassment would continue forever if I didn't come to my senses and go home.'

'You're not thinking of going back, are you?' asked Hannah, clearly horrified.

'No, I'm not. But, you know, I think life was actually easier when I was there?'

'Mattie!' screamed Hannah.

Mattie flinched and held the phone away for a second. 'God, Hannah. Do you mind?'

'Don't you *dare* give in to that bastard! Don't you dare!'

'I *said* I wasn't going to,' replied Mattie, too tired to be cross. 'I was just trying to explain how I . . . never mind.'

'Don't even think about it.'

'Hannah, be reasonable. I'm trying my best – it's just hard, that's all. Do you know I had to drag Max to school crying all the way? He begged me to let him stay home with me. He actually *begged* me. Do you have any idea how that felt?'

'No,' said Hannah quietly. 'Jesus.'

'Yes. And the truth is that it probably *would* be better for the kids if I went back.'

'Not in the long run.'

'Yes, even in the long run. That is, if Jake is serious about never giving up. Hannah, this could be my life for the next ten years. Do you understand that?'

'Yes.'

'And look, I appreciate everything you're doing for me, I really do, but are you going to be able to keep this level of support up for *ten years*?'

'Definitely,' replied Hannah quickly. 'For however long it takes.'

'That's easy to say.' Mattie sighed quietly and then fell silent for a few moments. 'You remember that magpie?'

'How could I forget.' Hannah's distaste was evident in her voice.

'Well, he didn't kill it after all. He found it like that.' Mattie didn't know why she was bringing this up, except that it felt important to let Hannah know.

'*That* makes it okay then?'

'I didn't mean that. I just . . . doesn't matter.'

'Do you want me to come around?'

'No. Really. I had a shocking sleep last night so I'm going to crawl back into bed in a minute. Then tomorrow I think I might go back down to Dandenong and see if I can get the interim orders moved up a bit.'

'That's a great idea,' said Hannah enthusiastically, pleased to grasp something positive. 'Then you'll get it done well before Christmas.'

'Christmas?'

'Yeah, Christmas,' Hannah laughed. 'Don't tell me you haven't noticed Christmas is creeping up on us again?'

'I just . . . well, forgot for a minute, that's all. So anyway, don't worry about me, I'll be fine for the weekend. Jake won't come around while he's got the kids.'

'I told Stuart,' said Hannah softly. 'He was absolutely shocked. Horrified. And he's going around there tonight to try and talk with Jake.'

'I don't think that's a good –'

'Look, Mattie, you said yourself we need to be more proactive. And I know they've never been best friends or anything, but they *have* always got on. It's worth a shot.'

'I suppose,' said Mattie doubtfully.

'Listen, has Liz rung?'

'No. You asked me that last week. Why the sudden interest?'

'I just thought it'd be nice for you, that's all. Anyway, how about I pop around on Monday?'

'That'd be nice. Thanks.'

'Don't mention it.'

Mattie hung up the phone and went over to the calendar hanging by the fridge. And Hannah was right, it was December already and Christmas was only three weeks away. How had she not noticed the decorations? The increase in catalogues? The shopping frenzy? The bloody festive spirit? And she had no money, no gifts, and no desire to buy any. Which was fine because she probably wouldn't have the children anyway.

As she let the calendar flop against the wall, the phone rang again. Thinking it was Hannah having forgotten something, Mattie answered it quickly.

'Hello? Hannah?'

'No. Sorry to disappoint you.'

'Jake.'

'The one and only.'

'What do you want?' Mattie was surprised to find herself speaking evenly.

'Just wanted to see how you liked my little present last night.'

'Better than I liked the one the night before.'

'Well, that's understandable,' Jake chuckled. 'I admit that that one was probably a bit extreme. But it was worth it to see you sleeping. You always look so cute sleeping.'

Mattie was silent. There was really nothing to reply to that, although her stomach lurched at the confirmation.

'I do love you. You know that, don't you?'

'You've got a funny way of showing it,' said Mattie bitterly. 'Taking the money, taking my children, sneaking in here and leaving dead birds on the table for your *daughter* to find. And you reported me to Centrelink, didn't you?'

'It was my civic duty,' replied Jake righteously. 'You're not supposed to have men virtually living with you while you're sponging off the taxpayers.'

'You're *not* living with me. Virtually or otherwise.'

'But I *should* be. You're my wife. Remember?'

'How could I forget?'

'And all this can stop in an instant. All you have to do is say the word.'

'What word is that?' asked Mattie, already knowing the answer.

'That you'll shift back home. Where you belong. And everything can go back to normal.'

'That's what I'm afraid of,' said Mattie quietly, winding the cord around her finger.

'It was better than what you've got now though, wasn't it? Come on, be honest.'

'But you're the one who's *making* it so bad!'

'No, *you* are. I'm just doing what has to be done. And I won't stop either. Not till you come to your senses. Because I'm not just doing this for me, I'm doing it for the kids *and* I'm doing it for you. I love you, Mattie, and throwing that away just isn't an option. You're my wife, you *belong* with me.'

'But what if I don't *want* to be there?' wailed Mattie desperately.

'You don't really mean that,' Jake said confidently. 'Your problem is that you don't know what's good for you. You never have, and that's why you need me.'

'Jake, listen to me.' Mattie pulled the cord off her finger and held her hand out, watching it tremble. 'You can't do this. If I'm meant to be with you, then eventually I'll come back. But you have to give me this time to decide for myself. You can't *force* me. It's not fair.'

'Ah, but all's *not* fair in love and war. There's no decision to make anyway, because you're my wife. I love you, and you love me. And you *belong* to me.' And then he hung up.

Mattie was surprised to find she wasn't as flustered as she'd expected. Her hands were still shaking but that seemed to be a permanent state now. And she had a headache, but she got those quite frequently as well. Apart from that, she felt rather calm. Almost fatalistic, in fact. Because in an odd way it was a relief to talk to Jake like this, calmly and reasonably, and to be told that he was doing all this through love and not hate, because that meant he *wasn't* trying to destroy her. Only trying desperately to convince her to come back. Maybe, just maybe, it was even flattering.

Mattie put the kettle on to make herself a cup of coffee. She took a few painkillers while she was waiting for it to boil and then, just as she was filling the plunger, the phone rang again. She finished what she was doing and then answered it.

'Hello?'

'Hello, Mattie?' The voice was breathless and familiar.

'Yes.'

'Hi there, this is Sharon. Whimsicalities, remember?'

'Of course. How are you?'

'Good. Very good. Just ringing to remind you I'll be dropping off your parcel on Monday. Is the morning okay?'

'The morning's fine. See you then.'

Mattie hung up and poured her coffee. Then she went in search of the list of who owed what from the party. She found it on the fridge, together with the money collected so far. Liz was the only one who hadn't paid and Mattie figured she could cover that, just, although she was a bit surprised that she hadn't heard from her since the party. Then again it took two to tango, and she hadn't rung Liz either. She hadn't even thought of it. But now was as good a time as any, and Hannah was right, she needed friends. Mattie looked up the phone number and dialled it.

'Hello?'

'Liz? It's Mattie! How are you?'

'Oh – Mattie.' Liz sounded strangely noncommittal. 'Good, I'm good. How about you?'

'Never better,' lied Mattie.

'I suppose you're ringing about the money for the wind-chimes and stuff? I'm so sorry I haven't got round to sending it over. I'll do it first thing tomorrow. Promise.'

'That's fine.' Mattie felt awkward. 'No rush.'

'No, I should have done it by now. I totally forgot. You know what it's like with babies around.'

'And how is the little miracle?'

'He's fine, thanks, just fine.'

There was an uncomfortable silence after this that lasted several moments. Mattie tried desperately to think of something to say to fill it but the awkwardness itself inhibited her. Finally Liz spoke.

'Look, I had a ball catching up with you at the party. And maybe when Thomas is a bit older, when I don't have to juggle him and work, we could catch up again?'

'That'd be nice,' said Mattie flatly. It suddenly occurred to her that the reason Hannah had been asking about Liz was because *she* had already told her. Liz knew, and was making it rather clear she wanted nothing to do with it.

'Yes, I'll really look forward to it. And in the meantime . . .' Liz paused for a moment. 'Take care of yourself, Mattie.'

'Hang on!' Mattie had to know for sure. 'Did . . . did my sister ring you? About me?'

There was a long pause before Liz spoke, which answered for her. 'Yes, she did.'

'I see.'

'No you don't,' Liz burst out. 'You're going to think I'm putting you off because of *that*, and it's not true, Mats, really it's not. It's just I'm so busy at the moment. And I don't have any experience with anything like that. So what good would I be anyway?'

'Look, it's okay, Liz, I don't blame you. Really.'

'And I wish you all the best, truly. If you ever need to talk, don't hesitate to –'

'That's fine,' interrupted Mattie, closing her eyes briefly. 'And besides, Hannah was overreacting as usual. In fact, everything's resolving itself really quickly now. No problems.'

'Oh good,' said Liz. 'That's really good.'

Mattie wound the cord around her finger and tried to summon up the words to end the conversation.

'And Jake rang too.'

'What?' Mattie frowned.

'Jake rang too,' Liz repeated in a bright, chatty voice. 'It wasn't long after Hannah rang. Alan was at soccer training. He said how lovely it was that you and I had caught up again, after all this time. And that he'd heard about Thomas and was so pleased for us. How nice it was to see us rewarded with a child after all those years of trying. Then he said he'd keep his fingers crossed for us that nothing ever happened to the baby, because that would be terrible. Devastating.'

Mattie stared at the kitchen wall. She didn't know what was worse – the shock, the embarrassment, or the shame.

'Are you still there, Mats?'

'Yes, I'm here,' replied Mattie dully.

'That was nice of him, wasn't it?'

'Yes. Sure. Listen, Liz, just send the money when you can and I'll post the wind-chimes out to you, okay?'

'And we'll definitely catch up at some stage. Maybe next year?'

'Absolutely.'

'And you can meet Thomas.'

'Can't wait.'

Liz paused for a moment. 'Look after yourself, Mattie.'

'Don't worry about me,' said Mattie breezily. 'You just take care of that baby. And we'll catch up in another year or so.'

'Looking forward to it.'

Mattie hung up, leaving her hand on the phone for a few moments as she stared at the wall. Then she pulled herself together and wiped at her eyes, still feeling sick but unwilling to dwell on what had just happened. She pushed it away. Because it wasn't flattering, not at all. Not to anybody. Her coffee had gone cold so she poured it down the sink because she couldn't be bothered heating it up. She rinsed the cup out and, because her hands felt sweaty, washed them at the sink and shook them dry. Then she put the list and the money back on top of the fridge and went into the lounge-room to watch some television.

The next phone-call didn't come until early afternoon, just as Mattie had started watching a segment of *Oprah* about women who had lost staggering amounts of weight. It was nice to watch other women with problems so dissimilar to her own, but who were conquering them with sheer perseverance. She got up heavily and went to answer the phone.

'Hello?'

'Is that Matilda Hampton?'

'Speaking.'

'This is Jan MacFarlane, Matilda, you'll remember we spoke a while ago? About your son, Max.'

'I remember.' Mattie closed her eyes briefly, wishing she'd left the phone to ring out.

'Now I've been meaning to contact you again as promised but, well –' Jan MacFarlane paused and then sighed, as if to indicate the demands on her limited time. After making this point, she went on briskly – 'but now I think we need to make it a priority to meet and talk some things through.'

Mattie frowned. 'Why the sudden urgency? Has something happened?'

'If you'll remember, Mrs – Matilda, *I* wanted to meet with you some time ago. So there's no "sudden urgency" as you put it, just a desire to follow through.'

'So nothing's just happened?' persisted Mattie, ignoring the woman's obvious attempt to shore up her professionalism.

Jan MacFarlane hesitated for a moment. 'I take it the principal hasn't contacted you yet?'

'No,' Mattie took a deep breath and then let it out as silently as possible.

'Ah. Well, I believe there *was* an incident today at lunchtime. A fight with another boy. It appears that Max tried to choke him in the end and he actually has some rather nasty bruising around his neck.'

'Oh my god. Is he okay? What about Max?'

'As you'd expect the boy is quite shaken up. As for Max, he's fine. However, I'm afraid the other parents are very upset, they're even talking about pressing charges. At the very least I'd say there'll be a suspension. So you see I really must insist on talking with you and your husband.'

Mattie's eyes, which had closed again as the other woman spoke, suddenly flew open. 'My husband?'

'Yes – that is, if there's . . .' Jan MacFarlane hesitated and Mattie could hear the sound of pages being turned. 'It says here that Max's father lives at home, with you. Is that correct?'

'That's correct,' said Mattie quickly, not wanting the woman to make a separate call to Jake.

'Well then, I think it's essential that you both come together. Now I'm only here Tuesdays and Thursdays, so shall we say next Tuesday?'

'Tuesday's fine,' said Mattie dully.

Mattie heard more pages flipping. 'Oh, sorry. No, Tuesday's out, but Thursday is okay. Say – ten am?'

'All right. I'll see you then.'

Mattie hung up the phone and it rang again, almost immediately. She put her hand out to answer automatically and then snatched it away again as if the phone was red-hot. It was highly probable that it was the principal ringing to tell her about Max's suspension. And she didn't want to know. After all, it didn't really matter whether she answered or not – Jake would still find out either way. Because there was no hiding this and if she didn't answer they'd have to catch Jake at school, rather than her having to ring later to tell him.

Mattie watched the phone as it rang, and rang, and rang. Finally it stopped, and she went back to the lounge-room to see if her program was still on. But now, of course, she couldn't concentrate. Max – her gentle, loving Max. She tried to picture him choking another child and just couldn't do it. But would this make a difference? Would the fact that his son had behaved in such a way show Jake what he was doing to the children? Could he be so hypocritical as to punish the boy for doing the same thing he'd seen his father do?

At three-thirty, Mattie stared at the clock, wondering what was happening. How was Max? He'd been so upset this morning that this would devastate him. Especially with the dread, ever since lunchtime, of knowing his father was coming to collect him. And would be informed. Guilt now began to stalk Mattie. Guilt that she hadn't kept the boy home, or answered the phone, or done something other than sit on the couch all day and stare at the television. To counter the guilt she kept telling herself that it wouldn't have made any difference. But that didn't help.

The last phone-call of the day came at six-thirty. Certain that by now it wouldn't be the principal and pretty confident it was Jake instead, Mattie snatched the phone off the wall.

'Hello?'

'Mattie, dear, you sound like you've been exercising.'

'Mum. How are you?'

'I'm fine. And yourself?'

'Good, thanks. Listen, sorry I haven't been in touch or dropped around or anything. I've just been so busy . . .'

Mattie's mother laughed lightly. 'I understand, dear, but I thought I'd ring just to make sure you're still in the land of the living!'

'Well, I am. And I promise I'll pop around next weekend and see you.'

'That'll be lovely. Will you be bringing the children?'

'Ah – no. Probably not.'

'Never mind. Now the other reason for my call was to let you know I haven't forgotten the money I owe you for the things I ordered.'

'That's fine, Mum. Hannah's already paid for you.'

'Oh, good. Funny she didn't mention it when I saw her today. We had a lovely chat.'

'What about?' asked Mattie suspiciously.

'Oh, this and that. And did I tell you how much I enjoyed your party?'

'Yes, you did. But thanks anyway.'

'No, thank *you*. Actually, I'm even thinking of hosting one myself. I could invite Beryl from next door, and some of the ladies from the bowls club. And Mrs DePosito. And Hannah and Charlotte would love to come again, I'm sure. And you would, wouldn't you, dear?'

'Sure I would, Mum.'

'Then I think I will. Yes, I will. Now, I won't keep you. See you next weekend.'

Mattie hung up tiredly. Her lack of sleep was catching up with her, together with her worry over Max. And the mixture of the two was making her feel nauseous. The only silver lining was that with the children at Jake's tonight, she should be able to get some sleep without worrying that he was in the unit. But it was a silver lining she would have traded in an instant to have them beside her, knowing they were safe.

Hannah rang again on Friday to see how Mattie was and she managed to sound upbeat and reassuring. As she hung up she wondered if Stuart had gone around to visit Jake, as promised, and why Hannah hadn't mentioned it. Not that Mattie was placing a great deal of hope in the outcome of such a visit. While she recognised that Stuart was an excellent partner for her sister, Mattie herself had always found him rather boring and ineffectual. And she knew that Jake felt exactly the same way.

One of the problems was that Stuart was an overly tactile man whose constant need to touch those he was speaking to actually robbed his words of impact instead of, as he seemed to imagine, giving them added emphasis. And he was no match for Jake. Stuart was too straightforward, too trusting, and far too moralistic to appreciate the complex side of humanity. He also had some rather didactic views on men, women and marriage, which he called traditional but were actually quite old-fashioned and rather sexist. Added to that was the fact that he was a physically unprepossessing man of below average height and above average weight, so that nobody, least of all Jake, would ever feel threatened by his presence. Mattie decided the visit must have taken place but not been terribly successful, and that was why Hannah hadn't mentioned it. Even though she told herself she hadn't expected anything anyway, she felt a keen sense of disappointment that yet another avenue had been closed off.

In the afternoon she went for a walk in an effort to get herself going again. She missed the Mattie of two weeks ago, with her plans and her optimism, and knew she desperately needed to access her again, to feel confident and assured of her actions, otherwise she was going to be even more badly matched in the struggle to come. So she pulled on her black bike shorts and a sloppy red t-shirt and took off determinedly. She intended to cover about five kilometres but only made it to two before her thighs started to tighten tiredly and she began to worry that, on top of everything else, she was going to overstrain a muscle. So she turned back.

Nevertheless, it was a good move. For the first time in days she felt energised mentally and her thoughts came through clearly instead of being blurred and uncertain. And the simple action of walking along the bike path and nodding politely to other walkers made her feel far less isolated. On the way back, an elderly man stopped her to let her know that there was an aggressively swooping magpie up ahead and it might be a good idea to cross the road. And as Mattie thanked him and followed his advice, she felt a deep appreciation out of all keeping with his actual deed. He had connected with her, reached out. Cared.

The postman was just pulling away from the units as Mattie turned into her road so she stopped at her letterbox on her way inside. Then, kicking off her runners, she sat down with a glass of water and the mail. The Centrelink review was there, with an ultimatum that she had only a fortnight to return the review forms, otherwise her parenting payment would be stopped. There was also the school account for the following year, including stationery items, and a gas bill, already. One letter that had Mattie momentarily puzzled was a letter from the Environment Protection Authority that stated her car had been sighted emitting overly high exhaust fumes and she was requested to look into it immediately. Then she smiled grimly and threw it into the bin. *Good one, Jake.* The last letter was from the Dandenong Family Court, with the date for her interim orders hearing. It was set for 13 December, in exactly ten days' time.

This last was a ray of hope in an otherwise depressing collection of mail that severely depleted the optimism she'd built up during her walk. But Mattie clung to it for the rest of the day. Whenever she thought about the situation, or the children, or how she was going to cope with Jake's ongoing harassment, she would remember that at least in ten days' time one thing would be solved. She'd been proactive and found a solution for the custody issue, so why couldn't she do the same for all the rest? It would just take time.

She decided to celebrate the impending hearing with a glass of wine. Which turned into another, and another. But when Jake turned up a little before ten o'clock, she still wasn't drunk, just filled with a sort of lassitude that was almost debilitating in itself. She'd been lying on the couch disinterestedly watching a rather inane reality television show. And when the knock came, her first thought was that it was part of the show, so she took no notice. But when it came again, and more insistently, she leapt off the couch, her lethargy forgotten as she stared wide-eyed at the door.

'Hello, Mattie? You home?'

It was him. Mattie blinked, trying to dispel her confusion, and glanced at the clock. Where were Max and Courtney then, if he was here? In the car? She walked slowly, softly, across the lounge-room until she stood in front of the door, listening carefully for the sound of a key.

'I know you're home. Your car's here. So you may as well open up.'

'Where are the children?' asked Mattie, in a reasonably controlled voice.

'At home. All the more reason for you to open the door quickly.'

'Who's with them?'

'No-one. So the sooner you open up and let me in, the sooner I can go home again.'

Mattie shook her head, disbelieving. 'You left them alone?'

'Sure.' Jake's voice had a smile in it. 'I have to use every weapon in my arsenal, don't I? So let's get this over and done with.'

Mattie fervently wished she hadn't drunk all that wine, because her thought processes seemed inhibited, slow. 'I don't believe it.'

'Trust me.'

'What if I ring the police? Tell them you've left an eight-year-old and a six-year-old at home alone?'

Jake laughed cheerfully. 'Then I'll just tell them that you rang me in a panic about an intruder, so I checked the kids were asleep and came racing over here, but you'd set me up. And you've been drinking, I can hear it in your voice, so that'll just support my story even more.'

Mattie stared at the door, still confused. 'Why?'

'Because I wanted to talk to you. Face it, sweetheart, you're in a no-win situation. And I'll stay out here till you realise that. So it'll be your fault if one of the kids wakes up and finds out they're alone. Because you're just putting off the inevitable, and placing them at risk. Come on, I'll only take up five minutes of your time. Maybe ten.'

Mattie took a deep breath. The one good thing about the amount she'd drunk was that she felt no fear at all. In fact, if anything, she felt a sense of anticipation. Butterflies crowding her stomach. After all, he *loved* her, didn't he? She reached out to unlock the door and was surprised to see that her hands were trembling so much that she fumbled the first try and had to start again. Finally she clicked the deadbolt back and the standard lock simultaneously and the door swung open. She stepped away as Jake entered and shut the door behind him. He was still dressed in his navy suit pants, with a crisp white shirt that had the top few buttons undone and the sleeves pulled up enough to show that his scratches were healing nicely.

'I can't believe you left them alone.'

'I told you I'd do what it takes.' Jake smiled at her affectionately. 'But you just don't seem to be able to accept that. Nice outfit, by the way. Hope you didn't go out in those bike shorts.'

'This is between you and me, not them.'

'Don't be naive. They *are* involved, because everything you do affects them. You leaving home – don't you think it affects them?'

'That's different –'

'Doesn't matter.' Jake waved a hand dismissively. 'I don't want to get into another argument. That's not what I'm here for.'

Mattie felt a surge of relief that almost made her light-headed. 'Then what?'

'You, of course.'

'Me?' Mattie took another step backwards, instinctively.

'Yes, you. It *has* been about two weeks, you know.'

'What are you talking about?' Mattie frowned, pretending ignorance, but deep down she suddenly knew exactly what he was talking about.

'You should be flattered.' Jake grinned down at her. 'Because the thought of someone else leaves me cold. And besides, you don't want me having to find someone else now, do you?'

'Yes, I do,' said Mattie tightly, but she was appalled to find she did feel a shaft of pain at the thought.

'You don't mean that,' said Jake confidently. 'Now, do you want another drink first? Or shall we just get straight into it?'

'I am not having sex with you.'

'Yes you are. It's just a matter of when.'

'No.' Mattie shook her head firmly. And suddenly she knew that, despite her unease at the thought of him with someone else, she *didn't* want to have sex with Jake. The very idea made her feel cold with humiliation. Disgusted.

'Look, the longer you play games, the longer those kids are alone. So just let me know when you're ready, okay? I'll be waiting.' Jake walked over to the couch and sat down, crossing his long legs casually and raising his eyebrows at her glass of wine before turning his attention to the television.

Mattie stared at him. The wine turned in her gut and she felt ill. She didn't know what to do. Should she simply walk out and go around to Hilda's? Or Hannah's? But the wine she'd consumed shamed her, and limited her options. And she felt deeply embarrassed by the very fact that her husband was here, on the couch. Maybe she should call his bluff and ring the police? But the time for that had been when he was still outside, because now, even if she tried to go for the phone, he could simply prevent her. And the truth was, she wasn't sure which she found most distressing – the possibility of annoying him, or the sex.

Her groin tightened uncomfortably at the thought of sex, but she didn't want to know what that meant. Instead she focused on the children. They weren't prone to waking once asleep, but it did happen now and then. Could she take that risk? If she just sat down on the end of the couch, away from Jake, and tried waiting him out, how long would he last? But she already knew the answer to that. He would wait as long as it took. And if she got up to go to bed, he would simply come along too. Jake didn't lose, ever.

But nor was he a rapist. In all their years of marriage, he'd never forced her, not once. That is, if you didn't count cajoling, bribing, sulking and generally making it clear that if she wanted a pleasant day, then she had better put out. Sometimes it simply felt like an extra chore and she would get it over and done with early so she could go on to other things without it hanging over her head. But he'd never forced her, not physically.

Jake was still watching the reality show, every now and again chuckling at something one of the characters said, as Mattie stood by the kitchen doorway, staring down at her feet trying to decide what to do. Or trying to face the fact that she had no real choice. And even though deep down she recognised, but refused to acknowledge, a frisson of excitement at what she was being forced to do, she hated him. Hated him with an intensity that made her want to kill him – not slowly, but quickly, furiously, painfully. And never see him again.

'Ready,' said Mattie bitterly, walking towards the bedroom without glancing back.

She felt betrayed by her body. Trying to see it as a separate entity that had stabbed her in the back and twisted the blade within her flesh despite her pleas. And she hated it for what it had done. She hated herself. Even though she had lain passively with her head turned to one side, it – she – had let herself down when it really mattered. And although she knew Jake had been determined to bring her to orgasm, and in fact ensured that it happened before intercourse even commenced, she still loathed herself for it. Telling herself it was a physical response in no way reflective of her feelings made little difference. And it hurt more than the beatings, more than the insults, more than anything. Like he had reached into her core and snatched at her essence, leaving it torn.

Jake left quickly afterwards, which suggested he was perhaps not as nonchalant about leaving the kids as he made out. But first, after he dressed, he came over and sat on the side of the bed, running his fingers gently through her hair for a few minutes. Then he sighed, almost sadly, and bent to kiss her tenderly on the lips before leaving. And it occurred to Mattie that if anybody had been watching, they would have supposed him a devoted husband profoundly concerned about his wife.

And for good reason. Because as soon as the front door closed behind him, Mattie, seriously nauseous now, ran to the toilet to vomit. She knelt in front of the bowl, crying piteously and gagging, but nothing came up. Just the rancid taste of sour wine deep within. So she stuck two fingers down her throat until she felt bile rise, and then let it flow. Her stomach cramped as she retched, and retched, until finally nothing was left except clear mucus-like fluid that she spat into the bowl. With her head throbbing painfully, she went into the bathroom to wash her hands and stared at herself in the mirror. Her cheeks were flushed, yet around them the flesh was pale, and her eyes were bottomless wells of darkness that swallowed her pupils. And the memory of that brief frisson of excitement, and the thrusting of her orgasm, branded itself shamefully across her face. *Pathetic. You really are pathetic.*

She was flushed, and had broken several blood vessels in her cheeks. And she looked sick, but not as sick as she felt. Because she'd expected that the vomiting would make her feel somehow purged, but instead it just added to the abhorrence. She still felt nauseous, but it was such an innate nausea that she was not really surprised it remained. It felt like a fundamental part of her which had permeated every inch, from her stomach acids to her bone marrow. Irremovable. She washed her hands again, and again, before going into the children's room to touch each of the walls and kiss their pillows, crying miserably as she did. Then she finally went back to bed and curled up, hugging her knees to her chest in an effort to make herself as small as possible. And the fact that the sheets, the bed, the whole *room* smelt deeply of Jake seemed fitting. No more than she deserved.

Mattie stayed that way throughout the night, and through all of the next day. She only rose a few times, twice to go to the toilet, once to make a piece of toast that she ate quickly, over the sink, before crawling back into bed, and once, at the end of the day, to conduct her ritual in the children's room. Most of the time she was curled up in a foetal position, but sometimes she lay flat on her stomach with her face to the side, pressed against the sheet. And although she did little sleeping, neither did she spend her time thinking. Instead, she blocked any invasive thoughts as soon as they floated near and concentrated on just existing, willing the hours away.

She recognised she'd entered a depression that blunted all else, but she quite simply didn't care. And didn't have enough energy or willpower to fight it. So instead she gave in to it, almost gratefully, because it excused her lethargy and inactiveness. Even the thought that no doubt *some-thing* would happen on Saturday, just as it had every other day, failed to rouse her from her lassitude. And she also failed to appreciate the irony that on this day, when she simply didn't care, nothing eventuated and she was left alone.

Despite having spent the day in bed, Mattie slept better that night than she had all week. But she still woke with a profound tiredness that made her feel far heavier than she really was. The sheets smelt of sweat, and sex, and were pulled together in the centre of the bed with ridges and creases that imprinted themselves on her flesh. She got up in the late morning with the vague thought of straightening the bed out, or changing the sheets, but then simply couldn't be bothered. Instead she took a few painkillers and stood in the bathroom, staring at the shower and trying to decide whether she wanted one or not.

Eventually she did pull off her t-shirt and climb into the shower, turning it on and then letting the freezing cold spray hit her body like a torrent of tiny shards of ice. Mattie gasped, holding on to the taps to keep her balance. And as the water warmed, so did she. Enough so that she was able to think clearly about what was happening to her, and face the fact that she was falling apart. But not enough to profoundly care.

She stayed under the shower, holding her face up to the spray, until the hot water ran out. Then she dried herself, brushed her hair and pulled on a clean baggy white t-shirt that had a huge smiley face on the front and the words, *Make my day!* She forced herself to change the sheets and pillowcases. Carrying the armful of dirty linen out of the bedroom, she thought about shoving it all into the rubbish bin, but her natural frugalness took her through to the laundry, where she pushed them inside the washing machine, added some laundry liquid and turned it on.

And that was as much as she was capable of. Her brief surge of energy from the shower had now dissipated so she returned to the bedroom, pulled back the newly made covers and climbed inside again. And she was still there four hours later when Jake returned the children, right on time, knocking sharply at the front door.

Mattie was in a half-sleep in which everything was blurred and indistinct, so it wasn't until the third knock that she realised what was happening and scrambled out of the bed to answer the door. Max and Courtney came in first, with their schoolbags in tow. Max was wearing board shorts and a red t-shirt while Courtney was back in her favoured tutu. Behind them came Jake. He looked at her and threw his hands up, in a fair imitation of shock.

'Good god, sweetheart! You look like death!'

Mattie glanced at him and then back at the two children, who were rather quiet. Even Courtney did not seem to be able to make eye contact.

'Go on, guys!' Jake laughed. 'Say hi to your mother!'

'Hey, Mum,' said Max, staring at her bare feet.

'Hello, Mummy.' Courtney smiled tentatively and then, dropping her bag, threw herself forward. At the same time Mattie bent down so they met on the same level, and hugged back fiercely. Almost desperately.

'Max.' Mattie put out an arm towards her son and he came forward, but only to touching distance, not enough to join the embrace.

'Now, you two –' Jake picked up Courtney's bag and held it out towards her – 'remember what we spoke about? About making yourselves scarce while I talk to Mummy for a bit?'

'Okay.' Max backed away and then turned towards his bedroom. Courtney, after giving her mother a wet kiss on the lips, took her bag from her father and followed. Mattie stood up and looked at Jake tiredly.

'What do you want now?'

'Just a chat.' Jake looked at her with some annoyance. 'Don't get excited.'

'I'm not,' replied Mattie, stating the obvious. She walked into the kitchen, expecting him to follow, and sat down at the table facing the door. Somehow it seemed less relaxed and informal than the couch in the lounge-room. After a minute or so, Jake came in and pulled out the chair opposite, sitting down.

'What? No offer of a cuppa?'

'Whatever.' Mattie got up and put the kettle on. 'Tea or coffee?'

'Tea, please.'

While she waited for the kettle to boil, Mattie put a teabag and one teaspoon of sugar into one mug and prepared the plunger for herself, putting the other mug beside it. Jake watched her in silence while she did this, and Mattie fancied that he was rather perturbed by her attitude. But in her current state of lethargy, she didn't really feel any sense of victory at this, just a sense of dull acceptance.

When the water boiled, Mattie poured it into the plunger and over the teabag, stirring until the water took on the deep honey colour that Jake preferred. She threw the teabag into the bin and passed him the cup before pouring her own coffee. Then she sat down again, her hands wrapped around her mug so that he wouldn't see them tremble. And waited.

Strangely, Jake gave in first. 'You're in a funny mood.'

'I suppose so.' Mattie shrugged. The heat from the coffee mug was starting to make her hands throb, but she kept them there, almost enjoying the pain.

'Anything you wanted to talk about?'

'No.'

'Look, Mattie, I'm really trying here. I even brought the kids back early for you.' Jake frowned at her. 'I *am* making an effort.'

'Yeah. Sure.' Mattie almost laughed.

'Okay, we can go back to being enemies then. Have it your way.'

This time Mattie did laugh. 'Have it *my* way?'

'Yeah, like always.' Jake stared at her narrowly. 'I'll say what I came to say, then I'll leave. *That* should make you happy.'

'Then just say it,' said Mattie tiredly.

'Okay. Fine. I just thought we should have a chat. Set out some things, so that we both know what to expect.'

'Okay.'

Jake looked at her intently. 'Like the chat I had with your mate Stuart last week.'

'He's not my mate.'

'Not now he's not.' Jake smiled. 'Now that he's been told a few home truths. But I must admit I'm a little surprised by you confiding in your sister so much. I never thought the two of you were so close. Never mind. I suppose it was her who gave you the idea to file for interim orders last week. Think you're clever, do you?'

'Not really.'

'You're right, you're not. Because let me tell you something, Mattie, I'm glad you got your first taste of the family court. Because you're going to be seeing a lot more of it. If you don't come to your senses, I'm going to be dragging you there every other month. The system is a beauty, and I've already studied up on it. Plenty of loopholes if I'm willing to pay the price. And believe me, sweetheart, I'm willing.'

'Why?'

'What do you mean, why?' Jake seemed a bit nonplussed. 'I've already told you why. You're my wife, and I'll do what it takes to get you back where you belong. See, if you think those orders will be worth the paper they're written on, you're wrong. All they do is give me another string to my bow. And I'll play them just like I play you. Have you thought how much it's going to cost you in lawyers' fees by the time I'm finished with you?'

'No,' said Mattie, rather wearily.

'Well, start thinking.' Jake picked up his mug and took a sip, smacking his lips as he put it back down. 'I haven't been sitting twiddling my thumbs, you know. I've been doing research. A *lot* of research. Like, did you know you're still entitled to some child support? Even though we're sharing custody? Amazing how geared the system is to you females. But don't think for a moment that it'll be worth it for you to apply, sweetheart, because I'll quit my job before you even finish the paperwork, and then I'll just work from home and take most of it under the table. Lucky I'm an accountant, isn't it? So I'll declare an income just over unemployment benefits, which'll entitle you to the grand sum of about five bucks a week.'

Mattie said nothing. She looked down at her hands, which had started to go numb.

'Because I'm giving you fair warning here. If you think things have been bad over the last week or so, think again. They'll get a whole lot worse if you don't come home. A whole lot worse.'

'Don't see how,' said Mattie with a harsh laugh.

'Then use your imagination. You'll be watching over your shoulder every moment you're outside, and you won't even feel safe in here. See this?' Jake put his hand in his pocket and pulled out a set of keys. When Mattie looked closer, she realised that they were her keys, from her handbag, with her distinctive gold *Matilda* tag. Jake slid her car key off the key-ring and passed it over, and then the original key to her unit.

'How . . . ?'

Jake shoved the remaining keys, with the tag, back into his pocket and shook his head at her sadly. 'You don't *think* enough, Mattie, that's your problem. Leaving your handbag in the lounge-room with me was really pretty stupid. Even for you. So what now? Change all the locks again? Must be getting expensive. And I bet your landlord doesn't know, either. Might have to give him a ring tomorrow.'

'God.'

'I won't give up, you know.' Jake leant closer to emphasise his words. '*Ever*. So your choice is between a life like this, or a life with me. And you have to admit that it wasn't that bad. We had our good times. Lots of them. Look at last night – you can't pretend you didn't want me too. Come on, Mat, what do you say? We can even get counselling if that's what you really want.'

Mattie shook her head, unable to say the words.

'Christ.' Jake stared at her, clearly irritated by her stubbornness. 'There's no pleasing you, is there?' He sighed, sat back again and then watched her closely. 'Well, I'll tell you something else for free. If you get any bright ideas about double-crossing me somehow in this hearing in a couple of weeks, like going for full custody instead of shared, then one weekend I simply won't bring them back. I'll take off with them. And you'll only have yourself to blame.'

Mattie frowned. 'What are you saying?'

'That you're not going to take my kids away from me. No bloody way.'

'You *can't* take off with them. The police'd be after you like a shot.'

'Want to try it and see?' Jake smiled at her challengingly. 'The only way you'd ever see them again would be if I got caught, and then you'd be seeing them in a casket.'

'You're not serious.'

'I am deadly serious.' Jake took another sip of tea and then looked at her again. 'Read the papers. Blokes do it all the time, because it's much more effective than just doing away with the wife. This way you hit her where it hurts, and leave her to live with it. She can regret what she did for the rest of her life, and it serves her bloody right. And don't for a moment think I wouldn't do it. You're not having them, Mattie. Face it.'

Mattie shook her head. 'You wouldn't.'

'Want to try me? See, your problem is that you want everything to go your way, and when anyone throws a spanner in the works, you act like you're a victim. Look at what you've done lately. First you convince me to let you move out, and you say it's only temporary, then as soon as I help you get settled, you announce that it's all over.' Jake's mouth thinned. 'And you expect me to just roll over and take it. You're trying to destroy our marriage and you're also trying to destroy our kids, just because that's what you *think* you want at the moment. But you're only thinking of yourself, as usual. By the way, did you know our son's been suspended?'

Mattie had been trying to let the words simply wash over her without settling, but this last question bit deep. She stared at Jake, stunned into silence by the fact that she had totally forgotten about Max's suspension. What did that say about her?

'That's right,' continued Jake, clearly pleased to get a reaction. 'For beating up some other kid. He's not allowed back to school till Wednesday. So you can chalk that up to your leaving too. Well done. But I've already disciplined him, not that you look like you care.'

'I *do* care,' flashed Mattie, as her mind ran a trailer of Max, standing in front of his father and stammering as he tried to explain his aggression. She clenched her hands around the mug and felt the hypocrisy churn in her gut. And all of a sudden her lethargy broke apart, like a cocoon, to reveal a blind fury that had been growing within it all the time, disguised by the blandness of its shell. She snatched her hands away and they felt like they were on fire. 'You're nothing but a fucking hypocrite.'

'What?'

'You heard me.' Mattie glared at him, her teeth grinding together so hard that her mouth trembled.

'*What* did you say?'

Mattie prised her teeth apart and felt her nostrils flare instead. 'I said you're a fucking hypocrite. And you are. You beat up on me all the time, but that's fine. Yet you have the damn gall to discipline him when he copies you. You should be ashamed of yourself.'

Jake was looking at her, astounded. 'Why, you bitch.'

'And you keep saying that it's all my fault for leaving but that's only because you don't have the guts to admit the reason I left was because you're such an arsehole. A fucking bully who beats up on people smaller than himself whenever he doesn't get his own way. Or just intimidates them, like ringing up Liz and threatening her *baby*. What a fucking hero you are. You know, we had everything, we *could* have had everything, but you fucked it up. Not me, idiot, *you*.'

As Mattie momentarily ran out of steam, Jake leapt up from his chair, pushing it away so fiercely that it rocked back on its two rear legs and teetered for a moment before settling again, with a thud. Mattie watched him without moving. Instead of fear, she felt fatalism. What will be, will be. And a stray thought shot through her mind that at least now Hannah would be pleased, she'd be able to get her photos after all. This thought struck her as incredibly funny, and a giggle bubbled up in her throat, bursting out with a slight edge of hysteria.

'I'll teach you to laugh at me, you fucking *bitch*!' Jake lunged across the table, knocking his mug flying, and grabbed Mattie by the hair. Then, by sheer force, he dragged her up out of her chair and across the table. Her own mug was pushed over the table and fell to the floor, where it smashed. She felt the spilt coffee and tea saturate her t-shirt as she slithered over the table and then she was pulled up so that her face was inches away from his.

'You low-life bitch. How *dare* you talk to me like that.'

Mattie stared into his face, which was so suffused with fury that the veins in his forehead were visibly throbbing and the grooves either side of his mouth stood out like wounds themselves. Then she did something that, if possible, stunned her even more than him. She gathered together every bit of phlegm she could muster and spat, full in his face.

Jake's eyes widened with shock and he pulled back, smacking her full across the face at the same time as he finally let go of her hair. Mattie flew sideways, tumbling straight off the table and onto the floor, where she felt a shard of pottery slice deeply into the palm of her left hand. She stared at the hand as the two edges of her flesh peeled back, just like a ripe peach, and then almost immediately the crimson blood welled up within the cut. And just as it started to spill over and drip down onto her bare legs, suddenly she was being lifted by the hair again.

This time her hands shot up automatically to scrabble frantically at the hand buried within her hair and blood splattered as she clawed. Then she saw, over Jake's shoulder, Max standing in the kitchen doorway. His face was so pale that he looked like a corpse, and his eyes were huge wells of disbelief. Enormous. Mattie opened her mouth to tell him to go, but nothing came out but a cry of pain.

'Daddy! Daddy! *Stop*! You're killing her!' Max ran behind his father and then Mattie couldn't see him anymore, but she could feel him, in the movement of Jake's body as the boy pummelled at him.

Mattie's scalp felt like it was about to be torn loose, and her forehead was stretched so tightly she couldn't blink. She hit at the hand furiously, ferociously, and when that didn't have any effect on his grip, she pulled her uninjured hand back, made a fist, and shot it forward with all her might, with the strength of years, and aimed it straight for where she estimated his face to be.

She felt it connect with a blunt force that jarred her hand, and then suddenly she was released, falling back down to the floor. She landed hard, and looked up immediately to see Jake reel backwards, clutching his face. As he did, he cannoned into Max, who was still hammering at his father's back, and the boy was knocked flying, landing by the doorway on his bottom with his head hitting the wall behind with a loud, solid crack.

Jake whirled around immediately and was clearly aghast when he realised what had happened. He put a hand out to Max, who was looking dazed, and then pulled it away again and turned to Mattie, staring at her with such hatred on his face that she drew back. His right eye was already starting to swell.

'You fucking *bitch*. Call yourself a mother?' Jake, copying her earlier gesture, spat straight at her. 'You're no mother. You're scum. And you'll pay for this.'

Mattie felt the spittle hit her warmly on one cheek and flinched, but didn't take her eyes off Jake. For a moment, she thought he was going to spit at her again but then he just turned and, without even glancing at Max, walked out. A second later, the front door slammed behind him.

'Max? Are you all right?' Mattie wiped the spittle off her cheek as she crawled across the floor towards her son, who was still sitting in the same spot.

'I think so.' Max looked at her and then his gaze dropped to the floor, and the trail of bloody handprints she had left behind. 'You're bleeding.'

'I'm okay.' Mattie knelt next to Max and stared into his eyes, trying to remember whether small or large pupils meant concussion. Anyway, his looked normal.

'Mummy?' Courtney stood in the doorway, staring at her brother, her mother, the blood. Her bottom lip trembled and she started to cry.

Mattie, still kneeling, reached out her arms and Courtney, after a wary look at the bloody hand, climbed into them. She buried her head against her mother's shoulder and Mattie patted her head with her good hand. The other she rested by her leg, where it dribbled blood onto the floor in a puddle. *Needs to be washed. Scrubbed clean.* Mattie glanced at Max and smiled at him, wanting him to know how proud she was. He grinned back, but his face was still pale.

The kitchen looked like a disaster had just unfolded there, which was exactly what had happened. But, to Mattie, it was also a triumph. And, in stark contrast to her depression and lethargy of the past two days, she felt jubilant. Victorious. They'd fought back and won. He was gone. Then, just as her exultation started to warm her, she remembered the words that had preceded the violence and it vanished. In its place were the threats he had made against the children. And she realised that all she had won was a brief reprieve. If that.

*S*he called the baby Riley, a good unisex name because she would never know whether it had been a boy or a girl. Nor would she ever know if her lifestyle had contributed to Riley's lack of survival. All she could do was give it some sort of identity and then bury it deep, where the tentacles of grief had to really stretch to entrap her. But the questions that surrounded the event could not be buried. Instead, they were added to all the others that, like a child's set of Lego bricks, had been building on each other throughout her marriage. Questions that she was sure would have answers if only she looked a little harder, deeper, longer. Questions like what made someone act that way? Where was her Jake when the other one came out? Why couldn't he do battle for her? And protect her? Why would someone deliberately sabotage something he said he held dear? What had she done to deserve it? What could she do to make it right?

There had to be answers. Somewhere. Or maybe the questions she was asking were simply the wrong ones. Maybe she just had to sit Jake down, one more time, and try to explain. Try to make him understand. Surely, if she phrased it right, explained herself better, picked the right moment – surely then he would understand.

EIGHTEEN

On Monday Mattie kept the children home again. With Max she had no choice, as he was suspended, but with Courtney she simply couldn't be bothered. She didn't want to have to get her ready, or drop her off, or talk to anyone. Instead, they could all stay home for the day and pretend that the outside world just didn't exist. Drink hot chocolate, watch television, talk about everything except what really mattered.

Her depression gradually returned after Jake left, but surprisingly it was not as severe as it had been. Perhaps because it couldn't be, not when the children were at home and their needs demanded priority over her own. She'd cleaned her hand with antiseptic and then bandaged it, even though she suspected it might well have needed stitches. She had lost quite a bit of hair, again, and despite piling on the foundation, displayed a large bruise that ran down one side of her face and puffed over the corner of her right eye so that it was semi-closed and quite sore. Max, fortunately, had no injuries. No visible injuries anyway.

During the morning, Mattie tried several times to muster the energy to organise a game or something with the children, but each time sheer weariness anchored her to the couch from where she stared rather blankly at the television. Nor did Max and Courtney complain of boredom or demand entertainment. Instead both lay across the beanbag watching cartoons, followed by the preschooler shows, without saying much at all.

Mattie would have dearly liked to block out her thoughts as easily as she was blocking out activity, but they kept filtering through. And chief amongst them was the knowledge that she had to make a choice – either stay here and go on like this, or return to Jake and make the best of it. There was no doubt that, all things considered, she'd been both happier and safer before she moved. Even with the persistence of the pattern and the occasional flare-ups, it had been less stressful, less injurious, less costly, and less physically and emotionally draining. And the predictability of the pattern meant that she could anticipate, more or less, what was going to occur and when. Not like now, when she felt bombarded and totally lacking any control over her situation.

As for Max and Courtney, when she'd been living at home she had been able to hide a great deal of the actual violence, so that although they probably intuited some of what was occurring, they were able to thrust it aside and continue on with it *shading* their lives but not actually colouring it. Now, within a few short weeks, they had become changed children. Alongside the intensification of Max's reserve was an aggression he had never displayed before, and Courtney's effervescent nature had become dimmed. Disturbingly, she'd even begun to copy Max's habit of not maintaining eye contact, so that one minute her eyes would be focused, and the next they would be flitting away nervously.

So it came down to a choice between two evils, with the vote going to whichever was the lesser. And the lesser, it seemed, was for Mattie to return home. It was a decision that filled her with no joy even though, deep down, she still thought she loved him. Or felt *something* for him – loyalty, constancy, affinity, a deep and irreplaceable sense of shared history. Not for the man who had planned and carried out this campaign of ruthless vengeance, but for the other man, the one she'd married. Or thought she'd married.

About mid-morning, Sharon, from Whimsicalities, came to drop off the box of ordered goods and pick up her payment. She exclaimed sympathetically over Mattie's face, and seemed to readily accept the story of an accidental fall. Mattie paid for Liz's order herself, although that left her with only coins in her purse, nothing in the bank, and very little in the cupboards either. This seemed to underline the choice she'd already made, and lent it a righteousness that almost, but not quite, balanced out the claustrophobia.

But she dreaded telling Hannah of her decision, and Hilda, and, for that matter, the children. She already knew that they would all see her as giving up, whereas she was merely giving in. They wouldn't see that she had no real choice. They wouldn't believe the system was unable to protect her, or that she couldn't live with the likelihood of Jake acting on his threats. They would just see it as letting him get away with it. Rewarding his bad behaviour. And they wouldn't appreciate that every so often her weariness was being pierced by a mental image of Jake's face when he was told of her capitulation – and the smug triumph that she imagined would be written there was enough to cause her dormant anger to flare like acid indigestion, leaving behind only the sour taste of defeat.

Mattie had forgotten Hannah's promise to drop around, so when her sister arrived, shortly after Sharon left, she felt a brief surge of self-pitying irritation. *Why me? Can't I have one break? Just one?* It was another thing to cope with on a day when she felt particularly incapable of coping with anything. She watched, from the couch, as her sister strode confidently up to the front door. Hannah looked every inch the white-collar wife today, with a calf-length layered brown skirt and a baggy cream t-shirt with a wide, low-slung leather-weave belt sitting just below the waist. To complement the bohemian look of the outfit, she wore chunky gold bracelets and a chunky gold chain that was tied in a knot between her breasts.

Mattie took a deep breath and got up to open the door.

'Hel-*lo*, how are you?' Hannah grinned happily and then her jaw dropped as she registered Mattie's bruised face. She stopped, just over the threshold, and stared.

'Come into the kitchen,' said Mattie, glancing across at Max and Courtney, who were watching silently.

'Jesus, Mattie! What happened?'

'Come into the kitchen,' repeated Mattie, closing the door.

Hannah, following Mattie's gaze, took in the two children lying across the beanbag. She pulled herself together and smiled at them. 'Hello, you two. Day off school, hey?'

While Hannah chatted brightly with her niece and nephew, Mattie went into the kitchen and put the kettle on, now accustomed to using only the fingertips of her injured hand to manage tasks. She got the plunger ready and was just filling it when Hannah came in. She went straight up to Mattie and took her by her face, putting her hand on the unbruised side and tilting it slightly to examine the extent of the damage.

'Jesus Christ. That bastard.'

'Mmm.'

'And your hand! Look at your hand!'

'Yep.'

'When did this happen?'

'Yesterday afternoon, when he returned the kids.'

'Did you ring the police? You *have* to ring the police.'

'What for?' Mattie poured hot water over Hannah's teabag. She felt annoyed that she even had to explain. 'Then it'd just get worse. And worse. Besides, I'd have had to drag Max into it all, because he was here too.'

'This is ridiculous.' Hannah thumped her handbag down onto the kitchen table and started rummaging through it. 'You need to start acting against him, Mattie. But we'll talk about that later. For now, I'm going to take some shots of this.'

Mattie put the two mugs on the table and sat down. For a moment she thought of telling her sister how, at the height of the violence, she'd thought how pleased Hannah would be to have something to photograph. But she didn't, because it would just have been something else to explain. Besides, perhaps it wasn't really that funny.

'Okay, hold still.' Hannah removed a small digital camera from her bag and leant forward with it in front of her face. It clicked once, twice, three times. Then she bobbed down and took another three photos of Mattie's bandaged hand.

'Hannah –' Mattie smiled, amused despite herself – 'what does that prove? It's a bandaged hand, and there might be *nothing* underneath the bandage.'

'You're right.' Hannah frowned and put the camera down. 'Undo the bandage.'

'Is this really necessary?'

'Yes.' Hannah already had hold of the end of the bandage and was unravelling it gently. She rolled it up efficiently and very soon Mattie's palm was exposed, with a deep purple-lipped laceration running across it diagonally that was smudged with dried blood and crusty antiseptic.

'There you go,' said Mattie, flinching as the fresh air chilled the open wound.

'Jesus.' Hannah held the hand gently. 'I think this needs stitches, Mattie.'

'Just take the photos.'

'Okay, it's your funeral.' Hannah raised the camera again and took a series of shots from different angles. Then she put the camera away in her bag and sat down opposite her sister, who was rebandaging herself awkwardly.

'Happy now?' asked Mattie.

'Do you want me to do that?'

'No, almost done.' Mattie wrapped the last section around her palm and then tucked the end in. 'There we go. Good as new.'

'Bastard.' Hannah shook her head with a sort of wonder. Then she looked at her sister grimly. 'Now tell me what happened. Everything.'

Mattie took a deep breath. This was what she'd wanted to avoid, because it wasn't like Hannah could help, or make a difference. And this time the load wouldn't be any lighter for sharing – if anything it would be heavier, because then she would have Hannah's condemnation on top of everything else. But apart from all that, and despite all he had done, telling anyone anything that put Jake in such a horribly bad light still made Mattie feel disloyal, humiliated and plain foolish.

'Come on.'

'Okay then.' Mattie frowned at Hannah's impatience. 'He came in when he dropped the kids off and said he wanted a chat. To set me straight about a few things. But what it really amounted to was a series of threats. Like he's already studied up on the court system, and child support and all that, and is going to use it all against me. Take me back to court all the time. Quit his job if I go after child support. Just generally make life pretty miserable.'

'He won't get away with that.'

'Why not?'

'Because, well, the system won't allow it.' Hannah looked doubtful. 'Will it?'

'Actually I think it might.' Mattie hefted herself out of her chair and went over to the fridge to retrieve the manilla folder that Jake had dropped off. She selected the personal account he'd particularly emphasised and passed it over to Hannah wordlessly. Mattie sat down again while her sister read it. She sipped at her coffee and just wished that this was all over. Everything.

'Jesus.' Hannah said when she'd read it. 'Where did you get this?'

'Jake. He dropped it off the other night.'

'He's trying to scare you.' Hannah put the sheet of paper down. 'Don't let him.'

'Too late.' Mattie smiled and shook her head. 'And there's more. He said that if I ever went for other than shared custody, or tried to take the kids off him, he'd shoot through with them one weekend. And the only way I'd ever see them again would be in a casket.'

Hannah's eyes widened. 'You're kidding. He means he'd . . .' She shook her head. 'No, he wouldn't.'

'Probably not, but he gave me a detailed explanation of why so many men do away with themselves and their kids after a marriage bust-up. He said simply doing away with the wife isn't as effective. You need to hit her where it hurts, and then leave her to live with it. *That's* effective.'

Hannah was still looking at her disbelievingly. 'But he wouldn't actually –'

'Who's to say?' Mattie snorted. 'I wouldn't have thought he'd do *any* of this but I was wrong, wasn't I?'

'You need to ring the police.'

'God, Hannah.' Mattie sat back in her chair and frowned at her sister with irritation. 'You've got this amazing trust in the powers of the police, haven't you? Have you ever thought that they might just make things worse? Actually force his hand? Besides, what are they going to *do*? They'll get my story and then he'll just say I'm lying. And he can be *very* persuasive. I should know. Which reminds me, did Stuart go around to see him the other day?'

Hannah looked at Mattie evenly and then dropped her gaze. 'Yes, he did.'

'And?'

'And that's not going to help. I'm sorry.'

'Just tell me what happened. Come on, I won't get upset.'

'Okay.' Hannah sighed and finally looked up, shaking her head. 'I'm so angry with him but . . . well, he went around there on Thursday night all riled up about everything and came back saying how there's two sides to every story and we shouldn't get involved. It seems they sat out on the patio and drank beer and chatted. And Jake denied everything.'

'Everything?' asked Mattie. 'What about picking the kids up early? Coming around here? The magpie?'

'Apparently he only picked the kids up because they had a doctor's appointment and he only comes around here when he's invited. And according to Stuart, Jake had no idea about the magpie stuff until he told him, and then he was really concerned. Says that you've got a habit of leaving the windows open and he's been worried about it for ages.' Hannah flipped her plait forward and started playing with the ends. 'And he also said you've got a drinking problem, and mood swings and a tendency to fabricate. He even said you'd been known to self-injure. Not often, but every now and again when you were really depressed. He said you need help.'

'I need help?' Mattie closed her eyes and felt a smile tug at her mouth.

'Yes. And that the real reason you left was because he was insisting on you getting some, because he was worried about the kids.'

'God. He's good, isn't he?'

'I'm not sure how much Stuart believed, but it was enough to convince him he didn't want to get involved. I'm sorry, Mattie. He thinks you need counselling as a family.'

'See what I mean?' asked Mattie. 'If Jake can convince Stuart, who *knows* me, then what hope do I have with the damn police?'

'Wait till he sees these photos.' Hannah narrowed her eyes in a manner that boded ill for her husband. Then she clicked her fingers. 'What about *his* family? What about telling *them*, or showing them the photos?'

Mattie paled at the thought but then, as Hannah watched her expectantly, she made herself examine it from every angle before shaking her head. 'No, they'd never believe me. He's their bright-eyed boy. And he'd just make something up, like with Stuart. He's very good at it, you know. I think he even convinces himself.'

'Still think it might be worth a shot,' said Hannah stubbornly. Then she glanced down at Mattie's hand. 'And you haven't said how you got *that* hurt.'

'Oh, it happened towards the end.' Mattie looked down at her hand as well and wiggled her fingers. 'See, Max got in trouble at school for being aggressive, and he got suspended. So Jake was telling me how this was all my fault too, when I sort of lost my temper and told him a few home truths.'

Hannah nodded approvingly. 'Good on you.'

'Easy for you to say. Unfortunately, Jake doesn't take home truths very well so he . . .' Mattie waved at her face. 'And a coffee cup got broken and I fell on it. Hence the hand. But the worst this time was . . .' Mattie hesitated, unsure whether she should confide this part.

'What?'

Mattie sighed, and went on. 'The worst part was that Max came in and started hitting his father on the back telling him to stop. And I thought he was going to get hurt so I hauled off and punched Jake full in the face. But that made him go backwards and he knocked Max flying against the wall.'

'Jesus! Was he hurt?'

'Luckily no. But you should have seen Jake's face. I know you won't believe me, but he was absolutely appalled at what he'd done. So he left.'

'So it's okay for him to beat up on you, but he draws the line at the kids?'

'Something like that.'

'What a hero,' said Hannah bitterly.

Before Mattie could respond to this, there was a sharp knock at the door. She and Hannah stared at each other, and both rose from the table.

'I'll get it,' said Mattie. 'You stay here.'

She left her sister standing by the table, looking worried, and went into the lounge-room to answer the door. Both children were looking towards her and she smiled at them reassuringly as she undid the dead-lock. It was Hilda.

'Hello there. Just thought I would pop in and –' Hilda stopped and stared aghast at Mattie's face. 'Oh my. What happened?'

'I'm fine, Hilda, really. Hannah's here too, so you may as well come in and have a coffee with us. And I've got that Whimsicalities stuff too, so I'll give you your order.'

'All right.' Hilda's eyes were still on the bruise. Then she glanced down at Mattie's hand and drew a sharp breath. '*Gott* in heaven.'

Mattie ushered her in and Hilda walked past, smiling at the watch-ful children as she went towards the kitchen. But as Mattie started to close the front door, she saw a police car turn into the driveway and, to her intense surprise, draw to a halt by her unit. For a moment, Mattie thought Hannah must have used the intervening few minutes to ring the police. Then she quickly realised that was ridiculous. Nobody had a response time that good. She watched as a policewoman got out of the passenger side of the car and walked up the pathway towards the porch.

'Can I help you?'

'Matilda Hampton?' It was the same policewoman who'd come before, with her tight but wispy blonde bun. She stared at Mattie's bruise for a second and then maintained eye contact.

'Yes, that's me.'

'I have to serve you with this.' The policewoman held out a single sheet of paper, which Mattie took hesitantly. It looked very official, with a number of handwritten sections interspersed within more formal rows of type.

'What is it?' Mattie started to read, but it didn't seem to make sense.

'It's an intervention order,' the policewoman explained. 'Against you.

Filed by your husband. It means that you are not allowed to come within a certain distance of his home or work, or any place that you know him to be. Do you understand?'

'Not really.' Mattie looked up, totally bewildered. 'Why?'

'Because he claims you assaulted him.' She spoke slowly, her eyes flicking back to the bruise momentarily. 'He made a police report and then went to court this morning to get a temporary IO, which you have there. And there'll be a hearing for a permanent one very soon. You'll be notified of the date and you have the right to attend. In fact, I would urge you to attend.'

'He said I assaulted him?' Mattie's legs felt weak.

'Yes. And he had a nasty black eye to prove it. But you . . . look, Mrs Hampton, if he caused those bruises on your face, you should make a police report as well. At the very least you can get a joint IO. This way –' she waved at the piece of paper – 'it looks like you're the sole instigator.'

'Okay.' Mattie looked over at the police car, where another police-woman sat in the driver's seat, waiting patiently.

The policewoman standing on the porch followed her gaze. 'I'd better get going. Do you understand what I've said?'

'Yes.' Mattie nodded. 'Thank you.'

She watched as the blonde policewoman walked briskly back down the path and climbed into the police car. Then they took off, driving up and over the bump at the gutter and down the road. Mattie looked at the form in her hand. An intervention order. *Against* her.

'What did they want?' asked Max, who was kneeling on the couch watching the police car disappear from view.

'Nothing much.' Mattie smiled at him mechanically. 'Just some paperwork, that's all. Nothing to worry about.'

'Oh.' Max didn't look like he believed her. He glanced across at his sister, who was watching her mother wide-eyed.

'Are they gonna put you in jail, Mummy?'

'Of course not, Court, didn't you hear what I told Max? It's nothing to worry about. Really.'

Max clambered back down and went to sit on the beanbag again.

He shoved Courtney roughly to one side and settled himself without glancing at his mother again. Mattie watched him silently and then shrugged. She would deal with that later. Even one thing at a time felt like more than she could manage at the moment. She went back into the kitchen.

'I've just been filling Hilda in on the latest,' said Hannah, who was by the kitchen bench making fresh tea and coffee. 'Hope you don't mind.'

'No.' Mattie shrugged again.

'Who was at the door?'

'Police.'

'Police!' Hannah whirled around, the plunger in her hand. 'What for?'

Instead of answering, Mattie held the intervention order up in front of Hannah's face. She started reading it with a frown.

'What the hell is this, Mattie? And what does it mean the complainant is *Jake*?'

'It means Jake made a police report about me punching him last night. And then followed it through with an intervention order to prohibit me from going near him, or his home or work.' Mattie put the form on the table and started to wash her hands, forgetting about the bandage until she felt it dampen. She stared at it, and then pressed her other fingers against the wet edges, to squeeze the water out. It felt even more uncomfortable now but she tried to ignore it as she slid back into her seat.

Hilda had picked up the form and was reading it. '*Mein Gott.*'

'That *bastard!*' Hannah slammed down the plunger angrily. 'How *dare* he?'

'Easily, it seems,' replied Mattie, feeling quite untouched by the news.

'It says here that you're not allowed to ring him, or contact him,' said Hilda. 'What about when he has the children? Can you not phone to see how they are?'

'Obviously not.'

'That bastard,' said Hannah again. 'Then *we* need one of those too!'

'Why?' asked Mattie wearily.

'Because it's not fair, that's why!' Hannah stared at her sister crossly. 'He's the one who's violent, not you! All you did is retaliate, and I hope you hurt him!'

Mattie smiled. 'The policewoman did say he had a nasty black eye.'

'Good.' Hannah picked up the plunger again and started pouring out two coffees. 'I hope he loses his sight.'

'Mattie –' Hilda pointed at the IO – 'would this affect your hearing? For the children?'

'I hadn't thought of that.' Mattie looked at it, and tried to care. 'Probably.'

Hannah put a mug in front of Hilda and a refreshed one in front of Mattie. Then she took her cup of tea and sat down again, frowning at her sister. 'You don't seem very worried about this.'

'I'm not. Not really.'

'How can you *not* be?' Hannah shook her head, perplexed.

'Because it won't make any difference, not in the long run.' Mattie took a deep breath. 'See, I'm going back to him. And before you start, I've thought about this long and hard, and I'm not being rash. It really is the only way.'

'No!' Max burst into the room and ran to his mother. But instead of flinging himself on her, which was what she half expected, he stopped about a foot from her and stood with his fists clenched, staring at her furiously.

'Max, let me explain –'

'No! You can't!'

'Max, come on! *Look* at us!' Mattie waved her good arm towards the lounge-room to take in Courtney also. 'We can't go on like this. We just can't!'

'Then I'm running away.' Max glared at her, and then suddenly kicked his bare foot out, connecting hard with her shin. Mattie gasped and held her hand out to stop him doing it again.

'Max!' Hannah jumped up, shocked.

'You're as bad as he is! I hate you both!' Max ran from the room, his footsteps echoing up the passage and into the children's bedroom. The door slammed.

'He *kicked* you!' said Hannah, staring at Mattie.

'He's just upset.' Mattie rubbed her shin and felt tears shimmering in her eyes. Although the kick itself had not been terribly painful, the fact that Max – *her Max* – had lashed out like that was almost unbearable.

'He is unhappy,' said Hilda, stating the obvious. 'He does not want you to go back to his father. He thinks you will be hurt again. He thinks he might lose you.'

'He's more likely to lose me if I *don't* go back to his father.' Mattie knew she should go to her son, talk to him, but could not summon the energy to face his anger.

'You can't be serious.' Hannah looked at her with thin lips.

The tears in Mattie's right eye stung the swelling in the corner and it started to throb. Mattie got up and washed her uninjured hand as well as the fingertips of the other before taking two painkillers. She glanced through the kitchen doorway and saw that Courtney, too, had vanished. And she was glad, because it meant that at least someone had followed Max.

'Mattie? Tell me you're not serious.'

'God, Hannah.' Mattie glared at her sister, so frustrated that it felt like even her blood was overheating. 'At least *try* to understand. How am I going to live like this? Look at my hands.' She held out both her hands and they trembled visibly, like an old lady's, with the wet part of the bandage now hanging loosely. 'I can't go on like this. There's something else every day and this is only the start. And it's not just me, the kids are wrecked too. Absolutely wrecked.'

'But we're gaining ground!' protested Hannah. 'Like changing the locks and –'

'He's already got the keys. Stole them out of my bag. And would you like to know what he did on Friday night?'

'What?'

'Came around here and left the kids at home, alone. Then he said he'd wait on the doorstep until I let him in, so the longer I took, the longer they'd be alone. I threatened to call the police and he laughed, said he'd tell them I'd rung him all panicked because there was a prowler or something. That I'd set him up to make him look bad.'

'What did you do?' asked Hilda softly.

Mattie snorted as she slid back into her seat. 'What could I do? I let him in. And you know what he wanted?'

'What?'

'Sex. That's what. It'd been two weeks, see, and he wanted his conjugal rights.' Mattie spoke sarcastically, but her eyes shimmered and she looked at the window over the sink as she spoke. 'And when I refused, he ran the same story. The longer I held out, the longer the kids would be alone.'

'So you did.' Hannah made it a statement, not a question.

'Yes. Of course I did.'

'You poor, poor girl.' Hilda reached out and laid her fingers gently over Mattie's injured hand. 'This man is a rotter.'

The old-fashioned word made Mattie glance at Hilda and smile, despite herself. But still the tears that had been filming her eyes for the past few minutes spilled over and she started to cry. Or maybe it was *because* of the sympathy, rather than in spite of it.

'But if you go back, he becomes even more powerful,' said Hannah, less aggressively this time. 'And you're putting yourself at risk. Terrible risk.'

'No, I'm not. It won't be as bad,' Mattie hiccupped wetly, pulling a tissue out of her pocket with her spare hand and blowing her nose. She folded the tissue over awkwardly and wiped her eyes, treating the right one very gently, but the tears just kept coming. It was like a slow, continual purge that could not be turned off until it was spent.

'She can't go back.' Hannah looked at Hilda. 'She just can't.'

'But she feels she cannot go on like this either,' said Hilda, still patting Mattie's hand.

'The law's an ass.' Hannah picked up the intervention order and threw it, but it only travelled about a foot away before curling over on itself and then fluttering to the floor, where it lay flat and easily readable. *Complainant – Jake Hampton. Aggrieved family member.*

Hilda stared at the paper and then released Mattie's hand and sat back. 'But maybe he made a mistake with that. After all, does it not help Mattie if they can never be together, yes? That she must stay away from him?'

'Not really.' Mattie rose and threw the scrunched tissue into the bin. Then she got the tissue box down from the top of the fridge and took it back to the table. 'He doesn't care about what the paper says, he just wants to intimidate me. And it'll make him look good for the interim hearing. Like *he's* the victim.'

'Bastard.' Hannah glared towards the kitchen window and then suddenly clicked her fingers. 'I know! What about if you move in with me temporarily? All three of you?'

Mattie tried to smile at her sister's generosity but the effort failed. 'Thanks, but it wouldn't work.'

'I don't see why –'

'You just don't get it.' Mattie grabbed another tissue and wiped her left eye roughly. Then she dabbed at the other eye and looked at her sister tiredly, her earlier frustration having dissipated. She took a deep breath. 'See, he really *does* think he's the victim. He really does. He thinks that I've done the wrong thing, that it's all my fault. I'm his wife, he loves me and I *belong* to him, I'm his property – just like the money, the house, the kids. And *I* left *him*. Therefore whatever he does to get me back is wholly justified. For *my* sake as well as his. And don't for a minute underestimate the lengths he'll go to accomplish that. Hasn't this last week shown you anything? Don't you get it?'

'But that makes no –'

'It doesn't *have* to make sense,' wailed Mattie, even while tears dribbled down her cheeks. 'And I didn't say he was right, did I? I just said that's how he feels. And that's why he'll never leave me alone. *Never*! He'd rather see me *dead,* or the kids *dead,* than give up! *Now* do you get it?'

There was silence after this outburst, the only noise being Mattie's continued snuffling and the rasping noise the tissues made as they were pulled from the box. Hannah looked down at the table as if an answer might lie in its wooden surface, while Hilda drank her coffee and stared over towards the window. After about five minutes, Hilda spoke.

'The way I see it, you have only one choice.'

'That's what I've been trying to tell you.' Mattie started crying even harder. She put an elbow up on the table, rested her forehead against her uninjured hand and just sobbed, too miserable to feel embarrassed.

'Oh, no. Not *that* choice.'

'What do you mean?' Hannah sounded suspicious.

'Why, the same as young Max before. *He* had the right idea.'

'By kicking me, you mean?' Mattie laughed wetly and heard the edge of hysteria scuttle along the ridges of the humour. She hiccupped, and felt drunk.

'No, of course not. By leaving. Running away.'

Mattie uncovered her face and stared at Hilda with disbelief. The older woman passed her another tissue and pointed at her nose. Mattie blew it noisily.

'What do you mean?' Hannah nudged Hilda to get her attention. 'Are you serious?'

'Very serious,' replied Hilda calmly. 'It is the only way.'

'For god's sake, how can I run away? It's impossible.' Mattie shook her head dismissively, almost annoyed at the ludicrous suggestion. She took another tissue and wiped at her eyes, forgetting momentarily that the right one was swollen. The pain was harsh and instantaneous, and she flinched.

'Nothing's impossible. It just takes a little planning.'

'Where would she run to?' asked Hannah, seriously.

'Does it matter? As long as it is away from here?'

'I suppose not.' Hannah stared narrowly down at the table and then glanced back over at Hilda. 'You *are* serious, aren't you?'

'I said I was. She could take as much as she can fit in, say, three suit-cases when she leaves. Start again somewhere else.'

Hannah stared. 'But won't she . . . ?'

'Look –' Hilda leant forward – 'you know how he told her about just taking off with the children? Well, why not her first? Lord knows, she's got a better reason to than he does. And she will not be the first, there are a lot of women, and some men, who just take their children and disappear. Some have good reason, like her, and some do it just to be spiteful. But how often do you read about someone being tracked down who *wanted* to vanish, yes?'

'He'd find me,' whispered Mattie, scrunching the tissue within her hand and feeling her nails dig into her palm. 'Eventually he'd find me.'

Hannah glanced across at her sister and cringed at the sight of her blood-red, inflamed eye. 'Jesus,' she muttered, shaking her head.

'No, not necessarily,' replied Hilda. 'He is not superman. And really, what have you got to lose? Spending your life wondering, each weekend, if you will ever see your children again? Or having a life with him, and who knows how that will end? So what do you have to lose?'

'Nothing!' said Hannah excitedly. 'She's right, Mattie!'

'You're talking about packing up and leaving, with the kids, and starting again somewhere else with next to nothing.' Mattie tried to make it sound as ridiculous as it was. 'Just . . . leaving. Just like that.'

'Exactly!' Hannah thumped a fist onto the table. 'And what's more, you won't even be doing anything illegal because there're no orders yet on Max and Courtney! In a few weeks, when the interim ones are handed down, *then* you'd be breaching them, but now – nothing! There's nothing!'

'Beat him at his own game,' added Hilda, her black eyes shining. 'Just like there was nothing to stop him picking up the children last week when it was not his turn.'

'And you'd be doing this for the children as well as yourself,' added Hannah. 'Because you're right, you *can't* go on like this. But neither can you go back to him.'

Mattie held up a hand. 'I really appreciate the fact that you both care. Really, I do. But what you're talking about is impossible. I mean, the kids would *never* see their father again, do you realise that? And I know you think I'm signing my own death warrant or something by going back, but you're wrong. Things only got really bad *after* I left. It wasn't like that before.'

'God, Mattie.' Hannah frowned crossly. 'It mightn't have been as bad but he was still *hitting* you. Well, wasn't he?'

'He said he'd get help. He said if I go back he'll get counselling.'

'A leopard cannot change his spots,' said Hilda darkly. 'Not spots like those anyway. And what sort of example are you setting for those children?'

Mattie ignored her. 'Besides, what you're talking about . . . the logistics are –'

'Not that bad,' finished Hannah. She reached out suddenly and grabbed Mattie by the wrist of her good hand, holding it up so that they could all see the tremor for a moment before Mattie snatched it back. 'And besides, that boy in there would never get over it if you went back. Hilda's right, think of what you'd be showing those kids. That violence pays off.'

'And Lord forbid if anything happened to you.' Hilda crossed herself. 'Then where would they be?'

'She'd have to do it as soon as possible.' Hannah ran her fingers through her hair while she thought. 'Those two kids shouldn't go back to him after this. It's too risky.'

Mattie stood up and went over to the sink, putting some distance between herself and this outrageous suggestion, which Hilda and Hannah seemed to be taking so seriously. She stared out of the window as the discussion continued behind her and tried to imagine starting all over again somewhere new – and couldn't. The very blankness of the future was frightening. Then she tried to imagine continuing on as she was, and knew that was not an option. Last of all she tried to picture herself back in the house with Jake, watching him and knowing how he'd forced her to return. The lengths to which he'd gone, regardless of their effect on her or the children. And she paled. But surely the counselling would help there. Surely.

Mattie licked her lips nervously, and turned on the tap to wash her hands. She kept the still-damp bandage away from the water and let the water trickle between her fingers. Then she allowed her thoughts to drift towards Hilda's bizarre suggestion. The thought of leaving, with two children and a couple of suitcases, and simply fleeing to another part of the country. There to re-establish themselves with next to nothing. Except an ongoing fear that every corner they turned, every door they opened, might have *him* standing on the other side. Mattie shook her head. Far better to live with him and know where he was. She turned off the tap and then leant against the sink, watching the other two as they continued their conversation with growing enthusiasm.

'And the lease doesn't really present a problem.' Hannah undid her plait and ran her fingers through her hair, fluffing it out. 'Because

Charlotte broke a lease last year when she changed universities. All she had to do was advertise it, and then pay the rent until someone new came in. We can do the same here, so we might end up out of pocket a month or two of rent, but that's a small price to pay.'

'So she takes only those things she cannot do without,' said Hilda, draining her coffee. 'Photographs, documents, things like that. Leave behind things she can replace.'

'And I'll just call in a second-hand dealer and flog him the lot,' put in Hannah, flicking her hair over her shoulder and leaving it out. 'Then send her the money.'

'Ah, yes. Money,' said Mattie sarcastically. 'Perhaps that might be a problem?'

'I'll lend it to you,' said Hannah promptly, 'And don't say no. You can't afford to. But don't forget you'll be selling your car for cash, that'll bring in some. See, here's the way I think it should work. I've got a set of suit-cases at home, we'll use them. Because we can't afford to have them here in case Jake comes around and guesses what we're up to. So we move what you want from here by plastic bags and pack the cases at my house. But don't take anything that'll indicate what's going on – like photos from the walls and that. Don't forget he's got keys now so he'll probably let himself in at some stage. You need to stay at my house until you go. Keep *both* kids out of school just in case. Now, today you sort out what you want from here, and I'm taking you to the doctor's. You need stitches, and I think that eye needs attention. Plus, it gives medical sup-port to what we're doing just in case we ever need it. Then tomorrow we sell the car and tie up loose ends. And tomorrow night you're off.'

'Tomorrow night!'

'Yes, you can't afford to wait any longer. That'll give you a two-day head start before Thursday. Besides, if you wait any longer, you run the risk of Jake pulling another stunt and us having to call it off. Like he refuses to bring the kids back until the hearing or something.'

'Hannah is right, Mattie,' agreed Hilda, nodding.

'And obviously you need to give a false name,' continued Hannah, frowning with concentration. 'Which should be okay because you'll only be going interstate. And don't go direct to wherever it is that we decide is the best. Instead, use a plane or bus or whatever first, to say Sydney, then use a different mode of transport to somewhere else. Zig-zag across country for a day or so. In fact, I'd zigzag until Thursday if I was you.'

Mattie shook her head in amazement. 'This is a joke.'

'And she needs to finish up in a capital city,' added Hilda, ignoring Mattie's interjection. 'That way she will not miss the car for a while. And it will be easier to just blend in.'

'That's right,' said Mattie sarcastically. 'I'll simply turn up in Sydney, or Perth or wherever, with a couple of suitcases and two children and then settle in under some lamp-post, shall I?'

'Don't be ridiculous,' Hannah waved a hand at her sister dismissively. 'You'll get emergency accommodation to start with. In fact, as soon as we decide where you'll end up, I'll start making some enquiries and I'll get you an address, or a phone number.'

'Which is another reason to end up in a capital city.' Hilda nodded. 'It will be easier to get emergency accommodation. And there is sure to be a domestic violence centre.'

Mattie recoiled. 'Domestic violence!'

'That is what it is, you know,' said Hannah softly. 'Domestic violence.'

Mattie didn't want to think about it. Even the words left a bitter taste in her mouth. She stared at Hilda and Hannah, becoming increasingly frustrated by their inability to see how ridiculous they were being.

'Do the children have passports?' asked Hilda suddenly.

'Why? You want me to go overseas now?'

'No, of course not.' Hilda smiled. 'But we could make him *think* you have, yes?'

'Sorry to be a killjoy, but they're at the house.'

'Can we break in?' asked Hannah, looking fierce.

'You're mad,' said Mattie, with a flat laugh.

Hannah looked disappointed. 'Oh well, we'll have to do without. Never mind. But if we do this right, Jake won't know you've gone till Thursday, when he tries to collect the children after school. And then he won't believe you've done a runner for a while.'

'He certainly won't,' agreed Mattie. For a moment, she embraced the image of Jake standing at the school, watching all the other children file out and slowly realising that his own weren't among them. And then having to search for them, growing increasingly angry, and frustrated, and powerless. Just as she had last week. Mattie shook the image away and looked at her sister questioningly. 'You realise that this great plan of yours means I'd never see you again? Or Mum?'

'I have no doubt that if Mum knew, she'd approve. She might be old-fashioned, but she'd be appalled to think of what you've been through. Absolutely appalled. As for me, well . . .' Hannah stared at Mattie in silence for a moment before continuing. 'I'll really miss you, but at least I'll know you're safe.'

'And it will not be forever.' Hilda shook her head dismissively. 'Things change. The children will get older, become less vulnerable. And Jake might find someone else.' Hilda narrowed her black-button eyes. 'Or die.'

'Remind me never to cross you,' Mattie grinned, warmed by the camaraderie despite the subject matter.

'We need to make some lists,' said Hilda efficiently, getting up and reaching for Mattie's notepad off the top of the fridge. It was the same one that she had used to make her 'to do' list. A lifetime ago.

'Yes.' Hannah nodded approvingly. 'We need to be practical. Think of every contingency.'

Mattie leant back and stared at them both in wonder. One was a sister who'd never been terribly close until recently, and the other was a woman she hadn't even known for that long. Both were willing to go to extraordinary lengths to help her, even putting themselves in danger. She felt her eyes mist and blinked to clear them. Enough was enough.

'I really, *really* appreciate all this.' Mattie gave them a wide, heart-felt smile, which made the bruise on her right side pucker around the edges. 'But I'm not doing it, you know.'

'You have no choice,' said Hilda. 'Not really.'

'Yes, I do. And with counselling, it'll work out. I know it.'

'You really think he will go through with that?' asked Hilda, raising an eyebrow. 'The counselling? That he is not just saying it for you to return?'

Mattie looked from Hilda to Hannah earnestly. 'I honestly don't know how I can convince you both that I know what I'm doing here. So I'm going to have to ask you to give me the benefit of the doubt and just trust me. Okay?' She stood up. 'And now, if you'll excuse me, I'm going to go and check on the kids.'

'Good idea.' Hannah stood up and put the kettle on again. 'While you're gone, we'll start writing everything down. Go over the plan. Fine-tune it, see if there's any more snags. And I'll make more tea and coffee, we're going to need it.'

Mattie shrugged. As she was leaving the room, she glanced at the fridge and the lone motivational saying caught her eye: *The obstacles of your past can become the gateways that lead to new beginnings.* She thought about reading that aloud, to illustrate to Hilda and Hannah that negatives *can* become the foundation of a new life, but she didn't. Only because she suspected they could just as easily use it to support their own suggestion.

Mattie left the room, with the other two already deep in discussion again, and almost skipped the three short steps to the children's door. She opened it and looked inside.

'Hey, Mum,' said Courtney immediately. She was sitting on the floor with the entire contents of her cardboard toy-box spread out around her. 'I'm seeing what I want to give to the poor people. Most of these I don't play with anymore.'

'Well, we'll discuss that later.' Mattie smiled at her. 'Where's Max?'

'Up on his bed.' Courtney pointed.

Mattie could now see the hump of his body underneath the covers. He had his back to her and was facing the wall.

'He's not talking to you,' added Courtney helpfully.

'I can see that.' Mattie climbed up the ladder and sat on Max's bed, next to him. Then she bent over and whispered to him. 'I'm sorry, Maxie. Do you want to talk about it?'

'No.'

'But I need to explain it to you.'

Max shuffled his body around and looked at her with a tear-stained face. 'I hate you.'

'No, you don't.' Mattie touched one damp cheek. 'But you do need
to trust me.'

'That's what *Dad* says!' Max glared at her and then turned, burying
himself back underneath the bedclothes.

'He does too,' said Courtney conversationally. 'All the time.'

'You know I wouldn't do anything to hurt you.' Mattie stared at the
humped bedclothes but when Max didn't answer, she sighed sadly and
bent forward to drop a light kiss on the covers. Then she clambered
back down the ladder. She kissed Courtney's head too as she was leaving and closed the door again, so they wouldn't be able to hear the
conversation out in the kitchen. Then she went to the bathroom to
wash her face. The cold water felt refreshing on her warm, flushed skin
and even the bruised section felt better for it.

After she'd finished, Mattie found a fresh bandage in the vanity and
rewrapped her hand awkwardly. She threw the wet bandage into the
sink and then stood back and stared at herself. Was their proposal
really so ludicrous? Could such a huge step be even remotely feasible?
Domestic violence. She rolled the words off her tongue and let them
hang before her, a separate entity to be either seized or dismissed. Then
she held out her good hand and watched it tremble. How long would
it take before all that stopped? Or would she still be looking over her
shoulder for the rest of her life, wherever she was?

For a moment she lowered her defences and allowed herself to
imagine arriving in a strange city with Max and Courtney. With few
belongings, borrowed money and no idea where to go or what to do
when she got there. It would probably be night, and she would emerge
from the airport, or railway station, or bus terminal, and stare into the
darkness as her children clutched a hand each and waited for her to
provide some answers. Which she wouldn't have.

The idea was so petrifying that Mattie watched herself visibly pale
in the mirror. And was reminded suddenly of how she'd looked when
she stared at herself after the sex on Thursday night. Her body a core of
contradictions, with disgust at her own frailties warring with an impo-
tence that was more painful than any physical maltreatment. She let
each of the options filter through her mind once more as if they *were*

options, and she had not already decided. One by one they embod-
ied themselves and proffered their ramifications, without bias, and she
allowed them to play themselves out without flinching.

When they were done, Mattie took a deep breath. She still didn't have
the answers but she did know that whatever she did, her life would be
bracketed by guilt. Guilt about things she had control over and things
she didn't. Guilt that she'd gotten into this mess, and guilt from trying
to extricate herself. Guilt because of the possible repercussions on the
children of any decisions she made. And huge, gut-wrenching guilt that
she was even entertaining the idea of taking his children away, and robbing him of the chance to change. To make things right.

But she'd lived with guilt for a long time now, and was used to it.
Her choices needed to be made only with what she opted to construct
within those boundaries. A finite balance of regret and resolve. Because
the bottom line was that whatever she did she would be hurting someone, and it was simply a case of minimising the number who were
harmed and maximising the number whose lives would be improved.
As this rumination crystallised, Mattie's mouth dropped open and she
stared at herself wide-eyed in the mirror. Because that was it. *Exactly* it.
And, what's more, it suddenly and irrevocably made her choices crystal
clear.

Mattie let this realisation permeate until it metamorphosed into an
unexpected but very welcome determination that washed away her
lethargy and gave her strength coiled around righteousness. And she
grasped it tightly, hugging it within her, so that she could carry it back
out to the kitchen and explain it to the others. So that they, too, could
appreciate that she wasn't going to change her mind.

The year that Mattie was about fifteen or sixteen, one of the 'in' words of her group was 'anguish'. 'Did you hear about Michael Hutchence and Kylie Minogue? I'm in anguish!' or 'Dad, if you don't let me go to Mandy's party, I'll be absolutely anguished! Truly!' And they bandied the word about with the least excuse, never stopping to think about the accuracy of its use, just liking the sound as it rolled off the tongue. Anguish.

Ten years later, Mattie finally learnt the true meaning of the word. And she came to realise that anguish was a rare word, a unique word, a word that rang out with the same despair as its meaning. You could roll the second syllable downwards and then draw it out as if it would last forever. Or collide the last few letters together with a finality that writhed in misery. And the word's proximity to 'anger' only gave it more effect, so that you could repeat it over and over again and never lose the impact. True anguish didn't just happen, it stabbed and scathed and scarred.

Because anguish is losing a baby, even if it didn't really exist. Or watching a premature one struggle for breath while you are holding hands with the very person who caused it. And anguish is continuing to believe that something will work, only to be injured by your own stupidity. Anguish is hiding in the darkness with your heart beating so loudly it knocks against your ribcage and then hearing those footsteps coming closer. Anguish is desperately wanting respect and not receiving it from anyone, not even yourself. Anguish is the absence of options, the absence of hope. And anguish is wanting something so badly that you would sell your soul, only to discover, like Faust, that the price is just too damn high.

NINETEEN

Mattie sat in her car with her arms folded against the steering-wheel as she stared at her mother's house. For some reason, just after she had parked in the driveway, she had started recalling the six days she spent there last time she left Jake, just over a year ago. How reluctant she had been to seek sanctuary here, how dubious of her welcome. If it had not been for the fact she had only twenty dollars in her purse, and not a single credit card, she would have taken refuge in a motel, or a caravan park, or just about anywhere else – except home.

So just after nine o'clock that night, and with two wide-eyed children in tow, she had arrived at her mother's house. The bruises hadn't been on show, but her fear and uncertainty had been hard to hide. And she was quite sure that her mother suspected that there had been a lot more going on than just a need 'to take a break for a little while'. But she hadn't asked, and Mattie hadn't told. Instead they lived for six days just beyond reality, where there was always a pot of tea to hand, and biscuits were eaten off chintz-patterned porcelain lined with paper doilies.

And the funny thing was that she hadn't hated it. Not at all. It was like being a little girl again, playing make-believe in a land where happy ever after was a context that framed the entire game, rather than being an ephemeral concept that remained just out of reach. But Mattie wasn't a child anymore, and she could not hold reality at bay. Gradually it began to seep through and decisions had to be made. So six days after arriving, Mattie and the children returned home. But she took with her a closeness to her mother that she hadn't felt for many years. And although it was something that proved transitory rather than a building block for the future, she still held the memory close, and treasured it.

Mattie smiled grimly, then took a deep breath and opened the car door with her unbandaged hand. She picked up her handbag from the passenger seat and slung it over her shoulder before gathering up her mother's Whimsicalities parcel and getting out of the car. She slammed the door shut with her hip and then headed towards the house. The front door opened before she even reached it and her mother appeared, looking concerned.

'Mattie, darling, I was wondering what –' She stopped abruptly as she caught sight of her daughter's face, with its long purpled bruise that ran up one cheek and finished underneath her eye with a swelling that cupped it.

Mattie put out her good hand quickly and placed it on her mother's arm reassuringly. 'It's okay, Mum. It was just a little accident and it looks a lot worse than it is.'

'But . . . what happened?'

'Me, that's what happened,' Mattie laughed. 'One of those stupid things. See, I was running up the front steps and tripped somehow. Probably over my own feet. Anyway, I managed to put one hand out, which broke my fall, otherwise I would have done some real damage.'

'It looks like you already have.' Mattie's mother stared at her daughter's face and then dropped her gaze briefly to the bandaged hand.

'Could have been worse,' said Mattie cheerfully. 'I would have whacked my cheek directly against the step if I hadn't put my hand in the way.'

Her mother flinched. 'Ouch. You poor thing.'

'Probably serves me right. Anyway, can I come in?'

'Of course, how silly of me.' Mattie's mother stepped back and closed the door after her daughter came through. 'I'll put the kettle on.'

Mattie followed her mother into the lounge-room and then sat down in an armchair as her mother went through into the kitchen to make a pot of tea. Mattie slid her handbag off and let it fall to the floor by her feet but kept the brown-papered Whimsicalities parcel on her lap. She closed her eyes briefly, the left eye immediately feeling less stretched and puffy.

'Would you like a piece of date loaf, Mattie?' called her mother, from the kitchen.

'Sounds lovely,' replied Mattie. She gazed across at her mother's selection of framed photographs, which were arranged in a semicircle on top of her crystal cabinet, directly opposite Mattie. The outer edges were predominantly made up of older, sepia-tinged photographs, grandparents sitting stiffly on wicker chairs and grim-faced family groups in which even the children looked pained. Then there was a selection taken during the early lives of Hannah and Mattie: black and white ones that showed babies wrapped in crocheted shawls, a pigtailed Mattie holding hands with her big sister, and a couple of school photos that spoke clearly of the awkwardness of adolescence.

But it was the photos in the centre of the semicircle that drew Mattie's attention today. These were the more recent ones, of Hannah and Mattie as adults with their own families. Full colour testimonials to the subterfuge of the camera. In Mattie's family grouping, which stood just to the side of Charlotte's debut, Jake stood tall and proud behind a white wicker sofa that contained Mattie, with Max and Courtney on either side of her. All of them were smiling, and not the fake, tight smiles that often marred those kinds of photographs, but big joyous grins that spoke of happiness and contentment and a sense of all being right within their world.

'Here we are then.' Mattie's mother came in bearing a well-laden tea-tray that she placed carefully down on the circular coffee table. She picked up the gently steaming teapot and poured out two cups before adding a splash of milk to each and passing one over to Mattie.

'Thanks.' Mattie added a teaspoon of sugar and then leant back, stirring her tea.

'Have you been to the doctor about that eye, darling?'

'Yes.' Mattie took a sip of tea and then put the cup back down on the coffee table, next to a plate of lightly buttered date loaf. 'He said it looks nastier than it is. Give it a few days and everything will be back to normal.'

'Well, make sure you put plenty of cream on it. You don't want the skin to dry out.'

'Okay.'

Mattie's mother looked critically at the coffee table and then nodded before lowering herself slowly into the armchair opposite her daughter. Once settled she looked curiously at the parcel on Mattie's lap. 'And what's that you've got there?'

'Oh, your order from that party I had.' Mattie passed the small parcel over. 'It arrived the other day.'

'Lovely!'

Mattie sipped her tea as her mother peeled the sticky-tape from the brown paper and then folded the sheet open to reveal an inner layer of bubble-wrap. Soon that too was off and Mattie was surprised to see an autumn-toned ceramic frog just like the one she had ordered, complete with splayed, gold-tipped feet.

'Isn't it beautiful? I couldn't resist.'

'Very nice,' said Mattie with sincerity. 'Very nice indeed.'

'Do you really like it?'

'Yes. Very much. It's gorgeous.'

Mattie's mother rewrapped the frog loosely in the bubble-wrap and held it out. 'Then you have it. As a present.'

'But . . . it's *yours*.' Mattie shook her head and kept her hands on her lap.

'No, I'd rather you have it. Really. It would make me happy.'

Mattie stared at the sincerity in her mother's face as she reached out and silently took the frog. It was too late now to say that she already had one, just like this, as her mother would probably think that Mattie was making it up as an excuse not to accept the gift. She placed the frog on her lap and ran a finger over the porcelain, made bumpy by the bubble-wrap. Then she glanced back at her mother. 'Thanks, Mum. He's beautiful.'

'My pleasure.'

Mattie dropped her gaze to her mother's hands, and the ropey blue veins that ridged them, splaying out to run up and over each knuckle. Today, she noticed, her mother was also wearing her engagement ring, a solitary diamond grasped securely by golden claws that winked with reflected light as she reached down to pick up her teacup. Mattie watched the diamond as her mother's fingers curled around the handle of the cup and, with her other hand holding the saucer, lifted it towards her mouth. 'Mum, were you and Dad happy?'

'Pardon?'

'Were you and Dad happy? As a couple, I mean.'

'What a funny question.' Mattie's mother gave a small frown as she rested her cup and saucer on one knee. 'Of *course* we were.'

'But . . . you must have had times when you were annoyed with each other or whatever. Like – did you ever argue? How did you resolve things?'

With the frown still in place, her mother stared back at Mattie and then she laughed lightly, breaking the mild tension that had started to build. 'You *are* in a strange mood today, aren't you? Maybe it's because of your eye. Is it giving you pain?'

'It's not because of my eye. It was just a question.'

'Well, if you must know, we *didn't* argue. Your father was a most reasonable man and marriage is, after all, based on give and take. Now, enough of that.' Mattie's mother took another sip of tea and then put the cup back down on the coffee table before struggling back to her feet. 'It occurs to me that having given you a present, I should do the same for the children.'

'You don't have to do that,' protested Mattie, as she watched her mother walk over to the walnut sideboard by the door and open up one of the narrow drawers.

'I know I don't *have* to, but I *want* to.' Mattie's mother rifled through the drawer for a moment and then brought out two folded twenty dollar notes before closing the drawer securely and bringing the money over to Mattie. She held it out with a smile.

'Mum, really, you don't –'

'Holidays are coming up soon,' said her mother, putting the notes down on Mattie's armrest, next to her cup of tea. 'So you tell Max and Courtney to use this for something special, or for their Christmas shopping. Whatever they like.'

Mattie stared down at the two folded notes and blinked. 'Thanks, Mum. They'll love that. It's very nice of you.'

'And it's very nice of you to drop in on me like this,' replied her mother, still standing by the chair. 'We should do it more often.'

'Yes. We should.'

'And now I'm going to top up our teapot. Then I'll tell you about my outing with Mrs Gardiner from up the road.'

Mattie watched silently as her mother picked up the teapot, which was still half full, and took it out to the kitchen. Then she looked back down at the money lying on her armrest. She took a deep breath and let it out with a rush that fluttered the notes and sent them sliding towards the edge. Before they could fall, she picked them up and then, leaning over, collected her handbag, which she put in her lap so that she could get her purse out. She opened the purse up and slid the money into the notes section, where there was a folded piece of white paper. Although she already knew what it said, Mattie took the paper out and unfolded it slowly, staring down at the address and phone number written in Hannah's distinctive sloping handwriting.

She read it through, and then read it through again, as if committing it to memory. Then, with a sudden rush of frustration, she crumpled the paper up with her good hand and closed her fist over it so that not even an edge of white could be seen. She gazed down at her straining knuckles for a few moments and then relaxed them as she opened her hand and watched the paper partially open again, like a flower slowly coming into bloom.

The sound of the kettle's whistle in the kitchen broke her reverie and Mattie hurriedly straightened the piece of paper and folded it back over. Then she shoved it into the rear of her purse, where it could not contaminate her mother's generosity. And where she couldn't see it either. With that accomplished, she pushed her purse back into her handbag and dropped it onto the floor again, by her feet. And prepared herself, for just a little while, to play make-believe.

Mattie put the empty cardboard box down on the carpet by her wardrobe and then started removing clothing from the hangers and folding them neatly. Her good hand automatically compensated for the limitations of the other by performing anything that required dexterity and only needing occasional support. She worked methodically, without letting herself think too much or too deeply about what she was doing. When she had a stack folded on the bed, she moved it into the box and started again.

After only about fifteen minutes she had filled two boxes, with her shoes piled on top to weigh the clothing down. Mattie pushed the boxes against the wall by the doorway and went into the lounge-room to fetch another empty one from the stack by the couch. She carried it into the bathroom and opened the vanity, peering at the contents within. Most of it, she decided, could be dealt with later, so she just took her essential make-up and threw that into the box before straightening and catching sight of herself in the mirror. She lifted one hand slowly and touched a finger to the corner of her eye, where the swelling was still angry and the bruising began, widening as it traversed downwards over her cheek. She stared at herself evenly and then dropped her hand to grasp the near-empty box, taking it through to the children's room, where she stood in the centre and looked around for a moment, from the neatly made pine bunks to the tallboy, from the now cluttered desk to the navy-blue tab-top curtains. It was hard to believe that they had only been living here for a few months when it all seemed so settled, so familiar.

Mattie swallowed, and then slowly touched each of the walls as if that would bring her some much-needed luck. Her superstition made her smile, but she still ensured she finished the ritual before turning to the wardrobe. She looked critically at the row of clothing hanging within. Most of it, she surmised quickly, could just as easily go to the charity bin. She flicked through the coathangers, sending them rattling along the pole, and selected a couple of pieces that had come over from the house to fold neatly within the box. Then she turned to the tallboy and extracted some items, including Courtney's precious tutu. Couldn't leave that behind.

She plucked the Harmony Bear from Courtney's bed and the floppy, loose-limbed dog from Max's and tossed them into the box also. Then she collected a few toys from the floor, some matchbox cars, a Rubik's cube, and a family of Polly Pockets, and placed them in the box before

sitting down on the bottom bunk and sighing. Once the sigh had
depleted her, she let herself flop backwards until she was lying down,
staring up at the wooden slats that formed the base of the upper bunk.
Her stomach rumbled lightly and she thought, briefly, about having
lunch but dismissed the idea because she simply didn't feel hungry.
Instead, she swung her legs idly, listening to the bed creak noisily
beneath her, so that she didn't quite register the sound of the keys in
the locks until it was too late, and the front door was already swinging
open.

   Mattie froze, unwilling to believe what she had just heard and so
certain that she was incapable of movement. With her heart thudding
painfully, she strained every nerve to listen for any follow-up noise,
until the weight of the silence became unbearable in itself. Then she
forced herself to sit up, slowly, and stare towards the doorway, absolutely positive that he would materialise there, blocking her only exit
while he fed off her terror.

   Minutes passed and the unit remained quiet so that Mattie was able
to convince herself that she'd imagined the keys turning, and the door
opening. That she was alone, and safe, with a job that needed to be done.
Clasping her injured hand protectively, she stood up, still keeping her
movements deliberately slow and quiet. And the sound of a floorboard
creaking came like a rifle shot from the lounge-room, followed quickly
by footsteps coming towards the children's room. Mattie's throat seized
and, in the space of a second, she ran through her available options.
But a second was all it took, as the footsteps continued to approach.
She was still standing by the bed, staring, when Jake came through the
doorway.

   He stopped just inside the room and looked at her, an almost puzzled
frown creasing his brow, and then he glanced at the half-filled cardboard
box by the wardrobe. Mattie knew she had to speak, say *something*,
but the blockage in her throat was preventing the words from forming.
Instead she stood facing him, hugging her left hand against her chest
so that she seemed to be adopting a boxer's pose, with one fist ready to
attack and the other positioned to defend.

   Jake stared at the bandaged hand and then his eyes flicked up to her face, and travelled along the length of the bruise, stopping only to dwell on the swelling, and the partly closed eye. He closed his own eyes briefly and then opened them to hold her gaze as she watched his reaction. They stood in silence for a few moments until the obstruction within Mattie's throat began to melt, washed away by the urgency to explain.

'It's not what it seems.'

'You're packing.' Jake glanced down at the box once more. 'And there're more boxes in the lounge-room. What's going on?'

'I'm coming home.'

Jake's eyes widened. 'You're what?'

'I'm coming home.' Mattie sat back down on the bed without taking her eyes off him. 'You win. Okay?'

'I win,' repeated Jake expressionlessly. He ran a hand through his hair, an unconscious action that emphasised his receding hairline, and then walked over to the cardboard box and picked out Courtney's tutu, rubbing his fingers on the tulle. He turned back to Mattie. 'Actually *we* win. All of us. When did you decide this?'

'Yesterday.'

'Have you told the kids?'

'Yes.'

'Are they pleased?'

Mattie suddenly pictured Max, fists clenched and eyes flashing as he kicked her in the shin. And she glanced across at Jake with something close to pity. 'What do you think?'

'Yeah, I guess so.' Jake dropped the tutu and picked up the Rubik's cube. He started to manipulate the squares idly as he glanced into the wardrobe. 'Still got a lot to go, haven't you? Want a hand?'

'No, that's fine. Most of it can go straight to the charity bin. It was only old stuff, anyway.'

'I remember – in fact I even helped them pack for this move.' Jake grinned down at the box and then glanced across at her, keeping the grin in place and testing its reception. The Rubik's cube continued to click.

'I thought you might have,' said Mattie lightly, his grin relaxing her even while she maintained her guard.

'Well, we'll have a clear-out. Get rid of all this and go on a shopping spree. The kids'll love that. Get them some new clothes.'

'Yes.'

'And you too, if you like. Get some new outfits, hey?'

'Okay.' Mattie smiled again, because she knew she wasn't speaking enough, knew she had to make much more of an effort if this was ever going to work, but it was quite difficult. The *click, click* of the Rubik's cube seemed even louder in the stillness, almost as if it were a timer, counting down the seconds. She glanced at it and wondered, for a moment, if he was nervous.

'And you're sure you don't need a hand? With the packing?'

'Positive.'

'What about the furniture?'

'I'm just going to get a second-hand dealer in. He can make an offer on the lot.' Mattie glanced at the bed-head of the lower bunk and remembered how proud she had been when she had managed to assemble it. She looked back towards Jake, then dropped her eyes quickly to watch the coloured squares on the Rubik's cube again as they moved around rhythmically. *Click, click.* 'I hate those,' she said suddenly.

Jake glanced up, surprised, and then realised she was staring at the toy. 'Do you? I quite like them, myself.'

'I'm going to take off all the little sections and then just rearrange them.' Mattie kept her eyes on the cube, but Jake had stopped playing with it.

'That'd be cheating.'

'Tough,' she replied lightly, glancing up at him. 'At least that way, I'd win.'

Jake threw the Rubik's cube into the cardboard box, then crossed over to the bed and sat down beside her. After a few moments, he reached over and picked up her injured hand, tracing his fingers softly over the bandage. Mattie watched him, feeling the fingertips echo through the protective dressing and touch something deep within. When he stopped, her skin immediately felt cold. He gently put the hand down again and picked up her other, uninjured one, which he took over to his lap and held tightly. Mattie tried to think of something to say but couldn't.

'We'll make this work, you know,' he said confidently. 'Trust me.'

'You said you'd get counselling.'

'And I will. If we're still having problems in a few months, I promise. But, do you know what, I don't think we're going to need it.'

Mattie looked up at him, at the crinkling eyes and self-assured smile. 'Though you'll go ahead with it if necessary?'

'I said I would, didn't I?'

'Yes. Yes, you did.' Mattie smiled back.

'So when's the big day?' Jake grinned. 'I'm going to have to make sure the house's clean, otherwise you'll accuse me of letting the side down.'

'I thought – Thursday. By then, I should have this place all packed up.'

'What about the lease?'

'I've already arranged to advertise it. And I only need to pay the rent until someone takes it. Shouldn't be too long.'

'You've been busy, haven't you?' Jake looked at her admiringly. 'My little Miss Organisation.'

'That's me.'

'You'll need the keys.' Jake let go of her hand and dug deep in his pocket, pulling out a small beeper to which several keys were attached. He started extracting the front door and the security door keys.

'I don't know that I really need them yet,' replied Mattie, watching the keys as they were freed. 'Unless I take some stuff over tomorrow. I suppose that'd be a good idea.'

'That's what I thought.' Jake passed the keys to her and then pushed the others back into his pocket.

Mattie held the two keys and stared at them for a moment. They both felt cold in the palm of her hand. Foreign. She put them down on the bed beside her and turned back to Jake, who was smiling at her. He took her hand again and wrapped it within both of his, making it immediately feel warmer.

'And I tell you what else. Don't you do anything for tea Thursday night. When I get home from work, we're going out for dinner. A celebration.'

'That sounds lovely.' Mattie made the smile travel up to her eyes, and it wasn't as difficult as she'd thought.

'Maybe we could even get a babysitter after tea, and you and I could go out. Dancing or something.' Jake removed one hand from hers so that he could use his fingers to stroke across the area just under her knuckles. 'You could be my Waltzing Matilda again. What do you say?'

Mattie watched the fingers move up and down, leaving a sensuous tingling in their wake. Then she glanced back up at him. 'Let's play it by ear. One thing at a time.'

'Okay. Fair enough.'

'It's just that –'

'I know. It's okay.' Jake grinned at her and then, perhaps reading something in her face, the grin faded and he sighed. 'I really do understand. One thing at a time, hey?'

'Yes.'

'So no sealing the deal?'

'No. Not this time.'

Jake fell silent and stared down at her hand as he continued his gentle stroking. He turned it over so that the palm was uppermost and began making circles with his fingertips. Mattie was reminded of a game they used to play with the children when they were small. *Round and round the garden goes the teddy-bear. One step, two step . . .* She closed her eyes for a moment and opened them again to find Jake gazing at her, his expression candid and sincere. And terribly vulnerable.

'You won't regret this, Mat. Trust me. You've made the right choice.'

Mattie reclaimed her hand and used it to gently touch him on the cheek, on the same spot as the bruise bloomed across hers. Then she smiled as she replied, 'I know.'

She'd worn white to her wedding. Huge clouds of frosted white that billowed around her in the wind like fairytale snow. Against her waist she held a bouquet of milky roses that dripped with clusters of tiny white gypsophilia. And the limousine was white too, inside as well as out. So that when the door opened and she looked out at the guests milling around the church steps, she merged perfectly into the background but for her red-lipped smile. An elaborate concoction of alabaster and lace.

Just before she entered the church, the photographer darted forward and took a shot when a gust of wind wrapped the white satin around her body like a sheath, picking up the veil and spreading it across the cloudy sky behind.

In the photograph, now living in an embossed gold frame, she has one hand up trying to harness the flyaway veil, and the other holding her bouquet down by her side so that the blooms brush against the cobblestoned portal. And she is still smiling, a broad open-mouthed smile that shows all her teeth and beams a message of delight so uninhibited that, even trapped in time, it remains infectious. So infectious that she hoped it would act as a balance against the other flashbacks and enable her to remember the good as well as the bad. So she folded it amongst some clothing and packed it with her ceramic frogs, a set of studio portraits of her children and some paperwork. Like their passports, birth certificates and a small typed note that read: The obstacles of your past can become the gateways that lead to new beginnings.

TWENTY

Jean Eltham pulled at the heavy glass door with some effort, and then her husband grabbed it by the handle and wrenched it towards him, making it easier for her to pass through.

'Thanks, Doug,' she said lightly, standing just inside the bus terminal and looking around.

'Humph,' replied Doug, still glowering.

Jean blithely ignored his bad mood knowing, with the experience of forty married years, that it wouldn't last long. He was only cross because they were so early, and he'd wanted to spend another three-quarters of an hour at home, in his favourite armchair in front of the television, before leaving. But Jean had been so excited, and nervous the traffic might be heavy or the bus early, that she'd badgered him until he finally gave in. And he'd been sulking ever since.

The bus terminal was a huge, plain building with lots of glass and chrome and functional furniture. Banks of black vinyl seating lined the walls, with some clustered in the centre around low formica tables. In one corner was an enquiry counter with nobody behind it and, to its right, a large board with expected arrivals, departures and estimated schedules. Doug headed over there immediately.

At the far end of this first section, with the seating and the counter, were three steps that led up to a second, more rectangular room. To the immediate left up the stairs was a well-stocked snack bar painted the colour of percolated coffee and hung gaily with advertisements for chocolate bars, ice-creams and decadent drinks like triple chocolate mint delight. Opposite the snack bar were small islands of tables and chairs, some set up along the balustrade that divided the two rooms. Then, past the snack bar and the tables was another counter with a luggage carousel next to it. The far wall, behind the counter, was made completely of glass and through it several buses could be seen, either having just arrived or waiting to depart.

Lip service had been paid to the fact that Christmas was just around the corner, and standing next to the downstairs counter was a small artificial tree decorated with a couple of red baubles. The upper level was slightly more festive, with a plastic Santa Claus cut-out stuck to one wall surrounded by gold tinsel, and a large red and green card-board banner was suspended from the ceiling with fishing line. It read: *Merry Christmas to all our Valued Customers! Enjoy your Trip!*

While Doug checked the arrivals board, Jean scanned the people waiting in the terminal just in case their daughter had arrived early. There were not terribly many. In the first room there was only an elderly man, who sat leaning forward on his walking stick near the counter, a middle-aged woman with a multitude of shopping bags, and someone who looked like a businessman, a newspaper spread out in front of his face. There were more in the upper area, sitting opposite the snack bar. From where she stood, Jean could see two families, one with a very young baby that still had that piteous newborn wail, a young couple who were draped over each other, several boisterous teenagers, and a young mother with two children.

Doug came back looking grim. 'Not only are we ridiculously early anyway, but the damn thing is running ten minutes late.'

'Oh, well.' Jean smiled at him brightly, not letting his mood touch her. 'You never know, do you? I mean, it *could* have been early, or the traffic worse than it was, or something. Let's find a seat.'

'Not up there.' Doug nodded his head towards the upper section. 'If I have to listen to that bloody baby crying for an hour I'm going to throttle you.'

'If it makes you feel better, go ahead. At least I wouldn't have to listen to you sook.'

'And look at those teenagers.' Doug glared at the upper section. 'I reckon they've got alcohol with them in those paper bags. Now when *I* was on the force –'

'Nobody under eighteen *ever* drank,' finished Jean sarcastically. 'Goodness, Doug, you've only been retired for five years, not fifty.' She pointed at the seats against the far wall. 'How about over there? It's away from all human contact. That should suit you.'

'Humph,' said Doug, mellowing enough to roll his eyes at her. Jean smiled at him sweetly and they walked over to the seats, settling themselves down comfortably.

'Quite snug, aren't they?' Jean wiggled approvingly.

'They'd better be.'

'You really are turning into an old grump, aren't you?' Jean shook her head at him. 'I hope you're going to lighten up when Rebecca gets here.'

'Course I will.' Doug's face lightened at the thought of his only daughter.

'And treat David nicely, and don't get irritated when the girls get a bit excited.'

'Would you like to write all these instructions down?' grumbled Doug, taking off his glasses and polishing them with a corner of his cardigan. 'Just in case I forget how to behave?'

'Perhaps I'd better.'

'Humph.'

Jean looked over at the snack bar. 'I know, let's have a cup of tea. It'll help pass the time. And maybe a muffin.'

'Want me to get it?'

'No, that's okay. I'll stretch my legs.' Jean got up out of the chair and smoothed her skirt down. Then she walked across the room, past the middle-aged woman and towards the stairs. Once up those, she stood back to look at the menu and see what was on offer. The prices, she noticed immediately, were exorbitant. One of the women at the tables had risen as well, and she stood behind Jean politely.

'You go ahead.' Jean took a step back. 'I'm still thinking.'

'Thanks.'

As the woman passed, Jean glanced at her face and only just stopped herself from gasping out loud. Because she was a pretty girl, with a cloud of dark brown hair and lovely brown eyes, but she had a long and livid bruise running down her cheek, which had swelled up the corner of one eye so that her face looked lopsided. While the woman moved up to the counter and ordered a chocolate milkshake, Jean stared at her surreptitiously. Apart from the bruise, one of her hands was bandaged tightly with only the fingers showing. And it was obviously painful as, while she paid for and then took the milkshake, she only used her right hand, with the other tucked against her waist as if for protection.

'Can I help you?'

Jean dragged her eyes away from the young woman and looked at the pimpled teenager behind the counter. 'Um. Oh, two cups of tea please. And one of those banana muffins.'

While he prepared her order, Jean glanced over towards the young woman again. She sat back down next to her two children, a boy of about eight or nine and a girl a few years younger, and handed them the milkshake which they shared, silently. It was an unnatural silence, Jean decided, that made them seem rather odd next to the children of the two larger families, who were running around and climbing over chairs, quite out of control.

The front glass door of the terminal banged shut as someone else entered and Jean was rather surprised to see the young mother and both children tense visibly and stare towards the door with what seemed to be fear. As soon as they saw who had entered, they visibly relaxed and the mother smiled down at her two children reassuringly.

'Here you go then.'

Jean turned around as the attendant put the muffin and two cups of tea on the counter. She was pleased to see they at least used china cups and not those dreadful polystyrene things that always made the tea taste of cardboard. Jean paid with a ten-dollar note out of which she got very little change and picked up two of the sugar sachets and a plastic stirrer for her husband. Then she put the muffin in her handbag and carried the two cups carefully. On her way to the stairs, she couldn't resist one more glance at the trio and saw that the little girl had crawled into her mother's lap and wrapped her arms around her.

Jean concentrated on the steps and took the cups over to her husband. She passed him one and settled herself back into her chair.

'Thanks.' Doug tore open the two sachets and poured them in simultaneously. Then he stirred it, took a sip and sighed. 'What they need here is a telly. Or at least a radio.'

'Look,' Jean hissed loudly, pointing covertly towards the upper section. 'See that young brunette with the two children?'

Doug craned his neck. 'Where?'

'By the balustrade. For god's sake, don't be so obvious.'

'The one with the little girl on her lap?' Doug frowned. 'What about them?'

'They're running away,' announced Jean firmly.

'Oh my lord. How do you know that, woman?'

'It's perfectly obvious. Look at her face – she's been beaten up. And her hand is bandaged too. I'd say it was the husband.'

'It's always the husband with you.' Doug stopped looking and took another sip of tea.

'I'm serious, Doug. When that last person came through the door there, you should have seen them all jump. They're worried the husband'll find them before they can get the bus. And they won't be able to escape.'

'You watch too many movies.'

'*You're* the one who's always in front of the telly,' snapped Jean crossly. 'Now use your eyes, Doug, that young woman is in trouble.'

'Even if you're right, what are we supposed to do?'

For the first time, Jean looked doubtful. 'I'm not quite sure.'

'There you go then.' Doug gestured at her cup. 'Drink your tea before it goes cold.'

'We should do *something*.'

'It's none of our business.' Doug bit into the muffin, chewed with a frown and then looked down at it disdainfully. 'What's this supposed to be? Boiled cardboard?'

'Banana.' Jean was still gazing at the upper level. 'Don't eat it if you don't like it.'

'I'm hungry,' muttered Doug, taking another bite.

'What if I went up there and asked her if she needed any help?'

'You can't stop yourself, can you, woman?' Doug rolled his eyes again. 'If you do that, she'll probably just tell you to get lost. And she'd be right.'

'But what if she doesn't? Shouldn't I at least try?'

'No,' replied Doug shortly, taking another bite.

Jean glowered at him. 'And what if it was Rebecca? All alone somewhere with the girls. Wouldn't you hope some stranger reached out?'

'Rebecca?' repeated Doug slowly, finally taking his eyes off the muffin and looking back up towards the young woman. He saw that the little girl had now closed her eyes against her mother's chest while the woman patted her with her good hand. And the boy had pulled his chair so close that there was barely any space between them. He sat swinging his legs and staring at the floor. Every now and again he would glance towards the front door with clear apprehension, and then down again.

Doug cleared his throat noisily and passed the rest of the muffin to his wife. 'There you go. Your half.'

'Half?' Jean held it up and raised her eyebrows. 'You call *this* half?'

'Get another one if you like,' said Doug gruffly, taking his glasses off again and examining them.

'I'm right, aren't I?'

'Probably,' admitted Doug reluctantly, blowing on his glasses and then polishing them with his cardigan once more.

'So what should we do?'

Doug sighed. 'Ask if she needs help, I suppose.'

'I agree.' Jean nodded firmly. 'If more people did that, we wouldn't have the problems with this sort of thing that we do now. Everybody always crawls under that old excuse "it's none of our business", and that's why these brutes get away with it.'

'Are you just going to lecture me, woman?' Doug slid his glasses on and looked at his wife with his eyebrows raised. 'Or are you going to do something?'

'*Do* something.' Jean got up and waited patiently for Doug to rise also. Then she turned, ready to lead the way up the steps. But that was when she noticed that the table the young woman had been sitting at was now deserted. She and the children were no longer there. By her side, Doug also paused. They both looked over towards the snack bar and then back to the table. But the little family were gone. And it was too late.

ACKNOWLEDGEMENTS

The main character in this book, Mattie Hampton, is wholly fictional and yet wholly real. She lives alongside the rest of us with nothing particular to make her stand out. She might be the woman who just stood behind you at the supermarket checkout, or the one whose child plays basketball alongside yours, or the old friend from high school who was always thought of as the most likely to succeed. She might be your next-door neighbour, your best friend, your sister, your mother – or she might even be you. Or me.

She is our past, our present and – unfortunately – our future. She is all the women who have ever been abused, and those who reach out with their experiences in the hopes that by doing so they might be able to help another woman somehow, somewhere, someday. She is the lesson we try to teach our daughters, and the person they never believe they might become. She is a tapestry – not just of pain but also of endurance, and resilience and the incredible capacity of female love. She is a hundred, a thousand, a million women around the world – and yet she is also just one. Standing alone because she does not realise she is many.

And it is the voices of all of these women, whether they are whispering a message that can barely be heard or screaming so loud it seems impossible that so many can tune them out, that have given birth to Mattie. She exists because of them.

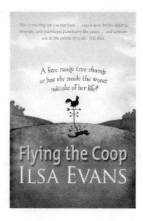

Deborah Robertson
Careless

Pearl and Riley closed the door behind them. From inside they could hear their mother crying. They were five storeys in the air and it was a hot day. Riley's lips quivered.

'What will we do?' he said.

She looked down. And then she smiled for him the Madonna of smiles; serene and consoling, a smile so at odds with her own true feelings that only a grown woman should have been capable of it.

Eight-year-old Pearl tries very hard to get things right. She watches over her small brother and manages her mother's happiness, while carefully guarding her private passions. But the events of a summer's day are about to change Pearl's life, and nothing may ever be right again.

In a cooler, greener suburb Sonia is learning to live alone after the death of her husband, and at the edge of the city, close to the beaches, the young artist Adam Logan is hoping that his recent celebrity will open the doors to a new life. In ways connected but unforseen, Pearl's tragedy will soon affect the worlds of these two strangers.

Combining the intimacy of a family's heartache, with the suspense of a thriller, *Careless* is a gripping, seductive novel about the ties of caring and responsibility that are formed, and broken, in our society.

It is a novel about our times.

'What a heart swell of a book, so much wisdom and compassion, loveliness and sadness in it . . . It's a winner'
NIKKI GEMMELL, author of *The Bride Stripped Bare*

'Deborah Robertson dissects human emotion in ways dark and provocative. She exposes the nakedness of emotion, the viscera of pain'
THE AGE

'Robertson's prose is seamless, seductive and a joy to read'
WEST AUSTRALIAN

Katherine Scholes
The Stone Angel

Stella Boyd is a successful journalist who reports from some of
the world's most exotic and dangerous places. She's young and
independent, and 'home' is wherever her work takes her. She has her
life under control.

Then an urgent fax arrives and six words bring her world crashing
down.

Your father is missing at sea.

Within days, Stella is back in the small Tasmanian fishing village where
she grew up. She hasn't been to Halfmoon Bay for fifteen years and
she doesn't want to face the memories that await her – or deal with the
long-hidden failures of her controlling father and the lost dreams of her
mother, now exiled in her home by the edge of the ocean.

But as Stella takes part in the search for her father, she finds herself
taken back to 1975. The summer she met Zeph, a young man sailing
the world alone. The extraordinary summer that ended in tragedy . . .

In a place of stones and driftwood, where the sea gives and takes away,
secrets can't stay buried forever. Stella must confront old anger and
pain. Only then can love and fate begin to work together . . .

'Scholes crafts her fiction with such care and subtlety'
WEEKEND AUSTRALIAN

'A truly absorbing book filled with secrets and conflicts'
WOMAN'S DAY

'A beautifully descriptive read and a soul-searching take on human
relationships'
NEW IDEA

Joy Dettman
One Sunday

Early one Sunday, the town of Molliston wakes to the news that a young bride is dead.

The year is 1929. The Great War with Germany has been fought and won, but at an immense cost to the small community. Death is too familiar here. So many sons were lost. So many daughters would never be wives; so many grandchildren would never be born. Racial hatred is like a bushfire in the belly of some.

And the dead girl is found only yards from the property of old Joe Reichenberg, a German.

Tom Thompson, the local cop, lost his two sons in Gallipoli. He believed he had come to terms with his bereavement – until that Sunday.

Slowly, the true face of Molliston is exposed. By midnight, a full moon is offering its light – and glimmer of hope.

'Joy Dettman is an adept storyteller. Reading one of her books is like sitting at the kitchen table with a cuppa while she recounts a tale of family secrets and small-town survival, usually with a dark and surprising twist'
SYDNEY MORNING HERALD

Liz Byrski
Belly Dancing for Beginners

Gayle and Sonya are complete opposites: one reserved and cautious, the other confident and outspoken. But their lives will be turned upside down when they impulsively join a belly dancing class.

Marissa, their teacher, is sixty, sexy, and very much her own person, and as Gayle and Sonya learn about the origins and meaning of the dance, much more than their muscle tone begins to change.

Belly Dancing for Beginners is a warm-hearted, moving, and often outright funny story of what can happen when women, and the men in their lives, are brave enough to reveal who they really are.